Praise for Jessica Dotta

"With a voice you'll love, Jessica Dotta paints a vivid portrait in words, drawing her readers through an unexpected maze of plot twists. *Born of Persuasion* is a story of betrayal and perseverance, rich with unforgettable characters."

CINDY WOODSMALL
New York Times bestselling author of *The Winnowing Season*

"A fascinating cast of characters and breathless twists and turns make this story anything but predictable. Mystery and romance, sins of the past and fears of the future all combine for a page-turning experience."

LIZ CURTIS HIGGS
New York Times bestselling author of *Mine Is the Night*

"*Born of Persuasion* is the sort of book in which readers of historical fiction long to lose themselves: rich with period detail and full of intrigue and deception. Jessica Dotta skillfully paints a vivid, moving portrait of a young woman who finds herself trapped in a perilous situation, facing surprises at every turn. Fans of Philippa Gregory and Sarah Dunant will fall in love with this arresting story."

TASHA ALEXANDER
bestselling author of *And Only to Deceive*

"Filled with romantic twists, social intrigue, and beautiful writing, Dotta's *Born of Persuasion* is an alluring debut that will leave fans of Victorian fiction clamoring for more."

TOSCA LEE
New York Times bestselling author

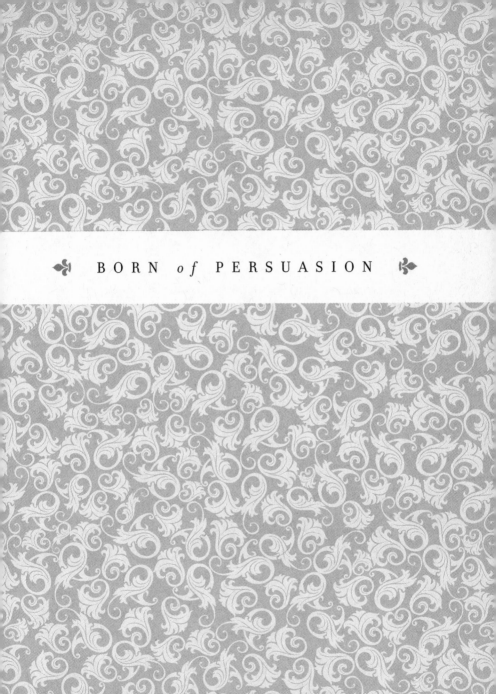

BORN *of* PERSUASION

BORN
of
Persuasion

Tyndale House Publishers, Inc., Carol Stream, Illinois

JESSICA
DOTTA

Visit Tyndale online at www.tyndale.com.

Visit Jessica Dotta's website at www.jessicadotta.com.

TYNDALE and Tyndale's quill logo are registered trademarks of Tyndale House Publishers, Inc.

Born of Persuasion

The author is represented by Chip MacGregor of MacGregor Literary Inc., 2373 NW 185th Avenue, Suite 165, Hillsboro, OR 97124.

Scripture quotations are taken from the *Holy Bible*, King James Version.

Born of Persuasion is a work of fiction. Where real people, events, establishments, organizations, or locales appear, they are used fictitiously. All other elements of the novel are drawn from the author's imagination.

Library of Congress Cataloging-in-Publication Data

Dotta, Jessica.
 Born of persuasion / Jessica Dotta.
   pages cm
  ISBN 978-1-4143-7555-7 (sc)
 1. Orphans—Fiction. 2. Guardian and ward—Fiction. 3. Great Britain—History—19th century—Fiction. I. Title.
 PS3604.O87B67 2013
 813'.6—dc23   2013010592

Printed in the United States of America

19   18   17   16   15   14
 8   7   6   5   4   3

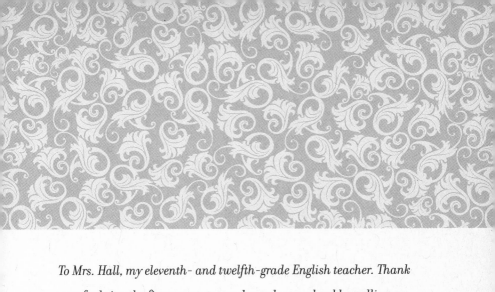

To Mrs. Hall, my eleventh- and twelfth-grade English teacher. Thank you for being the first person to speak my dream aloud by pulling me aside before class to tell me that I had the makings of a writer.

One

LATER, WHEN I ALLOWED MYSELF to confront the memories, to dwell on the particulars, I realized my arrival at Am Meer marked the beginning.

Not the mysterious letters that drained the life from Mama.

Not her suicide.

And not the two men arriving at dusk, stomping mud from their boots in the foyer, bearing ill tidings.

Nay—not even the disconcerting news that I had a guardian, one who intended to keep me sequestered.

For those happenings were not my story. I was sinless there. They were the end result of events set in motion long before I arrived at the cottage. I could no more have stopped their unfolding than I could have prevented my own birth.

Those of you who were alive that year might well remember the early frost of 1838. My arrival coincided with the hardship faced by the farmers that August. Though harvest hadn't quite begun, an overcast sky stretched over the rolling farmlands bringing a reminder of winter's cruel bite. How well I remember the coach jostling down the familiar lane, its wheels grinding through the familiar ruts. I felt no premonition of danger, only relief, sharp and undefiled. At Am Meer, home of my dearest childhood memories, I hoped to find that which I needed most—a respite between the past and my uncertain future.

The cottage stood beautiful as ever at the end of the pebbly drive. A thick, thatched roof covered grey stone walls with Breton blue shutters. Sleepy sunflowers nodded over amethyst larkspurs. Ivy and roses cambered over the sides of the house, rambling into holly bushes. For the first time in months, happiness swelled within my breast as I spied Mrs. Windham bustling about her herb garden.

Above her, Elizabeth pushed open wooden shutters and leaned over the planter boxes filled with begonias. Her reddish-blonde hair glinted in the sunlight as she watched the coach. Uncertainty passed over her features before she disappeared, leaving the window open.

There was scarce time to notice her dismay, much less interpret it, for the coach braked, swaying me forward. Without waiting for the coachman, I attempted escape and ended up clinging to the nickel-plated handle as I tripped upon layers of petticoats. I hastily wiped away the tears that wet my cheeks.

"Oh, Julia! Oh dear!" Mrs. Windham tottered down the stone pathway, holding scissors aloft. Beneath the crook of one elbow she clutched an oversized basket, and with her free hand, she clutched an apron full of clippings. Breathless, she reached over the wooden gate and unlatched it. Scatterings of rosemary and lavender fell about her feet, scenting the air. "Julia dear, what on earth? Tomorrow, tomorrow, not today. Depend upon you to come early. Oh, and I had such a lovely dinner of stewed pigeon planned, too. Now we shall have to eat rabbit pie and cold beef. Oh, it's all been ruined."

Talc filled my senses as she clutched me to her overlarge bosom. I shut my eyes and forced back tears. Too soon, she held me at arm's length and surveyed me. Wrinkles creased her fore-head and her mouth pressed into a firm line. While I had never fulfilled her ideal of beauty—only Elizabeth, a younger version of herself, measured up in that regard—I knew why she frowned. Months of pacing empty rooms stagnant with grief had taken their toll on me.

Since Mama's death, I'd warded off callers, withstood Sarah's fears that our crime would be discovered, and endured endless hours with the parish vicar, who gobbled up a day's worth of food in one sitting as he lectured me on the danger of my eternal damnation.

"Shame on you, Elizabeth." Mrs. Windham twisted and looked over her shoulder as Elizabeth approached. "Hiding Julia's intentions to arrive today. I thought you had outgrown such pranks."

"Mama, surely you don't think I had an idea of this?" Elizabeth laced her fingers together.

I gripped Mrs. Windham's sleeve and silently entreated Elizabeth for news. Words were unnecessary. She knew the information I sought.

Her gaze, however, shifted downwards and focused on a clump of woundwort, which she bent to harvest.

"But, what on . . . ? Julia, where's your carriage?" Mrs. Windham pulled me close and glared at the coachman untying the cords which held my trunks, as if he were to blame for my humble arrival. "Mercy! Tell me you haven't travelled alone. And by coach! I cannot conceive it. Where is Sarah?"

I shook my head. A lump in my throat rendered me unable to speak. Earlier that week, my guardian had discharged the woman who'd first been Mama's nursemaid and then mine.

Elizabeth noticed and took my hand. "How selfish we are. Poor Julia must have travelled through the night. You must feel exhausted."

"Selfish?" Mrs. Windham's chest swelled. "I'll have you

know that I instructed Hannah just today to air my best wedding linens for her room and—"

The driver approached, removing his hat, clearly expecting a tip. Color rose through my cheeks. Though I'd managed my fare yesterday, I had nothing left.

"Harry," Elizabeth called to the manservant who arrived to carry my trunks. "Run along and fetch a crown for the driver." Her eyes widened with questions she did not ask. "Come, dearest."

෴

"I am quite vexed with you." Mrs. Windham placed a slice of lard cake on a plate. She eyed my dress hanging loosely over my frame, then added another sliver alongside a gooseberry tart. "Why did you not tell us your mother was ailing? Had I knowledge, I would have visited before she passed; indeed, I would have."

My hand faltered as I reached for the plate. While I'd known the topic of Mama's death was unavoidable, I had not expected it so soon.

"Mama." Elizabeth cast her mother a disapproving look over the rim of her teacup. "You can scarcely blame Julia for it."

"Blame Julia?" Mrs. Windham dabbed her eyes with the corner of her gardening apron. "What a notion, child." Then to me, "Did she linger in much pain? Did she send me remembrances? Did she call for me in her deep despair?"

Tightness gathered in my chest as I sought for an explanation, knowing full well the Windhams wouldn't be fooled into believing Mama had pined herself into an early grave over my father's death.

I placed the plate on my lap, then set about tearing the cake into bite-sized pieces. "She called for no one. The cholera took her quickly."

Elizabeth froze, midsip, as if detecting my lie. Mrs. Windham frowned, but I wasn't certain whether she sensed deception or simply disliked being robbed of the notion that Mama had died crying out for her.

Mrs. Windham turned toward the window, pressing her lace handkerchief against her mouth. "Well, if you're going to try to spare me, I am sure there is nothing I can do." Her voice trembled. "I have lost my dearest friend, but why should anyone consider me?"

A long silence ensued, during which Elizabeth frowned and I twisted my cup in its saucer. We both knew trying to start a new conversation would be useless until her mother had been properly indulged.

After a minute, Mrs. Windham's mouth puckered. "Humph. Well, do not think yourself cleared on all accounts. I am even more outraged you agreed to have this . . . this guard-ian. I scarcely believed my own ears when I heard the tidings. Nothing, no, nothing, could have made me believe you would choose this person over me. Whatever are you thinking?"

I tore the cake into yet smaller pieces.

Elizabeth darted an apologetic look at me, wrapping her hands about her cup. "Mama, you can scarcely blame Julia for whom her parents selected as her guardian."

"What else am I to think? Especially when Lucy wrote me a mere month before her death begging me to care for Julia should this very thing happen. Well, all I can say is that Julia has cer-tainly made it clear whom she prefers. Surely this person has no tie, no claim over you. I never heard of such an odd thing in all my life. Not give a name, indeed! And that man who came. That rude man! Is it so unreasonable to assume your guardian would have taken it into account that I have a daughter, and as such made allowances? Seen if I merit approval? Of all the insults." She snorted into her half-empty cup.

I shot Elizabeth a questioning look. She'd not written any-thing about my guardian sending someone to Am Meer. Instead of meeting my eyes, her gaze drifted to the open windows.

"I never met such a rude man as that Simon." Looking at my untouched food, Mrs. Windham fluttered her handkerchief at it. "Indeed, I wish we'd begun dining amongst higher spheres before I listed our acquaintances. That would have swept the smug look off that Simon's face."

Elizabeth let out a short sigh. "His name was Simmons, not Simon."

"I think I should remember better than you, missy. I tell you it was Simon, and I cannot imagine a more disdainful or trying butler."

"Butler?" I asked, more perplexed than ever. "Are you saying my guardian's butler came here?"

"He was no butler, trust me," Elizabeth said. "He dressed the part of a gentleman. I think he was a solicitor."

"You can hardly expect a butler to wear his black tie when travelling. Take my word, the man is a servant, one who holds much too high an opinion of himself."

"But, Mama, think upon it. What sort of person sends a servant to make those types of inquiries? Who would run the household during his absence?"

"Are you never to tell me of what you are speaking?" I finally said. "What does this man and his lists of acquaintances have to do with my guardian?"

Elizabeth gave her mother a look that plainly asked if she was satisfied now that I was upset. "Well, we were not supposed to mention the visit." She glared a second longer at her mother. "Three months ago he arrived, stating he'd come to make certain Mama was a suitable chaperone for a visit."

"Very rude, he was, too. I should not have thought there was such a rude man in all of England."

Elizabeth took a sharp, annoyed intake of breath. "He gathered the names of all our acquaintances—"

"He dared to ask what we required as compensation for keeping you here for a month or two. The very idea, expecting to be reimbursed for keeping Lucy's child! He made it sound as though you were living on—" Mrs. Windham stopped suddenly and eyed the patch on my threadbare dress. The tinkling of the wind chimes was the only sound filling the space for a half minute.

"I heard nothing about this visit," I said, forcing an even tone. "Pray, did he happen to mention the name of my guardian?"

"No, indeed. This is all very strange." Mrs. Windham spooned more sugar into her tea. "I think your guardian must be very ill-mannered. What sense can there be in keeping one's identity hidden, I ask?"

She paused, eyeing me for all she was worth. But I had no suitable answer. I no longer even wanted to know about the man who'd been sent here. His visit only increased my unease, making it harder for me to find the nerve to do what I must. If I succeeded in accomplishing my goal, then this Simon or Simmons person mattered little.

A soft knock on the door interrupted us.

"Yes?" Mrs. Windham sank back into her chair, glaring. "What now?"

"I beg pardon." Their stout housekeeper managed to open the door and curtsy at the same time. "Only the room's ready, and Miss Lizbeth asked me to come fetch her."

"Thank you, Hannah." With undisguised relief, Elizabeth stood. "Mama, poor Julia must be exhausted. Surely you will excuse her."

Mrs. Windham waved me away with her handkerchief. "I have no wish to talk further regardless, what with her upsetting the household. My poor heart is pounding after such a distasteful tea. When you wake, I insist you write your guardian. Tell him this whole affair upsets my digestion, and that you wish to be transferred into my care. For I cannot conceive he wishes such vexations upon me. And—"

"What shall we do about a lady's maid for Julia?" Elizabeth

had the mercy to interrupt. "Betsy scarcely has time in the mornings to arrange our toilette, much less someone else's. What about that girl Nancy?"

"Yes, yes, anyone will do," agreed Mrs. Windham, picking up her teacup. "I am quite certain Julia shall not mind."

That night, I startled from my dreams to the sound of rain slashing against the window. I blinked at the tall furniture casting long shadows over the bed, trying to reorient myself. Then recalling I was safe at Am Meer, I turned over.

I'd slept long past the hour of dinner, evidenced by the plate of food next to my bedside. My stomach soured as I evaluated its contents. The hare had dried and shrunken from the bone. Granules of fat clung to the potatoes, and what looked like a petrified lump of dough served for bread.

I wrinkled my nose, sliding from the crumpled bed linens. My nightgown and hair were damp from perspiration, so I took up the heavy, woollen shawl draped over the end of the bed.

The dreams were always the same—wraithlike visions of Mama, tortured and frenzied in the netherworld, trying to warn me from across a vast chasm.

I sank before the expiring coals and rested my head against the cool fireplace tiles. Though I never heard what Mama was trying to tell me, I didn't need to. I tightened my shawl recalling my last visit to Am Meer, three years previous.

And how very different that trip was.

Mama had been with me, head high and erect. I suffered no anxiety for my future then, no fears or rejection. Instead, I felt certain of what was to come. I'd begun wearing stays, which decreased my waist size, enhancing my femininity. My hair was swept up and coiled in glossy, thick locks. At fourteen, I was old enough to be wed. Certainly old enough to enter a betrothal, which had already been promised me when I reached this age.

Poor Mama never suspected my exhilaration had little to do with Am Meer. How placidly she watched the sheep grazing over the windswept hills, her eyes seemingly fixed, her thoughts spreading far from me.

Our carriage had scarcely arrived before Elizabeth tore from the cottage and sprinted down the flagstone path. Crimson ribbons freed themselves from her hair as she ran.

"Julia! Julia! Oh, Julia!" She grabbed my hands, knocking me off balance, then swung me around and back to my place. Excitement flushed her cheeks as she bounced up and down on her toes. "Oh, you'll never guess. You cannot guess!"

With a slight smile, Mama shook the dust from her skirts.

My heart pounded, for I knew by the gleam in Elizabeth's eyes her news had to do with our favorite topic—Lord Auburn's sons. I gave her a slight, panicked shake of my head, which she failed to note.

"Edward . . . learned of your arrival." She paused to catch her breath, and as she did, she grinned—a grin only achieved by youth unaware of how quickly hopes can be blighted.

With a look of horror, Mama froze. Until that moment, I'd taken great pains to keep her from suspecting my attachment to Edward, the younger son. Our lazy afternoons had been kept far from prying eyes in leafy, cool coppices. The hours had been private ones, dwindled away chatting, safe within haystacks, or with our bare feet dipped in the icy waters of gushing brooks.

Elizabeth pumped my hands to bring my attention back to her. "Edward postponed a visit to his aunt—and she's a viscountess, too—simply refused to go, to make certain he saw you. He said to tell you he had something important to discuss." Her voice rose with excitement as she said the last line. "Had you seen the look on his face, there can be no doubt, none whatsoever, what he intends to ask. If we go now, right now, I bet we can find both Henry and Edward in the village."

Doubtless, Elizabeth would have riven me from Am Meer

and had me flying down the lane had not Mama's hands clutched my shoulders.

"My word," she said, sounding as if she'd been struck and could scarcely breathe.

The weight of my betrayal increased as I drew my eyes up to her, but she was not looking at me. Her face, emptied of color, turned toward Mrs. Windham. Though Mama kept her voice pleasing, an intense shudder rippled through her arms as she tightened her grip on me. "Edith, surely you knew nothing of this. The girls are far too old for such antics. There might be rumors, misunderstandings."

I could scarcely draw breath. My only hope lay with Mrs. Windham, which did not promise much. Poor Mrs. Windham. At that time, her highest ambition was to keep Elizabeth's name linked with the Auburns'. She looked nearly as dismayed as I felt.

"Well, upon my word, Lucy," was all she managed at first, tottering to join us. "Surely no one would mistake children . . ." Ill-advisedly, she gestured to Elizabeth, whose panting chest filled out her dress rather well. Mrs. Windham must have thought so too, for she frowned and quickly turned in my direction. Her eyes darted up and down my flat bodice before fluttering the lace she clutched in her hand toward me. "They are mere children. Who could possibly mistake their capers for more than that?"

"Mr. Henry Auburn is nineteen now, is he not?" Mama's voice was steel.

Elizabeth, impatient to be off, rolled her eyes. Mama had never stood in her way; therefore she could not perceive the storm gathering above us.

"Well . . . as I breathe," Mrs. Windham said, "I am sure I cannot recount Master Henry's age. Certainly he cannot be—" her face drooped—"as old as all that."

"Elizabeth?" Mama's voice took on a crisp tone.

The impatience drained from my friend's countenance as realization sank in. Her face turned scarlet. "Ma'am?"

"How old is Master Henry?" Mama did not ask Edward's age, for I think even then she could not bring herself to speak his name.

Elizabeth glanced at me for help. I felt like crying. Our perfect afternoons were ending, and there was nothing I could do.

"He is nineteen, ma'am."

"Ah." Mama fixed her stony gaze on Mrs. Windham. Her disapproval chilled even the misty air. "Surely you knew nothing of this scheme."

Mrs. Windham blinked as her mind absorbed the abrupt change. When Mama arched her eyebrows, Mrs. Windham seized her only chance of separating herself.

"Upon my word, Elizabeth." She grabbed Elizabeth's upper arm and walloped her through her thick petticoats, propelling her toward the house. "Such notions! Such carrying on! Such a thing I would not have imagined from you." She looked over her shoulder at Mama. "I had not thought she would suggest such a brazen act. Go find the Auburns in the village, indeed." She raised her hand and larruped Elizabeth's backside. "Get in the house! Do not let me hear one peep out of you. Of all the indecent, bald-faced . . ."

Elizabeth wore too many petticoats to be much disturbed. She cast me a determined look that promised we would see Henry and Edward this summer, no matter what.

Mama caught her meaning too, for her hand stopped trembling on my shoulder. From that moment forward, she became my jailor. Gone were my afternoon walks and Elizabeth's and my trips to the village, where we wove through the merchant stalls and cried out greetings to those amongst our class.

Mama found excuses not to visit Am Meer thereafter. The horse had clubfoot. The rain made it too muddy for safe passage. We needed to tend our garden. Her excuses were as lame as she claimed our horse was.

Mrs. Windham faithfully sent her yearly invitation, and

pain creased Mama's face as she read each missive. Not even a stranger would have mistaken Tantalus's hunger in her eyes. To this day I ache when I consider the cruelty she endured to keep me from Edward—the drunken rages, the swift, savage hand of my father. She could have escaped, spent her summer afternoons sewing in peace amongst Mrs. Windham's roses. But Mama held firm to her belief that Edward would devastate my life. Of all people, Mama should have known that we have no control over fate, not even our own.

Her efforts were vain, regardless. For despite her keeping me under lock and key during our last visit to Am Meer, Edward had managed to find me.

My faith in Edward had been so strong that even the afternoon I learned I had a guardian, I scarcely listened to his terms. That afternoon, I still had not been able to weep over Mama's death, as it was self-inflicted. I walked in a blur. Thus when Mr. Graves, my solicitor, informed me I had a guardian who intended to send me to Scotland as a widow's companion, I sat expressionless as he read my guardian's instructions.

My calm must have disturbed him, for when he finished he looked over the page and frowned. "Did you understand any of what I just read?"

"I understood." I kept my hands folded on my lap, refusing to change expression.

He clearly hadn't expected this, for he paused, looking annoyed.

I swallowed hard, wondering what a normal response was. Did he expect me to object to my lower status? Was I supposed to weep and wail? Or was he waiting for me to thank my guardian profusely for overseeing my future?

Twice Mr. Graves cleared his throat, an indicant he wished me to speak. Tugging his cravat, he stared, waiting. "Well, haven't you anything to say?" he finally demanded.

A slow smirk crept over my lips as I fought the urge to shriek with laughter. *Say?* I mused. When had it ever mattered what I said? My words were as empty as air. No one consulted me about concealing Mama's suicide, addressed the cost of the funeral, or even bothered to tell me that should my parents die, I'd have a guardian. No, I would not speak. I'd learned early that women did not escape their bonds. But neither would I thank my guardian. I would do nothing except sit here, hands folded.

Mr. Graves was not a particularly insightful personality. Instead of recognizing someone worn down from grief, he saw a girl who smirked when he didn't want her to. He wrinkled his nose in disgust. "Well—" he stood, stuffing papers back in his bag—"I'll take my leave, then."

I remained motionless until his footsteps died. Even as fear slowly curled through my body, a ray of sun sliced through the dust and landed near my feet. It was as warm and shining as my last hope—Edward.

The smattering of rain on the panes recalled me to Am Meer. I shook off the shawl and pattered to the bed, where my satchel lay. Stashed within the first compartment was the portrait of the life Mama had left me.

The page had come to me during the last meeting with Mr. Graves. When he stood to leave, it fluttered unnoticed to the floor. It had taken all my effort not to stare at it as he turned and walked from the room.

I opened the paper that I had folded and refolded so often the words had rubbed clean in the creases and could only be read from memory.

As far as I could tell, the letter was written to my guardian and discussed the conditions of my going to Scotland. It read:

> . . . *for if she's unused to Scotland's damp air, I daresay,*
> *she'll suffer without proper wool, boots, and cape.*
> *Also, it is imperative the girl remains in full mourning.*
> *Mother and I are most severe upon this point. Your charge*

likely expects to make the transition into second mourning before her arrival. But such frivolity will little suit her life with us.

You wrote that you are concerned about whom the girl associates with. Allow me to assure you, neither Mother nor I tolerate intermingling amongst the classes. I do not encourage those beneath our station to look above their rank. In the rare event of guests, Mother will especially require the girl's presence in the sickroom. Naturally, the same level of expectation shall continue where the staff is concerned—no mingling shall be tolerated. When Mama is sleeping, I personally shall make certain the girl's free time is filled with useful employment lest she grow lazy and idle.

While I'm on this topic, Isaac wrote that she's to be given a small allowance at your expense—enough to content the feminine mind. Sir, I cannot disagree more heartily with him upon the matter, and implore you trust my opinion as a woman over his. He is much deceived as to the nature of females. Not a single woman amongst my acquaintance defines her happiness as stemming from the substance of things. It would be a dangerous precedent to set. Your protégé would needlessly spoil the girl, and with it, give her an air of discontentment. If she is penniless, work alone secures her future. If she is friendless, let discipline structure her thoughts. She must be taught that only through usefulness shall she find security. This offers her far greater contentment than mere baubles. Indeed, I have often observed—

Whatever had been observed, I thankfully was spared from learning. The page ended.

I clutched the note against my stomach, glad for the lingering hours before dawn. Every time I read the letter, fear assailed me. Much depended upon the next few weeks of my life. My guardian had given me two months before I left for Scotland. If I were to find a husband first, I needed to act quickly.

My summers at Am Meer had always been interludes of peace, golden drafts of mead. The halcyon summer days blended with country dances, laughter, and girlish dreams. And Edward had always occupied the center.

Now he was all I had left.

A child's whimsy.

One that I desperately needed to make real.

Two

I WOKE TO A STRANGLING SCREAM.

Bolting upright, I found my room in the half-light of dawn. To my astonishment, a girl with long, russet tangles of hair was trying to reach the shutter latch behind a cockerel perched in the window. "Shoo," she hissed, "afore ye find yourself in a pot."

Her efforts were greeted with a flurry of beating wings and shrill crowing. The girl turned her face but somehow managed to close the shutters. The tips of the quill feathers remained, causing the rooster to emit discordant shrieks and thrash about all the more. The maid reopened the shutters enough to release him, then leaned outside. "And I did it a-purpose too. Maybe that'll teach ye to behave."

I pulled my unbound hair over my shoulder, too bewildered to speak. Beneath my window, hens clucked and the annoying rooster crowed again, this time sounding indignant. Yet even that horrible noise was balm.

The girl laughed, dusting her hands, then turned and saw me. "Don't be minding that old bird. His whole brood is such-like. 'Tis about time ye woke anyway. I'm to be in the kitchen afore the hour ends."

I rubbed my forehead, probably looking more severe than I intended. Ignoring her, I anxiously searched near the hearth for the page I'd been reading the night before. I loathed the idea of others learning I'd been reduced to the role of a lady's companion. I had told no one, lest Edward learn of it and regret our secret engagement.

The girl's mouth twisted when I said nothing. She knelt before the hearth and brushed the ash. "Miss Lizbeth sent me to be your lady's maid. She says ye travelled without one."

I grabbed a silk wrapper and stole from bed to rifle through my satchel. I breathed relief upon finding the letter stashed in its rightful place.

Free from that worry, I rubbed the sleep from my eyes and considered my room. Sun stretched over the birch floor, making it glint like a polished piece of citrine. At the washstand, I scrubbed with a bar of oatmeal soap. The room never changed between visits, but I liked the old-fashioned jade-colored walls and cream bedding. The only harsh colors were the ones I brought. My weather-stained trunks were piled in one corner, and the black garments I had strewn over the floor still lay where I'd dropped them. Yellow roses were crammed into an aged vase atop the writing desk. Since it seemed unlikely Mrs. Windham remembered they were my favorites, I concluded Elizabeth had overseen the detail.

I turned my attention back to the maid, who extended a linen towel, arching her eyebrows and seemingly waiting for comment.

"Your name?" I inquired, burying my face in the soft linen, satin-stitched with flowers and ribbons.

"Nancy."

I patted my face dry and then with mild alarm took in her soot-stained fingers and freckled face. "Have you experience as a lady's maid?"

Her smile increased as she lifted on her toes. "I got natural knack. Me mam says so."

I stared in dismay. Never before had my need to be lovely been so pressing. This girl scarcely looked as though she'd combed her own hair. Yet there was one comfort. Had she been qualified, even with that accent, decorum would have demanded that I tip her.

Her smile fell with my silence.

To hide my discomfort, I hung the towel back on its bar, wishing I were more like Elizabeth, who befriended others easily. At best, I could be forthright. "You realize I shall not tip you. Your wages shall only be what the Windhams pay you."

She scowled askance, but then went to my luggage, squatted, and lifted the lids.

I shut my eyes, knowing what was coming next. I'd stripped my house of every piece of silver and wrapped my garments about the pieces to keep them from chinking. She must have unfurled the first dress, for clattering filled the room.

Mouth open and wide-eyed, she turned to stare at me.

Having no reasonable explanation to give, I turned from her and took a seat at the vanity.

"Eh," her voice said behind me, "is this all you got?"

I drew my eyes to the mirror and watched as she rummaged through the trunks a second time, removing the undergarments from the platters and candlesticks.

"Three dresses and a tea service?" Disappointment filled her voice. "Where's th' other gowns?"

"There are no other gowns."

"Then thou are as marred as that rooster and as beggarly as me," she mumbled, loud enough for me to catch, but not loud enough to merit a reprimand.

～～

Am Meer's dining room faced east, so despite the intermittent clouds, the large mirror above the mantel sent sparkles dancing over the rows of china encircling the pale-green room. I paused in the doorway to view my hosts.

"Now here is a pretty change." Mrs. Windham noticed me as she tapped her hard-boiled egg. "Do you not think that coiffure lessens the gauntness of Julia's face?"

Elizabeth's eyes widened as she lowered her cup. "Pay Mama no mind, dear. You always look becoming."

Mrs. Windham glanced up from her dish. "Be good enough to tell me when I ever called her unbecoming?"

"Mama, hush," Elizabeth whispered.

"Well, I never stated she was unbecoming." Mrs. Windham pouted, waving away her egg as if it were now intolerable. "That was you."

"I said no such thing, and you know it."

"Yes, you did. Just now." Mrs. Windham motioned me into the argument. "Did she not?"

I gave Elizabeth a wicked grin as I took my chair. "I rather think you did, just now."

Mrs. Windham pulled a dish of cold fowl toward her. "Let it be stated now, I'll tolerate no competition between you. Elizabeth, apologize."

Elizabeth gasped but before she could object, I clasped my hands over the table and leaned forward with a mock-expectant look. "Oh, fine." Elizabeth set down her cup and pummelled her skirt with her fists. "Julia, I apologize."

"And I accept—" I patted the braids that looped over my ears and met in an intricate knot behind my head—"since you sent me a lady's maid with a natural knack."

Elizabeth gave a half smile, though she did not look completely appeased. "Yes, well, I thought you'd like Nancy."

"Nancy?" Mrs. Windham stopped carving the fowl. "I should not have thought her that accomplished. When I agreed to allow her to dress you, I had no idea, though I supposed she could do no harm considering . . ." She paused to look over my dress, licking her fingers. Elizabeth nearly choked on her tea, but Mrs. Windham took no notice. "No indeed, I had not a suspicion. What a pleasant surprise. Julia, after we've fattened you up a bit, you'll almost look lovely."

Elizabeth glared at her mother, then swung her gaze to me. "Julia, you mustn't take offense. You—"

"Offense?" Mrs. Windham dropped her fork and knife. "How obstinate you are being this morning to keep insulting Julia and then blaming me. I shall bear no further abuse at my table. Save your breath, Elizabeth, to cool your porridge."

I suppressed my giggles in my napkin while Elizabeth squinted her confusion at me.

Later I intended to explain how difficult the months of near isolation had been. I was at Am Meer. Every detail was as I remembered it. Even Mrs. Windham's babble was music. I now had only to see Edward to be assured that all would be well.

Appetite awoke after months of slumber as I piled buttered eggs and leftover fowl onto my plate. I ate slices of plump, red tomatoes fried fresh from the garden, and then signalled for tea, taking delight in being properly served again.

We ate in silence for several minutes before the doors swung open and Mrs. Windham's manservant entered with a tray of mail. Elizabeth caught her mother's attention as she pointed to the ivory envelope on top.

"Oh dear." Mrs. Windham laid her utensils aside and picked up the missive, giving Elizabeth a worried glance. "Now what can she possibly want?"

I felt myself pale as Mrs. Windham broke the seal and shook open the post. With discomfort I recalled the stark terror that filled Mama's eyes each time the mail arrived.

"What do you think this means?" Mrs. Windham refolded the letter and handed it to Elizabeth. "Lady Foxmore sends her regrets, but she shan't come for tea on Tuesday."

"Thank heavens." Elizabeth opened the note for herself.

At first it was impossible for me to believe that I correctly understood them. Lady Foxmore was legendary—and the scandals involving her, even more so. Not that Mama allowed me to read those sections of the paper. But I had not needed to do so.

Viscountess Foxmore was the primary landowner in Elizabeth's district, and something of a sphinx—an ever-absent dowager who ruled her land from afar with strange whims and tempers. What genteel mothers didn't allow daughters to read behind closed doors, merchants and fishwives discussed openly, gossip being their only means of waging war in retaliation.

"Lady Foxmore," I said, unable to hide my disbelief, "was going to come here for tea?"

Elizabeth lifted her gaze from the letter with a glance communicating that the circumstances were far from comical.

"But that's impossible . . . ," I argued, then trailed off seeing that Mrs. Windham's face had pursed.

"We've displeased her." Her lips trembled as she turned to Elizabeth. "I told you she would think your remark flippant."

Elizabeth refolded the note. "She began our acquaintance displeased with us. So if she is angry, then I say good riddance." Seeing my astonishment, she explained. "Two months ago, she arrived home, stating she was bored and needed a change of pace. It would have been better had she remained in Bath or London. Amongst her other unspeakable deeds, she widened her circle to include us. I fail to see how we amuse, unless she finds entertainment in dominating our very lives."

"What nonsense, my pet," Mrs. Windham said in a whisper. "She has been most kind."

I shook my head, wanting to declare that none of this was possible. Yet despite my disbelief, all that came out was, "Are the rumors true?"

Elizabeth's eyes flicked to the servant before she whispered, "I wouldn't be surprised to learn she cooks and eats infants for breakfast."

"Oh, Elizabeth, fie!" Mrs. Windham flew to her feet, knocking the table, and then shooed the maid from the room. Once the door slammed shut, she sank into her chair, gasping for breath. "How can you say such things? Imagine what she should do if she learned we spoke ill of her over breakfast? She would never again receive us. And we might never see Mr. Macy again, our poor Mr. Macy, or his friend Mr. Greenham—"

Mrs. Windham stopped midsentence and turned toward me, mouth agape. "Good heaven and earth! Why have I not thought of this before? Elizabeth, do you suppose our Mr. Greenham might take interest in Julia? What a useful match that would make." She clasped her hands together, her former agitation draining at the thought of a potential match. "His income exceeds that of nearly all our acquaintances."

I gave Elizabeth a warning shake of my head, not to encourage her mother even in jest. I wanted nothing to interfere with my plans.

Elizabeth rubbed her brow. "Mama, please collect yourself. A second ago Lady Foxmore was never speaking to us again, and now you're planning matches with her acquaintances."

"Hush, I need to think." Mrs. Windham held up a hand. "Just consider the advantages Julia should have if Mr. Greenham took pity on her."

Elizabeth opened and closed her mouth twice before managing, "Oh, nonsense. He's far too reserved to even notice her. We've dined twice with him, and I'm still not convinced he knows we exist."

Mrs. Windham positioned her hands near her ears, as if about to cover them. "Be so good as to remain quiet, love. Now that Edward's out of the question, I must do something. Lucy would expect it."

The dining room dimmed as my fork clanked to my plate. *Edward's out of the question.* I stared at Elizabeth, demanding explanation.

To my horror, Elizabeth only winced. "Mama, please! Now is not the time to speak of this."

"Why ever hadn't I thought of Mr. Greenham before?" Mrs. Windham spoke more to herself than to us. "We could have spent the last month dropping helpful hints to him. Yes, the more I think upon it, he is the very thing!"

I scarcely heard her. I tried to remember the last time Elizabeth had managed to wedge a bit of information involving Edward into a letter. Knowing Mama would also read the posts, she'd taken great care to give hints only I understood—a scarlet oak leaf, an odd phrase that could only have come from Edward's mouth. After Mama's death, very little had been forwarded by my guardian; therefore months had gone by without news.

Mrs. Windham rapped the table with her knife as she blathered about the merits of a match with Mr. Greenham. I willed Elizabeth to look at me, but she kept her gaze on her plate of eggs.

∽

At Mrs. Windham's insistence, I followed her from the breakfast chamber to the sitting room. I'd become her pet project, and she wasn't willing to relinquish my company while the idea of finding me a match was still fresh.

Though it was still morning, the room sat dark. Elizabeth gave a long sigh as Mrs. Windham opened her sewing basket and then indicated for me to choose something to hem from the assortment of linens.

I lifted out a sheet. One thing was certain: Mrs. Windham intended to have an audience as she sewed. It might be hours before Elizabeth and I escaped; therefore I did my best to check my emotions as I sank into the nearest seat.

"Elizabeth, pull aside the draperies. See if more light can be gained." Mrs. Windham settled into her chair.

Sidestepping me, Elizabeth crossed the room and pulled the heavy drapes further apart. Meager light seeped through the room. Outdoors, murky clouds now roiled in the sky.

For a minute, Mrs. Windham squinted, trying to see her embroidery hoop. Against my great hope, her fingers located the needle lodged beneath her work and picked up where she left off. Elizabeth likewise sighed with disappointment as she settled into the window seat.

My fingers moved of their own volition against the sound of Mrs. Windham's babbling voice. While she spoke of fulfilling her duty to my poor mother, my needle coursed through the linen in my hands, working from left to right. My mind, however, was like wool being carded. Hundreds of tiny teeth pulled my thoughts in various directions.

Too little information had been provided. *Now that Edward's out of the question.* Whatever had that meant? Much as I longed to ask, I knew I could not endure hearing my dreams crushed by Mrs. Windham's tongue. It should be Elizabeth or no one. Yet my mind demanded occupation.

The thought of an accident befalling Edward made my hands quake, but I'd no sooner given vent to that fear before mother wit would rise and demand that I acknowledge the possibility that Edward wished himself liberated.

He had been young when he pledged his hand to me. During my long absence he'd been at university cavorting with friends, larking about the city of London, and doubtlessly mingling with the best of society. Did he regret his troth?

The very idea he might regret our betrothal was loathsome to me, but not in the way one might expect it. From a young age, I'd been singled out and pecked upon for being different. Unlike those in my parish with their simpleminded beliefs, I kept no faith in a God who sought out the broken pieces of humanity and rejoiced over each shard collected.

My feet had been established upon reason, upon intellect.

My father wasn't a believer in fairy tales but amongst those who'd embraced the Enlightenment. The one gift he'd given me.

Yet even that morsel came at a high price.

Though my father's writings were celebrated elsewhere, the vicar in our parish had vowed to drive away the evil from his flock. Thus, Mama and I suffered more than my father. When we walked to our village, parishioners jeered us. Merchants' bills were always higher than the quality of goods received. No one outside my father's circle received us, and Mama refused to allow me to mingle with those within it.

Even as I sat and sewed that day, pressured with the knowledge that I would soon find myself in Scotland, I vowed to myself that I would not tolerate pity—even Edward's.

For what seemed like hours, Mrs. Windham prattled about every possible match in the neighborhood, always ending with reasons why Mr. Greenham was far superior, and why I must not consider whichever young man she'd spent the previous half hour discussing.

Each time I rethreaded my needle, I felt as though I might explode with a scream. The room grew unbearable. I needed to learn what happened to Edward or be left in solitude to think. Had I been home, I would have grabbed my shawl and stepped out into the bracing air. There, with the numbing winds serving as ointment for my mood, I would have been able to wrestle with the notion that my plans had already failed.

I glanced at the window, wondering what would happen if I asked to be excused, but flecks of rain spattered against the glass.

From her seat in the window nook, Elizabeth likewise glanced out the window. "Mama, since the light is gone, do you think—?"

A solid rap on the door checked her tongue.

Nancy poked her head into the room. She gave me a sidelong glance, as if surprised to find I did, indeed, belong to the upper class, before curtsying to Mrs. Windham. "I begs your pardon, ma'am, only th' vicar is here."

I groaned, lifting my sewing closer to my face. Had I believed in God, I would have chosen that moment to curse him and die. Undoubtedly, somewhere during the course of his visit, the vicar would learn I was the daughter of the famed atheist William Elliston. They always did somehow. Too often had members of that race belittled me by asking baited questions, as if defeating me were one and the same as defeating my father.

Firm footsteps in the hall informed me the brute was already nearing the door. There was no escape. Mrs. Windham rose to greet the newcomer, and being obliged, I likewise stood but kept my sewing in my hands. My only recourse was to be unapproachable. I would sew, ignoring all conversation, making no eye contact, giving unintelligible mumbles to all polite niceties. In short, I would be as prickly as a burred chestnut.

"My dear boy!" Mrs. Windham rushed toward the widening door. "Come in, come in. What on earth are you doing walking about in weather such as this?"

Silence met her greeting.

Even with eyes downcast, I felt the intense gaze of the vicar upon me. My mouth turned to cotton wool. Was I so soon discovered? No, I decided, my morning had been trying enough. I would not look. Let this clergyman learn from the beginning I'd have nothing to do with him.

Elizabeth's hand fluttered to my shoulder in support. With a hollow, guilty-sounding voice, she greeted him for both of us. "Reverend Auburn."

I startled as the name rattled through my brain like a familiar word whose meaning refuses to be grasped. Inwardly, I knew what my mind still declined. My spirit sank to the dust as I lifted my head to greet the man I'd not seen since the night of our betrothal.

Three

EDWARD'S HAZEL EYES MET MINE. What I once expected our reunion would be, I no longer recall, but this I know: that day utterly destroyed my childish illusions.

Gone was the youth who wore his wealth like a second skin. Gone was the boy who'd laughed with joy as he pledged me his troth beneath our ancient oak. In his place stood a man I knew not. No comradery flickered over his countenance. No happy greeting issued forth.

He regarded me with the telltale sternness that marked all vicars. His single-breasted black cassock pleated and flared at his waist like a skirt before falling to his mud-encrusted feet. A faded, silk-fringed cincture wrapped his torso, hiding three of the thirty-nine pewter buttons symbolizing the thirty-nine articles of religion—all of which I vehemently rejected.

My mouth trembled, but not from fighting tears. I desired to throw my sheet on the floor, to stomp on it, and to scream my accusation that he was worse than Judas Iscariot. I longed to fly at him and beat his chest, demanding he say to my face that

Mama was in everlasting torment, to make him say that I like-wise was destined for the flames of hell.

Elizabeth's hand gripped my arm and gave it a squeeze, restraining me.

"Do come in, Reverend Auburn." Mrs. Windham pulled his sleeve. "Sit by me and tell me the neighborhood happenings. It's been ages since your last visit."

At first, I did not believe he'd heard her, or even felt the tug on his arm. His gaze stayed fixed on me.

"Girls, for heaven's sake, sit." Mrs. Windham motioned us down. "Your gawking is making me nervous."

I fell to my seat, feeling so jarred that the chair felt as if it were floating. My fingers shook as I leaned over my sewing to help collect myself. A vicar? My precious Edward? One of those pompous, strutting swindlers! As I searched for my needle, I pricked my finger and drew blood, but I felt no pain. I was too angry.

This was the man who once swore he would never force church upon me? This was the same boy who grew so full of choler at the church's mistreatment of my family that he'd smashed a branch against a tree, unable to hear more? Once more I desired to rise and decry him as the worst of traitors, to pelt him with every last object in the sewing basket.

Instead, I shot him an accusatory glance and found his steady stare fixed on me.

Avoiding eye contact, I shifted my glare to his shoes, where worn leather peeked from beneath his cassock's ragged hem. This was no sudden change. Clearly, he'd made the decision to join the church shortly after our betrothal, days even, for he'd been on the verge of returning to school when we parted. He would have needed time to study, pass his tests, and then serve long enough for his outdoor lay to become ragged.

I drew an armful of the sheet toward my chest, as if it could shield me from the ache growing there. Tears welled like floodwaters threatening to lap over the side of a dam. In another moment, I knew I'd break and be swept away in the torrent.

"Will you take tea?" Mrs. Windham tugged on his arm again. "Edward?"

With a jerk of his head, he looked at her. "No." He blinked rapidly, touching his forehead with his fingertips. "I meant, no thank you. I shall stay no longer than necessary to return the five pounds Henry borrowed."

From the window seat behind me, Elizabeth gave a sharp hiss.

Mrs. Windham's brow furrowed. "Five pounds?"

"The money," Edward prompted, turning scarlet as he tucked his curled hat beneath one arm and reached inside a purse affixed to his cassock, "I believe he borrowed last Sunday. After church? Was it not urgent it be repaid by today?"

"Last Sunday! Good heavens, Edward. Are you accusing us of breaking your parents' edict?" Mrs. Windham's baby face pouted. "You know I would not. We have had no contact with Master Henry in months. I swear it."

Disbelief lit Edward's eyes but was soon followed by a jut of his chin that made his face look constructed of granite. His eyes shifted to Elizabeth, who breathed heavily as she worked over her sewing.

"I assure you—" Mrs. Windham wrung her hands, following his gaze—"Elizabeth has not seen Master Henry either. On my troth, she spent the entire of last Sunday by my side."

Shifting his weight, Edward gave me a sidelong glance. Severity tightened his features yet further. His gaze travelled over my face and dress, where he lingered the longest over the patch on my elbow.

My fingers lost the needle, obliging me to search my skirts. Tears blurred my eyes, but I forced aside the pain. I would never allow myself to feel anything again.

"Perhaps it was one of the Wilsons," Mrs. Windham

suggested when silence filled the room. "The more I consider it, the more convinced I am it must have been them. For I am certain we stumbled upon Mr. Wilson and Henry quarrelling only last Tuesday. Did we not, Elizabeth?"

Elizabeth merely gave her mother a flippant look.

"You must tell your parents it was the Wilsons." Mrs. Windham took Edward's arm and motioned him to the door. "Make certain they know I would never condone such behavior. No, indeed, even should he call in person, I would not open my door to Henry, but refuse him on the grounds of . . . your . . . parents' . . ."

Head bent, I waited to hear Edward's departing footsteps, but as Mrs. Windham's babble died, I slowly drew my eyes upwards.

Edward stood regarding me, his fingers crushing the brim of his hat. The tendons in his neck stood out as he spoke. "Forgive the bold inquiry, Miss Elliston. You're here. Why?"

Even had the thickness in my throat not forbidden speech, I should not have answered him. He had betrayed me, but that he should glower at me as if I were the traitor was unbearable. I returned his withering stare, then returned my focus to my sewing.

It was Mrs. Windham who finally filled the void. "Ah, I see you remember Miss Elliston. Did I neglect to mention her parents' passing and that she was coming to visit?"

I grew cold and then hot in succession. Her words were salt to a raw wound, for it wouldn't take him long to guess the reason why I'd come. But he seemed to scarcely note that I was now alone in the world.

"Yes, you did fail to mention it." His tone became stern as he looked at Elizabeth. "As did your daughter. Did you likewise forget?"

"No." Elizabeth sounded obstinate as she moved her gaze from her handiwork to him. "No. Henry forbade me to tell you."

"Henry!" Mrs. Windham spun in her direction. "When did you last see Master Henry?"

Elizabeth shrugged, still silently challenging Edward with a sullen look.

For a moment, he only mashed his hat between his fingers. When he finally spoke, his vocal cords were strained. "I am late. My errands are urgent." He kept his singular glare on Elizabeth. "Yet you and Henry would willfully conspire to cast extra burdens upon me?"

Elizabeth yanked her thread so hard, the fabric pulled.

Edward waited for comment, but when none came, he turned to me. He bowed his eyes, both guarded and apologetic. "I pray you will forgive my misguided brother. You have my word, I shall not disturb your visit by calling upon Am Meer again."

Glaring once more at Elizabeth, he shoved his crumpled hat onto his head, turned, and left.

"When did you last see Master Henry?" Mrs. Windham demanded again in an angry whisper as the door shut. "You know you're not supposed to. If Lord Auburn and—"

"Oh, Mama, hush!" Elizabeth threw her sewing down. Tears filled her eyes. "Who cares about them?" Her face sympathetic, she turned toward me. "Julia, I am so sorry. I had not an idea that Henry would . . . No, you mustn't leave. Dearest, we must talk; I must explain."

But I would have none of it. I shook my head, dumping the contents of my lap to the floor. My self-restraint had left with Edward.

❧

That night, I sat empty of faith, staring at the fire. My only comfort was one of the dogs I'd coaxed into my chamber an hour or two after Elizabeth stopped pounding on my door, demanding I come out.

Ordained, my mind said over and again. *Edward is ordained.* The bulldog soughed and stretched in his sleep as I ran my fingers over his bristled fur. It was all just too horrible to believe.

Edward was now one of those churlish men who thought nothing of crushing others from their man-made pulpits. It was unthinkable. Nearly as unthinkable as Edward's standing before me callous and impervious.

I envisioned him walking about in that ridiculous-looking cassock, visiting his parishioners while I'd been lectured and bullied by his brethren. I picked up the nearby poker and jabbed the fire with vigor, then when the dog jumped to attention at my motion, I rubbed his ears.

No vicar could wed William Elliston's daughter. Edward had to have known that when he took his orders. He had known he was discarding me.

And what of Elizabeth?

I hugged my knees and stared at the ceiling lost to the dark, feeling a roiling of emotion. Her betrayal was beyond belief. How could she have remained silent all those years, allowing me to think my future was set, when in reality, it was falling apart? Her actions were unconscionable. Unforgivable.

A warm tongue licked my hand. Looking down I realized I'd ceased petting the dog. Red-rimmed eyes looked soulfully upon me.

"Et tu Brute?" I hugged my knees tighter as my voice choked. "Are you just waiting around in hopes of seeing me cry?"

A long tongue and happy panting met my question.

No longer caring that it wasn't proper, I lay on my side and accepted the dog's warm kisses and energetic wagging of his tail. With nudges of his wet nose and high whines, he invited me to take consolation in his company and to have a good cry.

⁓

"Eh. Thou'll have fleas now if thou didn't before."

I opened my eyes to find the girl from yesterday leaning over me, her nose inches from mine. Her red curls hung like curtains on either side of her face. When she moved, sunlight flooded my face, forcing me to shield my eyes.

"Thou'll smell, too." Nancy wrinkled her nose before reaching down and grabbing the bulldog by the scruff of the neck. "Ga on, off with thee."

As I struggled to a sitting position, the events of yesterday flooded back. I glowered at the maid, displeased she'd found me in yesterday's wrinkled dress, lying brokenhearted on the floor with a bulldog.

Nor did she seem pleased with me. With the tone of a martyr, she planted her hand on her hip, saying, "And just this morn I gats permission to see me mam." She stamped her foot. "Now look at thee. I need to wash your dress before I can ga."

I opened my mouth to apologize but then clamped it shut, too forlorn to care. At least she was going to remain at Am Meer, while I'd soon be sent to Scotland.

Scowling, she opened the cedar wardrobe and gathered my second-best dress in her arms, but then to my surprise, her face softened as she turned and studied me. "Ye might as well be hearing th' gossip from me first." She nudged the door shut with her hip.

I wrapped my arms about my knees, looking toward the window, where sunlight streamed into the room.

"Th' butcher boy tells me Lord Auburn's sons gat in a row last night 'bout thee. Th' reverend was hot 'cause Master Henry knew about thy mam and didn't tell him. Chased Master Henry about the stable with a crop, he did." The maid's voice brightened. "Even though he's the younger of th' two, he whipped his brother soundly."

I felt like crying as I tried to picture Edward so stern and angry he'd punish someone in such a manner. Then I groaned. If this maid knew as much, likely enough other servants also gossiped about it as they emptied chamber pots and stirred porridge.

Hot anger tingled through me. For three years, I'd taken care never to mention Edward's name aloud, never to give Mama or Sarah the slightest hint that we were betrothed. And now, when marriage was no longer a possibility, when I'd be snickered at behind my back for entertaining such a great hope, Edward had made a spectacle of us!

Nancy cocked her head, waiting for a response as my fingers closed in fists. If I wasn't careful, even my sleeping with the dogs in the ashes would soon be common knowledge.

"I don't care for servants' gossip," I said, rising.

I ignored her scowl, then stood and brushed off my skirt, resolved to add no more fuel to the fire. At the washstand, I damped my face, careful to soak my eyes on a cool cloth to reduce the redness, then scrubbed hard to give my cheeks bloom and to make certain no trace of ash remained.

Being the daughter of William Elliston had its advantages. The role of outcast was familiar enough. While I did not relish the hard look that would settle upon my face, nor hearing whispers as I passed vendors, at least it wouldn't break me. I knew better than most how to maintain a frost around my heart. Only until that day, I'd never needed its protection at Am Meer.

In the mirror, my green eyes glinted with steely determination. I recognized the girl staring back, but disliked her. She was the girl my parish vicar had termed "shockingly wicked and hard-hearted."

I turned from the looking glass, determined that no one would see how crushed and how deadened I felt.

೬৲৴৶

It was difficult, however, to remain aloof at breakfast.

Mrs. Windham said nothing about Edward's strange visit yesterday, but instead chatted about a thick letter she'd received from her cousin who was visiting London. She read aloud the bits concerning the latest fashion of bonnets and shawls, then moodily declared that had it been Elizabeth in London, she would have managed to find more dance partners than her cousin's daughter. Elizabeth waited for my acknowledgment, wearing a bruised look upon her face.

With a growing sense of shame, I kept my gaze as far away from her as possible.

"Mama," Elizabeth interrupted Mrs. Windham midspeech. "After breakfast, will you excuse Julia and me so we can walk?"

Mrs. Windham didn't stop reading her letter. "To be sure. Now, where was I? Listen to this part. . . ."

But Elizabeth, with her own brand of communicating, silently demanded I acknowledge her. I finally turned. She wasn't laughing. She looked as anguished as I felt. My wall crumbled.

Once I became willing to speak with Elizabeth, breakfast stretched long.

Mrs. Windham continued to read from her pile of mail, well after the dishes had been cleared. She finally collected her posts, declaring her morning would be spent answering them.

In the hall, Elizabeth selected two heavy shawls from pegs, one of which she handed to me.

"Are you not wearing a bonnet?" I asked as she opened the door to a swirl of wind.

"No. We shall not be seen. We'll go over the hillock by the oak."

I grabbed mine regardless and hastily tied it beneath my chin, then draped my black crepe mourning veil over it. A young widow in my parish had trimmed her gown with color a fortnight early and had been shunned for months. I would not risk my reputation, not with servants' gossip on my heels.

With heavy feet, I followed Elizabeth to the top of the knoll and gazed at the vast farmlands sprawling in every direction. Brown cows picked their way across the fields. Sheep clustered near haystacks, like ships at harbor amidst a sea of grass.

"It's my fault. I debated telling you yesterday afternoon when you arrived." Elizabeth's shawl fluttered in the wind. "I should have warned you, only I hadn't the heart. I saw you'd been through an ordeal and needed at least one night's rest. Edward hasn't come to Am Meer in over a year. I swear it. I never would have allowed that to happen. I thought Henry had more sense than that."

Weary, I leaned against the boulder and twisted to observe Am Meer. The brim of my bonnet blocked the view of the lovely gardens I should soon have to leave. "Why did you not write me about it long ago?"

She faced me, her voice and face pleading. "Because you never would have come back here if you knew. Because you are our only hope of bringing Edward to his senses. You have no idea. He's completely absurd now. He can deny Henry and me, but he can't deny you."

I frowned, for the situation sounded like one of Henry's harebrained schemes. "You honestly think I have no more pride than that? That I wish to force myself upon Edward?"

"Force yourself? Ha! Surely even you could not have missed his great joy at seeing you yesterday."

I gasped. "Joy? If that was joy, then you've all gone mad during my absence. I saw only anger. Someone who no longer wants—" The rest of my words were choked.

"Julia, I swear it's not you, dearest." As gentle as her voice, Elizabeth's hand came to rest upon my shoulder. "I swear on my life. There are scarcely words to describe Edward's . . . his . . . well, fanaticism."

I pinched my mouth shut, wishing I had never come to Am Meer, wishing I'd never learned this. It would have been better if I'd believed Edward had died. Then at least I could have comforted myself with the thoughts of what could have been.

"You must believe me." A gust of wind freed wisps of hair, which she pushed back with determination. "Dearest, he's not, well . . . simply put, he's not normal anymore."

"Are you saying he's softheaded?"

Elizabeth frowned. "Soft? If only. He's harder than nails nowadays, but he's miserable. You've not been here to see for yourself. There's no explaining." She jerked her head and stared moodily at the landscape. "One Sunday Edward commanded the upper crust move to the back of the church and give their seats to the poor. Had you seen him when we refused . . . well, he wept, calling upon the mercy of God for our hard-heartedness."

I stiffened at that particular word, but Elizabeth failed to note it.

Her face and neck turned scarlet as she admitted the next part. "He tore his robes when we refused, claiming he'd set the example himself. It's why he never visits the upper class anymore, why I could not have fathomed that he'd call on us yesterday. The next week, he'd removed the dividers from the pews."

I tried to imagine Edward—the boy who'd swung me in circles and tormented the local butcher by setting his pigs loose in the garden—rending his garments. "Did anyone sit anywhere different?"

She recoiled. "Of course not. But you can imagine the stir it created. His parents are at a loss and have forbidden him to dine with them unless he wears the clothing of a gentleman, but he clings to that dreadful cassock; thus he only eats with the cottagers or at the workhouse. Even Henry is at a loss as to how to communicate with him. Edward listens to no one, never speaks to us now, unless it's to lecture us." She fell silent, waiting.

Her words wrought different results in me than she intended. Instead of softening my outlook toward Edward, they hardened it. I'd encountered his type before and seen their converts. Edward belonged to the sort that had persecuted me. He had become my worst enemy. Even friendship between us was now impossible.

On my right, the leaves enshrouding the sprawling branches of the ancient oak tree rustled in the wind—covering the very place where he asked me to become his wife. I wanted nothing more than to fade back in time, to speak to the Edward that I remembered, to seek his solace and advice.

"Well?" Elizabeth leaned forward.

I found my clarity. "Well, what? What do you expect? I have my own troubles now. I warrant he has no wish to see me again either."

Elizabeth's nose scrunched like a hare's. "Have you not heard one word? Not a day passes that he does not fear for your health, or worry about your environment. There are entire nights he can't sleep for thought of you. Every day, every single day, he struggles with this desire to go to your village himself, to ensure for himself that you are being cared for. Without fail, every day your name appears in his journals as he agonizes—"

"Journals? Elizabeth!"

"Well, *I* don't read them. Henry does. It's for Edward's own good."

I stopped my ears, starting toward the cottage. Edward's privacy—at least when I knew him—was sacred. To listen further was treachery.

"Julia, listen." Elizabeth grabbed my arm. "Please."

I stopped. "And will you be reading *my* diaries next?"

"That's harsh. How can you ask me that?"

I picked up my heavy skirts and started downhill. "What other conclusion am I to draw? You're reading his journals!"

With hurried, small steps Elizabeth managed to overtake me. "You must aid us. You owe it to Edward. This is nothing more than a fever he suffers from. He wasn't the only one infected at university. But it will pass. He's your betrothed. You can still compel him to acknowledge you. When this fades, would you rather be his wife, or have lost him forever?"

I gave an empty, bitter laugh to the wind. Elizabeth's shoulders drooped with disappointment. She would never understand, for it was to Edward's ears alone that I'd confessed what

I'd suffered at the hands of the church. Well, let him rot there now.

Yet my throat ached with tears as I hastened down the grassy slope.

"Julia!" Elizabeth lost no time in stumbling after me. "He's going to have to confront you sooner or later. I tell you, you still hold power over his heart. Oh, don't run, for heaven's sake—you know I can't keep up. I—"

Thankfully Elizabeth had never been a good sprinter. I managed to escape her—and the madness that seemed to be affecting her and Henry, as well as Edward.

Four

❧

MINE WEREN'T THE ONLY HOPES blighted that August. While cottagers and farmers scrambled to salvage a few baskets of their produce, left stringy and tasteless by the early frost, dark clouds congregated and released incessant rain.

Handfuls of ripening corn were sole survivors of entire fields. Wheat lay flattened and drowned. The poor and desperate gleaned what they could despite the icy rain and their painfully numb fingers, yet their harvest amounted to little more than lingering coughs and cellars filled with moldy vegetables.

Mrs. Windham also suffered loss. She bemoaned her garden, often walking from window to window lamenting her dead vines and barren flowers, speculating how many years it would take to recover the damage. It being too wet and cold for venturing outdoors, Elizabeth and I endured hours listening to her endless tirades, which inevitably concluded in tearful outbursts.

It was, therefore, with relief that I entered the drawing room one afternoon to find a merry fire crackling against the cold and an elaborate set upon the tea table. Mrs. Windham's best china, brown transferware, sat adorned with frilly lace napkins and matching tablecloth. A fourth cup promised a guest.

"Ooh!" Elizabeth's eyes grew wide as she likewise took in the room. "Who on earth would call in this weather?"

Unable to conjure anyone foolish enough to ruin her dress by embarking outdoors, I shook my head.

Mrs. Windham's rustling skirts sounded behind us as she emerged from her bedchamber, smoothing her bodice. Upon spotting us, her eyes narrowed at me. "For heaven's sake, Julia! What on earth are you thinking, wearing that?"

I glanced down at the dress I'd worn every day this week. After my father's death, I'd dyed it black because the sleeves were already too short. Mama hadn't ruined any of her good dresses either, stating there wasn't need, as we were not truly mourning.

"Why?" Mrs. Windham's mouth trembled as her eyes screwed up with tears. "Why would you wear that?"

I gave her a slight curtsy. "I had not an idea it offended you."

"Oh, for heaven's sake!" Mrs. Windham's tears dried as suddenly as they had appeared at the sharp rap which sounded on the front door. "Make haste! Do not stand there babbling. Have the goodness to go change. Hasten back."

I obeyed, listening to the bustle of the house as I started to unbutton my dress. When Hannah's trundling footsteps sounded in the hall, I knew tea had been delivered. There was no time. I gave up, rebuttoned myself, and grabbed a shawl to hide the deficiency before hurrying down the hall, wondering whose visit had caused such a commotion.

As I opened the drawing room door, however, I caught sight of Elizabeth, sitting arms crossed. Giving me a look as black as thunder, she silently communicated all was not well.

". . . you'll soon see for yourself," Mrs. Windham was saying, still shielded from my sight by the door. "Such a charming young lady. Such air and grace. Ah, I believe she is here now. Julia, please enter."

Enter I did, though in utter confusion.

Mrs. Windham gave me her evil eye upon finding me in the same clothing, but I scarcely noted it as my gaze was drawn across the room. The woman seated there was nothing like the normal guests who flowed through Am Meer, plump and gaily dressed. Her narrowness made her elbows and shoulders seem as though they stuck out at odd angles. Drenched ostrich feathers hung limply from her hat and straggled down her back. She clutched a stained drawstring purse against her stomach. Her mouth soured as she stared at me. "This is the girl?"

"Yes. Quite lovely, is she not?" Mrs. Windham forced a laugh, waving me forward. "Step into the light, Julia. Let Miss Pitts better view you. As you can see, she's modest. Holds her tongue, keeps her place."

"Fifty pounds, you say?" Miss Pitts's tone was clipped.

"Yes, fifty." The false sweetness disappeared from Mrs. Windham's voice.

I felt like stone as I stared in horror at this strange apparition. Then it flashed in my mind where I'd seen her before. Once, Elizabeth had pointed her out while we were at market, stating she made her living by arranging marriages amongst the lower classes. Even then, I'd inched closer to Mama, wondering who would trust such a miserly looking creature with their future.

"That's not per annum, mind you," Mrs. Windham said, moving toward me when I did nothing but stare. "This is coming straight from my purse. Just a one-time dowry, you understand."

"Has she experience tending children?" Miss Pitts's beady eyes blinked as she continued to examine me as one might a pig at market. "Hugh Kellie gots more'n he can handle. Think she can manage young Abe?"

Mrs. Windham made a snorting noise, pulling me two steps into the room. "No, indeed! I'll only pay twenty if it's to the likes of him. Haven't you a merchant, at least? I tell you, she's as good as a gentleman's daughter. Too good for Hugh Kellie or his ilk."

I turned my dazed stare on Mrs. Windham, wanting to remind her that I *was* a gentleman's daughter, yet words fled me. All I could think was that my fortune had sunk so low that my only choices were to marry lowborn or become a servant.

Miss Pitts frowned. "Aye, but Kellie would be willing to start the banns this coming Sunday if the girl's agreeable. You said the sooner the better. Fifty pounds would set him up right well and rid you of yer problem." Her sharp gaze turned on me. "Hugh Kellie might not be a merchant, but his farm always turns a decent profit."

"I tell you—" Mrs. Windham lifted both hands as if to push the idea away—"I shall not pay more than twenty for him. I do not like the man."

Miss Pitts's mouth twisted, but she appealed to me. "What say you?"

My mind whirled to comprehend this situation. Which was better—to take a husband, even a cottager, or to be banished to Scotland to nurse a bedridden woman? I felt myself flush scarlet as I confronted my dilemma, something I'd avoided brooding upon since learning that Edward had taken orders.

I started to shake my head in confusion. Then the stubborn part of my personality that neither my father nor my vicar—nay, not even Mama—had ever managed to squash rose up, fierce and protective. My voice trembled with anger as I turned to Mrs. Windham. "I will marry a gentleman or not at all. How dare you invite this woman here!"

Mrs. Windham's mouth fell open. She tottered back a step, for she had never seen me in temper before.

"Oh, a hoity-toity one, ain't she? Holds her tongue, keeps her place, indeed." Miss Pitts stood and placed her hand on a protruding hip bone, giving me a long, hard look before she turned and gathered her wet shawl from where it was hanging over the chair. "Not a penny to her name, but only a gent will do.

Too high-and-mighty for charity? Well mebbe I'm too good to offer her my services!"

Mrs. Windham gave a tittering laugh and hied from me to her. "Do not leave. I . . . I fear I made the mistake of mentioning Macy and Greenham on her first morning here." Her mouth quivered as she laid her hand on Miss Pitts's arm. "The child cherishes a notion of marrying one of them. It is a romantic fancy, nothing more. 'Tis all she speaks of. Mr. Greenham this, and Mr. Macy that, from dawn till dusk."

I opened my mouth in disbelief.

"Ah, so you fancy her ladyship's visitors, do you?" The visitor gave me a rude smile. "Aye, you and half of London are ready to seize those fortunes. But we must stay realistic." As hastily as she'd taken up her shawl she put it down and retook her seat. She held out her hand, making known her wish for tea, which Mrs. Windham obliged.

"'Tis the first rule." Miss Pitts stirred sugar into the brew, never taking her eyes off me. "Why, even in this here village, most of the girls hope I can persuade one of Lord Auburn's lads to wife 'em. Not that I wouldn't fancy that young vicar at nights for myself, aye?" To my horror, she gave a ribald laugh, exposing her rotted teeth and gums. "Not one of my girls married that high yet, missy, but as yer good friend Mrs. Windham can attest, I've found right many of them proper husbands, and most of 'em robust young lads too. Not a ol' man amongst 'em, least not the dirty kind."

I folded my hands over my bodice, unwilling to dignify such a speech with an answer. Mrs. Windham could not force me to marry, and I would not waste my breath acknowledging such a woman. Elizabeth also glared from the window seat.

"Good girl." Miss Pitts gave me a nod and then turned to Mrs. Windham, who anxiously watched me. "Got common sense, leastwise. Knows a good argument when she meets it." She gave me what I think she intended to be a friendly smile while I stiffened. "Can't live here forever, can you, what with the price of meat the way it is? Trust ol' Nellie to find you a proper husband. See if I don't."

"I'm determined," Mrs. Windham said in a teary voice, mistaking my scorn for compliance, "to do right by her. She has not a soul in the world, except us. Lost her mother only five months ago and her father barely a year before, though that was no great loss. A more severe man I have yet to see. Used to speak to her and her mother terribly. I assure you, it quite curdled my blood to hear him rant so—"

"Mama," Elizabeth hissed from her perch.

"Aye, that's the wicked way of things." Miss Pitts ignored them both, spreading her skirt over her lap. "As if we haven't got enough problems of our own, and then someone offs and leaves their kin to live at yer expense. There's no excuse for it."

"I warrant you find her too thin and pale," Mrs. Windham continued on her own vein. "I cannot present her to my acquaintances looking as worn as a shadow. But surely you know someone who won't mind."

I trembled with anger. Perhaps I ought to have picked up my skirts and swept from the room, but for some reason I wanted to know exactly how they evaluated my situation. What was being said there was likely the truest picture of everyone's thoughts.

"'Tis bad enough birthing a daughter nowadays," Miss Pitts said, her chair creaking despite the fact a good wind could have knocked her from her feet, "but to keep no dowry for 'em? Not a thought of who they'll marry without a brass farthing to their name."

"Mama." Elizabeth's quiet voice interrupted them. Her tone was soft but her cheeks blazed. "What has Julia's guardian said about this arrangement?"

"Oh, do not speak to me of that dreadful man!" Mrs. Windham twisted to view her daughter. "Why should he care if we secure Julia a husband? Why else would he send her here?

Even if he did protest, I am determined to fulfill my duty to poor Lucy."

"But how do you think she will marry without her guardian's approval? She's not yet one-and-twenty."

Mrs. Windham's face grew purple as she gave Elizabeth a look that clearly demanded she remain quiet. "No one in this village cares about that. Do not bother me with your vexations. What objection can be raised if a merchant takes Julia on as his common-law wife?"

Elizabeth's mouth dropped as she sprang to her feet. "Do you not think he'll feel it his duty to investigate the matter and press charges?"

Miss Pitts paled, but Mrs. Windham found her feet. "Of all the nonsense. Out! Both of you. You know nothing of these matters."

She gave another tittering laugh over her shoulder as she gathered and then shoved us toward the door. A moment later, Elizabeth and I found ourselves in the hall, excommunicated.

"I can't believe Mama!" Elizabeth kicked the door once. "Twenty pounds for Hugh Kellie, indeed! I wouldn't sell him a sheep I intended to slaughter."

With angry tears gathering in my eyes, I said nothing. I knew the deeper betrayal belonged to Mama. She abandoned me to these circumstances. At least Mrs. Windham was making an effort to secure my future, which was more than I could say of anyone else.

"What I'd like to know," Elizabeth said as Mrs. Windham's voice carried through the wood, words muffled, "is what on earth Edward thinks he's doing! It's been nearly a fortnight." She perched her foot on the bottom step, but instead of going upstairs, she pressed her ear against the door and listened as the women inside continued their dialogue.

I retreated to the nearest chamber, a small room that held books and a desk where Mrs. Windham replied to correspondences. With only the company of a stiff wind rattling the windows, I sank into the chair behind the desk and took stock of my situation. I wasn't sure whom to direct my choler toward—Mama for forsaking me, Edward for taking orders, or Mrs. Windham for being the first to acknowledge my true status.

I drew my shawl tighter, wondering if things had always been this way and I was only now waking up to it.

During my childhood, on summer evenings here, Mrs. Windham often pushed back the furniture in the drawing room so Elizabeth and I could practice dancing. Those nights were amongst the best of my memories. As I sat in the cold office, I recalled how the open windows framed starry skies and laved the room with the scent of roses. Had I been encouraged, I might have become an accomplished dancer. With hands posed femininely in the air, my feet took on a grace of their own as they chasséd back and forth to Elizabeth. Our nightgowns were swirls of white as Mrs. Windham swung her arms in three-counts, baa-baaing a minuet.

But sometimes between the twirling ribbons and peals of giggles, I'd catch sight of Mama and wish I hadn't. Her expression reminded me of Sarah's the time she was forced to drown a sack of unwanted kittens. I'd stumble in my steps, confused by her reaction, but by the time I spun again, she'd be focused on her needlework.

Miss Pitts's vulgar laugh pierced through the wall, drawing me back from my memories. I leaned against the chair and wondered what I had done that caused Mama to leave me to fend for myself. I rested my head against the wall and deliberated whether marriage to Edward was still an option. Whether I could allow the church to become my asylum after all.

Five

❦

FOUR LONG DAYS passed after Miss Pitts's visit—raw, dreary days where cold air permeated every stitch of clothing and seeped into bones. Rain pounded the landscape, delaying the delivery of coal and wood so that Mrs. Windham sanctioned fire for our use only in the morning room, where Elizabeth and I bided our time, sewing with numb fingers.

Mrs. Windham scarcely seemed to notice the cold, as her mind was full of the possible matches her efforts might secure me. While she sewed, she conjectured aloud which Tom, Dick, or Harry from the village I might find agreeable. I endured without comment, choosing instead to ruminate on the requirements Edward might place upon me.

I felt fairly certain no vicar could wed William Elliston's daughter unless she publicly repented and joined the church. But would Edward care if I truly believed? And if so, should I pretend? During those endless hours, I'd often rise and pace the room to stretch my aching muscles. Each time I passed the rain-beaded window, my gaze traced down the dirt path that led beyond Am Meer and into the spinney of birch trees lost in the swirling haze. I'd wonder whether I'd ever truly be free again. In Scotland, would they allow me long solitary rambles? Or if I did manage to marry Edward, what sort of restrictions might he place upon me? The vicar in my village was notorious for making his wife and children spend two hours a day in Scripture reading and another hour in prayer.

Often, as I wrestled with these thoughts, I'd feel Elizabeth's sympathetic gaze upon me. I hated that moment worst of all. In those pitying glances, I sensed her thoughts as easily as a gypsy detects a gullible client. It made little difference what Edward's expectations for his wife were, for thus far, he'd kept his vow and stayed clear of me.

How things might have eventually concluded, I cannot say. In the end, I slipped through my circumstances in a way I could have never anticipated.

⌒〰⌒

"Open!" A man beat his fist against Am Meer's door, in the dead of night, then shouted, "Open, I say!"

I sat up in my bed, gasping as dogs' frantic howls reverberated through the cottage. I made a movement to slip from my bed, but sheets entwined my legs.

"I said open up!" The man clanged on the door knocker.

"Hold your horses," the manservant, Harry, shouted as he passed my door. His feet slurred over the floor and I envisioned him buttoning trousers. "I'm coming, I'm coming, you filthy bog trotter."

Recovering from my shock, I rose and pulled on my wrapper, unable to fathom what was happening, for no catastrophe could merit waking us in such a manner. Am Meer was too far from the village to be disturbed over a fire, and the Windhams had no family close enough for it to be a death announcement. Hearing Mrs. Windham's voice at the end of the hall, I procured a light and proceeded to her.

She stood at the entrance, reading a missive by candlelight. A single, brown braid threaded with silver hung from beneath her nightcap. Her bare toes with thick, yellow nails protruded from beneath her nightgown. Elizabeth clung to her arm, reading over her shoulder. The coming years melted as I gauged how altered Elizabeth should appear twenty years hence.

Elizabeth looked up first, her face ghostly. "Oh, Julia."

I eyed the note, fear tingling through me. "I've been ordered to Scotland, haven't I?"

"Scotland?" Mrs. Windham looked over her note, her puffy eyes squinted.

"Worse." Elizabeth left her mother to link her arm with mine. "Her ladyship has ordered us to attend dinner with her on Thursday. She desires . . . to meet you."

I clutched my wrap tighter. Even in the murkiness, I recognized the distinct ivory stationery. "Lady Foxmore sent you a note at two o'clock in the morning?"

"Like as not, she has indigestion and wishes us to suffer alongside her," Elizabeth whispered, causing Harry to choke on laughter.

Mrs. Windham looked over the page at her manservant and hall boy, both swallowing back grins. Her eyes narrowed as she waved Elizabeth and me back down the hall.

"All right, all right. Back to bed, everyone. Nothing to make such a fuss over."

But when we turned the corner, she grabbed Elizabeth's arm and hissed, "You must never forget how terrible servants' gossip is. Imagine what her ladyship would think if she heard."

"As if Harry would repeat anything."

Mrs. Windham released her and addressed me. "Do not trouble yourself over meeting Lady Foxmore. Put the thought from your mind and go finish your slumber, like a good girl."

At my bedchamber, Mrs. Windham left us and returned to her own room, still reading the note.

"This is the fifth time," Elizabeth whispered, "that her lady-ship has seen fit to send a message in the dead of night. One would gather we'd imposed the acquaintance on her and this is our punishment. I'm convinced she instructs her footman to wake the entire household. Don't you dare start giggling. There's nothing humorous about it."

"What did the note say?" I asked, unable to keep the amuse-ment from my voice.

"It was dreadful. First, she berated Mama for not seeking her counsel before allowing you to live here." Mirth crept into Elizabeth's voice despite herself. "She wrote that she is uncer-tain as to whether Mama is adequate for the task, and she shall determine on Thursday whether she approves of the scheme."

I covered my mouth to restrain my laughter.

"You haven't heard the worst yet," Elizabeth chided. "The dinner is at Auburn Manor."

Aghast, I looked anew at Elizabeth, then sank in a chair situ-ated at the desk. "Why there?"

"Because she's the most horrid woman alive. Worse than even Miss Pitts. It's her own brand of tormenting Mama. She's perfectly aware that Lord and Lady Auburn found one of my love letters to Henry and no longer receive us."

I stared at her, horrified. "She can't order us there, then."

"She can do whatever she wants. Wait until you meet her. I'd sooner endure a caning."

"Well, I'm not going." I crossed my arms. "I won't attend. She can't force *me*."

Elizabeth straightened, unfolding her feet. "Mama will go into hysterics if you refuse."

"It's Edward's house, Elizabeth!"

She sagged against the bed. "That is exactly why you must go. Think of it—in her beastliness, she's provided you a chance to speak with Edward."

I shook my head, feeling the heaviness of my rag curls. The

idea of reuniting with Edward before peerage, before his parents, was unthinkable. "I thought he no longer dined with the gentry."

"He'd come if you wrote and asked him to." Elizabeth's voice became urgent as she knelt before me.

"You think I would act so desperate!" I cried too loudly.

"Girls!" Mrs. Windham's voice carried from her bedchamber.

"Well," Elizabeth whispered, rising, "something has to be done to change these circumstances."

I sat in silence as the cold embraced me. All week I'd clung to the desperate hope that Edward would call upon Am Meer and miraculously things would somehow fit together again.

The balm of such a fantasy was that Edward would beg, and be granted, my forgiveness. But that I should be the one to plead . . .

I crumpled my nightgown in my fist. It was vinegar on a wound.

"*Och,*" I recalled Sarah, my nursemaid, saying at her departure, her gnarled hands wiping tears from my cheeks, "*I pray yer'll find some manner of happiness, child.*"

At the time, my confidence in Edward was such that I'd looked her in the eye, trying to communicate that I had a plan, I'd be fine. Her mouth remained tight, however, as my solicitor moved forward to separate us.

I schooled my thoughts away from that unhappy event and returned to the matter at hand. Better Edward than some farmer. If it took begging, then I'd beg.

At the writing desk, I lifted a sheet of stationery, which Mrs. Windham generously supplied. It took several drafts, for my first attempts were steeped with hurt and bitterness. But by the time the pearly light of dawn flushed the room, I had composed a letter which I felt confident would move Edward to compassion—if any part of him that I'd known still existed.

I delivered the note to Elizabeth, still abed, requesting that she find a way to put it into Edward's hand, then returned to my bedchamber to attempt to catch an hour of sleep.

∼

Four days later, I braced myself in a swaying carriage as sobbing wind and great sheets of rain assaulted it. Elizabeth glumly watched trails of water cascading down the window while Mrs. Windham mouthed words, making graceful waves of her hand and elegant head nods as she continued to practice my introduction to Lady Foxmore. All week I'd endured Mrs. Windham's fluttering handkerchief as she declared herself a fit of nerves over my introduction.

For my own part, I sat quiet despite my screaming thoughts. It had been three weeks since I first arrived at Am Meer. I hadn't much longer before I'd be shipped to Scotland. If Edward failed to make an appearance tonight, I had no recourse.

At the crunch of gravel, I leaned forward, anxious to view Edward's childhood home. It might seem odd that I'd never glimpsed Auburn Manor, given our relationship, but the residence was gated, and as a rule, Mama's prejudice steered her clear of all titled gentry. Edward likewise kept our trysts far from his parents' land, lest through discovery our hopes be destroyed.

The house stood at the end of a row of chestnut trees. Welcoming lights poured from mullioned windows and glimmered over the wet grounds. Enthralled, I touched the coach window. It was lovelier than I'd imagined.

"Do not ruffle me." Mrs. Windham batted me from the window with her closed fan as the carriage stopped. "If my gown wrinkles, my entire evening will be ruined."

"And here I thought you in such a state that tonight was spoiled, with or without a crinkled gown," Elizabeth replied moodily. "Let her look if she wants."

"Don't be impertinent, or I shall send you both home."

"What, and defy her ladyship's orders?"

Mrs. Windham gathered her ballooning skirts, ignoring Elizabeth. "Julia, you mustn't oppose Lady Foxmore's opinion, no matter what nonsense she utters. I daresay, she shall be in her fault-finding humor, but do as she bids. Why are we not moving?" She shuffled forward, treading on our dresses.

The carriage rocked as Harry jumped from the box seat. After several minutes, he opened the door. Rain plastered hair to his forehead and dripped off his nose. "Lady Foxmore's carriage is parked under th' covered terrace. Her man has instructions not to move it."

"All evening?" Elizabeth asked.

"Begging yer pardon, miss, but he dinna say when she planned on leaving."

"Oh, honestly." Elizabeth pounded her lap. "Just once, I'd like to openly defy her ladyship."

For a moment it appeared Mrs. Windham might do so. She said nothing as water poured from the roof of the carriage and fell in loud splashes to the puddles beneath us, before finally saying, "Well, standing here accomplishes nothing. Fetch an umbrella, Harry." She pulled the hood of her mantle over her hair as Elizabeth grimaced in disgust.

"We shall have to dash for it, girls." Mrs. Windham looked over her shoulder. "Such a shame too, the very idea of the gentlemen seeing mud over your petticoats."

"I have no intention of the gentlemen viewing my petti-coats, with mud or otherwise." Elizabeth leaned backwards to accommodate her mother readying her skirts. "Honestly, if Lady Foxmore wishes to end our acquaintance, why does she not discontinue her invitations, rather than insisting upon humiliating us?"

She received no answer. The manservant returned with an umbrella and assisted Mrs. Windham first. In her absence, the carriage became a sanctuary. Elizabeth smoothed her skirts, while I felt my hair, ensuring the style held. To Nancy's credit, the curls she'd toiled over remained. When Harry next opened the door, he offered his hand to Elizabeth.

Alone, I picked at the hole in the fourth finger of my glove, recalling how I'd once hoped to arrive at Auburn Manor garbed in bridal attire and received as a daughter. It seemed ridiculous compared to arriving in the rain, an unwelcome guest in threadbare clothing.

When the carriage door opened again, Harry's nose was red. "Here, miss." He offered his drenched hand. "Watch yer step. Best take me arm. Me apologies it's wet. Wait, that water's deeper than it 'pears."

Soggy leaves bogged around my foot as the manservant extended the umbrella over my head. Rain pounded on the silk canopy as I edged toward the house.

Inside, a well-lit hall with burnished floors stretched beneath amber lanterns. Above, dark beams were braced by intricately carved corbels. Light spilled over the polished hall floor from behind closed doors, tempting me to explore. A smile tugged my lips as I wondered whether this was the hall in which, as Edward had once confessed, he and Henry played King Arthur and Lancelot. It was easy to picture two boys holding up wooden swords, declaring the suits of armor their captives.

"Julia, do not straggle." Mrs. Windham frantically waved me to follow the retreating butler.

When I was a child, there was a certain fairy tale Mama sometimes told as she tucked me into bed. In it, a young lady had fallen deeply in love with a foreign dignitary who was soon to return to his native country. The girl had one last opportunity in which to win his affections, for he planned a ball the night before his departure.

Lovesick, she spent every cent she had to commission a resplendent gown. Here, Mama always paused before finishing. The day of the ball there was a great storm, which toppled trees and made roads impassable—therefore the gown never arrived.

The girl, desperate to see her beloved, borrowed a second-rate dress.

At the ball, she was forced to watch as the dignitary danced with only the most beautifully dressed ladies—one after the other. That night he became enraptured with a girl whose love for him was but a shadow compared to the heroine's.

Here, Mama would end the story, kiss my forehead, and then, wearing a hardened expression, lift the taper and leave.

I used to lie awake long afterwards and imagine the unfinished part—the following morning when the gown finally arrived. How it must have felt to open the box and see golden layers of satin and tulle, knowing her plan might have worked. I used to wonder whether she could still admire the gown's beauty, or did it crush her?

I learned, that evening, it was neither.

Six

⚜

DARK VELVET DRAPERIES muffled the sound of rain and absorbed the candlelight emitted by the ivory tapers. Polished woodwork stood out against settees and sofas upholstered in colors of ocher and scarlet, making their indoor autumn friend- lier than the one outdoors, as three people turned to greet us.

I hadn't realized the hope I'd placed on seeing Edward until I noted his absence. Mrs. Windham marched to the center of the room, where she curtsied to our hosts in a great sweeping motion. Elizabeth, still holding my hand, followed.

No one wishes to look upon his greatest loss—a burned-out cottage, a drowned team of oxen, one's child in a coffin. Such scenes are approached with eyes averted, faces turned. I was no different. To stand inside Edward's home and greet his parents, knowing I should have been their daughter, was as agonizing as it would have been for Mama's fairy-tale girl to have explored every tuck and frill of lace on her gown.

In desperation, my gaze travelled to the only object in the room not associated with Edward. I distinguished Lady Foxmore immediately.

An old woman, a clinging remnant of the previous generation, she sat with her hands clasped over her walking stick. White powder caked her face and wrinkles. In stark contrast, streaks of rouge smeared her cheeks while a darkening element had been applied to her thin eyebrows. Even her hoary hair, styled in standing rolls, was powdered. Though she sat near the flame, a mantle of ermine covered her shoulders, over which heavy pearl necklaces drooped.

She stared at me for an eternity, and then from deep within, raspy chuckles broke through, though she kept her lips pressed together. She rested her forehead on her hands as her shoulders shook with silent mirth.

Mrs. Windham finished her greetings to Lord and Lady Auburn in a tremulous voice. Every time Lady Foxmore regarded me, she laughed anew. At length, Mrs. Windham led me to the grand dame.

"No, Edith." Lady Foxmore waved her back, and though she was tiny, her voice rang with authority. "I am in no mood to tolerate hysterics tonight. Take that seat there by the door, and for mercy's sake, bite your tongue. Elizabeth, make our introductions."

Elizabeth's brow furrowed but she dutifully took my side. "Miss Elliston, allow me to introduce you to Lady Foxmore."

"Tell me—" Lady Foxmore gripped her cane—"did she purposefully dress like that to annoy me, Beth?"

Elizabeth's eyes clouded, for she hated being called Beth. "No, ma'am. She's in mourning."

"Humph. Is it now fashionable to wear rags as well as black?" Lady Foxmore's eyes screwed as she peered through her lorgnette. "Child, why not parade about in sackcloth with ashes smeared over your face? If you're going to be dramatic, you may as well do so fully."

There was a pause, a hollow expectation for me to fashion some manner of reply. I kept my face insolent.

"If her dress seems thread-worn," Elizabeth filled in for me, "it's because she's been in mourning for a very long—"

"Oh, hush!" Lady Foxmore lifted a hand to her ear. "You grow as cackling as your mother. Leave. Go take a seat by her. Try not to speak. If you manage it, perhaps I shall send my footman over in the morning with a seedcake as reward."

Every muscle in Elizabeth's face tightened, but she gave a low curtsy and withdrew.

"Just what we lacked," Lady Foxmore muttered, watching her, "another magpie." She rapped her walking stick, demonstrating her foul humor, and then focused on me. "Sit down, child. I desire to study you. No, not there. Here, at my feet, where I can best view you."

She indicated a footstool that had been fashioned for a child. I considered walking straight from the room, back to the carriage, and waiting out the evening there. Yet four days of hoping to gain her ladyship's favor held me fast. I sat, my dress billowing up around my knees.

"Now—" Lady Foxmore lifted her lorgnette, the crow's-feet deepening about her eyes—"tell me for whom you mourn, and I shall determine whether it's worth walking about looking as you do."

Though my head was bent, I looked up enough to give her a long cool gaze.

"Nonsense. Is that how you wish to form our acquaintance? You dislike me, no doubt, for being richer and prettier, but is that any way to treat your betters?"

My face must have looked as tight as Elizabeth's as I smoothed my skirts. "No, ma'am," I finally decided on. "I am simply hoping to earn one of your seedcakes."

Amusement twinkled in her eye, but her mouth turned downwards. "Humph. If I thought you'd eat them, I'd send you a box." She poked my shoulder with the end of her lorgnette. "You lack substance. Let us hope it doesn't carry over to your mental faculties. But come now, my patience wears thin. Tell me for whom you mourn."

"My mother," I said, recognizing she'd not relent. I had no desire for her to apply to Mrs. Windham. The less said by her, the better.

"Your *maman*?" Lady Foxmore gave an approving nod. "Good. William doesn't deserve anyone's tears. His temper was too uncontrolled."

Hearing my father's first name, I gave her a surprised look.

She leaned back and surveyed me with a slight smile. "You didn't think I knew whose daughter was lurking in my parish?"

The door banged, giving me an excuse to turn. A gentleman dipped his head as he entered, yet still his shoulders barely missed scraping the lintel. From the way Mrs. Windham caught my attention and pointed urgently to him, I understood him to be Mr. Greenham.

Never had I seen such a person. Were I to take the population of London, I doubted more than a handful of men would have been his equal in height. He was not only the tallest gentleman I'd ever seen, but also the most dapper. Compared to his, my garments were rags. Though it rained, his shoes were dry without a speck of dirt. His every hair was in place. His coat was made of choice wool; his waistcoat, rich, full brocade. At his collar, a large diamond pin sparkled as it held no less than two cravats.

"John," Lady Foxmore cried, lifting her voice, "do come here. I wish to introduce you. This is the darling creature I desired to meet tonight."

He glared but obeyed.

She chuckled. "Well, John, give us your opinion of her."

There was no time for embarrassment. While he gave me a long, fixed look, I gawked as though he were a jinni who suddenly appeared out of thin air. When his eyes finally met mine, I read pity. He cast Lady Foxmore a silencing look, then slumped in the nearest armchair.

"He's charmed," Lady Foxmore said to me.

"Mr. Greenham," Mrs. Windham cried as a second set of footsteps rang in the hall, "do I hear Mr. Macy approaching? Stand, Elizabeth. Smile!"

Mr. Greenham pinched the bridge of his nose.

"If you don't answer," Lady Foxmore said, "she'll continue talking."

"It is not." Mr. Greenham's voice was weary. He shut his eyes, as if experiencing a headache. "Mr. Macy awayed this morning on business. I'm to beg excuses."

"But if it's not Mr. Macy," Mrs. Windham persisted, "who is it?"

Mr. Greenham opened one eye. "How the devil should I know?"

"Well, have the goodness, at least, to tell me whether or not it's a gentleman," Mrs. Windham demanded, frantically signalling for Elizabeth to continue smiling.

Before more could be said, Edward entered, securing gold cuff links to formal attire. His jaw tight, his gaze darted over the room's occupants, stopping on me before proceeding to Lady Auburn.

"Mother." He bent and kissed her cheek. "May I join tonight's dinner?"

I shut my eyes to regain composure, so I only heard Lady Foxmore thwack her cane as Edward's footfall struck the floor behind me. "So, you've finally decided to come back from the dead, have you, boy?"

"Not yet," was Edward's measured reply. "Although someday I intend to. Lady Foxmore. Mr. Greenham."

"Do not presume to greet me, Edward." Lady Foxmore's words were sharp. "There is no excuse for interrupting a conversation. I suppose you're fishing for an introduction to the girl so you can try to save her soul next."

Edward said nothing but stooped, placing his hand on my

elbow. "No, Juls," he whispered in my ear, using his pet name for me. "You're not sitting on a stool, not in my house." Then louder, looking directly at Lady Foxmore, "I need no introduction to Julia. I daresay she has a far stronger claim on me than anyone else here, thank you."

Were he not supporting my elbow, I should have doubted my ability to stand. The shocked silence intensified as Edward led me near the door and took his stance next to me.

My face burned. Edward's use of my first name combined with his speech was as good as an announcement of our betrothal. With a sternness I'd never seen him exhibit, he returned their stares, one by one, with a glower of his own.

"Well, Edward," Lady Foxmore said, recovering first, "you certainly are amusing, if nothing else." Turning to Lady Auburn, she said, "Perhaps you'd best start dinner, dear."

Lady Auburn seemed unable to move. Wide-eyed, she clutched her husband's arm, her gaze circling between Edward and me.

When his parents did nothing, Edward presented me his arm. "May I have the honor?" He nodded to the footman to open the door. During that short walk to the dining room, there was little I could say or do with everyone watching except construct a mask and retreat behind it.

Candlelight bedecked the room we entered. A mahogany table, easily large enough to accommodate thirty, was lavished with china, fine linens, and crystal. Green boughs decorated the mantel, filling the chamber with the fragrance of spruce.

Within a few minutes, curls of steam, laced with scents of lemon, thyme, and sherry, escaped from the tureen carried in by the butler. While the footman ladled soup, Edward sat rigid, staring at his soup bowl with such intensity it was a marvel the fragile china did not crumble.

"Well, boy," Lady Foxmore eventually said, tearing apart bread, "no one wants to inquire why it is that you are so familiar with Miss Elliston. By and by, we shall uncover this mystery, but not just yet. Give us at least the first course. In the meantime, since you stole the conversation before dinner even started, have the decency to supply us with a new one."

He lifted his head as if with great effort. "Dinner conversation? You want dinner conversation?" He glanced over the table occupants and settled on Lady Foxmore. "This very moment I was thinking of how callous we are, to gather and eat seven courses, when less than a mile from here, six cottager's children shall go to bed with empty stomachs."

Lord Auburn stirred, his cheeks ruddy with anger. "Son."

"Remain with us awhile longer, Miss Elliston." Lady Foxmore pointed her spoon at Edward. "That one is full of dreary statements nowadays. Only take care he doesn't steal your appetite. You're too thin as is."

Edward seemed to recall me and looked at my untouched food. Compunction softened his features. "No, not you," he whispered. "Eat, Juls."

Lady Foxmore laughed outright. "You disappoint, Edward, for I refuse to believe you remain unaware of her heritage. Why is the atheist allowed to eat unharassed?"

"Leave her be." Edward took up his wineglass. "At least she does not claim to embrace Christ while ignoring his teachings, as most here do."

Both Lord and Lady Auburn stared anew at me, and I saw they were puzzling out my name. In an effort to compose myself, I placed my hand over my bodice. My father was notorious for retaining his composure while under attack. Yet I knew I'd lose steadiness of mind should anyone mention the other scandalous topics my father wrote about.

Lady Foxmore's eyes twinkled as if reading my thoughts, but she took mercy and steered the conversation elsewhere. "Edward, I insist you come along the next time I go to Bath. You may make all the dreary statements you wish. Indeed, I hope you'll preach at us as we dine, rend your clothing as we dance, and at the opera, you can stand upon your seat and call down fire and brimstone. My friends pay well for their amusement. I personally promise a thousand pounds if you convert one, or even one of their servants."

Edward turned deaf, his eyes not so much as flickering in her direction as he returned his attention to his soup bowl.

Lady Foxmore chuckled as she salted her soup. "Tell me, boy, by any chance am I correct in assuming that all six of those starving children drank tea today?"

Edward's head reared up. "And what has that to do with anything?"

Satisfied that he'd taken her bait, she made him wait until she'd set down her salt spoon. "With such a high duty on tea and sugar, one would hope they'd forgo the pleasure and buy food instead."

"You know full well—" his voice held a cold fury—"they're buying your secondhand leaves." He grated his mother next with his gaze. "As they do yours, madam."

"Yet," Lady Foxmore persisted, "if they were truly starving, a little gruel should prove more useful. As far as your demands we give away our used leaves, I never shall. I do not condone the waste. During the tea hour, every field and every garden is empty, and for what? So they can sit, doing nothing?"

Edward clenched his teeth, though his voice sounded calm. "You take the only respite offered them in their miserable, unhappy lives—the only hour they gain a moment's rest from backbreaking labor, and you dare to condemn them for it?"

Lord Auburn leaned forward, seemingly ready to unleash a rebuke, but Lady Foxmore held up a hand for peace. "When it steals my guests' appetites because their children starve, yes."

Edward fell silent, casting his gaze back upon his empty bowl. To anyone who knew him less well, it might have seemed he had no argument in reply, but I knew he was too angry for words.

"Well," Lady Foxmore said after an awkward silence, "are we empty of conversation so soon? How delightful. Dare I ask you to try again?"

A bell jangled in the hall, as though someone were clamoring on it with all his might.

Edward cringed, shutting his eyes.

"What's this? Surely we are not expecting more visitors." Lady Foxmore turned to Lady Auburn. "Who dares to call upon you at this hour in such vulgarity?"

"Yes," agreed Elizabeth. "It's almost as vulgar as waking someone in the dead of night for a mere trifle."

Mrs. Windham tittered, while Lord Auburn glared at Edward. Less than a minute later, his accusation was confirmed by the appearance of a footman slipping into the chamber to bend over Edward.

"Sir." He breathed as if able to feel his master's displeasure boring into his back. He presented a soiled note between our chairs. "I beg pardon, but this just arrived."

For a moment, it seemed Edward would not pick up the paper, but then, moving as if he had to break invisible ropes tying his arms to the chair, he took up the note.

"Thank you, John." Edward met the footman's eye before unfolding the page.

With everyone else's attention focused on Edward, I finally had my first opportunity to study him myself. His face, though hard and set like flint, also revealed strain. Lines of worry etched his brow. He blinked tired eyes as though he fought valiantly to force them to remain open. His hands were not the smooth white I remembered, but were stained, nicked, and scarred. Even his shoulders drooped with fatigue. I doubted he'd have looked more battered had he been drawn out of the sea after being cast adrift for days.

Compassion stirred me, and I understood Henry and Elizabeth's compulsion to stop him. If he continued this madness, he'd work himself into an early grave. Were we alone, I'd have implored him to fill his stomach and then stretch before the fire to sleep with his head upon my lap, where I could guard his slumber from interruption.

"Has something happened?" Lady Foxmore asked. "Worthy enough to disturb dinner?"

Edward nodded, then crumpled the paper, his features tight.

"Well, what is it? I demand to know." Lady Foxmore set down her spoon with a clatter. "I may have made you vicar, but this is still my parish."

"An infant died at the workhouse." His tone was hollow as he placed his napkin on the table. "If I may be excused."

"Lovely." Lady Foxmore beckoned her soup to be removed. "Starving cottagers and dying infants. I'd rather forgotten how delightful your company was. 'Tis a pity you don't join us more often. Honestly, Edward, if the child is dead, what difference is another hour or two? My last incumbent never even held services for those under the age of eighteen, much less tramped through a stormy night to mark their passing."

"Yes, and so the sheep were scattered because there was no shepherd." Edward rested his thumb and forefinger over his eyes, as if trying to summon the energy to rise from his chair. "Was it not you who instructed me on the sacred duty of tending this flock?"

Lady Foxmore snorted. "Bosh. It was the standard speech I give all incumbents. Unless you have a particular tie to the bastard child—one strong enough to compel you to venture out into this muck—remain. I wish you here. It's not as though this were an uncommon occurrence."

I hadn't thought it possible for Edward's appearance to grow more austere, but it did. "My tie to that babe is no more and no less than that of any other member of my parish. Shall I so easily break troth with them in order to dine with you?"

"Me?" Lady Foxmore spread her bejewelled hands in mock

surprise. "Well, now I am flattered, indeed! And here I thought it was that scrawny girl sitting there who lured you back to civilization." She clutched the ermine mantle at her throat, her voice deepening with anger. "At least you'll find that I am free from paltering. I shall be direct. Be aware, Edward, I summoned the girl in order to judge for myself whether I'll allow her to marry Hugh Kellie—for you know, do you not, that he's agreed to wed her for the dowry Mrs. Windham is offering?"

Edward, it appeared, did not know. His countenance grew so still, so severe, he could have been a statue of Mars. Even Elizabeth drew back in her seat.

"Have no fear on that account." Lady Foxmore dipped the tips of her fingers in her finger bowl. "No one here likes Hugh Kellie, least of all me. I have decided to replace her matchmaker with myself. This scarecrow of a girl promises quite a career and requires an equally extraordinary chaperone. Already she's managed the feat of reintroducing you into society, and she has utterly captivated Mr. Greenham, has she not, John?"

The silent giant roused long enough to give her a scathing look.

"Well, she has," Lady Foxmore said with humor. "He just has yet to discover it. So, Edward, will you really so willingly abandon your lady to me?"

I scrunched my skirt as once more the company's shocked stares focused on me.

"You waste your breath," Edward eventually said to Lady Foxmore, rising. "Only a fool would invest further trust in you."

"Edward!" Lord Auburn rose in rebuke to his son.

"Father—" Edward bowed—"if you'll excuse me."

His hand skimmed the top of my chair as he left the room while I sat mute in disbelief. Through the closed door, I heard him bid a servant to have his coat and Wellingtons fetched.

"Go bring him back." Lady Auburn looked at her husband. "There is nothing he can do tonight. We need him here."

While Lord Auburn followed his son into the hall, where their voices carried in uproar, Mrs. Windham declared herself a fit of nerves.

"Well, child?" Lady Foxmore asked, drying her hands with her napkin and ignoring the others. "What have you to say on the matter?"

Still stunned that Edward had abandoned me to such a pit, I opened my mouth but remained at a loss for words. I had no doubt Edward expected me to rebuff Lady Foxmore with cold disregard—and after days of contemplating what to expect from him, I finally had an answer. He was hard and unyielding, all fire and ice with little else between.

He'd not asked one question or sought after my health. He'd made us a spectacle and then waltzed away, leaving me to explain. Ignoring everyone else in the room, I drew a deep breath. There had been no pledge to keep his betrothal, no discussion about our grave differences.

Did he think me that desperate for him? That he could treat me thus and still retain my favor?

"Well?" Lady Foxmore's age made it impossible for her to keep her head perfectly still, and as a result, her diamond ear-bobs swayed, casting sparkles of light. Her mouth curved in roguery. "I was not in jest. Shall I find you a husband? Surely I can offer better than the Windhams or . . ." She punctuated her thought with a nod at Edward's empty chair.

I felt so jarred by my sudden change of circumstance that my chair felt as if it were floating. I stared. Compared to the rumors circulating about her, spiting her own vicar by finding a husband for his love interest was mild.

I do not know what I would have said were not the threat of Scotland looming over me. As I sat in my chair that evening, I saw possibilities open that had never been offered me before. Edward had already proven himself traitor by joining the church.

Why, I asked myself, should I not explore every possibility provided?

As I opened my mouth to accept her offer, Elizabeth silently shook her head.

"I should very much like to continue the conversation," was my simple reply.

Seven

THE NEXT MORNING, Nancy pounced on my bed before
sunrise.

"Be it true?" she demanded, her cap slipping off her head.
"Lady Foxmore is sponsoring thee?"

I pulled the covers up to my chin and groaned, too mired in
sleep to upbraid her. She grabbed a copper pitcher and skipped
over to my washstand, where she poured steaming water. "Cook
says with her, thou'll be married before a month's end."

I said nothing, surprised at the hurt I felt at the idea. The
previous evening, Mrs. Windham returned home wild over her
success. She'd gone to bed, prattling about how she convinced
Lady Foxmore to take me off her hands.

I swung my feet out of bed and plodded to the washbasin,
realizing why Mrs. Windham lived in terror of servants' gossip,
if news spread so quickly. "What else have you heard about last
night?"

"That th' reverend is wick with love over thee."

I dried my hands on a towel, shoving aside the stab of pain

and wondering how far the rumors had gotten. Deciding to test it, I asked, "Why do they think that?"

She hurried over to the wardrobe and shook out my second-best dress. Glancing back over her shoulder, a stupid look suddenly stole across her features, making her appear a dullard. "Think what, m'lady?"

I swallowed my smile, but in truth her ability to appear so daft amazed me. I dried my face, determined to remember the trick if I got sent to Scotland.

By the time I made my way to the dining room, it was nearing ten. Sun spread over the table as I dropped to my seat. Mrs. Windham nodded. Elizabeth chewed toast thoughtfully, but gave me a nod. The window sat open, affording a cool breeze with a tang of smoke.

"Did you oversleep, dear?" Mrs. Windham asked.

I nodded, though it wasn't true. After Nancy left, I'd remained in my bedchamber until the homey clatter of dishes, clink of silverware, and scent of buttery scones cajoled me to join them.

"This arrived." Mrs. Windham laid a missive beside my plate, and I saw with discomfort it was Lady Foxmore's stationery.

"Don't open it." Elizabeth set aside her toast. "Burn it. Disembowel it. Drown it. Anything except open it."

"Nonsense," Mrs. Windham said. "Go on, Julia."

Frowning, I turned over the creamy paper and broke the wax seal. Lady Foxmore's handwriting was fine lace.

"I'm invited for tea. She wishes to discuss her requirements before sponsoring me." Then, hating the idea of appearing before this woman again, I appealed to Elizabeth. "Come with me?"

"Was I invited?" Elizabeth extended her hand for the letter. "I thought she swore no Windham should ever set foot inside her estate."

I tucked the page beneath the table. If her ladyship could disregard the rules, so could I. "You're invited."

That afternoon the sun shone high in the cold sky as we hastened through the orchard shortcut. The ruined harvest had a profound effect on the parish. As we trampled over the rutted ground, men stopped their work and glared at us with crabbed expressions. No hats were doffed, no knuckles scraped against foreheads.

Elizabeth avoided looking at them, keeping her determined gaze straight ahead, but at a proper distance, I stripped off my veil and continued my study of the men. During my past visits, the workers had been merry. Legs had dangled over tree branches, swinging in rhythm as men sang songs. Boys ate tawny, dripping fruit on their breaks, while girls hauled pails of drinking water and shyly hinted at upcoming dances.

Elizabeth seemed to guess what had upset the parish, but I did not inquire, fearing to learn that it was Edward's strictness that caused their great unhappiness.

My reservations increased when Lady Foxmore's house loomed into view. The gravel walks and manicured boxwoods leading to her doorstep seemed a world apart from the pastures starred with cosmos.

Inside, the butler took our wraps and left us in the antechamber. A French king could not have ordered a grander entrance. Apricot walls painted with exotic parrots and long-beaked birds contrasted against scrolling chairs and marble busts. Leaf-green portières blocked all other views of the house. I eyed the space with satisfaction, recalling how my parish vicar said God would punish me by bringing me to the meanest level of society unless I repented. How I longed for him to see me standing here.

"Welcome, child." Head bobbing, Lady Foxmore stepped from behind a curtain. No mischief twinkled in her eyes; no mockery curved her mouth. Anyone meeting her for the first time might have been fooled into thinking her a kindhearted, snowy-haired matron.

Expressionless, she stared at Elizabeth. "I had forgotten how deep attachments run between young girls. Next time, I shall invite your friend, so you need not impose on me. I would question your upbringing, Julia, had I not already found it inadequate."

With a slight touch on my arm, she indicated for me to follow and turned down a passage. Despite not having been received, Elizabeth accompanied me into the dragon's lair. At the end of the hall, Lady Foxmore opened the door to a room attired in white. Sheer window panels filtered daylight into the airy space. The walls were bone-colored, the upholstery cream. Tea was laid over a tablecloth of Brussels lace. The color scheme carried to the food. Whipped meringue shells with ivory rose petals and custards with curls of coconut had been arranged on delicate dishes.

Lady Foxmore pulled an embroidered bell cord, then invited us to take a seat. A uniformed maid brought the teapot. Lady Foxmore motioned toward the service. "Julia, show me your serving skills."

Mama and I rarely entertained; therefore I was unpracticed. When tea dripped over the spout, staining the lace, Lady Foxmore's mouth creased. "I see I shall have to find you a husband who has no disposition for tea."

"Or she could practice," Elizabeth said with an edge in her voice as I pressed a linen napkin into the stain. "Perhaps you'd best leave Julia to her own devices."

Lady Foxmore chuckled. "There is hope for you yet, Elizabeth. By and by, I may learn to forgive you your choice of mother."

I tucked the stained linen under the silver tray, feeling discomposed. Beneath Lady Foxmore's friendly facade, I sensed she was disgruntled, like a tiger eyeing us through the bars of her metal cage.

None of us drank our tea, and Elizabeth and I dared not risk blowing on it, so we sat silent for several minutes.

"I suppose," Lady Foxmore eventually said over the ticking clock, "you are wondering why such a crabby, eccentric woman would take on the challenge of finding you a husband?" Her eyes narrowed. "No, I see the thought never crossed your mind. Then I perceive you are only interested in what I might do for you. Find a wealthy husband; is that not so, child?"

I set my cup in its saucer, ready to counter the thought.

Lady Foxmore held up her hand. "Say nothing, Miss Elliston. It would shatter everything I like about you, were you to deny it, and there is precious little I like about you now. I owe this favor to your mother. Did you know I was well acquainted with her when she was your age?"

"My mother!" My amazement was so complete, I sat forward. "That's not possible. She never mentioned you."

"Nor would I have expected her to." Lady Foxmore cooled her tea, her expression smug. "And it was just as well. She had no right to claim status with me. Had she tried to call on me, I should not have received her."

"But—"

"After the death of her family in that fire," she continued over me, "your mother spent the following summer with my niece Isabella in Bath. I chaperoned them to numerous balls and assemblies. She was a great favorite of mine, though stubborn as the year is long. Had she trusted me, she wouldn't have married as low as she did and to such a dreadfully tempered man."

Mama never spoke of the past—never, not to anyone. I learned only a year ago, when I'd appealed to Sarah about my maternal grandparents, that her family had died in a fire. Sarah's face paled as she apprised me of their fate, telling me never to mention it, as it would upset Mama.

Finding a link to Mama's past in Lady Foxmore was so overwhelming, I had no response. Lady Foxmore moved in the highest spheres. It didn't seem possible that Mama had once belonged there. Suddenly, I wondered who else of consequence was connected to her past. Why that thought made me feel ill, I could not have said, but it did.

My face must have hinted at my nausea, for Lady Foxmore gave me a strange look. I sipped tea to distract her, burning my tongue.

"Did you . . . did you ever write my mother?" I asked, envisioning the slew of letters that drove her to suicide. "During this past year, perhaps—or know someone who might have?"

Lady Foxmore shut her eyes as if I'd blundered. "Gracious, no. After her marriage she was no longer acknowledged by society. Had she married higher, perhaps . . ." Lady Foxmore studied my face. "With her good looks, I have not a doubt she could have captured a very wealthy husband. I have far better expectations for you."

I looked down, still wrestling with the thought that Mama had known Lady Foxmore. All those visits to Am Meer, and all the times we'd listened to stories involving her ladyship, Mama kept their acquaintance hidden, usually ushering Elizabeth and me from the room, stating gossip wasn't suitable for young ears.

I looked at Elizabeth, but it was as if Lady Foxmore and I were two actors on stage and she had no role.

"Now, child—" Lady Foxmore set aside her teacup—"against my better judgment, I have agreed to find you a husband. But we still need to discuss my terms."

"Terms?" Elizabeth wrinkled her nose, giving me a warning look.

Had not my stomach felt as though my body had been pulled to dizzying heights, I might have admitted I was taken aback as well.

"Naturally. This is not the first time I've been paid to introduce a young lady, though generally the idea is to arrange wealth with title." Lady Foxmore clutched the crook of her walking stick. "First thing is first. My usual fee for finding one a husband—"

A firm knock sounded on the door, and Lady Foxmore gave a

gasp of annoyance before calling over her shoulder, "Come in, John. I know it's you."

Mr. Greenham opened the door. "Would I be interrupting?"

"Nonsense. Were you truly concerned, you wouldn't have disturbed us in the first place." Lady Foxmore struck her walking stick against the floor, then gestured to me with her heavily jewelled hand to pour him a cup. "Come. I can see you are as curious about this girl as I am."

Greenham's entry was as meticulous as his attire. His movements were genteel, his feet scarcely making a sound. He moved a chair near us, then studied me unabashedly. The way he slowly scrutinized my every feature drew a nervous response. Though the tea would taste bitter having brewed too long, I hastily poured a cup and handed it to him.

"Now," Lady Foxmore said, "my usual fee for introducing an upstart to society is one thousand pounds. Generally the hope is to crossbreed money with gentry, but in your case . . ." She made a gesturing wave over my dress. "My fee for you shall be two thousand pounds, which you shall agree to pay within a year of the wedding."

Elizabeth made a scoffing noise, then seeming to find the conversation too ludicrous, collapsed against the back of her chair and turned her face to the window.

Lady Foxmore smiled, stirring her tea. "Are we agreed upon my first condition, Miss Elliston?"

Mr. Greenham's stare remained fastened upon me as I focused on the pool of brown in my cup. The number was astronomical. Even were I not fated to be a lady's companion, which offered no wages, but say a governess, it would take me seventy years to pay such a sum. Yet she hadn't said I'd owe her money unless I wed. She'd want her money, so surely she'd work to find me a rich husband—but that still left the problem of explaining after the ceremony, to my still-unknown husband, that he owed her two thousand pounds.

"Will . . ." I took a breath. "What I mean is, if this person is unwilling to pay such a sum, would you accept jewelry, or perhaps an article worth that amount?"

Lady Foxmore burst into laughter, clapping her hands. "Good gracious, John. She's already planning to rob her new household." She laughed again. "Yes, I daresay, child, I'll accept payment in kind. Though I hope to marry you to a more generous husband than that. Consider the two thousand pounds my personal revenge for his using me as a matchmaker." Here, Mr. Greenham stirred in his chair, giving her an evil look. "So, are we agreed?"

I nodded, trying to ignore the strange manner in which Mr. Greenham watched me. Unknown to most, I still retained Mama's emeralds—the heart of a priceless collection, or so Sarah said. Each piece—hair circlet, necklace, bracelet, brooch, and varying other pieces—was matched with peerless diamonds. The value of the set was so great, Mama never dared to even wear so much as one ring.

"A verbal agreement, child. Do not leave our witnesses, John and Elizabeth, in doubt. Do you agree to my first term?"

I felt like a girl in a fairy tale making a bargain with a witch. "Yes."

Elizabeth made a choking noise while Mr. Greenham turned his attention to his cup.

"Good. Now for my next term. Nothing would induce me to present you to a person of consequence looking as such. Your garb is positively ghastly. You must start wearing color again."

"Oh, honestly," Elizabeth burst into our conversation. "You cannot expect her to defy society on your orders. Besides, this entire conversation is irrelevant. Julia is under her guardian's protection, and he'd never allow any of this."

"Guardian?" Lady Foxmore arched her eyebrows. "Who, child? I shall write this person."

After glaring at Elizabeth, I shook my head. "I know not. He wishes to remain anonymous."

"Rubbish." Lady Foxmore swept the air with her hand. "Anyone who refuses to reveal himself is hiding something and will not dare interfere with our plans. Had he been worthy in the first place, he never would have even allowed a visit to the Windhams. The next time I lay eyes on you, child, I expect you out of those ridiculous rags." She held up a hand, though I'd made no attempt to interrupt her. "I gather you have no funds, but you'll have to find a way to manage. I'm offering you a husband beyond the compass of your imagination. I expect to see a bit of fortitude on your part. Sell that locket if necessary. Just find a way."

My finger sought out the heavy, gold locket around my neck. Inside was a painted ivory of Mama and my father.

"She's not selling her locket." Elizabeth rose alongside her voice. "Nor is she going to allow you to choose her a husband! Do you honestly think she'll risk her reputation? We all know the rumors surrounding you, how more than one young lady in your charge has disappeared only to reappear after a questionable length of time, her middle thicker, never to marry."

Instead of appearing offended, Lady Foxmore looked rather amused. Her head trembled as she tried to hold still. "Am I to blame when young girls mishandle the freedom I give them?"

Elizabeth turned and gathered her shawl from her chair. "Come, Julia. We're leaving this conversation right now."

I fastened my gaze on a crackled ivory vase holding waxed roses.

"Julia?" Elizabeth sounded panicked this time.

When I sat unmoving, she picked up her skirts and hied to the door, her petticoats rustling. I envisioned her finding Henry. Doubtless by nightfall, Edward would learn what had transpired this afternoon, but I no longer cared.

"Do you accept my second condition?" Lady Foxmore asked.

My throat felt strained, so I nodded but then remembered it had to be verbal. "Yes."

"But she's not selling her locket," Mr. Greenham said in a firm voice.

"So, you are capable of speech." Lady Foxmore shifted to view him. "Good heavens, John, if you must make noise, wait and test your conversational skills on someone else. I do not like interruptions, especially from men who normally refuse to speak."

He set his untouched cup of tea aside and sat forward. After divesting his waistcoat of a pocketbook, he pulled out several pound notes. "I believe this should suffice for a new wardrobe, yes?"

"You know I cannot accept that," I said, staring at the notes. "No lady can acce—"

"Make no mistake, Miss Elliston," Lady Foxmore said. "We are no longer working within society's confines. If you wish to marry a husband on the top rung, you may find yourself compromising in many ways—"

"No." My throat grew even tighter. "There are some things I shall never do."

"Nor shall you be asked to," Mr. Greenham said through gritted teeth, glaring at Lady Foxmore. "Upon my oath, nothing shall be required of you which you are unwilling to do. If I may be allowed, let me restate my offer. Would you honor me by permitting me to purchase your locket? I shall retain it until you are capable of purchasing it back again."

"That's hardly showing fortitude on her part, John."

A vein in his neck emerged. "This is no game, and—"

"Temper, temper," Lady Foxmore said in a singsong voice.

His eyes flashed with a look of sheer rage, but unlike my father he found a place in which to tuck it away. He turned back to me in full control of himself and extended the banknotes. "Will you honor me by accepting my offer?"

Eight

⁂

THE NIGHT FOLLOWING my pact with Lady Foxmore, a smattering of pebbles bounced off the shutters, puncturing my dreams. I opened my eyes, realizing the sound had been incorporated into my last few minutes of sleep.

Another round of pebbles skidded across the wood.

Of all that had happened since my arrival at Am Meer, this sickened me the most, for I knew it was Edward. I guessed he'd learned about my visit with Lady Foxmore.

I wanted nothing more than for Edward to leave, but I knew him too well. If he wanted an audience, he'd stop at nothing short of plowing through the thatched roof.

Brushing aside the locks of hair cascading over my eyes, I threw back the covers and hastily donned my wrapper. Ignoring the ache in my legs from the long walk to Lady Foxmore's residence, I went to the window and threw open the shutters.

Clouds obscured the sky, but light from the waxing moon still served as an illuminant. Drizzle hazed over the withered vines and the rosebushes that had been cut back for the approaching winter.

Dressed in his cassock, Edward was bending over, retrieving more pebbles, but it was what came next that froze my blood. His elbow suddenly protruded from his shadowed form, and he both staggered and wiped his eyes. A sob rent the silence as he stumbled in his quest for more stones.

Intoxicated?

I drew in a breath of cold air. Experience had taught me men never sobbed except when drunk—and volatile. I clutched the windowsill, fearing not the violence Edward might be capable of, but his tongue. Sober, he was a gentleman and would never allow his words to cut, but drunk . . . ?

He straightened to strike my window again, but upon catching sight of me, his hand dropped and pebbles fell from it.

"Come down," he ordered, and then plodded toward the ancient oak.

My feet were stone as silence engulfed the night. It was foolishness to confront Edward in this state of mind. But I detested my own fear. I had sworn to never again feel weak, to never again cower before another's temper. Glancing up at the cloudy sky, I wondered how many times Mama had stood thus, cold tingling through her fingers as she summoned courage to confront my father. Yet she had always gone. Her face granite, her heart marble, she always went.

Gathering fortitude from her memory, I left the window to find slippers. I crept from my room and down the hall, where I shushed the dogs that stirred beneath the bench where the hall boy slept.

Outdoors, I made my way to the spinney, which at night seemed primeval. Gossamer webs clung to my hands and robe as I groped through the darkness. The marshy ground seeped into my shoes, causing my toes to ache with the chill. The scents invading the air were not those of my childhood meetings with Edward—but carried the foul odor of a bog.

Under a bower of our oak tree, I stopped and crossed my

arms, no longer fearing the woods or Edward's coming wrath. Drizzle rustled the leaves above me as mist coiled about my ankles.

I felt Edward's presence before I saw him.

"Look at me," he commanded from behind.

I obeyed, twisting to see over my shoulder, certain that defiance must be written over my every feature. Though it was dark, I saw him—and knew he saw me—although nebulously. Damp curls rested against his pale face. His countenance gave the impression he'd returned from the scene of a great tragedy.

"You went to her?" His cry was impassioned with pain, his voice hoarse. "You entered into an agreement for her to arrange a marriage?"

I said nothing as he circled to the front of me, though my stomach hollowed with the realization there was no stench of ale upon his breath.

"What of us, Juls? Why drag me to that godforsaken dinner if you had no intention of acceding to our betrothal?"

I tightened my wrapper, narrowing my eyes at him.

"What?" he shouted. "Are you going to deny that, too? We were never engaged? Was it not this very spot!"

"No," I slowly said in a tone that Sarah would have called quarrelsome. "I do not deny that we *were* engaged, only that you intend to honor the commitment."

He emitted a growling sound. "I'm not the one who walked away from here and never came back. It's been three years, Julia!" His bellowing caused birds to take noisy flight from their trees. "You're the one who refused to visit after learning I intended to enter the church. You're the one who couldn't stand to look upon me in my vestments. You're the one petitioning others to find you a husband."

"That wasn't me! That was Mama! And we didn't even know you intended to enter the church. But it was *you* who betrayed us. *You.* You knew what the church did to my family."

"Not the church. One man, one vicar. You know nothing about what you're rejecting alongside me. You're ruining our lives because of the actions of one person. One!"

"Do not presume to lecture me. You knew you were severing all relations with us. Well, take your accursed church. Take it and go. I no longer want you."

His eyes blazed as intensity marked his features. Until that moment I never noticed he stood a full head taller than myself, for he'd always seemed exactly my height. "Fine." He ground the words out. "Do not expect me to come grovelling at your next beck and call. May you find what you deserve with Lady Foxmore. She's as false as you are."

Turning his back to me, he stalked off into the ebon shadows.

I did not move, my face still twisted in anger and my body heated from our exchange. To an outsider, I might have appeared unmoved, untouched by the scene. But in truth, I struggled not to fragment into irrecoverable pieces.

I'd never told anyone, but conjuring Edward in my mind had helped me survive Mama's burial. While gravediggers dug the cold, wet earth, I'd stood in the rain, listening to their shovels chink against the bones of the excommunicated, trying to callous myself that in a few years hence Mama would likewise be disinterred to make room in the crowded yard.

The apothecary, Mr. Hollis, stuttering and turning various shades of red, had advised me to attend the body until the very end—here he'd been obliged to remove his spectacles and wipe them—because without my presence, someone might show their reverence to the church by taking their fury out on Mama's coffin, as they had my father's. The risk of her body being seen was too high.

For hours I ignored the reek of corpses by pretending Edward's strong hand cupped my elbow. To drown out the gravediggers' cursing, I'd made up encouraging words which Edward might have whispered in my ear.

That night, as I stood bareheaded in that dismal, dripping bower, memory of Mama's burial found me anew. The heartache I'd refused to make room for suddenly rose up, seizing me. Warm tears blended on my cheek with the cold rain. It was a strange breaking, to grieve that something imaginary wasn't real.

We are not meant to take gnawing pain and cocoon it inside, for the ache only grows. That first sob rent its silk envelope, releasing the reservoir of tears. Rare are the moments when we purge the anguish of our souls. There is nothing dainty or feminine about it. Harsh, bestial sobs wracked my body as I sank to the ground, finally acknowledging my loss.

I keened as I hadn't yet—for the loss of Mama, the loss of Sarah, the loss of who I believed Edward to be, and the future I once pursued.

"Juls." Arms wrapped me from behind as Edward knelt, gathering me from the marshy ground to settle me against his chest. "Do not weep," his voice lulled as he cradled me. "Forgive me; I meant it not."

But all I could see was Mama's dead face. I was reliving those numb, horrible moments of realizing she was gone, the harrowing silence of the house, and the necessity of locking away all emotion.

"Do not." Edward pulled me closer against him. "Do not."

Was I weak? Was it wrong? I clutched the back of his cassock as I sobbed against his sinewy chest. His clothing smelled like smoke, not the sooty scent of a coal fire, but of burning wood. It felt real and earthy—not bound in the past, but something present and alive.

Edward spoke into my hair, murmuring comforting words and pleas that I collect myself.

But I would weep until energy was spent, until I'd cried so hard my breathing refused to regulate itself.

"Be calm. Take slow breaths," Edward whispered to me. "It will pass."

All around us, rain tapped on the rustling trees above and on the slick ground. By the time my gasping subsided enough that I could distinguish the sounds, my nightgown was soaked, my eyes and throat burned.

As Edward continued to hold me and breathe his warmth into my hair, I closed my eyes, taking in the feel of his arms, running my fingers over his back and broad shoulders before twining them in his hair. I cared not that the moment was fleeting, that my path was barred from Edward's, and his from me.

"Juls." His voice grew strained as he pushed me away. Obediently, I withdrew, but in doing so caught a clear glimpse of him.

During our youth, a peculiar look would sometimes cross Edward's face and his body would stiffen. He'd grow resolute and would retreat to brood under a tree. Fear used to tingle through me that perhaps I'd upset or disappointed him.

That night, as I encountered the same expression, I learned my error.

Before he could veil his thoughts or mask his hunger, I saw his unbridled desire.

I leaned toward him, tilting my lips up to his.

No other invitation was needed. The boy who had always taken great pains to remain chaste with me lost his battle as a man.

He cupped my face with rough, calloused hands and kissed my forehead, cheeks, and eyes before finding my mouth.

I entwined my fingers in his curls as he drew me closer, pressing me tightly against him. Part of me marvelled at my own actions, while another part grew disquieted over his level of boldness. His mouth moved to my neck, both thrilling and alarming me. His hands quaked, as if I were made of delicate china and he was holding back his full strength. His hand slid down the curve of my waist, and his mouth to my collarbone.

All at once, common sense rose up and insisted I envision our future.

After indulging his desires, he'd blame me. Was I not the atheist? Would he not look back someday and remember me as the temptress? How well I could see him, standing behind a pulpit, relieving his conscience by condemning cottagers for their lust. This one act contained the means of securing Edward but at the cost of killing all love between us.

How, I thought next, could I be so rational and logical during a moment like this? It wasn't right. Yet, I reasoned further, as he tightened a fistful of my hair between his fingers, would I find love in Scotland? Was it not better to be the wife of a guilt-ridden vicar than to be banished and alone?

"H-h-hello?"

Edward's body stiffened, then slowly, noiselessly, he shifted in the direction of the voice.

A lantern bobbed near the edge of the spinney like a misguided faerie. In its light I recognized the Windhams' lanky hall boy, squinting as he peered in our direction, doubtless seeing the white of my nightgown. He took two steps nearer the woods, but fear of will-o'-the-wisps must have kept him, for he hesitated. "Is a-anyone there?"

"Caleb." Edward's voice was iron as he rose, revealing himself fully in the light. "Go back to your cot. Turn your face to the wall, and do not hear or see anything. Am I clear?"

No one, not even Mama in her most obstinate mood, would have disobeyed an order given in that tone. The hall boy didn't even nod, but set the lantern on the ground and plowed his way indoors.

Edward staggered to the nearest tree. Hand on hip, he pinched the bridge of his nose, his breathing strained. When he finally spoke, he scarcely sounded in control of himself. "Go back to bed now, Julia, lest I do something rash."

My legs were ungainly and wet linen clung to my body and water dripped from the ends of my hair as I stood. Even in the dark I could see bracken stained my nightgown. I hesitated, waiting for Edward to say something—anything.

His jaw firm, he kept his gaze fixed in the distance, as if determined not to see me in my soaked nightclothes.

"Edward," I pleaded, not certain what I needed him to say, what I needed to hear.

"Now!" he shouted.

Tears clotting my throat, I turned and raced back to Am Meer. To my mind, he had narrowly escaped me and knew it. He would not again risk such an entrapment.

The cottage hall appeared dark upon my reentrance. The hall boy's cot creaked as I plodded past. There was little doubt what the poor boy must have thought his vicar to be doing, and there I found a small morsel of comfort. Perhaps one mind might be set free tonight, if nothing else.

But once in my chambers, my legs gave way and I slid to the floor, where I covered my mouth, holding back tears of shame.

༄

The last day of Mama's life still presides over my thoughts. I have no memory of conversation, no recollection of the usual noises that would have filled the house—the clunk of shoes, the scrape of coal scuttles. Did I touch Mama that day? It frustrates me not to be able to recall. All I have are fleeting images, impressions at best, soft and blurred. Mama patting Sarah's knobby shoulder at breakfast. Mama bent over her sewing, the afternoon sun catching golden strands of her hair as she whiled away the last hours of her life. Darkness closing in about her as she blew out the flickering candle before retiring for the night.

Since my arrival, my days at Am Meer had melded into a routine of needlework, reading, and the various other trifles that fill rainy days. Yet memories of Mama oppressed me. At odd hours and during small tasks, I wondered why she never confided the contents of those mysterious letters, or what had caused her great fear. For I had not yet learned that some secrets destroy their percipients, and she no more would have told me what was happening behind the scenes than a general would reveal his battle plans to the infantry unit he planned to sacrifice.

Edward, on the other hand, was rather blunt about throwing me upon the altar.

The morning following our tryst in the woods, pale sunlight filtered through the house, lifting spirits, making it impossible not to hope that our shocking behavior from last night might end up for my betterment. Had I not felt it in the trembling of his body, the crushing weight of his kisses? Had he not been drawn back to me when I wept? Had he not gathered me tenderly toward him? Memories would haunt him, I knew, working in my favor.

By noon, I paced the house, certain that Edward would call. After the previous evening, he'd have to. He wouldn't be a gentleman otherwise. I occupied myself by imagining the secret looks we'd exchange while Mrs. Windham babbled. No doubt he'd be nervous, wondering how best to arrange a private moment with me—where I envisioned he'd fall to his knees, his voice contrite as he tried to explain what happened. And whenever I closed my eyes and relived the touch of his hands, the scratch of his cheek, the feel of his mouth on mine, it was impossible not to hope we'd find a way to renew the dangerous experiment.

I was unprepared, therefore, for the events that were set in motion during the early hours of that afternoon. Boots sounded in the hall, followed by a light rapping on the drawing room door.

"Come in," I called out, feeling breathless over my luck. Both Mrs. Windham and Elizabeth had gone over the hill to check on a neighbor. Not wanting to risk missing Edward's visit, I'd feigned a headache.

Full of anticipation, I watched the door open.

To my disappointment, Caleb, the hall boy, ducked into the

chamber, smelling of manure. Muck and straw clung to the bottom of his ragged trousers. His hair mussy and his face scarlet, he mumbled a few incoherent words and extended a sealed note.

To mask my bewilderment, I smiled. Pride lifted my chin as I took up the page, but my hands were ice. It boded ill. Never before had Edward sent me a note. He'd always come in person. With calmness I did not feel, I retook my seat and broke the seal.

I saw at once no gentleman had penned the letter, but a madman. The words were wild, scrawled in sporadic and uneven lines. Dried ink blotted the paper, revealing he'd not even tapped aside the extra ink before writing. Entire paragraphs were smudged and showed evidence that he'd carelessly rested his hand on the page.

Yet it was the words themselves that bore the strongest testimony of how deep Edward's madness went.

> J,
>
> How heavy my heart is within me. My hand barely manages to hold the pen, my eyes to see the page. Yet write I must. Too long have I neglected my conscience. Too long have I served my tenderest affections in its stead. In weakness, I acted as no gentleman, no servant of God ought. I have shamed myself, disgraced you, and caused one of my little ones to stumble.
>
> I am undone.
>
> How shall I instruct others to abandon all for the Kingdom of God when I cannot? I delude myself with lies. Yet I will free myself as my sense of duty, my sense of right demands.
>
> No more will I blind myself into believing that as a gentleman I cannot break troth with you. I have used my delusion to offer up a crippled lamb while withholding the pure and unblemished one. Did not Shechaniah put away

his very children and wife? Abraham withheld not his own son. Shall I do less? Shall I, a teacher, do less?

What utter nonsense you must think I write. And nonsense I will write, though you are blind and deaf. For even as I scrawl the words that will forever rive us, I cannot withhold my soul from you. You, who once were my very heart.

Would that you could see me and understand. This action rips my soul in twain; it severs my right hand. Mere ink stained on parchment cannot express my agony. Yet I will not come in person.

Long have I known what I needed to do, and I will delay no longer. Julia, release me from our betrothal.

I beg you,

E

I read and reread the note, half numb with shock, half sting-ing with rejection. Every remembrance of last night now felt foolish and cockeyed. With a flush of shame, I wondered how I had deluded myself into thinking otherwise.

"He . . . he said to wait for your answer." Caleb stared at his feet.

Harsh words, insulting words that my mother and father would have flung at each other, crossed my mind. I choked on them while smothering back angry tears. For a full minute, I remained silent, for it would not do for Edward to learn I'd crumbled at his rejection. When I could speak again, my words were hard and cold. "Tell him I shall give him whatever he desires."

Goggle-eyed, Caleb stood riveted.

"Go!" I commanded, not realizing at the time how my words could be misconstrued, nor dreaming that someday they would be printed and reprinted in every paper in the land, further sul-lying my name.

As the hall boy hied from the room, I stormed to the hearth. Out of countenance, I shredded the note, then lit a match and watched it curl in the flames. Over and over I told myself I didn't need or want him. But the sting remained.

❧

As momentous an occasion as Edward's first and presumably last direct letter to me was, it was the second letter, which arrived later that evening, that took precedence. After tea, a set of hooves filled the lane leading to Am Meer, followed by a banging on our door.

Elizabeth gave a gasp of annoyance. "Oh, what can that harridan want now?"

For once Mrs. Windham did not rebuke Elizabeth. Only it was not Lady Foxmore's footman who darkened the entry. A moment later, the housekeeper tiptoed into the room and whispered in Mrs. Windham's ear, handing her a brown packet tied with string.

Mrs. Windham peered at the name on the parcel, then stared at me. "Julia, what on earth? This just arrived for you, but upon my word, the sender had not the patience to send it post, but paid a horseman to deliver it." She handed the packet to me, then waved away her housekeeper and said, "Hannah, go tell the man that the lady in question received the package. You saw it with your own eyes. Send him away now. Tip him if you must."

Stirred from my stupor, I took up the mysterious parcel. For half a second, hope flared that Edward had come to his senses, but then I realized he'd have been more discreet. As the knot in the string was tight, I signalled for Mrs. Windham's housewife. Aware of my greater wish, Mrs. Windham retrieved only the scissors.

One thought beset all others as I severed the twine. My time had ended, and I'd failed. The week's end would find me in

Scotland. There hadn't been time for Lady Foxmore to find me a husband.

"Open it already," Elizabeth demanded.

A single sheet of parchment waited within, and to my amazement, a hundred-pound note fluttered to the table. Scrawled in a masculine hand, the letter read:

> *Provisions for your upcoming trip to Scotland. Purchase your needs for the next two years.*
>
> *Your Guardian*

While Mrs. Windham reached for the money, I crumpled the letter. Elizabeth's face scrunched. "Who on earth sent you money?"

Stunned, I stared at the amount, then recovered enough to say, "It doesn't say."

"Well, her guardian, obviously," Mrs. Windham said. "And I call it positively providential too. In another month, I might have had to sacrifice one of your gowns and dye it black for her."

My heart fluttered as it always did when I lied. "Now that I think upon it, it was mentioned he might send money for my wardrobe."

Elizabeth frowned, then half rose from her chair to squint at the address on the brown wrapping. "That doesn't match the handwriting from our correspondence with that Simmons person."

"It was Simon," Mrs. Windham corrected. "Of all the nonsense! Who cares if the handwriting matches?"

Elizabeth's eyes screwed. "If you ask me—ooohhh!"

"What?" Mrs. Windham gripped the arms of her chair.

"It's Greenham!" Elizabeth snatched the brown wrapping. "Mama, it's Mr. Greenham. I'm convinced of it." And then the story tumbled out of how he'd joined us while Lady Foxmore outlined her prerequisites, including my finding a new wardrobe.

When she finished, Elizabeth triumphantly handed the wrapping to her mother.

My face burned as Mrs. Windham unfolded spectacles and silently studied the handwriting. Elizabeth hovered over her chair, gripping its backrest, clearly waiting for the censure that was to follow. Though I knew Mr. Greenham innocent, I preferred to keep speculation on him and away from my guardian.

"Mr. Greenham in love with our Julia?" Wonderment filled Mrs. Windham's voice. "Just think, Elizabeth, how this could elevate us, too."

"Mama!"

Mrs. Windham slapped the parchment on her lap. "Mr. Greenham madly in love with our Julia. Oh, we must make haste. Oh dear, oh my! I am quite convinced he is most anxious to wed. Why else risk advancing her money? I always said he was a pernickety dresser and would someday require the same of his wife, did I not, Elizabeth?"

Elizabeth wrinkled her nose. "No, you did not. This is ludicrous. He is not in love with Julia. He's scarcely acquainted with her."

"Yes, yes, quite right." Mrs. Windham bit her thumbnail. "We must take careful pains never to let him see her true personality. Julia, on all accounts, you must not speak with him. Let him discover afterwards what he has married."

"Mama, that's not what I meant."

"This has the power to advance us all." Mrs. Windham waved the banknote high. "Elizabeth, on my troth, this will secure you someone far better than Mr. Henry Auburn."

"Oh, honestly, Mama!"

"By George, I will not tolerate languishing about for mere Auburns when within months we'll be traversing the highest circles."

Elizabeth ripped the money from her hands. "Julia is not going to accept this. Even you must acknowledge the impropriety. She can no more accept this than she can abandon mourning. She'd be shunned—"

"I acknowledge no such thing!" Mrs. Windham said. "There's nothing improper, so long as Mr. Greenham eventually weds her." She faced me. "Julia, you must take careful pains to submit to some of his caresses, but not all. Entice him, only be sure—"

"Mama!"

"Well, we must make some grains of allowance, considering the difference in station." Mrs. Windham removed her spectacles. "A man of his status rarely takes notice of an inferior, unless—" here she gave an uncomfortable bob—"but so long as you withhold—" she bobbed her head twice—"it will force him to wed you. Trust me."

Elizabeth's hands flew to shield either side of her face. "Mama, for shame! Fie, fie. Oh, imagine if Mrs. Elliston were here to hear you."

"Nonsense! Lucy would agree."

My cheeks burning, I shifted in my seat, thankful the money had not, in fact, been advanced by the man in question, and glad that I had refused his similar offer yesterday. Unease pricked me as I recalled her ladyship's statement that we'd be working outside society's confines. For the first time I considered the darker gossip whispered about how Lady Foxmore's matches were achieved.

In the foolishness of youth, I suddenly grew angry at everyone else for placing me in such a precarious situation.

"Julia." Elizabeth tugged on my skirt, breaking my thoughts. From her expectant expression, I gathered she'd been speaking.

"No, leave her be." Mrs. Windham pulled me from my chair and then escorted me to the door. "Have your lady's maid make a list. Not to mince the matter, but such an offer will never come along again. Accordingly, we shall make the most of it. What would you like for breakfast tomorrow? I daresay you haven't touched a bite of food all afternoon. Think up tomorrow's menu. Have whatever you like."

It was several minutes before I managed to stumble from the room, escaping them. I felt as out of sorts as when I made the decision to conceal Mama's suicide. If Mrs. Windham, who cared about me, encouraged such behavior, then what would Lady Foxmore expect?

I pulled my shawl tighter as I ducked into my chamber.

Alone, I sank to the hearthstone and turned my gaze outdoors. Yet why did I care? What were morals except what society made them? Had not my father railed against this very thing? Was I not free?

Languish about for an Auburn, indeed, I thought, clutching Mama's locket. My entire life had been spent hoping someone would pull me from my fate. And where had it gotten me?

I knew, in that moment, I'd reached an epoch. Mrs. Windham was right. No more would I try to be biddable, sweet, and compliant, as young ladies ought. If I truly believed myself free with an unhappy fate awaiting me, then I would fight back at all costs.

I kept isolated the remainder of the day, not wanting to know whether Elizabeth had tattled the day's events to Henry. Later I learned she had not. Unaware that Edward had cut our ties, she deemed he'd never forgive such a step on my part and kept the news to herself.

When dusk trickled into darkness, Nancy came to undress me. I carefully studied her face as she extracted my hairpins and unbuttoned the back of my gown. I wanted to gauge the servants' opinion on the matter. Nancy, however, carried out her duties with a blank expression, as if unconscious I'd planned my own social demise.

It wasn't until she slid my nightgown over my head that she finally spoke of the matter.

"Ye must not allow Mrs. Windham to oversee thy new wardrobe. She buys from th' Mallory sisters. I knows a needlewoman that will sew thy gowns for half th' price an' finish 'em right early too."

I gave a skeptical laugh. "How could your needlewoman possibly finish a gown in less time than someone in the trade?"

"'Cause many are starving here, so she'll hire out to have th' gowns before th' Mallory sisters can."

I lifted my hair as she buttoned me up. "Then why don't the Mallory sisters just hire out?"

"'Cause th' cottagers won't work for 'em."

Surprised at the vehemence in Nancy's voice, I turned. Generally, her expressions were bossy or full of self-assurance, but now something far stronger evidenced itself. "Why?"

A sullen look crossed her face, as if she debated telling me. "'Cause they obey Lady Foxmore's orders on th' doings of th' village. 'Tis better to starve than work with some."

"I rather disagree with that." I rubbed my arms against the chill as I considered Scotland. "You are aware, aren't you, of my association with her ladyship?"

The corner of her mouth lifted, as if she thought me a fool. "Aye."

I waited as she shook out my dress, but no further explanation came. "Well, then? Why speak ill of her to me?"

She looked at me as if I were daft. "Someone gats to warn thee."

"You forget—" I started brushing my hair—"I've already met her, which is warning enough."

Wondering how I'd gotten into a discussion with this maid to begin with, I turned, intending to order her to silence, when she did something extraordinary.

Instead of just shoving my dress into the closet, she opened the shutters and hung it in the light of the moon. She set a fluttering candle on the window ledge, then squatted before my gown, lifted its hem to her nose, and proceeded to squint over every inch, slowly working her way around and up. She rubbed a damp rag over places in which nothing appeared wrong. She sprinkled powder, which she'd kept tucked in her apron, to deodorize and then effectively removed all traces of it. Equal attention was paid to my shoes. The scent of sweet oil and vinegar filled the room as she rubbed her homemade potion where my toe had stretched the material white.

These are simple, everyday household duties, but what made it extraordinary was that none of this was required of Nancy. To her, I was an additional burden—one for which she received no compensation. No one would have blamed her if she'd just hung my dress and raced downstairs to enjoy the only hour of freedom servants are given.

It touched me. For the first time since Mama died, someone took pains over me. Inwardly, a rush of emotions threatened to unmake me, like a brook gurgling to be free beneath its sheet of winter ice. It affected me so greatly, my mouth trembled as she pulled a bottle of blacking and incorporated it into the worn areas of my shoes.

I watched motionless, feeling the cool evening air drift through the room as I realized that since my arrival, she'd re-dyed my faded dresses, making the patches less noticeable, and had even remade one of my bonnets.

Until now, I'd just assumed she'd been ordered to, perhaps by the housekeeper.

"Nancy," I said, then stopped for my voice shook.

She'd been so absorbed in her work, she blinked as though waking from a deep slumber before looking at me.

I turned my gaze to the fire, for I did not wish her to know that she'd touched me. "Be truthful. If I allowed your help in commissioning a new wardrobe, would you honestly know what you were doing?"

"Aye." Her voice contained her smile. "I knows th' merchants better than th' missus, and where th' best bits and bats are."

I stared harder at the flames devouring the coals. "All right, then; tomorrow I'll arrange for you to assist with my wardrobe. Now I want silence. My head hurts."

I averted my eyes, not watching as she made haste to finish, for I could not afford to feel again. There was still much to do to secure my future.

❧

As Nancy promised, within a fortnight, an entire wardrobe miraculously had been completed and was cabbaged in my room. Nancy surpassed my skill with her choices of color, trim, and accessories. The necklines she insisted upon revealed more, yet gave me a thin, delicate appearance. High waistlines accentuated my slender figure. Thick, pleated brocade skirts expanded in full circles to the floor, making me feel prominent and lovely all at once.

Every morning, however, I clad myself in crepe. Nancy silently protested by styling my hair into a simple chignon, making me look as haggard as my clothing. Mrs. Windham was worse.

From dawn till dusk, she followed me, fussing that I still dressed in rags. She'd scold, asking what Mr. Greenham would think. She'd chide me for not taking her nerves into consideration.

I knew eventually I'd have to wear the new gowns. The first half of the task was over. The money had been spent. I had disobeyed my guardian. I had given myself into her ladyship's care. Now, I only needed to complete the transition, and that harrowed me, for I had no idea what she planned. Thankfully the matter came to a head quickly. It started with footsteps clattering down the flagstone hall during our tea hour.

Our fare was simple that day, tea and scones, as the

housekeeper was busy scraping the grates and inspecting the chimneys in preparation for the winter months. It was with great surprise, therefore, that the door flung open and Hannah burst in, wisps of hair stuck to her sooty face. "Mr. Greenham is dismounting in the stable yard!"

Elizabeth dropped her scone and stared in disbelief.

"Girls! Oh, oh!" Mrs. Windham beat the air with her hands. "Julia, why oh why aren't you wearing at least one of your new dresses, the pretty one with bouffant sleeves. Oh, for heaven's sake, where's your common sense? Smile. He's going to propose and you look as grave and as ugly as a mustard pot."

Heart pounding, I allowed Mrs. Windham to pull me to my feet. Panic clutched at my chest, cutting off my breath. I never imagined Mr. Greenham would condescend to call on Am Meer.

I looked at Elizabeth, but she, too, appeared at a loss.

"Hurry! To the drawing room." Mrs. Windham seized my arm. The housekeeper squeezed tightly against the wall to prevent the soot on her clothing from touching us. Mrs. Windham kept a firm pace and we nearly tumbled into the chamber.

"There, Elizabeth. Sit there, by the chimney nook." Mrs. Windham scurried to her sewing basket. "No, Julia, the fireside chair. Leave him the davenport. He shall have an excellent view of you sitting in the sun. Not sewing—a book, a book. Pretend you are reading to us. The red one. 'Tis love sonnets."

I seized the volume and dropped to my seat. My fingers shook so much they scarcely managed to open the pages. Now that the deed was upon me, I felt ready to burst into tears. It was sheer madness. What if Lady Foxmore planned to match me with Mr. Greenham? What if he expected favors?

Mrs. Windham flung white material at Elizabeth and pulled out my fancy embroidery work for herself. Her chest heaving, she motioned me to read. With a choking voice, I faltered through a few lines. Surely, I reasoned, Mr. Greenham— melancholy as he was—wouldn't make that sort of demand upon me. Hadn't he promised that day at tea, nothing of that sort would be required of me? Besides, he knew I was looking for a husband, not a private arrangement! A lump swelled in my throat, growing so thick I paused.

"Read," Mrs. Windham hissed. She possessed neither needle nor thread but made the motions, pretending to sew.

I obeyed and stammered through another half a verse.

The door opened and the housekeeper entered. Though her face was streaked with soot and perspiration, she dipped with seemliness. "Mr. Greenham, ma'am."

Mrs. Windham looked up. "Ah, do show him in, Hannah."

The wood-beamed ceiling was so low, Mr. Greenham was obliged to remained stooped.

Mrs. Windham rose and spread her arms. "Mr. Greenham! What a welcome surprise. How devilish to give no hint you planned to call."

"Madam." He bowed. His face was stone, lacking his usual brooding. Some unyielding determination braced him.

Elizabeth noted it too, for she raised her eyebrows at me, but I couldn't read the strange twist.

"Please, sit." Mrs. Windham gestured to the davenport. "I am certain Julia will not mind entertaining you alone a moment. Come, Elizabeth, we shall find Hannah and instruct her to bring tea."

A frown stretched over Elizabeth's brow as I silently pleaded with her not to leave.

"I fear I cannot, Mama." She lifted her right foot. "My foot is numbed from sitting too long."

"You will do as I bid!"

"But I cannot." Elizabeth pointed anew to her foot and made her voice sound near tears. "I tell you, I cannot. I'll fall if I try to walk."

Her face turning purple, Mrs. Windham screwed her mouth shut, but I suspected she understood Elizabeth's resolve not to budge. "Of *all* the selfish things for your foot to do! I expect you to join me the minute it awakens."

She banged the door shut.

If Mr. Greenham found the exchange strange, he gave no hint but took a seat, making him appear more ill-suited to the room than Gulliver amongst the Lilliputians. His long legs, though bent, extended over the footstool and came to rest on the center of the mottled rug. His melton waistcoat and dark woollen suit stood out amongst the white doilies and mantel scarf. He clutched his whip and hat.

I sat stiff, too dry-mouthed to speak. Elizabeth fared no better. After a great length of time, made longer by our awkwardness, Mrs. Windham returned, glowering at Elizabeth. Harry followed with a tray of tea and the pear bread.

Mrs. Windham settled into her chair as Harry left the room, motioning for Elizabeth to distribute tea. "Now look over my table, Mr. Greenham. If you can think of but one morsel that would make it more complete, Elizabeth and I *both* shall walk to the village to fetch it if necessary." With a knowing smile, she leaned forward. "Julia, I am certain, can entertain you well enough *alone*. Now look carefully. You have only to name an item."

For half a moment, I feared I might faint. I gripped the chair arm, refusing to believe this was happening.

Mr. Greenham's eyes flickered in my direction, and then to my relief, he gave Mrs. Windham a look of disgust before taking a long draft of tea.

"I have come," he finally said, "as a favor to Lady Foxmore. This morning I received correspondence from Mr. Macy. He desires us at Eastbourne. Her ladyship wants Miss Elliston as her companion. Will you give her leave?"

I felt color drain from my face as I envisioned myself removed from Am Meer's safety.

Mrs. Windham fumbled her teacup. "Only Julia!" Then she

gave a wooden smile. "Perhaps Lady Foxmore is unaware, but Julia is in my care. I fear I cannot . . . Though perhaps if I went myself to keep an eye on her . . ." Mrs. Windham tilted her head, looking pointedly at her tea. "A-and of course, I'd need to bring Elizabeth."

Mr. Greenham tapped his long fingers on his teacup, giving her one of his rare second glances. "It could be arranged," he said slowly. "Only let us make sure we clearly understand one another. Lady Foxmore alone shall have full charge of Miss Elliston."

Mrs. Windham soured, whether because she finally realized the precariousness of my situation or because she disliked the idea of Lady Foxmore boosting my interests over Elizabeth's, I couldn't tell. She wet her lips. "I fear her guardian is particular. I am not certain—"

"Never mind then." Mr. Greenham made movement to rise. "Forgive me for not staying longer, but my time is stretched."

"What I mean—" Mrs. Windham placed her hand on his arm—"is that I'm certain her guardian would have no objections to Lady Foxmore, providing I was on hand . . . to . . . to consult, if her ladyship had questions."

"But not to interfere with her ladyship's methods, correct?"

For once, Mrs. Windham was stunned into silence, giving only a small nod of agreement.

He stared at her the way a man might look upon his over-drawn bankbook, then turned to me. The intensity in his eyes startled me. "Do you understand and agree, Miss Elliston?"

When I was twelve, Mama and I used to pass an enclosed bull on our way to the market. The way he'd lower his head, eye-ing us, pawing the ground, used to send tingles up through my spine, though Mama hushed me if I commented upon it.

Something about Mr. Greenham's bearing, the strain of his jaw, the whiteness of his knuckles, made me feel that the wrong answer would be the equivalent of setting that bull free.

I nodded.

A look of embarrassment crossed his face before he looked at the floor. "And your new wardrobe is ready? Yes?"

"Yes." Mrs. Windham recovered. "And I assure you, it is the most elegant—"

"Good. We leave at cockcrow tomorrow, wind and weather permitting."

"Tomorrow?" Mrs. Windham fanned herself with her hand. "But that's scarcely enough time to ready our dresses and set our affairs in order. Can we not leave the day after?"

Instead of answering, he set his remaining tea aside and gathered his belongings.

He left so abruptly we'd scarcely found our feet before he reached the door. Mrs. Windham managed to raise a hand-kerchief. "Well, ah . . . adieu."

The door clapped shut.

No one spoke or moved until the sound of hooves filled the stable yard; then Mrs. Windham jolted back to life. "Hannah!" she screamed, rushing into the hall. "Oh, what do you think! Lady Foxmore wishes to introduce Elizabeth! We must pack."

I set my tea aside and rested my forehead in the palms of my hands. Gratitude welled that thus far nothing had been required of me. When I looked up, I found Elizabeth, pale as a ghost, watching.

"What did he mean?" she asked. "I thought him about to tear down the house with his bare hands. What did you just agree to?"

Rather than admit I was uncertain, I shrugged. "You worry too much."

She clamped her mouth shut, and I saw the steely glint of dissatisfaction in her eye.

❧

That afternoon I wrote my guardian, in order to feign innocence if he learned about the trip. Penning the note, however, proved harder than anticipated as he'd strictly forbidden me to travel.

While I bit the edge of an ebony pen, Nancy lined my trunks, her face red from exertion. Her lips moved as she counted and recounted my new dresses. Down the hall, Mrs. Windham loudly bemoaned the fact that Elizabeth had no worthy gowns and there wasn't time to commission new ones, and for heaven's sake go ask to borrow mine, as I was supposed to be in mourning regardless. Elizabeth, it appeared, was flatly refusing to.

I dipped the nib in ink, finally deciding to state that I obediently remained in the safekeeping of Mrs. Windham while she took a brief excursion to visit a friend.

Ink smudged the edges as I pressed blotting paper over the note, then closed it. I tapped the folded page against my knuckles. If I were lucky, my solicitor would only glance at the letter and not bother to forward it.

"By gum," Nancy said, stretching the kinks from her back, "I can't see how thou'll do dressing yourself. Does thou want instructions for these here gowns?"

"Instructions?"

"Aye, which dresses go with which accessories and suchlike."

"Am I to be forever plagued with you?" I suppressed a smile and pasted a wafer over my letter. The sly vixen would find a way to join us. "I'll make the request for you to join us."

"Maybe I'll ga." She ran the back of her hand over her brow. "If thou asks me."

I looked over the desk, amazed at her brashness. "It makes little difference to me whether you go or stay. If I must, I'll borrow Elizabeth's maid."

She huffed and resumed packing. "Aye, and it would be a shame for thee. Thou'll have th' same style of hair as Miss Lizbeth th' entire trip."

I tucked the letter under my arm and stood. It was true. Elizabeth's style of hair rarely changed, and it wasn't a particularly flattering style on me either. Unwilling to show Nancy she'd won, I flounced from the room, but after dropping my post in the mail basket by the door, I tapped on Mrs. Windham's chamber door and begged until she granted me use of Nancy.

I did not know it then, but that day marked the last carefree day I ever spent at Am Meer.

Nine

"HURRY, MISS."

Nancy urged me from dreams cushioned by warm comforters. I groaned, opening my eyes. Once again, during the wee hours, Lady Foxmore's footman hammered on our door to deliver a note, this time demanding we travel in her ladyship's carriage.

Nancy shook me. "Make haste. 'Tis barely enough time to dress thee."

I rubbed my hand over bleary eyes. The clock indicated there wasn't time for breakfast or to have my hair fashioned in more than a chignon. I scrambled from the toasty covers and shivered.

"Where's the fire?" I demanded.

"Eh?"

"The fire." I jabbed the freezing air, pointing to the empty hearth. "The fire!"

She touched a match to the candlewick. "What? Does thou think I can learn th' tidings and keep thy blaze goin' an' all?"

"What tidings?" I plunged my hand into the basin and gasped at the frigid temperature.

"Th' butcher boy stopped with all the goin' ons."

I rubbed the gooseflesh over my arms. "Do you mean to stand there and admit you disregarded duty for servants' gossip?"

"Aye. What else would I neglect 'em for?" She threw a bundle of undergarments at my feet, then sorted through them. Since my chemise hadn't been hung before the hearth, it felt damp with cold. To save time, I brushed my own hair, regretting my decision to take this girl. My temper was such, I only caught what she was saying midprattle.

". . . th' gent arrived at two o'clock in the morn and forced Lady Foxmore from her bed to attend him. Can thou imagine such a thing?"

I yanked the brush, smarting my scalp. "Who did?"

"Mr. Rooke, th' other person joining th' party."

I gasped. "Someone is joining us? Who?"

Her brow furrowed. "I tole thee. Th' man th' servants say is tight-lipped, Mr. Rooke."

"Nonsense." I straightened, pulling my hair over one shoulder. "Why would a gentleman speak to servants? Do you have useful information about him? Marital status? Wealth? Something to justify waking me this late?"

Nancy shrugged. "Afore was gossip I listened to, but now what does thou think?"

"Hold your tongue—" I stopped short when she pulled a pale-green dress from the wardrobe. My voice fell to a whisper. "Not that dress. My usual one."

Her lower lip protruded. "What does thou suppose Lady Foxmore's reaction will be if thou arrives still in weeds? Who outside this here village knows thee anyway?"

There is no other segment of time quite like the moment we finally enact our prior decisions. It's like a wedding morn where someone realizes it is a grave mistake. But what is to be done after the trousseau is purchased, the dowry paid, the land transferred, the food prepared, and the gifts bestowed? I teetered upon a similar ledge as Nancy buttoned my dress. Nancy was right. I couldn't greet Lady Foxmore wearing mourning, nor could I refuse to make this trip. The carriages were packed and ready. Besides, if I failed to follow through, only Scotland awaited me.

"There." Nancy stepped away. "Look at yoursen."

I turned and considered my reflection. The green drew out the uncanny color of my eyes. The cut gave my neck a thin, delicate appearance and accented my tiny waist. I'd forgotten how it felt to be young and lovely.

"Are you certain?" I whispered, touching the neckline, but knew nothing would convince me to take off the gown.

"Aye." Nancy's eyes glinted.

⁓

Lady Foxmore's stable yard teemed with activity. A large bonfire in the center was a welcome sight amidst the brume rising from the ground. Servants packed carriages while grooms curried horses. Dogs yipped, scampering about.

As our carriage disturbed low-lying branches, orange and crimson leaves were set adrift in the thick, eddying fog. I eyed the brilliant foliage, my soul feeling equally unfixed and unattached.

Mrs. Windham's puffy eyes squinted in my direction as she reached over and plumped my skirt. After licking her finger, she scrubbed what must have been a shadow, for she frowned.

"For heaven's sake, Julia, have the mercy to smile. Here Mr. Greenham must be all anxiousness to see your new gowns, yet you look as long-faced as an undertaker. Smile, swish your skirts, laugh, and be merry this morning."

Elizabeth kept her mouth pinched shut.

"At your earliest convenience you must draw Mr. Greenham to your side. Bill and coo—"

"Mama!"

"Oh, what would you know?" was Mrs. Windham's nettle-some answer back. "Here you are, eighteen and without so much as one marriage proposal."

Elizabeth's eyes flashed; once again I suspected she was secretly engaged to Henry Auburn. She opened her mouth as if to contradict, but then snapped it shut again.

Our carriage jerked to a halt, but when the door opened we found Lady Foxmore's tone as vexed as ours. "If this is Chance's idea of a joke," she said in a terse voice, "he shall answer to me for this nonsense. One day's notice, indeed!"

Aided by their manservant, Mrs. Windham alighted and then Elizabeth.

Still safe within the carriage, I heard Mr. Greenham's deep baritone voice greet them. I steadied myself before gathering a fistful of the pale-green gown, then inclined into the swirling mist.

To my relief, Mr. Greenham appeared as taciturn as I felt. This man wanted no braw companion to cling to his arm. In fact, as I studied him I believed he found the idea of a match between us monstrous.

I gave a breathy laugh of relief, accepting his hand.

Tiny lines puckered over Lady Foxmore's mouth as she lifted her lorgnette. "Well, she's not in rags, at least." Her crow's-feet deepened as her eyes slid to Mr. Greenham. "But she blushes. You haven't wooed her without permission, have you?"

I felt fury rise through Mr. Greenham's body like a growing thunderhead, lifting his shoulders, raising tendons in his neck.

"Do not," he choked in a half-strangled voice, "*do not* test my patience one more time this morning. Or so help me, Adelia, I shall not be held accountable."

"Threatening a lady?" Lady Foxmore tilted her head back. "Good heavens, John, that's a new low, even for you."

Though I felt certain her ladyship's jibe rankled him, he said nothing but placed his hand on my back and directed me toward the fire. His ability to cap his temper amazed me. Had it been my father, he'd not have calmed until the entire house cowered. Even sober, my father kept a cruel gleam in his eyes.

Mr. Greenham placed me at the bonfire, then stalked to the other side and stood opposite.

I stretched my hands over the flames and studied Mr. Greenham anew. Overnight he'd changed again. Yesterday some force of will branded him. Today he eyed the crackling logs, lost in thought. Whether it was his true mood or the way shadows pitched his features, he looked hunted.

"John." A gentleman materialized. He started to speak but, noticing me, pulled back into the shadows. "Who's she?"

Mr. Greenham appeared too conquered by his thoughts to rise to the occasion, but finally said, "Miss Elliston, may I introduce Mr. Horace Rooke."

I inclined slightly, sizing the newcomer. He stood average height, only a thin beard to distinguish him.

"But who is she?" he demanded.

Mr. Greenham's glare turned feral. "Mind yourself, Rooke. The girl travels under my protection."

Rooke's eyes widened with astonishment.

"What is it you want?"

Rooke tore his stare from me, then blinked as if recovering from shock before speaking. "Southeast. One gent, one servant. Horseback. Three minutes."

Mr. Greenham's eyelids lowered for a fraction of a second before he gave a slight nod. The gesture must have meant something to Rooke, for he gave me one last confused glance, then trampled off, his woollen cape flapping.

"I-is he your friend?" I asked, marvelling at their singular exchange.

Mr. Greenham frowned. "Chance trusts him to carry letters."

"Chance?"

Mr. Greenham looked anew at me. For the first time, his mouth relaxed, his eyes smiled as if hearing a jest. "I meant Mr. Macy. The man whose estate we're visiting."

I studied him, wondering if he'd purposely avoided my original question. "But is he your friend?"

"Yes." Mr. Greenham sighed. "Chance is more familiar with my affairs than anyone else. I am anxious for your introduction."

I crossed my arms, thinking his idea of friendship curious. By that account, every gentleman's solicitor was his staunchest supporter. But I dismissed the notion and endeavored once more. "No, I meant that Rooke fellow."

Mr. Greenham shifted his weight, eyeing the gentleman in question. "I've not contemplated it. Nor shall I ever."

His tone held a command to cease talking about Rooke, so I did, and we fell back into silence. His friends, if nothing else, seemed singular.

A sharp whistle was punctuated with Rooke saying, "There."

Mr. Greenham did an about-turn and peered through the thick shrouds of murk. Eventually, over the nearest hillock, two grey forms appeared on horseback. With dismay, I recognized the gentleman.

As Henry crested the hill, penetrating the gloom, I steeled my emotions, cut off every tender feeling in an attempt to combat the disgrace of having hired her ladyship and agreed to take this journey with her.

Henry sat straight and tall in the saddle, but upon spotting me, he sprinted his steed forward. He'd grown into a man during my absence. Yet his eyes still danced with their old merriness, as if he rather enjoyed our circumstances.

The last time I laid eyes on Henry had been after Edward asked me to be his wife. The next day, as Mama and I travelled home, his steed appeared out of nowhere. Whooping and hollering, Henry spurred his horse alongside us, then pounded his gloved fists on the side of our chaise before burying us in his cloud of dust. I had to swallow my laughter then, know-ing he was only showing his excitement at the news, but Mama shut the curtains, stating one day he'd kill someone with his recklessness.

He approached, wearing his Henry grin. Though he seemed about the same height, his shoulders had broadened and filled out.

"Miss Elliston!" He took my hands and leaned in as if to kiss my cheek, but whispered, "Were I Edward, I would beat you very hard for this! Good show, Juls. This will finally get him off his duff if anything will."

Under different circumstances, I'd have corrected Henry's misunderstanding. As it was, I was too amazed by his speech to form thoughts.

Grinning, he saluted me with two fingers and stepped backwards.

"Henry?" Lady Foxmore's voice came from my right, sound-ing as trembly as she looked. The petite woman stepped into my line of vision. "What on earth are you doing here?"

Merriment crinkled Henry's every feature as he bowed. "I've come to join your party." He faced Mr. Greenham. "That is, if you'll have me, sir?"

"For what purpose?" Lady Foxmore demanded. "We both know you have no further need to find a wife, Henry. Even if you find yourself in need, come to Bath and I shall select you a plump, rich girl. Go home! I have no one for you this outing."

Henry grinned and nodded toward Elizabeth. "What about her?"

"Oh, I've had enough." Lady Foxmore's head quavered. "John, remove him."

Mr. Greenham, however, studied Henry with a look that brought back a memory of Sarah leaning against our rough-hewn kitchen door, eyeballing a starving dog, weighing con-science against common sense.

Still wearing his grin, Henry crossed his arms, waiting.

Lady Foxmore seized me with surprising force for such a helpless-looking woman and speared Henry with a glare. "You are as stubborn as your brother, only stupider if you still plan on pursuing a Windham. Of all the nonsense. Absolutely not. John, tell him I forbid him."

"We're leaving." Mr. Greenham turned his back, snapping his fingers toward the stables. A groom emerged with a chestnut stallion.

"What about Henry?" Lady Foxmore called after him as Henry raced to greet Elizabeth.

Mr. Greenham scathed her with his glare as he mounted his horse. With a cluck of his tongue, he reined his steed in the direction of Rooke.

"John!" Lady Foxmore's wig tilted forward as she yelled, but he did not look behind him. Stabbing pain shot through my arm as she dug her talons deep. I prepared to witness one of her famous tempers, for a streak of perspiration trickled down her face, streaking through her white powder. But she perceived the embarrassed looks upon the faces surrounding us and straightened.

"Fifteen years without a single visitor." Lady Foxmore prodded me along. "And what do I bring him? A scarecrow of a girl, a magpie of a woman, and—" she narrowed her eyes to where Henry approached Elizabeth—"a mismatched pair of lovebirds. How viciously low our circle has fallen."

I glanced over my shoulder as she pulled me toward the carriage.

Henry now stood near a shining-eyed Elizabeth. He leaned over her, whispering something that made her look like a white, fluttering butterfly, incapable of holding any more happiness. Envy pierced me and then unspeakable sadness as I considered how their attachment had always seemed dim compared to Edward's and mine.

"Climb in and take your seat," Lady Foxmore ordered as a servant placed wooden steps before the carriage.

The carriage rocked as I obeyed. Lady Foxmore followed suit and waved for me to make room for her. "On my troth, I shall not be seated to a Windham next. Move over, child."

I scooted into the seat she'd indicated as the first flecks of rain spotted the window and Mrs. Windham and Elizabeth broke off speech with Henry to hasten to the carriage. Behind them, I caught a glimpse of Nancy's white face as she clutched a handful of oil paper that was scarved over her head and beneath her chin. With misgiving, I looked at the roiling sky and hoped she had a decent coat, for doubtless she'd be forced to ride in the basket.

Elizabeth scrambled aboard first. Shadows enhanced her worried expression as she slid across from me. "Henry's joining us! Can you believe it?"

"The very idea," Lady Foxmore muttered, "of a Windham using the first name of Lord Auburn's son. Hold your tongue, Elizabeth, lest you give away far more than you wish to reveal."

Elizabeth grew scarlet. Before she could gather herself, Mrs. Windham's bonnet appeared in the door and two hands extended above her anxious face. "Girls, girls, pull me in. The steps have gone missing and the footman appears deaf."

～～

We reached the Dancing Toad an hour past gloaming. Rain had muddied the roads and hindered our progress. We lost additional time when a servants' carriage sank in the mire. We arrived bedraggled and famished at the already-bustling inn. Mr. Greenham paid handsomely to see we were attended and given a private sitting room.

While we dined, my attention stayed riveted on my former cronies. Henry, his cheeks still ruddy and his hair dishevelled from the wind, broke propriety by sneaking his arm around the back of Elizabeth's chair. Bacchus and one of his nymphs couldn't have appeared merrier as their laughing whispers competed with the chinks of silverware against porcelain.

I couldn't hear their banter, but reminders of Edward hung heavy about them. It was in the way Henry's eyes crinkled as he buried his nose in Elizabeth's hair to whisper, his crooked smile, his easygoing manner—all Auburn traits, all salt rubbed in wounds.

It grew impossible not to feel my loss. It was there in that dimly lit inn that I first experienced the cost of keeping composure against one's own best interest and disguising the true desires of one's heart. Later, I would become an artisan in this role, creating and fulfilling society's very definition of a lady, in a deadly game which forced me to hide in public, to become the very worst liar—or the very best, I suppose, depending on one's viewpoint. But this was my first lesson, my first bitter taste.

I watched them silently as the innkeeper's wife set before us goose roasted with sage and onion, vegetable marrow, and brussels sprouts. I was debating the idea of retiring when Lady Foxmore leaned to my ear and said in a private voice, "You have yet to ask me about our host."

I dropped Mama's locket, which I'd been clutching, and faced her. "Ought I?"

She made a noise of disgust in the back of her throat. "Good heavens! Here I am, planning to introduce you to the most sought-after man in the country, and you haven't enough sense to make inquiries. Well, since you seem satisfied with your information, tell me what you've heard. I'll correct the errors."

I tilted my head to show my confusion.

She gave an exasperated sigh. "What does that woman speak of all day? No! No, do not tell. I have no desire to learn. Just tell me what you know of Macy."

"Macy? You—you mean *Mr.* Macy?"

"Yes, Macy," she said in a quiet voice. She glanced at Mr. Greenham. "Surely you don't think the height of my ambition is to match you with that puddle of gloom? Have you no more faith in me than that, child?"

There was no proper answer.

Amusement twinkled in her eyes before she whispered, "Disappointed?"

"Well, no," I found myself replying too quickly. "Not at all."

She laughed loudly, then turned and announced to him in a loud voice, "Poor John. You're spurned and rejected at every corner. Not even the orphans want you."

"Eat so you can retire early," was his reply. "We rise before dawn."

Chuckling, she returned her attention to me. "Do you truly know nothing about our host?"

"Only that he is your acquaintance."

"*My* acquaintance?"

I swallowed. "Well, yes."

Her bitter laugh grated the air. "You greatly misunderstand the nature of our affinity if you think that." She pinched the bridge of her nose. "Fifteen years of being a recluse and what? I bring him an ungrateful toadeater who hasn't the sense of a gnat."

"Fifteen years?" I asked, determined to ignore the insult. "Am I to take it, then, that Mr. Macy's parents kept him from society?"

Her ladyship's eyes grew hard and small. "I know not whether I should berate or congratulate you for being the stupidest girl in England. In the future, you will make it your duty to learn everything possible—oh, why am I bothering. Just sit there and hold your tongue. Even dolts can accomplish that much."

As a shy person, it was already a daunting task to join a dinner party, but her ladyship's harshness scattered my ability to retort.

Elizabeth, however, felt up to the occasion. "Never mind her, dearest. Mr. Macy is Mama's age and highly unsocial." Her eyes directed toward her ladyship. "Although not as unsocial as some."

"He's not unsocial," Lady Foxmore snapped. "He's reclusive. The fancy seized him one night. When he was throwing a ball, no less." She skewered her goose with a knife. "He refused everyone at the door. It was the scandal of the season. Imagine, leaving the cream of society standing in the snow. Not even I was admitted."

"Why?" Henry asked. "What happened?"

"It's no use asking me. Did he ever tell you, John?"

Mr. Greenham's eyes slid to me, as if inquiring what I made of this conversation, but then retreated to his brooding self.

Her ladyship humphed. "Never mind, I forbid you to speak. In fact, I forbid all of you to speak. I may be forced to travel with this mangy, ragtag circus. However, nothing dictates I must listen to your ignorance."

"Well, I for one agree with you," Mrs. Windham said. "I even said to Elizabeth this morning that I thought the horses looked mangy. My exact words, were they not, my dear."

Elizabeth shut her eyes as Henry quickly buried his mouth in his napkin.

"And I would never dream of speaking after such a day of travelling in disagreeable weather. For goodness' sake, Julia, hold your tongue and stop pestering her ladyship. In my day, we knew better than to assault our betters. It isn't likely Mr. Macy would take note of you regardless, even with your new wardrobe."

Henry's eyes were all merriment, but Elizabeth met mine with a look that questioned whether I truly understood what I was getting myself into by aligning myself with her ladyship.

I stabbed a roasted brussels sprout, ignoring her. I had little doubt that if she realized Edward had broken our betrothal, her look would have been one of pity.

For a moment, I wasn't sure which was worse. To be pitied or to have them think I willingly submitted to such treatment.

My pride won.

Ten

⚜

PEOPLE HAVE ASKED whether I was in ferment during that journey, I suppose because we were travelling to one of Bedfordshire's most prestigious estates to be entertained by the elusive Mr. Macy.

The simple answer is no.

As our carriage slogged through muddy roads, I had no appreciation of the rarity of my situation. I had no inkling Lady Foxmore was about to accomplish what would one day be hailed as her greatest feat. I was ignorant that I was about to meet the only person in the whole of England brash enough to pit himself against my guardian.

Nor was there anyone to educate me; Mrs. Windham, Henry, and Elizabeth being equally unaware and Mr. Greenham having reverted back to his taciturn self. My only indication that something larger was afoot was the manner in which Lady Foxmore occasionally studied me before shaking her head in disbelief.

Little needs to be said about our second day of travel except that we arrived at dusk. Wet cobblestones reflected our carriage lanterns as we rattled down the lanes of the town bordering Eastbourne. The streets appeared uninhabited, except for the lights of those retiring for the evening. Past the village, I continued to catch sight of cottages tucked willy-nilly amongst the hollows.

"I recognize those very trees." Lady Foxmore indicated a line of elms arching against a gloomy sky above the carriage. "We should arrive at Eastbourne any moment. Time stands still. I recognize every landmark."

I leaned forward with Mrs. Windham and Elizabeth.

"There." Lady Foxmore pointed out the rain-flecked window.

Below, in the valley, a massive house sprawled in every direction, a patchwork of crumbling architecture. Ivy and creeping plants obscured much of the stonemasonry. Towers and spires, seemingly ready to topple, pierced the darkening sky.

My eyes traced the ancient structure as loathing fluttered through me. That someone lived there seemed impossible. Were it not for the few windows that twinkled amidst the derelict estate, I'd have assumed Eastbourne an uninhabited ruin.

"It must have a hundred rooms." Elizabeth sounded breathless.

"Over two hundred and fifty." Lady Foxmore joined me in peering through the window. The lines about her mouth softened as she viewed the estate the way a mother might look upon a favorite child. "It started life as a monastery, but over the centuries the estate has also become an influential house. If I know Macy, I warrant he's vastly improved it since I laid eyes on it." She turned in my direction. "Here we shall see whether or not I can raise you from your pitiful state."

I stared, horror-stricken, thinking her mad if she believed this mass of stones to be an influential great house. It was a devastating moment.

Her ladyship had brought me to a moth-eaten estate—not one of her grand acquaintances, not London, not Bath. For one wild moment, I feared I'd risked my guardian's wrath for naught.

A large gate forced the carriage to a halt beneath dripping pines. We waited several minutes before a guard admitted us, then proceeded down a winding lane. As we passed the first section of the house, gargoyles stippled with colored lichen and moss leered from their various perches.

Lady Foxmore inclined near me and in a low voice asked, "Well, what do you make of Eastbourne, child?" Her eyes shone with a softness I did not understand as she gazed up at the rustling ivy.

I measured my voice to hide my thick disappointment. "I wait to see the master."

She chuckled. "Yes, I'm rather waiting for that myself."

The percussion of rain ceased under the porte cochere. Mrs. Windham paled as she attempted to revive Elizabeth's curls.

"No need to worry over her appearance," Lady Foxmore said in an amused tone. "I'm certain Chance shan't care how she looks."

The driver opened the door and Lady Foxmore departed the carriage with a grace and bearing I could only hope to achieve. "Adelia?" A voice just outside the carriage took us by surprise.

I glimpsed her ladyship's face as she turned in its direction. Her expression was novel. Titillation, loathing, fear, and delight all seemed to coexist. Her hand flew to her chest, but it was impossible to tell whether the action denoted horror or delight.

"There you are," she said, recovering. Though she sounded shrill, her tone differed, bringing to mind a dog's last and desperate bark as its master jerks its collar. "Well, at least you're still sound in body—" her voice grew tart—"though I am convinced madness has seized your mind."

The most beguiling laugh was followed by an equally bewitching voice. "Do not presume to berate me, Adelia. Take satisfaction that after all these years, you're seeing your fondest wish for me fulfilled."

The full tone of the voice enthralled me. Each word was carefully enunciated, calling attention to the man's good breeding. Despite myself, I felt the delightful sensation of hope spread through me. Perhaps not all was lost.

"And since when," demanded Lady Foxmore, "was it my fondest wish to see you rendered insane?"

Another hypnotic laugh responded. "Is this not how it is supposed to happen? I thought rationale was always the very first thing to go."

Lady Foxmore stamped her stick, then stepped away from the carriage. "Well, it certainly fled in this case. Honestly, Chance. Miss Elliston, kindly step down from my carriage so I can make proper introductions."

I had not anticipated exiting before Mrs. Windham and cast her a guilty glance. The good woman gasped at the slight to her station while Elizabeth's eyes narrowed.

A hand reached into the carriage. Embarrassment burned my cheeks as I gathered my skirts. There was no helping it. I grasped the hand in order to alight.

Those of you who have seen Macy, even from a distance, can well imagine my wonder upon lifting my eyes. Nothing could have prepared me for the captivating master who waited in the thickening fog. It was as though a dark angel had swooped in and landed at my feet.

My shock at his appearance was so complete, I stood agog, halfway between the carriage and the ground. Lack of beauty had not played into his decision to withdraw from society. His symmetry was not that of classic proportions, but exotic and dangerous. Black hair, longer than generally accepted, curved over his brow.

The figure he cut was likewise devastating. There was nothing middle-aged or sagging. His frock coat was oxford grey but did not flare out in gathers, as was the style then. Rather it was a revival of an earlier cut, squaring at his ribs before tailoring into a single coattail, which fell to his knees. His waistcoat was pewter-colored and featured pearly buttons that ended with a silvery cravat amassed about his throat.

During our journey, our carriage had been suffocating, so that by the time of our arrival, I was gloveless and hatless. Heat registered over my cheeks as I realized my bare hand rested in his.

"Chance, I believe you need a formal introduction," said Lady Foxmore. "Miss Julia Elliston, may I present Mr. Chance Macy."

His gaze lingered longer than was proper before he bowed.

I opened my mouth, but shyness seized my words.

A hint of a smile dented the corner of his mouth as he finished his study and helped me to the ground. He stepped nearer, pleased. "You know, then?"

"She knows nothing. You've been away so long, you forget the effect you have," Lady Foxmore's scowling voice said beside me. "Honestly, Chance, if this is some perverted joke on me, cease now. It is sickening to watch. Of all the undeserving people!"

How Mr. Macy would have responded, I know not, for at that moment Mrs. Windham's voice hallooed him. "Oh, oh, my dear Mr. Macy!"

I turned and caught sight of her stooping in the doorway of the carriage.

She started to alight on her own, then grumbled over her shoulder, "Elizabeth, for heaven's sake, your foot is on my dress!"

One dark brow arched as Mr. Macy faced Lady Foxmore.

A slow, catlike smile spread over her features. "John's doing. Certainly not mine. I utterly detest them. She insisted her presence will satisfy prerequisites set for Miss Elliston's visit."

An incredulous-seeming Mr. Macy searched for Mr. Greenham and found him a short distance away.

Rain had dampened his hat and oiled coat to a rich brown that matched the circles shadowing his eyes. Whether it was his mood or the way the shadows pitched his face, he looked like the unhappiest man in England. Behind him, Henry slid from his mount.

"Lord Auburn's eldest, as well?" Surprise laced Mr. Macy's voice.

It was at that moment Mrs. Windham managed to free herself. Lifting her skirts, she stumbled from the carriage, nearly stepping in a horse dropping. "I cannot begin to tell you how flattered we are to have been invited! Indeed, we are the envy of our entire neighborhood! You have no idea how greatly you honor us!"

Behind us, Elizabeth's pale face emerged from the darkened carriage. Sighing, she took the footman's hand and hopped down.

"Such a trip," Mrs. Windham panted, fanning herself. "Upon my word, but I am fagged. Such bumping and swaying! I thought we should never arrive." Over her shoulder she called, "Hurry, Elizabeth, my smelling salts. Mr. Macy, I fear I shall need your arm. I feel faint."

"Mrs. Windham." Mr. Macy duly offered his arm, giving Lady Foxmore a bedazed look. "I daresay, we shall have an atmosphere that Eastbourne has not seen in many years."

"Know," said Lady Foxmore, "that I am opposed to this in every possible way."

Mr. Macy gave another beguiling laugh. "And yet here you stand." To everyone else, he said, "Shall we adjourn inside, then?"

"Elizabeth," Mrs. Windham hissed, pointing to Mr. Macy's free arm.

I blushed for Elizabeth's sake as Mr. Macy gave Lady Foxmore a second incredulous look, but offered his free arm.

"I think, perhaps—" Lady Foxmore clutched my arm and leaned her weight upon me—"I may yet learn to like the

Windhams. And to think that I berated John when he included them."

Questions pressed upon me as we trudged past two stone lions guarding the estate's grand entrance. By then, of course, I'd gained an inkling that something bigger was happening behind the scenes, something Mr. Macy and Lady Foxmore took no pains to hide from me in their private snatches of conversation.

The exterior of Eastbourne belied its interior. I braced myself to enter a downtrodden hall lit with rushlights and padded with bundles of reeds on the floor. Instead, the massive, pillared hall looked like a relic from the Byzantine Empire. The floors were inlaid with various colors of marble and resembled carpets. A pattern of animals—elephants, deer, and monkeys—all marched in a circle around a tree laden with fruit.

My amazement only grew from there. The hall was at least sixty feet in length with arches between the pillars, and above those a second story of arched pillars supported a third level, which cambered into a cathedral ceiling, where glistening gold-and-blue mosaics competed against frescoes of vengeful angels.

Servants lined the hall, at least sixty in number, all standing in perfect unison.

I gaped, experiencing my first sensation of being amongst the highest sphere. We all know wealth. As we sit to our china tea, it is not difficult to imagine silver, and as we don our serviceable dresses, it is not too far a cry to imagine silks. But it is quite another to be dressed in the best attire you've ever owned and still feel little better than the meanest maid. Gone was the dismay I'd experienced with my first glance at Eastbourne. I now felt Lady Foxmore had pulled me up far too swiftly.

Her rasping laugh brought me to my senses. "You always were ostentatious. Good heavens, Chance, what on earth have you done? Tell me, does it only grow worse from here?"

Mr. Macy never glanced at his servants as he dispensed orders. "Randal, find a chamber suitable for Mr. Auburn and give instructions concerning dinner." He turned to Rooke. "I need to look at your documents within the hour. Carry them to the library, then house in your usual quarters. John, accompany them."

Frown lines appeared over Mr. Greenham's brow as he glanced at me, but then he waved for the gentlemen to follow. Their dripping capes left shimmering trails of water. Mr. Macy waited until they disappeared, then dismissed his staff with a flick of his left hand. His black-and-gold onyx ring caught the light. He turned and nodded at the rest of us. "I shall personally escort you to your rooms."

His pace left little time for glancing at the wonders surrounding us. Collections of family portraits mingled with elaborately framed watercolors. The polished floors peeking from beneath foreign carpets were inlaid with rare woods. Priceless collections of artifacts and paintings were masterfully arranged. Cabinets contained vases, statues, and ancient-looking treasures. Later I learned Etruscan, Greek, Egyptian, and Roman treasures were numbered amongst them.

To my surprise, Lady Foxmore kept up with Macy's fast stride, though she dug deeply into my arm.

Stopping before a mahogany door, Mr. Macy unlocked it and handed Mrs. Windham the key. "These two adjoining rooms should suit you and your daughter."

He swung open the door, revealing a chamber with a bed surrounded by peacock-blue satin panels, stitched with silver crewelwork. The French furniture grouped in the large space appeared costly.

"Such a handsome apartment." Mrs. Windham stepped over the threshold. "Beyond a doubt, there is not a nicer bedchamber in all of Britain. I am certain of it."

"You are very kind." Mr. Macy bowed, releasing Elizabeth. "Now if you'll both excuse me."

"Mama!" Elizabeth blushed, then whispered in her mother's ear.

Mrs. Windham's eyebrows shot up. She motioned to the remaining door in the passage. "I beg pardon, but is that Julia's room? I need her key too. My mother always said—"

"No. I've arranged different quarters for *Miss Elliston.*"

Elizabeth gave her mother's arm a violent tug, widening her eyes.

Mrs. Windham licked her lips. "Ah, yes . . . but . . . well, you see, ha-ha, I am Miss Elliston's chaperone—"

"Nonsense," Lady Foxmore interjected. "Miss Elliston is under my care. John was quite plain in his terms. She is my charge, and for the record, I care not where Chance places the child, nor what he does with her."

Mrs. Windham straightened her shoulders. "Nonetheless—"

Arms spread like someone driving a flock of geese, Mr. Macy ushered the Windhams into their chamber. "Yes, yes, your objection is duly noted. On my word, no harm will come to Miss Elliston."

Mrs. Windham looked ready to protest, but Mr. Macy's expression must have changed her mind. She turned on me instead. "Such a fuss, Julia, about where your room is." She shooed me away. "I am certain you'll find your room suitable enough. I highly doubt Mr. Macy will place you too close to the servants!"

Mr. Macy, with a bow, shut the door. Annoyance flashed over his face as he narrowed his eyes at Lady Foxmore. "Remind me to have a word with John later."

In a nearby passage, he unlocked a door that revealed a chamber as ancient as Queen Elizabeth's reign. A huge bed with thick posts and a canopy sat amidst Jacobean furniture.

"Your room, Adelia."

She stepped to the threshold and took her time examining the space. Whether she approved or not was difficult to tell by her odd expression. "You do realize," she said, finishing her inspection, "I am quite your enemy now."

"Are you, indeed?" was Mr. Macy's amused reply.

Her earbobs swung as she addressed him. "I am in earnest, Chance, for I did not think you serious until this exact moment. You must know I am completely against this."

His eyes danced briefly to me. "Are you? Why?"

Lady Foxmore fully turned. "Shall I truly spell out my objections, here and now?" She gestured toward me. "Look at her. She's as ungainly and as unprepared for this as a newborn colt, Chance. Honestly, if you want my advice—"

"Do not pit yourself against me, Adelia. You will lose."

A brief narrowing of his eyes was all it took. Lady Foxmore stopped midspeech, though she looked none too pleased. I fidgeted, feeling little better than a servant being spoken about while she tends the fire.

Lady Foxmore lifted her petite stature to its full height. "Expect no mercy, then, from me."

He laughed in his mesmerizing way. "I never do, my dear. I never do. Now if you'll excuse me, my last guest still requires attention."

I met her ladyship's gaze, to plead silently that she not leave me alone with our host.

Lady Foxmore limped into her room, looked over her shoulder, and gave Mr. Macy such a baleful stare that my every hair stood on end. The door clapped shut.

The next few seconds were pure agony as I tugged on my sleeves and looked at the crack of light shining beneath her ladyship's door. Inside, the sound of her cane retreated toward the back of the room.

I fixed my gaze on the thin ribbon of light, overly aware of my windblown hair and scarlet cheeks. Mr. Macy stood motionless.

How long we remained as such, I cannot say, but to me it felt endless. Eventually, my senses attuned to the distant echo of rain and the footfall of servants running in the main hall. The scents of beeswax and soaplees were borne aloft on the cold draft.

Yet despite this, I felt the presence of Mr. Macy more than anything else. No air stirred near him; no scent carried from his body; he made no sound. Yet were I blind, I would have known he was there. The air fairly scintillated with his presence.

Feeling wretched at my shyness, I finally dared a peek.

No one wore pride like Mr. Macy. Ebony-colored eyes sparkled with delight. If such a thing is possible, he looked as charmed by my shyness as he was with my victory over it.

"Undoubtedly," he said in a soft voice, "you have many questions for me. I give you my word, we shall discuss this arrangement at length. Only now, as you've just arrived, it is not the proper time. Come, allow me to take you to your chambers."

I took him as meaning to soften my discomfort by being frank; however, I did not know what "arrangement" he spoke about. Stunned, I stared at him.

His brows scrunched for a fraction of a second, but then all at once he seemed to grasp something. With a look of irritation, he turned toward Lady Foxmore's closed door. "She wasn't in jest," he said softly.

He rubbed this thumb over his forehead, for a moment looking lost, but then he chuckled and placed his hand on his hip. "She neglected to inform you, didn't she?"

I folded my arms, drawing them close. When I spoke, I wished I hadn't, for it sounded weak. "Sir?"

He grew very still. "And you're frightened besides."

At first, I thought him angry, for his jaw tightened and he averted his eyes, but then as he reposed himself, I thought him hurt. "And why wouldn't you be," he asked more to himself, then swore under his breath. "What would I think, were I in your position?"

By this time the heavy wetness of my clothing combined with escalating emotions was taking its toll. I shivered, pulling the damp wool of my cape tighter.

He offered me his hand. "Come."

I have been much criticized for what followed next, the point being belabored that had I possessed more moral fiber, I would have refused to be led through a crumbling estate without a chaperone—especially as I had two on hand.

To my critics let me respond that I am not at fault for the disgrace that claimed so many over the next year. That storm already loomed on the horizon. I was little more than a wayfarer caught in the torrent without an umbrella.

As our footsteps rang through one long corridor after another, my mind reviewed the strange banter between Lady Foxmore and our host. To avoid looking at him, I pretended to study the master paintings that lined every wall. Soon bright plaster halls, lit from suspended lamps, turned into narrow stone passages. Lancet windows became smaller and were set in deeper recesses.

When we approached an arch etched with Roman letters, I hesitated, suddenly reluctant. Past that threshold the estate was stripped bare, without even carpet to soften our tread. Though I could not read Latin, I felt a dread of passing beneath those words. I pulled back. "Is my room not near the Windhams'?"

"No. It's on the other side of the house." He stopped walking and turned when I refused to continue. "Allow me to assure you, you are now far safer than you've been in months."

I lifted my face to study him. "I have been in no danger."

The cant of his eyebrows told me he found my answer unexpected. "If that is your belief, then it's urgent we talk."

"Sir!" A panting voice sounded behind me.

Mr. Macy lifted his eyes and gave a nod. "Approach."

I looked behind me as the butler turned the corner. With one elbow he leaned against the wall. "Forgive me, sir," he said between breaths, "but you have a visitor."

Mr. Macy looked at his manservant as if he'd gone mad, before asking me, "Is there another in your party?"

I denied it as Mr. Macy waved his servant forward, then took up the soggy card on a silver tray. He flipped it over.

For a full minute he said nothing as he stared. "Forrester." He tossed the card back on the tray. "My word, that man is relentless." His gaze flitted over me. "And of all the nights to make a nuisance of himself. Is Rooke still here?"

"Yes, sir."

"Good. I'll go find him. I grant you permission to take Miss Elliston to her rooms."

The butler bowed.

Mr. Macy looked about to make apologies, but then, with a flick of his fingers, said, "No, change that. I'll take Miss Elliston to her rooms. Find Rooke; tell him Forrester is here. He'll know what I want. Send them both to the billiards room. Tell them I'll join them shortly."

The butler bowed and turned. His footsteps quickly dissipated down the corridor.

"This is not the way I envisioned our first conversation," Mr. Macy said with a smile, though I sensed irritation. "At least let me see you to your rooms."

He quickened our pace, checking from time to time to see if I lagged. After it seemed we had crossed the length of the house, we stopped at a door at the bottom of a stairwell. With both hands, he pulled a ribbon out from beneath his collar and removed it from around his neck. On it was threaded a single key. His eyes sparkled as he unlocked the door. "Your room."

The chamber was larger than my drawing room, parlor, and foyer combined, but I saw no bed. Expensive silks, whose color and texture reminded me of honeycomb, dripped from the windows. The settees and chairs were upholstered in the same fabric. Above, the ceiling arched and slanted into domes. The firelight flickered off polished wood, evidencing the skills of past artisans. Confused, I crossed the threshold and realized this was only a sitting room and that several chambers adjoined it. The door to my right revealed a bed covered with satins.

Regaining my senses, I turned toward Mr. Macy and

found him leaning against the doorpost, appraising me with satisfaction.

"I cannot occupy this room."

"Nonsense. It's plain to see you are taken with it. I didn't refurnish this for mere extravagance." He straightened and entered. "I must hurry now, for I have an uninvited guest." He took my hand and placed the key in it, slowly closing my fingers around, making my heart flutter. He waited a moment, regarding me, then retreated.

When the door clicked shut, my world moved again. I pressed my ear against the door; however, it was too thick to hear his retreating footsteps. I sank to the floor with euphoria rushing over me, then moaned. This was impossible, unimaginable, unforeseeable. Forcing myself to breathe, I reviewed all the questions, all the peculiar conversations that rushed over me, all demanding attention at once. I wanted to know who Mr. Macy was, and why he thought I should know him. I felt as though I'd been lifted from a stupor into a strange new reality.

I cradled my hands over my stomach, feeling like a fool. Less than an hour ago I'd believed I was wrong to place myself in Lady Foxmore's care, but now I was buoyant with hope. I laughed aloud, suddenly understanding Lady Foxmore's demand that I show fortitude and abandon mourning.

Eventually, the sensible ticking of the clock and ordinary drumming of rain weakened my fascination. I sat forward, suspicious that Mr. Macy might, perhaps, take pleasure in trifling with women's affections. There must be a reason he remained a bachelor.

Loud rapping startled me, followed by Nancy's "Miss?"

I stood, feeling guilt flush my cheeks, and pulled open the heavy door. She waited in the hall, looking especially shabby with a drenched coat and hat with drooping feathers. Behind her, three men and my trunks waited.

"Good grief!" She tugged at the knot on her bonnet, staring

at the room wide-eyed. "I tried to get to thee before now," she said, entering, "only they was all arguing about whether they were allowed in this part of the house." She waved to the men behind her. "Come on with ye. Fetch th' trunks to yon corner."

The footmen eyed her with contempt until I nodded agreement, and they carried in the trunks. Having delivered the baggage, the taller one bowed. "I'm to inform you a servant will be sent in an hour to escort you to dinner."

"Escort me to dinner?" I asked. "Is that customary?"

Nancy squatted before the luggage. "How does thou think to find your way round this house without a servant and all?"

The footmen stiffened when she answered for me. I grinned, tucking a wisp of hair behind my ear, pleased somehow to find the girl was as brash here as she'd been at Am Meer. I waved them out the door.

Nancy shook her coat off. "We best hasten if I'm to have ye ready at an hour."

I nodded agreement, surprised how good Nancy's presence felt. She brought with her normalcy, the sense that everything hadn't gone topsy-turvy. While Nancy rummaged through trunks, I explored the chamber. The first door I opened held the greatest luxury of all. A large copper tub, filled with steaming water and rose petals, sat before a roaring fire.

I stared wide-eyed before gathering my wits. "Nancy!"

She came running, then gaped.

"Hurry!" I peeled off my stockings. It had been years since I'd had a proper bath, with Sarah too old to lug water and Mrs. Windham believing bathing was the death of people.

Nancy wrinkled her nose, then crossed the space. She touched a petal. "'Tis hot. How's that done? What if somewhat happened and we stayed on th' road another hour?"

"I couldn't care less how it's accomplished." I unbuttoned the cuffs on my sleeves. "Hurry, assist me."

She stared longingly at the water once more but then

unhooked my dress and started on my petticoats. I scanned the space while I waited, and then the room beyond it, which was entirely dedicated to writing. A large desk sat open with stationery and pens. Atop the desk, an elaborate grouping of yellow roses was arranged in a hand-painted bowl.

I froze, forgetting everything except the roses.

Their message was jealousy, so it was impossible that they were chosen to convey any sentiments. Yet the chances were remote that the exact flower adorned a writing desk here, the same spot they'd been featured my entire life, in my bed-chambers both at home and while visiting Am Meer.

Nancy piled my hair atop my head and pinned it. "Well? Is thou going to stand there or bathe?"

I shook off the thought and turned my attention to the bath. Never had I been afforded so much water at once. There was enough room, if I sank down, for the water to touch my chin. A nearby table held scrubs and perfumed soaps. I entered the fragranced water and felt my numb toes and fingers warm. I shut my eyes, submerging myself in the warmth. Later, I decided, I would ponder the roses.

Eleven

A GIRL IS TAUGHT from an early age her highest achievement is marriage. Her greatest ambition is acquiring a husband. While young men crowd classrooms stuffing their heads with Latin and mathematics, young ladies nest within the same four walls, learning it is they who cushion their husband's existence and who can create an environment of marital bliss.

It is likewise believed that marriage within one's sphere is the only right and reasonable union. What use has a gentleman for a frugal merchant's daughter? How would a highborn lady benefit a struggling baker? Shall clean touch the unclean? The very thought is unhallowed, defiled.

Yet that night, as I stood before my mirror, my thoughts tarnished society. Only weeks away from servanthood, I stood amidst unimaginable wealth, envisioning a new life for myself. I hungered to belong in this sphere—not just for the sake of belonging, but for the sake of my future security. Too long had I stood on the threshold of uncertainty, never quite sure how matters would work out.

Wisps of hair, damp from my bath, clung to the nape of my neck as I ran my hands over the close-fitted waist and touched my low neckline. A myriad of desires coursed through me—each as varied and as lovely as the sparkling treasures surrounding us. I knew as I stared back at my image I would do whatever it took to secure my place in this sphere.

My gown was pink *peau de soie*, frilled in the same material, with tight, small sleeves in lieu of the large mutton sleeves I knew the Windhams would wear tonight. When I had first tried on the gown for Nancy's needlewoman, I thought it too unusual, too modern. But now I saw Nancy's wisdom. My dress would be light and airy next to Lady Foxmore's stiff drapery folds, and young and girlish compared to the Windhams' excess of ruffles and lace.

My reveries ended with a rap on the door.

"'Twas scarcely above a half hour." Nancy regarded the sprigs of ivy she'd been entwining in my hair and wiped her hands over her apron. With a frustrated sigh, she looked over Mama's emeralds. "What about thy jewelry?"

"Leave it." I tugged her skirt as she turned, keeping her in place. "Nancy, do me a favor. . . . Keep a sharp ear. Learn everything possible about Mr. Macy."

Freckled cheeks rose with her grin. "Aye. And what does thou want to know?"

"Never you mind," I said, reclaiming as much distinction between us as possible. "Now answer the door."

I gave my cheeks a pinch and inspected myself anew. Surely, I thought viewing my dress, this night was a gift of the gods.

In the hall, an elderly man waited. His silver-white hair had been carefully parted and combed in place with bandoline. The creases around his blue eyes deepened as he smiled and bowed. "Are you Miss Elliston?"

I glanced sideways, but Nancy seemed as perplexed by him as I was.

"I am Reynolds, Mr. Macy's personal valet. It is my honor to escort you to dinner."

Confusion washed over me as to whether I should take his arm. He, however, did not offer it. With militaristic precision, he pivoted and waited for me to follow.

I dangled my key before Nancy. "Listen carefully. Unpack; touch nothing in the room. Find the butler and have him return this to me within the hour."

"I beg your pardon, miss, but I cannot permit that." Reynolds said. "Did not Mr. Macy instruct you about the keys?"

"The keys?"

"Yes. Outside of myself, servants are not permitted them in this household." He gave Nancy a head nod. "Not even abigails, I fear. I must forbid this." Though Reynolds maintained a bored expression, the determination in his eyes made it clear he would have his way, to the point of appropriating the key himself if necessary.

Nancy's eyes narrowed, and she stretched out her hand. "I ain't never stole nothing in me whole life."

I hesitated. It didn't seem possible an estate could run if servants didn't possess keys. I glanced at my chambers. Pandemonium had erupted during my bath. My wet trunks dotted the room and stood with lids open, their muddy water seeping into the rich carpet. Clothing lay piled over every article of furniture.

"Here." I pulled Nancy from the room. "I'll address it with Mr. Macy."

Nancy gave me an indignant stare as I locked my door. Then, not knowing what else to do with it, I wound the ribbon around my wrist.

"You'll find the servants' quarters if you turn right and keep walking the length of the corridor," Reynolds said.

Nancy huffed and turned.

"You forgot to say, 'Yes, sir.'"

She spun. "Eh?"

"We do not say 'eh' in this household. Neither do we feign deafness. You have ten seconds." He pulled out a pocket watch, flipped open the gold lid, and stared at the face.

Somehow, this small gesture finally penetrated her brashness. Her eyes widened, and for the first time in my memory, she bobbed. "Yes, sir." And then to me, "By thy leave."

He waited until she ran from sight before sliding his watch inside his waistcoat. "How does your housekeeper manage her?"

Too embarrassed to admit Nancy was borrowed, I shrugged.

He tugged at his waistcoat. "Never mind. Within a week, I'll have her spit-spot."

As Reynolds retraced our steps to the entrance hall, I shoved aside my lingering sadness over Edward and thoughts of Mama. In my new gown, I felt graceful and elegant. I envisioned Mr. Macy greeting me with admiration. The world felt magical as Reynolds opened a pair of doors. "The dining hall."

My slippers made no noise as I entered.

Like all of Eastbourne, the chamber was grand. A shimmering host of candles lit a painted ceiling awash in golden clouds and angels. A massive table was laden with an excessive number of articles. Heavy goblets in successive sizes, mother-of-pearl utensils, and gold chargers graced each place setting. I reached for one of the finger bowls, knocking a wine and water glass together. A shimmering sound tinkled through the room. I drew in my breath in awe, realizing the space was designed so that one could whisper and be heard. In the center of the table, an arrangement of ferns and almond blossoms sat in a silver urn.

"Fascination and hope?" I fingered one of the flowers.

"It was not my intention to send a message," came Mr. Macy's breathtaking voice behind me. "However, I'll acknowledge what they say."

I turned, unintentionally tearing a petal from the center-piece. Mr. Macy stood near the door, looking devastating in din-ner attire. Next to him stood a trolley laden with decanters and tumblers. In his right hand he held a tumbler containing amber drink.

"I thought myself alone."

"Yes, I know. Perhaps I should have made my presence known, but I desired to study your behavior when you thought yourself unobserved."

I broke our gaze and turned slightly to place the shorn petal on the table. "I . . . I'm early."

"Yes. I asked Reynolds to fetch you. There are matters we need to discuss." He set down his drink and approached. When I backed against the table, he paused. "No, now isn't right either. You still fear m—" His mouth curved upwards. "What the devil?" He laughed and caught my hand in his, running his fingers along the ribbon wound about my wrist. "Are you lacking bracelets? Shall I supply some?"

"Your . . . manservant—he wouldn't allow me to give it to my maid."

He closed his eyes and rubbed a thumb along his forehead. "Ahh, yes. Excuse me, please." He strode to the door and leaned out. "My good man, Miss Elliston reminds me I neglected to instruct my guests regarding their keys. Amend it. Also start bringing our guests. Fetch me John first."

Mr. Macy shut the door and returned to me with an amused expression. "Why on earth did you not bring a reticule? You are perfection, except for that key."

Still unable to look directly at him, I unwound the ribbon, uncertain what to do with it.

"I'll safeguard it." He held out his gloved hand. When I placed it in his palm, he clucked his tongue. "You are far too trusting. Never again give a gentleman your key, even if he owns the house."

My stomach dropped, but he did not offer me my key back. Instead, he looped the ribbon over his head and tucked it beneath his shirt. The doors opened.

"Mr. Jonathan Alexander Greenham," Reynolds called.

Though I estimated the door height to be twice the height of Mr. Greenham, he still ducked as he entered, no longer a rain-soaked traveller. This was as much his world as Mr. Macy's. He looked impeccable. His eyes, however, blazed as he tore through the doors. He stopped midstride upon spotting me.

"John, welcome." Mr. Macy's voice held admonishment. He went to the drink table and poured a beverage. "Please join us. Allow me to extend my gratitude. I trust I did not burden you by having you arrange the journey."

Mr. Greenham accepted the tumbler but avoided Mr. Macy's gaze. "The trip wasn't the burden and you know it."

"Good. There's more business we need to discuss. I fear I need another favor."

Mr. Greenham gripped his drink. "Yes, well, there's something I'd like to address with you too."

"Good; after dinner, then."

Next, Reynolds announced Henry Auburn and Mr. Rooke.

Henry entered first and viewed the dining room as Rooke went straight to Mr. Macy and whispered in his ear.

Henry joined me, then leaned over and matched their secretive tones, wearing a mocking grin. "So what did you think when I rode up and pounded on the side of your carriage? Did you laugh? I imagine your mother wasn't very pleased. What did she say?"

It was so like Henry to simply resume our relationship—as if we'd just seen each other yesterday and I were still destined to become his sister. I felt my lip quiver as I looked askance at him, silently imploring him to stop.

Something about his penetrating gaze made me think he remembered the girl I'd been. The girl who'd laughed beneath the warmth of the sun as Edward spun her around in circles, her hair whirling in the air, before she collapsed to the ground in peals of laughter. I'd never felt self-conscious around Henry before, but suddenly I realized if anyone were fully cognizant of my great change, it was he.

His jovial mood was replaced by sobriety as I hugged myself. "It will be all right, Juls. I swear it. Edward always was somewhat of a tomfool with his high notions, but I swear to you, he will keep his oath."

I felt my quivering bottom lip push out. I did not take the opportunity to inform Henry that Edward's and my engagement had ended. Anyone who knows Henry also knows he would have badgered me until he learned the whole story. At that particular moment, I didn't want Henry's pestering.

When the doors swung open again, Mr. Robert Forrester was announced.

Upon hearing the name, Mr. Greenham's head jerked up and he viewed the visitor with an expression of equivocal horror and relief.

I scarce have need to describe Mr. Forrester, as his notoriety continues to this day, but I will say this: even by his late thirties, he did not have his pants tailored; therefore they hung about his feet like the excess skin of pugs. His hair looked tangled. I am uncertain whether a comb had ever touched it in his entire life. Only the top buttons of his frock coat were fastened, adding to his unkempt appearance.

What utter depth of stupidity he exhibited too, entering the chamber. He tripped, and when he righted himself, he narrowed his eyes at Mr. Greenham, as if to place blame. "Gentlemen," he announced in that nasally, annoying voice of his, as though challenging the room. Seeing the drink table, he picked up a glass and ran ink-stained fingers along the bottom. Apparently satisfied, he poured a drink and waved it under his nose.

"By all means, help yourself," Mr. Macy said in a bland tone over his shoulder, then returned to his conversation.

Mr. Forrester set the drink down untouched, though he stuck one finger in and brought it to his mouth.

Henry laughed. "What a droll fellow."

Mr. Forrester's eyes darted to us, his hand over his stomach, seemingly nauseated. But those eyes widened upon seeing me. "I know you!"

Mr. Macy paused and looked up from his conversation.

In response to Mr. Forrester's forwardness, I turned to face Henry.

"I'm certain of it." Mr. Forrester took a few steps in our direction. "Yes, yes; I can see you remember me too. I demand to know where we've met."

Mr. Macy crossed the room and placed his hands on my shoulders. "Robert, may I present Miss Julia Elliston. She's my guest and not about to be harassed by your uncouth ways."

Mr. Forrester snorted but retreated two steps. The doors crashed into the drink trolley, and Lady Foxmore burst into the room, her face sour. Stopping before Macy, she stood on tiptoes, pointing toward his nose. "I shall not tolerate this! Not even from you. If your man does not return my key momentarily, I shall take my leave and take my charge with me!"

Mr. Macy's mouth twitched as he steered her back to the hall. "Excuse us, please."

Elizabeth and Mrs. Windham entered, wide-eyed. Elizabeth touched her hair, looking at me, asking my opinion on her looks. I nodded. Thankfully a smiling Henry hastened to greet her, doubtlessly glad for the circumstances to meet away from his parents' watchful eyes.

Legend has it that no one has ever bested her ladyship, but it isn't true. When Lady Foxmore returned with Mr. Macy, I saw in a glance that not even she had managed to secure a key for her servant. Beneath the powder, her face was a shade of puce, yet her dignity was a marvel to behold. Her shoulders square, she discarded angry looks as carelessly as a gentleman tosses coins to a beggar.

To my delight, Mr. Macy came straight to me and took my arm. He placed me in the seat of honor; then, holding the back of my chair, he announced, "Please, everyone be seated."

There were no place cards, no prior arrangements as to which gentleman should seat which lady. It took a full minute for the confusion to abate, and another until the men sorted it out.

One lavish course followed another, pigs' feet in truffles, garnished tongue, artichokes with béchamel sauce. Mr. Macy paused each time a dish was offered me; his eyes gleamed whenever I pronounced something a novelty. He took no efforts to hide his pleasure that the weight of the crystal goblets shocked me, or that I marvelled that each course was served upon gold chargers. Noticing I only tasted the wine, he whispered for it to be replaced with sweeter claret.

While his footmen toiled to keep every guest satisfied, Mr. Macy kept the conversation light and palatable. For the short amount of time he'd spent in the Windhams' neighborhood, his knowledge was uncanny. He knew the merchants and their wares. He was familiar with dances and dinner plans, even asking if one of the cottagers had yet managed to afford the hunting pup he'd been saving to purchase.

"Mr. Auburn," Mr. Macy said, "I understand you return to school soon. What subjects will you study?"

Henry dabbed his mouth, frowning. "According to my father, Latin, chemistry, political science, and botany."

"According to your father?"

Lady Foxmore laughed and pointed at Elizabeth with her knife. "Yes, Lord Auburn hopes to prevent unsavory relations by forcing the boy back to school."

Poor Elizabeth. Even I hadn't heard this news, but knew it was true by the way scarlet crept up her cheeks.

Mr. Macy noticed, gave Lady Foxmore a warning look, then

changed the topic. "Is it true your brother continues his studies as well?"

"Yes," Henry said. "Edward devotes his spare time to learning Hebrew and Greek."

Mr. Macy nodded approval, cutting his curried rabbit. "I hear his sermons are excellent. I regret not having had the time to attend one."

"Edward would say you could have made the time."

Lady Foxmore laughed, waving her dish away. "Henry, shame on you. Do not blame Edward for your rude statements."

Mr. Macy smiled. "I'm rather surprised he didn't elect to join us too."

Lady Foxmore smirked at me. "Yes, and more's the pity he didn't join us. He would have made a most amusing addition to our party. Perhaps John can tell you what you missed. Heaven knows he's spent enough time with my incumbent to be familiar with him." Then, with a malicious smile, she stabbed her fork toward Mr. Greenham. "You never did tell me why you started spending hours a day with my vicar."

"What's this?" Mr. Macy turned to Mr. Greenham with astonishment. "You wrote nothing about it."

"That's because it was nothing." Mr. Greenham fixed his gaze on his plate.

"Yet my curiosity persists," Mr. Macy said, his voice sterner. "What was so fascinating to you about the vicar?"

"Fascinating?" Lady Foxmore's voice barely contained her mirth. "Well, if that's the information you seek, you're applying to the wrong person. Try the child sitting next to you! Rumor has it no one knows him better than she. Surely, William Elliston's daughter must have some biting insight on our overzealous parson. Dazzle us with your father's brilliant wit. Amuse us with your opinion of our vicar."

I had known, of course, that Lady Foxmore could be as

vicious as she could be generous. But until that moment, I could not guess on which side of that balance I truly stood.

She smirked as she glanced toward Henry, who shifted in his seat and leaned forward. I frowned, confused about what she wanted.

"William Elliston's daughter?" Mr. Forrester's head snapped toward me. His brow furrowed. "Someone spoke about your father, just the other day. Who was that?"

"Well, child?" Lady Foxmore demanded.

I shook my head. "I have no insight worth offering."

Her walking stick thumped the floor. "You must think our faculties are dulled with age, if you think to befool us with an answer like that. Come, child, there's no need to play shy. We all were present when Edward declared that you—how did he put it?—have far stronger claim on him than any other. What did he mean?"

His brows raised, Mr. Macy angled his head toward me.

During the past week, Elizabeth had given me plenty of warnings about Lady Foxmore, but none of them had prepared me for this. I nearly choked as her game became clear. With the skill of a faro player pitting her opponents against each other, she'd cornered me.

She knew that Mr. Macy had demonstrated interest in me, and the tiny glances she flashed at Henry alerted me to what she hoped to accomplish. Henry's rumored tempers were secondary only to her own. Henry would consider anything less than the truth an affront to Edward's honor—and if there was ever a person ready to blindly defend someone's honor, it was Henry.

I drew a slow breath. While my illusion of Edward was destroyed, Henry and Elizabeth still believed in our foursome. They walked in the lie that nothing would ever tear us apart, that we were untouchable. It pained me to publicly shatter them.

Yet if I did not deny Edward, I feared I'd lose Mr. Macy.

I felt my face grow sullen as I faced her ladyship. "How should I know his meaning?"

"But you do know him? Yes?"

I wanted to deny it, but one glance at Henry, sitting rigid in his chair, red splotching his cheeks, told me that would be carrying it too far. "Y-yes . . . I've met him once or twice."

"Once or twice?" Bitterness pinched Lady Foxmore's mouth. "Very well, child, if you're going to answer like that, I shall confront this head-on. Are you or are you not betrothed to him?"

Mr. Macy's astonished gaze excluded everyone but me.

"Oh, nonsense," Mrs. Windham said. "If anyone would know about such a thing, it would be me. I tell you, Lucy would have never allowed it. She forbade Julia to have any contact with the Auburn sons. Simply forbade it."

I drew a deep breath, feeling gladder for Mrs. Windham's babble than I ever thought possible. But it did not last long.

"Nonetheless—" Henry's voice was grinding as knives being sharpened—"I'd like to hear Miss Elliston's answer."

Beneath the table, I fingered my napkin as I met his angry gaze. It was Henry's own fault he was here to witness this. I had not asked him to come. "There is no betrothal," I said evenly. "I scarcely even know Reverend Auburn."

Henry stood and sliced me with his gaze. Though he was angrier than I'd ever seen him, he managed to keep his temper in check and gave Mr. Macy a stiff bow.

"Henry," Elizabeth whispered.

He shook off her pleading touch, threw his napkin on the table, and stalked from the chamber.

Elizabeth's skirts rustled as she prepared to follow. She managed to cast me an exasperated look as she stood.

"Elizabeth," Mrs. Windham hissed loud enough for everyone to hear. "What will Lord and Lady Auburn say?"

Her face tight, Elizabeth narrowed her eyes at her mother before leaving the room.

"Think of the impression you're giving Mr. Macy!" Mrs. Windham paused to titter at Mr. Macy, then called out to her daughter's retreating form, "Elizabeth!" She placed her hands on the table and attempted to hoist herself, addressing us. "You must excuse us all a moment. I warrant Elizabeth detected something amiss with the dish and wishes to speak to the staff privately."

Mr. Macy cast Mr. Greenham a look of displeasure over the rim of his wineglass.

"To be sure—" Mrs. Windham rocked as she made her second attempt to rise to her feet, looking at Mr. Macy—"it is just like Elizabeth too. A more fastidious wife one could never find. Within a month, she'd have any household so well-managed a husband would never experience even a hint of embarrassment."

"What?" A malicious smile curved her ladyship's mouth. "Shall you never visit?"

Mrs. Windham did not register the insult as she hastened toward the door. She paused at the threshold and addressed Lady Foxmore. "I can assure you, Elizabeth is not breaking Lord Auburn's edict. When you speak to them of this matter, you must make certain they know that Elizabeth would never meet alone with Henry. That they have my personal word . . ." She trailed off as she shifted her gaze over the table.

Contempt registered on the face of every guest, except me. I felt myself color and pale in succession with embarrassment. Had she been my own mother, my mortification could not have been more complete. Mrs. Windham's smile drained for a brief second as she sensed the censure, but then she brightened and waved her lacy handkerchief. "Eat, eat! Do not feel obligated to wait for us. No sense in allowing the food to grow cold!"

For a brief moment no one spoke as she pattered down the hall and, in what I believe she thought a subdued whisper, called for Elizabeth.

Rooke recovered first, leaning back in his chair and reaching into a nearby crystal bowl before popping an olive into his mouth. He grinned, looking toward Mr. Macy and Mr. Greenham, as if waiting for them to join him in his amusement.

Mr. Macy slowly wiped his mouth, folded his napkin, and set it on the table. "John," he said in a quiet voice, rising, "a word in private, if you please."

Mr. Greenham stiffened and drained his glass of wine while Lady Foxmore laughed outright. "I warned him!"

I bent my head, feeling overwhelmed with a keen sense of regret and humiliation. Rare was the occasion that someone of my status attended a dinner in this sphere, but the odds of someone like Mr. Macy paying attention to that person were even more astronomical. All I could think was that Mrs. Windham had spoiled a golden opportunity, one that would never come my way again.

A warm hand came to rest on my shoulder, and I raised my head to find Mr. Macy peering down at me with an encouraging smile. He gave me a slight squeeze before stepping away. Nothing more was necessary. My misery lifted and I found my breath.

"I do hope I am present," Lady Foxmore said, as Mr. Macy and Mr. Greenham retreated, "when Thomas learns Henry is still disregarding his orders about meeting secretly with Elizabeth. 'Tis no wonder he fears that creature's daughter becoming the next Lady Auburn."

"Thomas Auburn?" Mr. Forrester gave her ladyship a dubious look, then indicated Henry's empty chair. "Wait a moment, are you telling me that was Henry Auburn, as in *Lord Thomas Auburn's* elder son?"

Lady Foxmore gave him an affirmative nod.

He pointed at me. "And the vicar discussed was his brother, Edward Auburn?"

Lady Foxmore arched her eyebrows, as if to indicate he was rather slow to only now catch up.

"I don't know who you are, young lady—" Mr. Forrester gave me a sneering glance as he polished his knife with his napkin—"but I'll thank you not to spread defamatory rumors about the Auburns. I've met the young man in question and can say with conviction he'd never have anything or anyone connected to your father." He looked at her ladyship. "And as for you, do not smear future MPs. I'll have you know I have it on the best authority that Master Henry Auburn is planning to marry one Miss Abigail Morris and they will marry by the year's end. Her father personally brought my attention to the fact three days ago. I congratulated the future bride myself."

I gasped, feeling bright with shock at the succession of untruths he had just unleashed, but then anger took over. "That is a lie! You are a liar!"

Lady Foxmore laughed too hard to speak. With one hand she clutched her chest, and with the other she waved me to silence. "Cease," she gasped between breaths. "Cease, child! You forget your manners, though I'm not certain you ever possessed any. Hold your tongue, for the Auburns keep me better informed of matters than you, apparently."

Two footmen entered, struggling to carry a silver platter holding a roasted pig with an apple in its mouth. It was large enough to feed an assembly. They placed it at the head of the table for Mr. Macy to carve, exaggerating his absence.

"Remove it," Lady Foxmore ordered, struggling from her chair. "I daresay this charade of a dinner has ended. Give it to the servants; surely they'll be grateful."

No one argued with her assessment. Mr. Forrester stood, wiping his hands over his jacket, eyeing the door Mr. Macy and Mr. Greenham had taken while he shuffled toward it.

The rap of her ladyship's stick interrupted my observation. "You will come with me, Miss Elliston."

I obeyed and was surprised to find that my legs felt weak as I lifted myself from my chair.

"This way," Lady Foxmore said.

I followed her to a small door in the back of the room. It led to a narrow, twisting passage, which she deftly navigated.

"I imagine Chance is most anxious to speak with you. You are to remain here." She tested a door, which opened to reveal a chamber with heavy beams. Stiff leather and horsehair chairs made it appear spartan. Firelight flickered on the swords displayed over one wall. A pair of archaic crossbows hung over the stone mantelpiece.

She stood a long moment, as if reliving a memory, then murmured, "He would leave this room untouched." She hustled me into the room. "Take that seat there, child."

I started to protest, but she held up a finger, ordering silence. "We have an agreement, Miss Elliston. Wait here. Touch nothing. I'll send word where he can find you. You'll be safe from discovery."

Without another word she shut the door, and her walking stick tapped down the hall.

Twelve

※

ALONE IN THE CHAMBER, I pressed the tips of my fingers against my brow, feeling sick for Elizabeth. No matter what Mr. Forrester had claimed, I could not, would not, believe that Henry was engaged to someone else. It wasn't possible. The idea of either Henry or Elizabeth marrying another was positively revolting. I found myself wishing I had ignored her ladyship in the dining room and confronted Mr. Forrester on its impossibility.

Drawing a deep breath, I raised my gaze and viewed the swords flickering in the firelight. For the first time I finally understood why Henry and Elizabeth had furiously plotted to keep Edward and me together. Some things were just meant to be. Had to be.

I tucked a stray curl behind my ear, feeling the stark severity of the space, its dark corners pressing down upon me. Our foursome had been so real, so tangible. How was it possible that tonight I'd denied knowing Edward and then found out that Henry was engaged to another? I half fancied that hundreds of miles away, Edward had looked up from his studies with an acute feeling of pain. For I'd felt the last cords of our relationship strain and snap, as surely as if they were physical.

To distract myself, I stood and paced in front of the fireplace, wondering if this chamber was always so oppressive. Even in daylight, little sun would come through the narrow windows, which had scarcely enough width to peer out. It wasn't difficult to envision this room was a prison of sorts during Henry VIII's time.

I deserved such a soulless room, I thought, viewing the ancient weapons. By allowing Lady Foxmore to bring me here, I'd been no wiser than the flighty young Catherine Howard, who'd followed Lady Rochford's leading. Like her, had I stepped too far outside the perimeters of society? I'd abandoned mourning, and I now waited to meet alone with a gentleman at night.

I frowned, rubbing the chill from my arms. Yet at the same time, I was nothing like the beheaded queen. I was not wed. Let me find refuge from the north, from my humble circumstances, and see if I'd be so foolish as to betray the savior-king who'd offered it.

I crouched before the fire and stretched my hands over the flame. My eyes drifted over the mass of antique weapons above me, catching sight of an axe, pockmarked with rust and iron pockets. I studied its splayed and flattened head. An execution axe.

"I die a queen, but I would rather have died the wife of Culpeper." Catherine Howard's last words drifted through my mind. Daft, Mama had called her, after I'd read the account of her execution. At the time, I thought Mama the most unromantic soul in England, for I fancied I understood the queen's sentiments. Culpeper had been her Edward, worth dying for.

The fire popped and hissed beneath my fingers and I withdrew my hands from the warmth. But what was love compared to survival? Despite Catherine's love of Culpeper, had she chosen survival, the orphaned girl might have lived out her days wrapped in fur and jewels—queen of England.

I jabbed the fire, causing the fiery log to crumble. No. I was no Catherine Howard. I wouldn't die for love either.

Placing my hand over my neck, I gave the axe one last disdaining look, for it was impossible not to feel it had claimed more than one life. It appeared ancient, so antiquated it possibly could have been the same instrument used for—

"Enough," I whispered, rubbing my heavy eyes.

Determined to think no more upon executions, I rested my head on my folded arms and soaked in the warmth of the fire. My life seemed unstable in that moment, as ready to crumble as the log beneath the fire's flame. If Mama could abandon me, if men as genuine as Edward and Henry could be proven false, then what was constant?

I lowered myself to the floor and leaned against the davenport, wondering how Elizabeth and I missed the clues that Henry and Edward would shrink back.

During my long absence, there was one memory in particular I was wont to reflect upon when I wanted reassurance. I'd recall as many details as I could about the Midsummer Night's Eve when Mama and Mrs. Windham attended a dinner, never suspecting their daughters had agreed to a tryst in the woods. The air had been crisp; Elizabeth and I stuffed our beds, then hand in hand raced into the night for adventure.

When we arrived at the edge of the woods, Henry jested that we were tempting Robin Goodfellow to flirt with our fates, and that if we weren't careful, we'd fall in love with the wrong person. Edward's skeptical look caused Henry and Elizabeth to shriek with laughter. Thereafter, to befool Puck, Henry picked fistfuls of sleeping bluebells, which he thrust in my hands, and Elizabeth wove Edward a crown of twigs, denoting her newfound love for him.

By the time we arrived at our destination, their gaiety had

dressed us in sticks, ferns, leaves, and wildflowers. Edward gave me a private glance and our minds were one. We had not fooled Puck, but rather he'd ushered us into his courts with welcome and overseen that we were bedecked as one of his folks. A rare honor indeed.

As sparks from our small fire floated into the night and blended into the starry canopy, Edward bowed and extended his hand. I nimbly curtsied.

A sound, like that of stone scraping against stone, caused us both to pause. The fire expired and the forest became black. Edward paled, backing away.

I already knew what was happening, for I had dreamed it a hundred times. Tears thickened my throat as I heard the crackle of flames. I turned, crying, expecting to see Mama across the vast pit. Only this time she had managed to cross the expanse. Her maggot-eaten face, still wrapped in her gauzy shroud, hovered before mine. She held out her hands, wailing in agony.

I sat up from my sleep, my feet sliding over the polished floor as birch trees dissolved into walls and windows. All at once, I realized Mama's dream wails were actually my own. With a sob, I covered my mouth.

Never before in my dreams had Mama crossed the chasm. I closed my eyes, trying to erase the image. Though I'd sworn I would never cry or mourn for her again, tears came unbidden.

No longer did the swords flicker in the firelight. The chamber was dark. While I'd slept, the candles had burned down to the wick. The light produced from the ruby embers behind me cast a hellish hue over the Turkish carpet.

To my great embarrassment, the door creaked open, sending light through the room.

"Miss Elliston?" Reynolds stepped in from the hall. "Are you all right?"

I gave him no answer, but signalled for privacy.

It was easy to see he was uncertain what to do. He started toward me but stiffened at the sound of rushing feet.

"What the dickens is going on in here?" Mr. Macy demanded, entering the room. "Who was that screaming?"

I turned away to wipe my eyes and nose on the sleeve of my dress.

"I beg your pardon, Mr. Macy, sir; only Miss Elliston—"

Before I knew what was happening, a pair of hands braced my shoulders and turned me. I attempted to rise, but his hands on my shoulders kept me from more than sitting. Mr. Macy's gaze probed every inch of my face. Under his scrutiny, memory of Mama faded as I grew conscious of my wrinkled dress and tearstained eyes. He exhaled, relieved. Barely audible, he asked, "Are you all right?"

My voice lodged in my throat, but I managed a slight nod.

His features became forbidding as he looked over his shoulder. "Might I ask why it is that one of my guests—*this* guest in particular—is here alone and unguarded?"

The silence that followed was pregnant with discomfort.

"I don't know, sir," Reynolds finally said. "I only just found her myself."

"What do you mean you only just found her?" He gnashed his teeth at his valet. "Did I not assign you to tend to her after dinner? What is she doing here?"

"I hardly know myself, sir. She'd already left the table by the time I arriv—"

"Quiet." Mr. Macy's gaze lingered on the room before he returned his attention to me. He tucked a stray piece of hair behind my ear and then cradled my face. He bent his head near mine and kept his voice private. "Of all the rooms in the estate, Miss Elliston, why did you choose this one?"

I'd been unable to recover my wits before Reynolds, but now, like forcing the final dress into a trunk and then latching it, I managed to quell my confusion and panic. As I became conscious of Mr. Macy's hands on my cheeks, they grew inflamed.

"Her ladyship brought me here." My voice sounded more wan than I liked. "Did she forget to tell you where I was?"

It was difficult to see his expression in the murk, but I gathered from the tension in his arm that he was displeased. He dipped his head, whether to think or to recover his temper, I knew not. "Reynolds, do not fail me again. You may leave now."

"Yes, sir."

"John—" Mr. Macy looked over his shoulder—"go find Adelia and make it abundantly clear I am not amused. Tell her no more games. I mean it."

Mr. Greenham bowed. "And when I finish?"

"Retire for the evening." Mr. Macy's eyes met mine as he brushed his thumb along my jawline. To my chagrin, as he viewed my mouth his eyes lit with amusement. It did not occur to me until later that it was because he read the desire that spread through me as a fire burns a page. "I've waited a long time to have Julia alone."

My stomach hollowed at his words, yet at the same time they also thrilled me.

"What?" Mr. Greenham lowered his voice. "Alone? Here?"

Mr. Macy slowly looked over his shoulder. "Is there a problem, John?"

"No, but we agreed that—"

"Then leave."

Mr. Greenham's mouth clamped shut, but he turned his gaze on me. He looked so feral that I half believed that should every servant in Eastbourne spontaneously attack us with knifes and pokers, he could have vanquished them bare-handed. In a sort of spasm, Mr. Greenham jerked his head, then retreated into the dark hall. Mr. Macy likewise watched him, only with an expression that better suited a hawk.

Once the sound of the slap of his boots faded, Mr. Macy

angled his head and studied me. "May I ask—" his voice was as beguiling as his appearance—"what message of yours Lady Foxmore failed to deliver? Were you waiting for me?"

I opened my mouth to respond, but a new kind of shyness seized me. I pleaded with my eyes not to be questioned.

He laughed as his gaze darted over the gloomy hall and darkened chamber. "And alone, too? You are either very brave or very foolish to follow her bidding. Tell me, are you very nervous?"

"Ought I to be?"

"Yes, with a chaperone as notorious as Adelia and no gentleman present to defend your honor." His nostrils flared slightly as if he were a starved man savoring a meal he was about to devour. Mr. Macy's gaze dropped to my mouth and then ran along my neck. When his eyes returned to mine, my stomach twisted with a new sensation, one of which I knew Edward would not approve.

Mr. Macy leaned forward, as though to kiss me. "You made a very foolish mistake, being caught alone in the dead of night, with a man, inviting his glances. Clearly your mother neglected to teach you the finer points of propriety." His voice grew jagged as his gaze moved along my collarbone. He picked up a lock of my hair and breathed in its scent. "What would you do, little one, if I were in no mood to correct her mistakes?"

Fisting my skirt, I watched him, wide-eyed.

With a chuckle, he released my curl. "Lucky for you, I am a man of restraint. Besides, it would be counterproductive, considering I brought you here to offer you my full assistance."

"Assistance?" My voice came out weak, my heart still pounding against my stays. "I don't understand."

His brows knit. "You must admit the odds are not in your favor at the moment and growing worse. It's nothing short of a miracle you've made it this far." My confusion must have been apparent, for Mr. Macy's face crumpled. "You mean no one's told you?"

"Told me what?"

He ran his fingers through his hair, glancing at the clock before his hand moved to his chin, which now shadowed a day's growth. He shook his head as though in disbelief. When he spoke, it was slow and thoughtful. "Forgive me in advance, Miss Elliston, but this may be a rather trying night for you. We haven't much time to act, and it appears you lack important knowledge." He stood with fluid movement and offered his hand. "The documents are in my study. Will you come?"

∿

Mr. Macy paused before a small door and pulled out a key ring. He gave me a nod of encouragement as the key twisted in the lock.

Inside, a merry blaze illuminated an intimate cedar-panelled room. Before the hearth, two worn leather couches faced each other. On my right stood a massive desk strewn with papers, some of which spilled over onto the floor. Scattered ash and the scent of cigars suggested a negligent smoker. Behind the far couch, a tray was set with liquors in sparkling decanters. Mr. Macy ushered me into the chamber, then relocked the door.

I folded my arms and drew them close as he locked his keys in a drawer.

"Cold?" Mr. Macy shook off his silk banyan, then held it in the air for me to slide my arms through. It was the first time in my memory someone had acted as though my well-being meant more to him than his own.

As I slid my hand over the raised embroidery and silk, he navigated his way around the papers near the desk. Nothing in my entire wardrobe was so costly. To the backdrop of decanters chinking against each other, I lifted the square collar about my face and breathed in his scent—cigars, brandy, and sandalwood. I hadn't realized I'd shut my eyes until he asked, "Brandy?"

I opened my eyes and found him watching me with pleasure. "For me?"

With a disarming smile, he turned over a glass. "So, they've not permitted you the drink of gentlemen, eh? Here, try it." He sauntered to me and pressed a full tumbler into my hands. "You'll find no such restrictions on you in my house."

With his head he indicated the nearby couch. "Sit."

I perched on the edge of the cushion and took my first taste of spirits, imagining the heart palpitations Mrs. Windham would suffer if she knew. The drink was strong, burning enough to sear the conscience as well as the tongue.

"Good?" he asked.

I nodded, knowing better than to speak, then coughed.

Mr. Macy gave his hypnotic laugh as he poured his own glass. "For the record, should you ever find yourself as compromised as you were earlier, protest. Loudly. The louder the better. Demand to be freed, then threaten the man with full retaliation from your nearest male relative."

I must have flashed him a look that told him the absurdity of his statement.

His expression went beyond my ken as he tilted his head. "Yes, perhaps that would have no effect on me, but trust me when I tell you that you are better protected than you realize."

He settled into the couch across from me, where he sipped his brandy, watching. That he waited for me to speak, I had not a doubt. But I didn't know what to make of him yet, so I matched his intake of brandy, sip for sip, making it clear by the jut of my jaw that I would not begin this conversation.

After a quarter hour, he finally set his drink aside and leaned forward, clasping his hands over his knees. His voice smiled. "I've waited a long time for this conversation, and now that you're here, I scarcely know where to start."

I allowed the hand holding the brandy to lower to my lap. "Then tell me what you meant earlier, when you said I was in danger."

He nodded, as if approving. "Quite the contrary—you're safer now than you've been in months." His brows drew together. "Yes. Why not. Let's begin there."

He stood, brushing his hands, and then went to his desk, where he unlocked a drawer and shuffled through papers. His onyx ring winked in the light as his fingers deftly maneuvered through files. "Perhaps you've heard I keep strange habits, or that I'm reclusive and so forth. My life is peculiar for good reason. It's rare I explain myself, yet with you, I will do so."

He selected two pages, stuck them in a brown leather folder, and relocked the drawer before reclaiming his seat. He waited until my attention shifted from the folder to him.

"I require something of you first. You must swear to me, everything discussed here remains a private matter between us. Have a clear understanding, Miss Elliston, when you make a contract with me, verbal or otherwise, I will hold you to it. So promise me nothing lightly."

I tightened my fingers about my tumbler. "You have my word."

His eyes sharpened. "You promised that very quickly."

His abrupt change of mood startled me. His eyes no longer smiled, and I sensed him offended, though it wasn't clear why. "Does that make it less valid?"

"Not as long as you understand the gravity. Yet I am hesitant, for what I wish to share with you has the potential to destroy many lives. You are rather young and have just proved how impulsive you are."

My young life had been difficult, tempered with my father's fist and our neighbors' harrying. I had lived divided, riven between the two people I loved the most, forced to hide all knowledge of Edward from Mama. Secrets I had kept. Lies I had told. All to protect two people who had ended up betraying me in every possible manner. My very flesh recoiled at the thought of being considered a frivolous youth, and it wrought a change in my countenance.

"You gravely mistake me, then," I said in a hard voice, ready to gather my skirts and leave.

Mr. Macy's face sobered as he tilted his head to study me. "Yes," he said slowly, "perhaps I do. Forgive me. I meant no offense. I forget how deeply entrenched you already are in this matter besides." He gave a slight nod. "All right, so we begin. Since I am uncertain how much knowledge you have, we'll start at the very beginning. Please do not think I am patronizing you."

I waited, hands gripping my tumbler on my lap as he reached behind him to the drink trolley. He poured himself a second helping and without asking, he extended the decanter and refilled my drink. He shoved the stopper into the throat of the decanter. "I assume you are aware you have a guardian?"

I started, a gnarled, hollow knot forming in my stomach.

"Yes or no, if you please."

"Yes, but how—?"

"Have you yet been informed that he's made arrangements for you to leave for Scotland to stay as a lady's companion to the late General Clark's widow—and very soon, I might add?"

I stopped breathing. Even I hadn't learned the name of my patron in Scotland.

"Yes, I can see you have. And judging by your face, you also know your guardian intends for you to meet with a fatal accident while in Scotland." He gave a bitter laugh, lifting his tumbler in a mock toast. "It is his way, is it not? Strip away all power and then remove his victim from anyone who might ask questions."

At first, like a pebble thrown into a pond and spiralling downwards but not hitting the bottom, his words made no sense. Then, as meaning penetrated, the tumbler slipped from my fingers and splashed its remaining contents over the couch and floor.

"Forgive me." Mr. Macy slid to the floor and crouched near me, removing his silk handkerchief. "Perhaps I should not have been so blunt. It is my habit to be direct, and I forget not everyone shares my tastes."

My fingers trembled as I clutched his sleeve. "Y-you . . . how could you know such a thing?"

"I know a great many things about your guardian," he replied with distaste, sweeping a pool of brandy from the couch to the rug.

Why tears rose at this juncture I cannot say, but my vision blurred. "But why would he wish me harm? I've done nothing to him! I don't even know who he is."

"You don't know—?" Mr. Macy dropped the sopping linen and turned to me, his face incredulous. "What? How can you not know his identity?"

My throat was too tight to speak as I struggled against the urge to cry.

"Forgive me. I've frightened you." He enfolded my trembling hands between his. "Had I known you were ignorant of this fact, I would have broken it to you differently. Forgive me. I assumed that since you knew about your guardian, you knew your peril. Didn't your mother tell you there was a dangerous man associated with your family?"

I wanted to defame the notion, yet before I could, I realized Mama had told me by the way her face paled with each letter, the way her breathing halted each time hooves approached.

"Here." Mr. Macy reached behind himself and brought forth the decanter. He poured me more brandy. "Take a sip; it will steady you. It's all right. You're perfectly safe, I can assure you. He hasn't even an idea of your current whereabouts."

I obeyed, glad for the burn in my throat. It took several gulps before I shook my head, disagreeing. "I told him. I wrote and told him I was coming here."

"Please, Miss Elliston. Be calm." Mr. Macy gave my hands a squeeze before retreating to the other couch. "You have nothing to fear." He took up the brown folder and pulled out one of the papers. "Here, see for yourself, though you may think me with-out scruples."

He held in his hand a folded sheet that was the same grain and texture as Am Meer's stationery. Familiar ink splatters, from where I'd carelessly moved the pen, confirmed its origins.

"That's my post," I exclaimed, holding out my hand. "But how?"

Mr. Macy handed it to me and sat back, crossing one leg over the other. "More than one of your guardian's servants is loyal to me. I've been intercepting all correspondence involving you since your mother's death."

As I stared at the missive, I felt as a sailor must the first time aboard ship, trying to find balance in a new world. To interfere with someone's private business was unheard of. I did not have to lift my eyes to know Mr. Macy was carefully evaluating my response.

Rather than address him, I shook open the missive and reread its contents:

> *Dear Sir or Madam,*
>
> *I obediently remain in the care of Mrs. Windham while she travels to Bedfordshire to visit a Mr. Chance Macy in his home, Eastbourne. The good lady departs on the morrow, leaving me no time to wait for your permission. I trust it is your desire I remain with my appointed chaperone. Should you disapprove, I shall immediately return home.*
>
> > *Your humble servant,*
> > *Julia Elliston*

"I don't understand," I said, refolding the note. "Why are you—were you—intercepting his mail? How is it that you are involved?"

His voice smiled for him. "Perhaps now is not the best time for that discussion."

I found my courage and met his eyes. "I demand to know."

"You demand?" One dark brow rose, as if to suggest I should not insist on more than I could handle. His voice smoldered. "You've already had one blow tonight. Are you certain you're ready to handle more?"

Completely uncertain, I nodded.

He picked up the brown folder and with a flick of his wrist, he presented Mama's stationery. "Be forewarned, the contents may shock you. Apparently there are a great many things your mother neglected to mention."

I eyed the black mourning band, which edged the paper with dread. The note had been penned after my father's death. My head cleared despite the heat of the fire and the effect of the brandy.

Ignoring the puzzled look that crossed Mr. Macy's face, I snatched up the page. My fingers trembled so much, I could scarcely open it. When I managed, I sought out the date. Thankfully she'd added it: January.

I crushed the letter against my chest, nearly crying with relief. It was months after the initial missive that set her strange behavior into motion.

Mr. Macy looked so perplexed, I explained. "Mama was corresponding with someone whom she feared. When I saw her letter, for a moment, I thought it was you."

His mouth slanted downwards. "Are you this rash in all your judgments? You only gave the post a fleeting glance. There couldn't have been time to read the contents. How can you be certain? You've not even seen my stationery to compare with the post she received."

I ignored him, returning my attention to what Mama had written. I'd observed her each time she received mail. The letters that frightened her, she would always read quickly, then fly to her writing desk and scribble a reply. One of those posts would have been ink-smeared or evidenced tearstains. This letter was nothing like that. Each word, each perfect letter, seemed labored over.

> *My dear Mr. Macy,*
>
> *My amazement to receive a correspondence from you could not have been more complete. The contents of your letter were even more astonishing. Indeed, I do remember you, though I was under the assumption you had no contact with society. You must sympathize with my great shock when you wrote of your partiality for my only daughter. I offer no objections to the match if she feels inclined toward it. Only grant me this: she is young and I have recently lost my husband. Give me time to prepare her. I plan to visit friends in Gloucestershire soon. When I return, introductions will be made on your behalf.*
>
> Mrs. L. Elliston

"But it makes no sense," I finally whispered, too embarrassed to address the fact that Mr. Macy at some point had asked for my hand. "She swore I'd never marry."

"Perhaps she had good reason for wishing you safely wed." Mr. Macy lifted the letter from my fingers and refolded it. "She was in the same danger you now face, which leads me to the primary reason I wished to meet tonight. I need to make further inquiries into her death. I've spent months trying to learn the cause. Her apothecary claims she died of a broken heart, pining after your father." His laugh was bitter. "Anyone acquainted with your father knows the absurdity of that statement."

I lowered my gaze. Memory of finding her corpse was still too raw for discussion. It was the fuel on which my nightmares burned. I shook my head.

Mr. Macy's tone lowered. "Please. If I'm to properly safeguard you, I must know."

Though I shut my eyes, memory enshrouded me like a slow,

creeping fog, and I knew if I couldn't force back the thoughts, things would spin far beyond my control.

He gently lifted my chin. "It's evident you're keeping back something."

A tear formed and trickled down my cheek as memory trumped reticence. Once more I saw myself gasping awake, saw the moonlight streaming through the windows as I silently raced toward Mama's room.

"Tell me," Mr. Macy persisted.

It was as though a weight crushed my chest, making it difficult to breathe. Then all at once my body took a ragged breath of its own accord. Tears streamed down my face as I confessed the very thing I'd so solemnly sworn to the apothecary never to reveal. "She killed herself."

"That, I can assure you, is not possible."

"I found her body." My nose ran as more tears spilled. "I know she did."

"Sweetheart." He slid from his couch and knelt at my feet. "Take my word on this: your guardian wanted her death too badly for her to have obliged him that easily. Tell me how you found her."

"I woke in the middle of the night—"

"What woke you?"

"I don't know." I pressed the back of my hand against my nose, ashamed of my appearance. "I just remember being alarmed and needing to see her."

"Was it a noise, perhaps?"

"I don't know. I don't. I just awoke. When I reached her room—" My throat constricted as I envisioned my hand on her door, pushing it open. "The chamber was so . . . so . . . cold, and her body—" my words came out serrated—"her body, her face, was all twisted, grotesque."

"Wait. Shh. Take a deep breath. Good. Why was her chamber cold? Was there no fire?"

"No, it was colder than that." I blinked up at him in surprise, visualizing her curtains billowing like graceful dancers over her body. "I think . . . the windows were open."

"Did you look outside?" He leaned forward, sounding hopeful.

"No." The realization made me nauseous. "But why were her windows open? She believed night air—"

"What happened after you entered the chamber?"

I pictured the milky liquid spreading over the floor. I had slipped and landed on Mama's corpse. I had screamed and screamed, seemingly unable to escape her. For in my panic, my own hands and feet kept sliding over the medicine.

What I was reliving must have been evident on my face, for in the next moment, I found myself wrapped in Mr. Macy's arms. "Shh. Wait until you've caught your breath," he whispered, his warmth bleeding into my hair.

I nodded, crying, burying my face against his warm chest. He rocked me, allowing me time to compose myself. When the clock chimed three, however, he placed distance between us.

He stroked my hair. "I am truly sorry to put you through this, but I need to know. What happened next?"

"I slipped on her medicine."

"Medicine?"

"The laudanum she used to kill herself."

"What?" He drew back. "How can that be?"

"The doctor dropped off a bottle the day before. She complained of headaches."

"How big was it?"

I showed him the approximate size with my fingers.

"Julia, sweetheart, are you aware how much laudanum one must consume to kill oneself?"

I did not answer him but just wiped away tears.

He pointed at a filled decanter. "She would have to consume a portion at least equal to a third of my Scotch. How much had spilled on the floor?" I eyed the whiskey as he lowered his voice. "Do you know how long it would have taken her to die from a laudanum overdose?"

Unconscious thoughts that had only crept about in my dreams began to seep outward. "No."

"She would have grown sleepy and died peacefully in her bed. Not dropped to the floor with contorted . . . Who is this so-called doctor? Surely he must have known."

"Sarah mopped up the elixir before he arrived. I-I know Mama was placed in her bed . . . I . . ." The thought Mr. Macy was suggesting finally formed. "Someone murdered Mama."

It was too terrible to consider. Yet I knew it. I recalled the snatches of the months leading up to Mama's death—they all proclaimed this truth. Had I known? I allowed my hands to fall empty to my lap. Yes, I decided, on some unconscious level, I had always known. How else could I explain my constant nightmare?

Horrified, I looked to Mr. Macy.

"I should have acted sooner," he soothed, lifting strands of hair from my face. "Offered her sanctuary here, perhaps. At least I have you under my protection now. I shall not fail again."

I felt too emotionally spent to even inquire what he meant.

His lips pursed as concern etched his brow. "Perhaps I've allowed you to ingest more brandy and knowledge than you were ready to handle. If I take you back to your chambers, do you think you could sleep? It would be your best remedy. We can continue our discussion later."

I struggled to my feet, dully nodding, ready to be alone.

He steadied me as I tottered too far to one side. "I know you're overwhelmed, but pay mind. I'll not be here tomorrow. There are matters requiring my attention. There is a man in my house, one not to be trusted. You met him at dinner. Robert Forrester. Avoid him. Do you understand?"

I nodded, rubbing my eyes.

"Aside from those in Adelia's village, few people know your whereabouts. We must hope your guardian also remains ignorant. Which is why we cannot risk causing a sensation by letting it be known I've finally become enamored, or your location would be learned far sooner. I propose we act normally and slowly introduce an attachment between us." His voice took on a teasing tone. "At least I pray you have no objections to my request to court you. After all, I can't exactly ask your guardian."

I nodded, scarcely hearing him. I spied my empty glass and realized I'd consumed more spirits than I originally thought.

"You can depend upon Reynolds with your life, as well as John."

I rubbed my eyes, trying to focus, but all my sluggish thoughts streamed in one direction—someone had murdered Mama, someone intent on harming me.

"You are very quiet. What are you thinking?"

I clutched his arm to keep my balance and found him watching me with concern. My condition led me to answer more truthfully than I would have liked. "Your conversation flows too rapidly from one extreme to the other. I can hardly keep pace."

He chuckled and cupped my elbow. "I think, my dear, when you've sobered, you'll see I was not the river of emotion, but the solid ground that kept you channelled."

I clung to his arm, too exhausted to make out whether or not his statement pleased me. Thankfully the study was in the same ancient section of the house where I'd been placed. Within a few turns, I recognized the hall that contained my bedchamber. Reynolds stood outside my door.

"Is he waiting for me?" I asked, confused.

"No." Mr. Macy's voice was low and amused. "He waits for me. I have an identical chamber at the top of the stairs, just above yours."

He unlocked my door and handed me the key. To my wonderment, the lamps were lit and a fire waited. Holding up a finger to Reynolds, Mr. Macy stepped inside with me, though he didn't close the door completely.

Feeling strangely shy again, I allowed him to pull me against him and tilt up my chin. He kissed me slowly but softly, teaching me to respond, and when I did, he deepened our kiss, pulling me close. Only when I had completely surrendered did he end our lingering kiss, keeping me loosely gathered in his arms.

"There's something I've been wondering," he said, "and while you're still tipsy, I'm going to ask. What on earth did you think you were doing with Adelia if you didn't know I had asked her to escort you to me?"

It took a couple of seconds to realize he meant her ladyship. "I have an agreement with her."

"Agreement?" His tone grew hard. "What agreement?"

I stared at the unfastened pearl button on his shirt. "To . . . to find me a husband."

"She did wh—? In exchange for what, might I ask?"

I could not look at him. "Two thousand pounds."

His shock was so complete he said nothing, though I felt his body cough. "Tell me you did not agree."

I blushed, not responding.

To my relief, Mr. Macy laughed. "She was in earnest when she called herself my enemy. Good night! Must I protect you from my acquaintances as well as our enemies? No more agreements with her ladyship. In fact, avoid her ladyship completely if you can. She's not what I consider a good influence."

"But she is my chaperone," I protested.

"And a very poor one at that, as evidenced by tonight." He kissed my forehead. "Now go find some rest. I'll see you tomorrow."

Thirteen

THE FIRST SOUND I became conscious of the next morning was tapping. Two top sheets were tangled about my ankles and a third had bunched under my stomach. Groaning, I kicked them off, then sat. Light stabbed my eyes while nausea twisted my stomach. The mantel clock marked the hour.

Six.

The knocking turned into pounding.

"Coming," I yelled, then winced at the pain that shot through my head. I stood, increasing my queasiness. More pounding followed. Frantic, I searched the dishevelled bedclothing for something to wrap around my shimmy. I gleaned my wrinkled dress from the floor and fumbled with it. "Who is it?"

"Who does thou expect but mysell?"

Nancy. I sagged against the bed frame and called to the door. "It's six in the morning."

"Aye!" returned Nancy's crabbed voice. "And if thou had seen fit to give me a key last night, instead of leavin' all th' work for morning, there'd be no want for me to wake thee this early." She hammered again.

Realizing she'd not be deterred, I stumbled into the main chamber and yanked open the door. She stood, fist raised, ready to pound again. She appeared as annoyed as I felt, but faltered under my glare. I stepped aside, allowing her to enter.

Her gaze swept to the bedchamber, where last night's dress and crinolines were spread over the carpet, and then to my pile of trunks.

"Well, 'tis a mercy thy fire is lit at least."

"Oh, hush," I said, in no mood for her. "You're the one who wanted to come."

She stomped into the bedchamber and bent, gathering the gown I wore last night, and then in the main chamber retrieved yesterday's travel gown. While she spread them before the fire to inspect, I stretched out over the settee and hid my face from the light with a velvet cushion. Every noise seemed magnified as Nancy began to brush the dried mud from the hem of my travel dress. The hard swish communicated her ire.

"Thou best hasten," she eventually said, "if thou wishes to be on time. Breakfast is at eight and thy hair weren't set last night. Thou'll have no curls today."

Not particularly caring, I pulled a second pillow against my stomach. Memory of the previous night rushed in like flotsam caught in the morning tide. Like waves after a storm, memory pounded on top of memory as I sorted through jumbled scenes. Dinner. The dark chamber. Mr. Greenham. Only then, as if my mind were determined to cushion each awful blow, did I recall. My eyes opened of their own accord.

Mama. Murdered.

Nancy looked over from her work. "What?"

Feeling ill, I rested my head in the palms of my hands. "Hold your tongue."

With a sniff, she continued the mad swishing of her brush. Knowing I couldn't hold the contents of my stomach, I stumbled to my feet and staggered into the room where I was sure to find a chamber pot.

Nancy's voice carried. "Thou did well to ask me to learn about this household."

I didn't answer except to collapse over the elegant china bowl and retch the sour contents of my stomach. When I finished, I lay down and stared at the ceiling through a blur of tears. What sort of coward would murder Mama? I covered my eyes, recalling her pale face as she blew out the candle that final evening. What had she gone and faced alone? What would cause a person to writhe in so much pain?

"'Tis a strange house, to be sure," Nancy continued, as if trying to bait me. "Never heard of such a thing as not allowing servants keys. Only that Reynolds chap is allowed to tend thy rooms. Can thou imagine? Me ma would say somewhat wrong with that, to be sure."

The stench coming from the chamber pot was acrid. I sat up and raked my fingers through my hair, which felt damp. A basin waited on the nightstand. I dipped my cupped hand into the cool water, then drank to wash away the sour taste.

Nancy joined me, carrying a dress between her arms. She froze at the threshold. Following her gaze, I spotted Mr. Macy's banyan half crammed into the corner.

Nancy stared at it with wide eyes. Like numbers being worked into an equation, she viewed my unmade bed, my clothing haphazardly strewn about the room before returning to the men's robe.

"You needn't bother starting servants' gossip," I said bitterly. "It's not what you think."

"Aye, is that what thou thinks? I gossip about thee? As if I haven't gat better things to talk about."

"Oh yes," I replied, feeling none too charitable, "I forgot. You have other domestics to chitchat about."

Her freckled cheeks rose as she scowled. "Thou wants

gossip? How about this? I have it on th' best authority, one of th' young ladies spent th' night with a gent." She leaned over and snatched up Mr. Macy's robe, which she shook at me. "I warrant she weren't up to no good. Then she was daft enough to insult her maid, atop of everything."

"Oh, hush!" I covered my eyes. Everything hurt.

"Come on with thee." Nancy gripped my upper arm. "Th' least we can do is make certain thou art first to breakfast, case word of this leaks out."

∼

There is a sense of comfort in pain, when it has been one's companion long enough. There's a familiarity to the sensation of being pulled down from rapturous dreams and having our feet mingle with the dust once more. I found myself on famil- iar territory that morning as Nancy dressed me. Mama had been murdered. No longer did I believe my starry-eyed dream of Lady Foxmore lifting me from my circumstances. Yet strangely, I found the heavy ache in my chest comforting. I knew far better how to navigate stormy waters than calm ones.

Even the throb of my head and the agitation in my stomach were a boon—they added to my collectedness. Who can indulge in fantasies of Adonis when suffering? Questions I'd been too inebriated last night to consider now accumulated. How had Mr. Macy known about me? He had said he'd be absent today, but where had he gone? What was the footing of our relationship?

I touched the dark crescents under my eyes as Nancy shoved the last comb into place. When she opened my jewelry case, a white box caught my eye.

"Eh? What's this?" Nancy picked it up.

"Here, give it to me."

She placed the cold ivory box in my hand. Inside, an assortment of bracelets waited, gold, pearls, sapphires—each seemingly more costly than the last. I clamped the lid shut, ignoring Nancy's stunned expression. That a gentleman had given me a gift, and of this value, was exceedingly improper; yet I felt a dart of delight.

I found Reynolds waiting outside my chambers, looking exactly as he had yesterday. Whether he had slept or changed clothing was indiscernible. Upon spotting him, Nancy paled and curtsied, hurrying from the room and down the corridor, giving him no time to speak.

He watched her leave with a decided frown before turning to me with a slight bow. "Please accept my deepest apologies, Miss Elliston. It was Mr. Macy's orders that you not be disturbed. She came without permission. I can assure you, it will not happen again."

I nodded, wrapping my shawl tightly about me. Nancy was the least of my concerns. "Is he still here? I wish to speak with him."

The blue of Reynolds's eyes was startling as he faced me, like frost against a brilliant blue sky. "I am sorry, Miss Elliston, but he's already absented himself. Shall I fetch Mr. Greenham? I daresay he can answer any question that Mr. Macy can."

"Mr. Greenham?" Already the name was foreign on my lips. In less than twelve hours, I'd forgotten the man who'd accompanied me here. I shot Reynolds a puzzled look. "He knows too?"

"Knows, Miss Elliston?"

I lowered my voice. "About last night?"

Reynolds shifted his eyes to a place over my shoulder. "I beg your pardon, Miss Elliston, but whatever did or did not happen last night is none of my business. Shall I fetch Mr. Greenham?"

I grew sullen as I wondered what exactly he thought had occurred in his master's study. "Yes, please."

Near the entrance hall, Reynolds stopped before a carved wooden door and opened it for me. "If you will wait in the breakfast chamber, I'll have him fetched straightaway."

Large windows framed the far wall and displayed dapple-grey skies. Rain hammered the grounds, so that the garden topiaries protruded like islands from amidst puddles. Inside the chamber, thick-framed Renaissance paintings dotted the walls. The largest of the set hung above a massive buffet where fruits, pastries, tea, and coffee waited.

I poured coffee into a Russian cup patterned in blue and gold, then sat at the immense table and shielded my eyes from the feeble light.

The sound of footsteps ended my musings.

Like spirit met like spirit as Mr. Greenham ducked into the chamber. In his grave manner, he studied my eyes, then stepped to the sideboard and poured tomato juice.

"This will help," he said, taking the seat next to me. He pulled a flask from his waistcoat and added its contents to the drink, then slid the glass to me.

I opened my mouth to protest.

"Trust me," he said.

To refuse, I saw, would greatly offend him. I took up the glass and smelled it, vaguely wondering what Mama would have thought to know I'd found protection amongst chronic drinkers. Like a father encouraging his child, Mr. Greenham nodded for me to drink.

The concoction tasted horrible.

"I should have warned you that Macy never feels the effect of drink and easily forgets himself," Mr. Greenham said. "He shall feel remorse when he learns you've suffered this morning."

I nodded, unwilling to examine why that statement brought so much comfort.

Over the next quarter hour, I came to believe Mr. Greenham had been in my condition a great many times. He said nothing as if sensing how each noise jolted my ears, how light stabbed my eyes. When he finally spoke, it was after my headache became manageable.

"Reynolds told me you were looking for Macy? Is there something I can help you with?"

I nodded but then felt tears rising, so I shook my head. He simply waited.

"How much do you know?" I finally managed.

He heaved a sigh. "I should imagine a great deal."

"About my guardian?"

"Yes."

"And that my mother was . . ." I couldn't bring myself to say the ugly word.

There was a slight pause followed by "Yes."

No tears, I thought, blinking them back. I would not cry. Not until I'd seen Mama avenged.

Mr. Greenham proved to be a patient companion. He waited, his tender gaze fixed upon me. When I could speak again, I asked, "You knew all this the first time we met?"

He gave a guarded "Yes."

It was an adjustment to realize he'd known about Mama during that dreadful dinner with Edward and his parents. He knew my guardian intended me harm while Lady Foxmore bargained her requirements for chaperoning me. *"This is no game,"* he'd told her through gritted teeth. No wonder he had looked so disgusted when Mrs. Windham contrived to leave us alone. Doubtless he had no other intentions but to transport me safely to Eastbourne.

"And Lady Foxmore?" I asked.

"She is in no danger of which I am aware."

"No, I mean, does she know?"

Mr. Greenham grew very still. "I do not know how much Macy has made her aware of."

Our conversation was broken by the heavy slap of boots. Mr. Greenham shifted forward to the edge of his chair, as if ready to stand. Only later would I learn to distinguish the unwelcome sound of Mr. Forrester's tread—a slight lilt between steps.

Knowing my eyes evidenced the effects of last night, I feared meeting the newcomer.

Mr. Forrester entered, wearing the same suit of clothing from the previous evening, only now more creased, suggesting he'd slept in it. Though I gave him a slight nod of welcome, he only wrinkled his nose and wiped his hands over his waistcoat, as if my greeting had soiled him.

Eyes narrowed at us, he poured juice at the buffet and then strode to our table. His bloodshot eyes hinted he'd slept no better than I had.

I silently studied him as he dropped to his seat and took a loud gulp from his glass before sneering at us. "Where's Macy?"

I dropped my gaze and Mr. Greenham only tapped his long fingers over the side of his steaming coffee cup.

Who at that moment could have known how inextricably bound our three fates were? What a thin thread that held us too, for we were dissimilar in every possible way excepting one—we were traitors. The cord binding us did not snap, either, until we each administered our Judas kiss.

"I know he's here," Mr. Forrester prompted.

Mr. Greenham and I united, our silence becoming a wall. Though it was unladylike, I placed my chin in my hand and made a point of looking arch, as if I thought him vulgar.

"His servants claim he's left," Mr. Forrester said. "But his horse is still here."

Again, silence reigned.

"All right, keep to yourselves." Mr. Forrester stood with a leering smile. "On the day you come begging to me for succor, know that you'll find me equally silent."

As he stood, he reached for his glass and picked up mine by mistake. Before I could stop him, he took a swig. His eyes bulged before he gave a gagging cough. His head jerked toward me. "Aww, nice, love. It's not even nine yet."

My breath caught as Mr. Greenham stood in my defense.

But Mr. Forrester backed toward the door, holding his hands upright.

"Remain here," Mr. Greenham ordered once we were alone, then slipped from the chamber, closing the door behind himself.

∼

A quarter hour turned into half an hour, yet Mr. Greenham did not return.

I sat looking outdoors, listening to the patter of rain. Eventually I folded my arms on the table and rested my head, feeling drowsiness weight my limbs. After another quarter hour passed, I sat back in my chair and decided to return to my bedchamber and sleep.

No one else had awakened for breakfast. Only now do I suspect that Mr. Greenham had only because Reynolds must have awoken him from his slumber to tend to me.

I slipped from the room, not knowing how long that day would stretch out. It is a curious thing to have your perception altered. I had lost my footing. I wanted no company, no comfort, yet neither could I bear to be alone.

Reynolds approached with a bow. "May I be of service, Miss Elliston?"

"I'm returning to my bedchamber to sleep. Would you carry that message to Mr. Greenham?"

Reynolds's head bobbed, as though approving of my plan. "Do you need help finding your bedchamber?"

I gave him a shy smile. "No, if you point me in the direction, I'll manage on my own."

"Very good, miss." He gestured down a hall. "You'll want to turn left at the end of the first hall."

I nodded my thanks and followed his instructions. It wasn't long before I reached a crumbling section of the house, although the worn stone floor did not look familiar. Slabs of rock jutted from the ground in a mismatched formation. There were few doors in this section of the house, and the ones I tried were locked. Eventually I found a hallway with the same sooty color as the walls near my bedchamber and took that passage.

Instead of my bedchamber, however, an arched door with studded nails waited at the end of the hall. The door was so ancient it bore a chain instead of a door handle. Its scrolled hinges sprawled over the door like decorative tree branches. Heart beating, I approached and gave the chain a tug. A groaning sound filled the air as the massive door swung open.

Inside was a medieval chapel—so aged that I knew I had found the heart of Eastbourne. Cold air swirled about me as I stood on the threshold. I eyed the decaying sanctuary. My father had sworn that I should never set foot inside a church. Sarah said that unbeknownst to him, when I was a babe Mama had carried me into one to be baptized. When Sarah protested in fear, Mama said she'd make certain my feet would never touch the floor. That story wasn't the only reason I believed Mama had entertained some sort of faith. During the last months of her life, she'd taken to kneeling before a torn book page bearing the image of the crucified Christ. Her lips moved silently, begging something of him, as his image grimaced in pain, looking elsewhere.

A rough-hewn beam had fallen from the ceiling in the chancel, but by some miracle, the ceiling remained intact. The air, though stale, had a trace of incense, as though decades ago someone had religiously prayed here. Only there was something more, something deeper. A sacred memory clung to this chamber. I stretched my hand inside.

Dust stirred in particles around my fingers.

What devout monks, I wondered, had built these walls, labored and bled over this mason work? They must have been men of a rare sort for traces of them to leave behind such a deep impression.

My gaze went to the altar and my thoughts turned toward Edward. What power on earth would convince the son of landed gentry to side with the commoners? What if it wasn't the monks I felt? What if, what if . . . ?

I shut my eyes, pulling back my hand, refusing to surrender to whatever it was. My father had spoken of the human need to create a feeling that God existed. I'd lost my family, my stability, and had only just learned of my danger. Surely this was nothing except my need to feel there was something worth clinging to.

Make no mistake, the heart of Eastbourne is a monastery, but the organ is stilled; it no longer beats. Gone are the Gregorian chants, the rising incense, the quiet, orderly schedule.

Grasping the door, I tiptoed back into the hall and gently shut the door. I wiped my hand over my skirt, willing myself to shake free all influences of the chamber. I chose the nearest passage and took several successive turns. Instead of leading me toward a section of the house I recognized, my steps took me into a closed-off area. Only shafts of light penetrated the wood boarding the windows, exposing the velvet carpet of dust coating the floor.

Here I sank to the floor in blessed silence. This place, this empty, dying hall suited me better than the rich furnishing in my chambers. I had graduated to new circumstances. Mama had been murdered. Here, I decided, I would collect myself. It was necessary. I'd moved into the heart of an intrigue which I couldn't quite grasp. Again I wondered who would murder Mama.

I opened the locket that held miniatures of my parents. My father's blond moustache was raised in a sneer and his blue eyes were cold and indifferent. But Mama . . . I kissed her picture. She looked young and afraid like me. I reflected and saw for the first time how cold and hard I'd grown in order to survive. I'd believed a lie, and like a hailstorm sweeping a field, it had flat-tened and crushed my opinion of myself. Knowing Mama had not callously forsaken me, however, soothed some of the pain and brought forth fresh grief.

Drawing my knees to my chest, I recalled the terror that had occupied her eyes in those final weeks. How could I not have known her life was in danger? She jumped at every noise. Checked every lock.

Only a beast would execute a woman in her own bedroom—a beast who looked to devour me next. Did she know I'd found safety? I opened my eyes and viewed the dark passage, remembering Mr. Macy's kiss. I touched my lips, thrilling anew at the memory.

From there, my thoughts turned to Mr. Macy. That he had written Mama and asked for my hand was as extraordinary as the fact she agreed. Neither made any sense. I suspected Mr. Macy's reasons were not based on love. How could they be? He'd never met me. The more I considered the thought, the more distressed I grew. What would make such an eligible bachelor desire an abandoned orphan? Duty? Guilt? Pity?

Like a cribbage player discarding unnecessary cards, I rejected each one of those suits. *Duty*—let Edward pay me duty if it were so important. *Guilt*—how horribly did that picture rise before me, for the eventual paths of such a marriage end in disdain. *Pity.* Here my face grew hard. Better I go to Scotland as a servant than accept pity. Yet with a quickening of my pulse, I remembered Scotland was no option.

So deep was I in my thoughts that at first I didn't notice the sound. The second time I heard it, however, I lifted my head and realized the identical noise had occurred just seconds before.

It was a shuffling. But not that of a rat or bird, which one could rightfully expect to meet in such a part of a house. Rather it was larger, more like a mastiff. I clambered to my feet as quickly as I could, aware that candlelight now flickered over the wall in a semicircle.

The intruder stopped, however, short of turning the corner.

From the way the light shrank, I deemed the candlestick had been set on the floor. Every nerve tingled, telling me to run.

Dreading my presence becoming known, I took a step backwards as the sound of metal scraping metal filled the air. It was followed by a string of curses from Mr. Forrester. "What does Macy do, weld the locks?"

My mouth dried as I realized it was the very person Macy told me to avoid. I took another step backwards, this time causing a pebble to skitter across the floor.

"Who's there?"

I attempted to run, but as in a nightmare where one's legs are bound by the sheets, my feet refused to move.

Footsteps fumbled toward me, but the light suddenly went out alongside a loud clatter, making me think he dropped his candlestick. This time, I fled.

In two steps, I was around the opposite corner and running. I ran down one haunted passage after another, uncertain of my way. My left side screamed as it cramped anew, but I pressed on. Tears of terror and exhaustion formed.

"Miss Elliston!" A firm grip on my arm forced me to halt.

Gasping, I whirled to find Mr. Greenham towering over me. I doubled over to catch my breath.

"Are you injured?" His searching eyes demanded explanation. "What happened?"

I winced, shaking my head. The cramp in my left side refused to cease.

"Please, Miss Elliston, I have a responsibility." Mr. Greenham placed a hand on my shoulder. "What were you running from? Tell me."

He was nothing like his brooding self. Aroused, he was fearsome. I believe he could have snapped a sapling in half had he desired. He placed a hand on his hip and waited for me to regain breath.

Recalling how he had looked at the unexpected arrival of Mr. Forrester, I shook my head. "It is nothing."

He stormed to the end of the passage and peered around the corner. His fingers flexed into a fist before he turned back. "What happened?"

"The house spooked me."

"Where were you?"

"Lost."

"Miss Elliston, please, I'm only trying . . ." He unclenched his fingers and returned to me. "What do you fear to tell me?" He knelt, this time taking my hands. "Is this because I left you in a compromising situation last night? I would not have done so unless I deemed you safe. I am your friend. You must believe that and—"

"John, is that you?" Lady Foxmore turned the corner to find my hands in his. "My goodness, what happened to the child?"

Mr. Greenham ignored her, keeping me in his grasp. "Why aren't you in your chambers? Reynolds said you were sleeping."

The brass end of Lady Foxmore's cane poked his knuckles. "Really, John, I must insist you release the child. Your manner is frightening her. She looks ready to faint."

When he did not, she wrapped her arms around my waist. "Child, your heart is pounding." She turned to Mr. Greenham. "She's shivering. What happened?"

He rose, towering over us. "She won't say."

"Well, go fetch Chance. He'll want to know."

"He's not here."

"It was nothing." I smoothed my bodice, something Sarah taught me, to attend appearances first when I needed steadiness of mind. "I was lost and heard a noise." I shifted away from Mr. Greenham's doubting stare. "I think a bird is loose in the house. It sounded like flapping."

Lady Foxmore blinked slowly. "Child, in elegant society, we do not run when frightened. Next time—"

"What really happened?" Mr. Greenham said.

"Give her space to breathe." Lady Foxmore frowned. "Trust me, you'll receive more information from her if you do."

"I'm better aware than you how to obtain information from someone."

"Apparently not." Lady Foxmore pressed me against her. "Come, child. We shall tour Chance's hothouses. The warmth will remove your chill. Then you and I shall partake of tea and—"

Mr. Greenham planted a hand on my shoulder, holding me in place. "She's not leaving my sight until I know what she was running from."

"So accompany us. Only I liked you better when you refused to speak."

"There are letters I must attend to today."

"Fine. Attend to them. We shall go without you." She leaned heavily upon my arm and carried her walking stick.

"Do not test me, Adelia. Miss Elliston remains with me. In this house, my word is law. Do not make me prove it."

"We shall see" was Lady Foxmore's response.

Fourteen

❦

THAT EVENING, I could scarcely keep my eyes open as Reynolds opened the dining room doors for me to join dinner. Each moment of my first day at Eastbourne was like an individual painting in a long hall that featured art. The hues and emotions kept changing the further along I went—as did the complexity of colors and subject matter. Had I truly dissolved all ties with Edward? Met with a gentleman late at night? Tasted brandy? Learned that Mama had been murdered? Felt something consecrated in the chapel? Witnessed a gentleman breaking into someone's rooms? Spent the day alone with Mr. Greenham, locked in a study?

I clasped my shawl tight, needing the cessation that only sleep would bring. My eyes felt leaded as I stepped across the threshold. The chamber was as opulent as yesterday, yet I no longer attended to the estate's wealth but scanned the room solely to learn its occupants. To my delight, and then dismay, only the Windhams had arrived.

Here was familiar! Only I did not start toward them. I hesitated, twisting my hands, realizing that I had not yet shared my bitter news about Henry. There scarce seemed a need. Moving as slowly as Sarah used to on mornings when her joints hurt, Elizabeth blinked wearily at me.

I stepped toward her, ready to comfort.

"I suppose," Mrs. Windham began in an injured tone, turning her head to face me, "that you've spent the day with her ladyship and thought to spare my feelings with a simple ruse."

"Ruse?" I asked, stopping short.

"Mama," Elizabeth said, but her tone was flat.

Mrs. Windham dabbed puffy eyes, her mouth scrunched with bitterness. "I daresay when you've lived the charmed life, you have no regard for the comforts of others. Never mind it was I who first took you in when you were an orphan."

Elizabeth approached. She took in my eyes, which still bore dark smudges of a sleepless night. Her brow furrowed before she bent her mouth to my ear. "Lady Foxmore sent a note to Mama this morning, stating she was in no mood to visit with the underbred, and then when you didn't arrive for lunch or tea—"

Mrs. Windham's voice turned shrill. "I am not as unaware as you think. I know what you are both whispering." Her chin quivered as she cast me an accusing look. "And I can very well guess where you spent your day. I should hope I will never think so much of myself that I would grasp and claw at my first opportunity to befriend peerage."

"Well, here's your proof, Mama," Elizabeth said, pushing me before her. "Julia did not abandon us. She's here now. Think of how lovely dinner will be."

"Humph." Mrs. Windham's bottom lip curled as more baby tears formed in her eyes. "You have it wrong. Now that Julia is here, we can very well guess Lady Foxmore is joining dinner. And you—" she gestured to me—"I suppose you're obligated to look surprised when you see her, when we all know you've probably spent the day most agreeably playing cards with her and Mr. Greenham, not giving one thought to your *true* friends."

"Mr. Greenham?" I felt my face grow hot as I realized how difficult it was going to be to play innocent. "You've not seen him either?"

"Oh, posh." Mrs. Windham fisted her lace, her face growing crimson. "You know perfectly well we have not. I can see by your face he's paid you attentions. And I may as well tell you right now, I know you're doing everything in your power to derogate us in a vain attempt to appear above your station."

I glanced at Elizabeth for help, but she stared at the floor silently counting. "I assure you, I've not said one word about you or—"

"No. I should imagine not." Mrs. Windham collapsed into a chair, her voice increasing in volume. "What with you doing everything possible to keep the attention on yourself at all times."

"Mama, hush," Elizabeth finally said.

I glanced toward the open door and prayed no servants were in the hall listening. While not common, such fits with Mrs. Windham were not uncommon either. More than once in the past, I had witnessed her escalate herself into a frenzied state of mind.

Tears rose in Mrs. Windham's eyes. "No! I will not hush! If Julia does not like being put in her proper place, then she ought to act more ladylike. How dare you tell your mother to hush. In fact, you hush! I forbid you to speak. I would forbid Julia, only she will disregard my order." Her mouth quivered. "Well, go on. Go on and prattle about your new friends. I certainly have not enough consequence to stop you."

I could have groaned aloud when the distinctive clack of Lady Foxmore's walking stick filled the hall. I already knew her mood was ill.

"Lucy never would have given us such a turn." Mrs. Windham scrunched her eyes as she dabbed them. "A dearer friend I've never had."

Her ladyship's tiny frame scarcely filled the doorway through which she hobbled. Ostrich feathers added a foot to her height. The glitter of her eyes and the smirk on her face communicated that she'd overheard Mrs. Windham.

She made a show of straightening her petite form, the stiff drapery folds of her dress remaining unmoving. "Child," she directed toward me, "I'm an old woman. Where are your manners? Help me to the table."

Jealousy filled Mrs. Windham's features as I complied. Her ladyship transferred her full weight to my arm. "You will sit by me," she instructed in a loud voice, "and we shall do our best to close our ears to—" she gave an airy wave in the direction of Mrs. Windham—"the feebleminded."

Mr. Forrester chose that moment to enter. With suspicion, he studied each occupant, his eyes narrowing on me as if surmising I'd been the one in the hall.

"Sit, child," Lady Foxmore ordered, tugging my arm.

I started to cast Elizabeth an apologetic look, but her mouth thinned and she crossed her arms, daring me to comply. It was the first time I'd been on the other side of such a look, although I'd seen her give it before cutting off acquaintances. It gave me pause.

"Did I see you earlier today?" Mr. Forrester demanded, stepping toward me.

Lightning flashed over Lady Foxmore's countenance. "How dare you speak to my charge! You've had no formal introduction." Her nails bit into my arm. "Take your seat, child. This instant."

I gathered my skirts to comply, then with a look tried to tell Elizabeth I'd explain later, but realized I was foresworn to keep the truth a secret. With a sinking in my stomach, I wondered how Edward would feel when he learned how quickly I'd replaced him. I took a draft of my wine, suddenly wishing I had told him about Scotland, so he'd at least understand.

That dinner stands in my mind as the most awkward of my life. Without Macy to bend the atmosphere to suit his mood, all goodwill crumbled. Mr. Greenham touched neither food nor drink, but remained buried in thought. Rooke alone ate with relish, as though immune to our tension.

Henry, thankfully, tended to the Windhams. Though they did not openly censure me, the angry glances he sent in my direction gave me cause to think he knew I'd caused their distress. Elizabeth refused to meet my eye. She stared at her plate, her brows knit. Under normal circumstances, I'd have felt crushed had it not been for Mr. Forrester staring at me, relentlessly, never eating, just staring.

~~~

"Did you enjoy dinner?" Reynolds asked me hours later as he escorted me to my chamber.

I rose from my thoughts as one awakens from the watery layers of slumber. With a frown, I pondered how to answer him. Not only had it been miserable, but long. It was well past ten by the time the footmen collected the last dishes and the butler announced that musical entertainment had been provided. Macy had hired an opera singer from London.

By that time, I could scarcely keep my eyes open, and thankfully Mr. Greenham took note and collected me from the table before Lady Foxmore did. As the others filed into the unlocked music room, Mr. Greenham gave Reynolds charge of me, stating I wished to retire.

I eventually decided on "It was very . . . nice." Then, seeing Reynolds's crestfallen look, quickly added, "The braised goose was sublime."

He beamed at the praise and I made a mental note to applaud future menus. He stopped before my bedchamber door and withdrew a key. I studied my surroundings, realizing I should have paid better attention to our route.

"Shall I fetch your lady's maid?"

I shook my head, having no desire to encounter her tongue on top of everything else that had happened today.

"Very well, then." Reynolds opened my door.

"Has Mr. Macy returned yet?" I asked, hesitating.

"Not yet, though I expect him home any moment. Shall I inform him you wish to see him when he does?"

Heat worked its way through my face as I imagined how bold such a request would sound. I almost couldn't look at Reynolds. "Yes, if it's not too much trouble."

Reynolds bowed. "Very good, miss."

Anxious to escape from my embarrassment, I ducked into my chambers, where a new surprise awaited. Though I suspected Nancy had not been permitted there, my trunks were unpacked and the mayhem gone. My dresses were hung and my scattered jewelry had been collected and organized. The lamp wicks were turned low, making the atmosphere inviting. Most lovely of all, arrangements of tropical flowers adorned the room, filling it with fragrance.

While Reynolds locked the door behind me, I entered, grateful for the respite. I unpinned the tightest coils of my hair, glad to be free of the combs digging into my scalp, then sank into the closest chair and spied a plate of chocolates.

Pleasure filled me. How on earth could they have known the exact chair I would choose? Too tired to even taste the confection, I shut my eyes, feeling sleep curl through my limbs.

☙

The strong scent of cigars woke me.

When my eyes fluttered open, Mr. Macy sat opposite me in a wing chair, his legs sprawled idly in front of him. The lamps had been extinguished, leaving only the glow of embers. A cashmere blanket covered me.

"You needed sleep," Mr. Macy said without bothering to

rationalize his being there. "I didn't have the heart to wake you. Besides, it gave me a chance to reflect." He rose and brushed my cheek with his lips. When I blushed, his mouth curled in a seductive smile.

I straightened, rubbing my eyes, tempted to tell him he was presumptuous.

He withdrew and went to the hearth, where he added a log to the remains of the fire, wiping the excess bark from his hands with a silk handkerchief before turning to me.

"I had assumed," he said, advancing, managing to sound mesmerizing even as he scolded, "that last night I made clear the dangers of being alone with a gentleman. Yet somehow, when I arrived home tonight, I learned you'd spent the entire day unaccompanied with John." He placed both hands on the arm of my chair and leaned over me. "Perhaps I failed to make a lasting impression of such dangers and need to correct it?"

My face felt scarlet as I gave him a guilty look.

The anger in his face lessened, though he kept his voice stern. "Have you any idea how precarious your footing is in this sphere? Or how many high-ranking gentlemen would mistake your intentions? No, do not attempt to quench my anger with looks of innocence, for I have another charge against you, and I'm not sure which angers me more, your recklessness or your betrayal."

"Betrayal?"

"How is it that John knows intimate details of our conversation when you gave your solemn promise never to repeat it?"

My mouth parted.

"Do you have any idea how angry John is? I'm surprised our little shouting match didn't wake you. How is it he knows details from our conversation?"

My mouth felt dry. "But I thought he already knew. Reynolds said—"

"Reynolds!"

"Yes, he said Mr. Greenham could answer questions about last night."

"Reynolds said that!" Mr. Macy crossed his arms, looking truly angry now. "He dared to speak to you about last night? When? What did he say?"

My fingers sought my locket, but with a movement so fleet I hadn't seen it, Macy caught my hand. "Tell me word for word what Reynolds said."

"He . . . he didn't . . . I mean, I did. He said it wasn't his business what we did or didn't . . ." I trailed off, seeing Mr. Macy's incredulous expression.

"Go on."

I shut my eyes. Already the Windhams were angry at me, and now I was about to sink Reynolds. "I hadn't thought . . . He only suggested Mr. Greenham when I couldn't find you."

"Find me?" His voice softened. "For what?"

I felt my face crumple as I recalled my morning: the sickening sensation in my stomach, the manner in which the room had reeled, the crushing knowledge of Mama's murder.

Mr. Macy must have glimpsed my thoughts, for he exhaled the remainder of his anger. "Ah, the condition John found you in." He reached down and with the tips of his fingers drew up my chin. "Yes, I can still see the marks of suffering." His face pinched before he released me and retreated to the hearth.

There, he withdrew a silver cigarette case from his waistcoat, which he turned over in his hands. From it, he withdrew a fag, then knelt upon the hearthstone to light it. He smoked in the same manner others chew their nails. Drag after drag, he stared at the fire, wrestling with his thoughts, until all at once he rose from his haunches, saying, "John is right. I make a poor replacement for a guardian."

I started to shake my head in denial of his evaluation, fear coiling in my stomach, but he did not look at me as he took one last drag. "I'll be hanged before I give anyone else the opportunity to say I've unfairly influenced you."

He glanced over his shoulder with a frown as I felt tears forming. Mentally I prepared for him to declare that my being at Eastbourne was not a good idea, that he'd made a mistake. Instead he flicked his cig into the blaze and returned to me, bringing with him the scent of tobacco. He took the ottoman and enfolded my hands in his. "I told you my intentions to court you, but I think it only fair you learn what is being offered."

More than once during that long afternoon, I had envisioned such a tête-à-tête with him, but in none of those imaginings had he worn such a self-loathing expression.

"My past," he continued, "is far from faultless. And though I have changed and tried to make amends, dark rumors about me persist. Some false, some true."

Every part of me stilled, and my hands went slack in his.

He paused, giving me opportunity to speak. When I did not, he adjusted our hands. "Should you choose this path, you may learn things about me you wish you had not. Are you willing to accept me, knowing this?"

My stomach hollowed. "How dark?"

His eyes glittered, sending a shiver through me. "Are you inquiring as to the degree of evil I fell to, or how black the rumors are in comparison?"

He stared at me with such intensity that I dropped my gaze. Tendons rose in lines over the backs of his hands, giving testimony to his agitation. A wave of doubt, like a sinister undertide, washed over me. It would be madness to agree to such a courtship, and I knew it.

"Allow me to offer assurances," he said, "that regardless of what you say, I will continue to offer you my full protection."

Once more he shifted my hands in his, only this time I noted how gently he encased them. That simple gesture lit my path. In it I read safety, no matter what secrets his past held.

I lifted my head and met him with my own brand of tenacity. "Your past does not alarm me, nor do I require any confidence of it."

He gave me a queer look and withdrew slightly.

It aroused my temper. "You doubt me?"

A ghost of a smile finally softened his mouth. "Yes, I rather do. You forget I have firsthand knowledge of how easily you disregard promises. Here, do not pull away. I can see you are serious. Forgive me if I seem confused, but does this mean you're accepting my courtship?"

I turned away as shyness espoused me. It was one thing to dismiss his past, but quite another to voice my desire to be pursued.

He drew my hands and rested his chin upon them. "Is that a yes?"

Without intending to, my eyes strayed to his mouth and my breath caught. In that instant, the atmosphere charged. Some say you feel the air tingle before lightning strikes. So it was in that moment. My innards twisted with a new, sharp sensation. Mr. Macy felt it too, for I saw pleasure and surprise light his face.

His voice thickened. "Is that a yes?"

I nodded, feeling as I had once when I wandered too near the edge of a cliff.

He turned my hand and ran his thumb over my palm. "Know then, that I am not accepting your dismissal of my past, for its secrets will not be kept. With your permission, I'd rather extract a different promise." He placed a kiss on my palm.

Pleasure thrilled through me, like a shower of petals in the breeze.

He eyed me, measuring my response before cradling my hand against his rough chin and shutting his eyes. The rasp of his skin as he nuzzled my hand nearly undid me. "Will you pledge instead to seek me first, when you hear strange reports involving my name? Rather than just accepting what someone tells you?"

Instead of waiting for my answer, he unbuttoned my sleeve and kissed the underside of my wrist before rolling up the cuff of my dress, exposing my bare arm.

Had I been better trained, I'd have pulled away with a provocation ready on my lips. But I was artless, and idiotically blathered the first words that came to mind. "Will you swear to answer truthfully?"

He laughed before kissing my arm near the crook of my elbow. He kissed the same spot again, more slowly.

"Is this how we proceed, a vow in exchange for a vow, a favor for a favor?" My sleeve would not push back farther than my elbow, so he leaned over to kiss my neck. My body screamed with awareness. "You . . ." I shut my eyes and swallowed, unable to hold back the sensations roaring to life. "You did not answer my question."

I felt him as he smiled near my collarbone. "Nor did you answer mine, but yes, sweetheart. I swear to answer questions truthfully." With his fingertips, he tilted up my chin.

All at once, the weight of his experience overbalanced my inexperience. What had happened between Edward and me was far different. Here, I felt like a fledgling, flapping on the edge of its nest, knowing it couldn't fly. Desperate to hide my awkwardness, I turned before he brought his mouth to mine.

I blurted out the first distraction I could think of. "Who is Mr. Forrester?"

Abruptly he sat back. "Forrester? I offer you unprecedented access to the remotest reaches of my soul, and you want to know about Robert? Why? What happened?"

My neck still felt cognizant of his kisses. With my hand, I reached up and covered the spot as if I could press back the stirrings he'd summoned forth in me. "I . . . Well, Mr. Greenham seemed rather surprised to see him."

"Yes, so I gathered." Mr. Macy's voice took an edge. "Why

did you ask that? Was there a scene between them? Did Robert speak to you?"

I felt like a child who'd been offered cake, but had no sooner tasted the icing before it was whisked away. I bit my lip, wishing I'd not been such a fool.

"Tell me," he insisted. "This may be important."

"It was nothing," I began, then offered, "This morning, Mr. Greenham made me a . . . a drink, to make my head feel better."

"Yes," Mr. Macy said dryly, "if anyone knows a cure, it would be John."

"Mr. Forrester picked up my glass by accident—"

"Did he taste it?"

My rising color was answer enough.

Chuckling, Mr. Macy drew me to him. "Good heavens, I leave you alone for one morning, yet somehow in that short span of time you nearly cost me John's allegiance and gave a sip of your spirits to the worst gossipmonger in the country with his own newspaper."

"He owns a newspaper?"

"Not just any newspaper, darling—one of the better-circulated ones."

I felt my eyes widen as panic rose.

Mr. Macy looked toward the mantel with a frown. "Do not fear. In the morning I'll put him on his guard about slandering you." He gave my features an appreciative glance, then lowered his lips near my neck again.

"There's more."

He lifted his gaze enough for me to see his dark, amused eyes. One thick brow rose. "Yes?"

"I saw him trying to pick one of your locks."

Mr. Macy's eyes sharpened and he grew still. "Was he now? Where?"

"Near the chapel. I was lost, trying to find my chambers. I don't think he saw me."

Mr. Macy fully disentangled himself from me and retook the ottoman. When he spoke, his voice was so low I scarcely heard it. "Yes, it's never beneficial to disturb a man when he's not acting honorably. Did John confront him?"

"I refused to tell him about it."

"Refused to tell him?" He tilted his head. "Does that mean John asked you?"

Looking at his shoes and stuttering, I explained how Mr. Greenham had found me running and wanted an explanation.

When I finished, Mr. Macy leaned forward, kissed my palm, then traced the spot with his finger. "What kept you from telling him? I've enlisted his help for your protection. No wonder John locked you in his study all day."

"Had it been someone else, I would have." I looked up at Mr. Macy. "The night we arrived, Mr. Greenham was elated to see him. He tried to hide it, but I saw his face as Mr. Forrester joined the dinner party."

Mr. Macy's brow creased, and he gave me an odd look. "Are you sure? I mean absolutely certain about that?"

I nodded.

Mr. Macy dropped my hand, rose from the ottoman. Once more his long fingers extracted the silver case from his waistcoat. He selected a cigarette and for several minutes ran the length of it with his fingers.

"Is Mr. Forrester dangerous?" I asked.

Mr. Macy chuckled, as if amused by the thought. "Yes and no. I would not have allowed him here with you if he were a direct threat. You have nothing to fear, at least. I would rather not disturb you with the details, but he holds something from my past against me."

I arched my eyebrows.

A look of resignation settled over Mr. Macy's face. He gave a weary nod, as if to say I could ask if I desired.

Instead, I fought back my curiosity. "Then I'll have nothing to do with him."

He looked touched by my loyalty. "I am your humble servant." He cradled my hand but paused instead of kissing it. He touched the bracelet adorning my wrist. "My gift pleased you, then?"

I gasped. I'd forgotten I was wearing one of his gifts. Earlier I had slipped it on, to admire the way it sparkled on my wrist. My intention had never been to accept them. "I should have thanked you. They are wonderful, but I cannot—"

He placed one finger over my lips. "I did not give them for recognition but for my own gratification. As far as I'm concerned, gifts are a necessary part of my courtship."

I started to object, but he kept his finger firmly planted.

"Besides, you are already wearing it. I'm going to bed. I'm very tired, as I've slept even less than you have. Tomorrow night after the others are in bed, we can speak further. Now, walk me to the door, and I'll kiss you good night, but only if you promise not to say another word."

I nodded and blushed at his implication that I desired to be kissed.

His smile grew. "It will be tragic the first day I cease to see you blush."

Fifteen

THE NEXT MORNING, blinding light caused me to bury my face. The draperies rattled as Nancy spread them further apart. I groaned, realizing Reynolds must have allowed her in.

"Best move on," she said. "Thou should have roused before now. As it is, thou'll be th' last to breakfast."

I squinted at the clock. Half of the morning had passed. "You are the most useless abigail!" I slid from the bed, taking the counterpane with me. "How could you let me sleep so late?"

"Let thee sleep? I banged on the door for ten minutes, I did, before Reynolds fetched Mr. Macy. I daresay, not havin' guests for fifteen years thou must've given him a fright. Last thing he wants is a sick guest—or worse."

"Or worse!" I glared as she gathered the coverlets on the floor.

She bent to collect my scattered petticoats, then turned and gave me a wide grin. "Has thou seen Mr. Macy?"

"What do you think?" I combed my hair from my forehead with my fingers.

"'Tis a comely man, to be sure. The maids twittered about his looks, but before today I thought 'twas all air."

"Enough chatter. Hurry," I snapped.

"Wait on the rest." Nancy pulled another petticoat over my head. "Mr. Macy bursts into thy room. Made bold to touch thee, he did. He stood a full minute, watching thou sleep, then brushed thy hair off thy brow with a glint of a smile. He tells Reynolds, 'Give her another hour. If she's disturbed, you'll answer to mysell,' and stormed out."

I paused, my arm halfway through my sleeve, doubting he'd said it in *that* accent. Realizing it was Mr. Macy's doing I had overslept, I plodded to the washbasin.

My mind recycled last night and I wondered how far things might have gone with Mr. Macy had I allowed it. Then, as I dried my face, it occurred to me that Nancy might have learned something of use.

"You never did tell me what you learned about this house," I called to Nancy.

I heard her give a cough of annoyance. "Aye, that I did. Only thou was too boozy to hear."

I tucked wet hair behind my ear, frowning. "Well, tell me again."

"There isn't anything worth repeating," Nancy argued. "Nor have I learnt more. These servants are th' most closed-mouth group I've ever seen. Not one word over dinner."

I chuckled, envisioning that the servants' dinner must have been eerily similar to ours.

"Don't see why thou would grin about that," Nancy said with a frown.

"Oh, hush." From my seated position I faced the vanity again. "Why should I care if domestics talked over dinner? All the servants can drown in the Thames for all I care. Have you learned anything useful?"

Nancy yanked on a section of hair as she narrowed her eyes.

"Aye! Only thou art too grand to hears about servants. So never mind it."

I grabbed that section of hair, then gasped at her in the mirror.

"A knot," she said, growing suddenly contrite. "If thou must know, I learned Reynolds is a tyrant about having things ready for thy chambers. Only he can touch thy dishes. Not even th' housekeeper can launder thy sheets. What does thou think o' that?"

I frowned, wondering how on earth Reynolds managed it. I knew for a fact he handled the menus as well. Then with a tingling chill, it occurred to me that I might not be as secure as Mr. Macy presented. Why else would his valet personally over-see my every detail—if not to ensure my safety? Had not Mama been poisoned?

I refused to consider it further. If I wasn't careful, soon I'd be afraid of my own shadow. Somehow it increased my desire to learn more about Mr. Macy apart from what he told me. With a frown, I realized how difficult that would be. Not even his ser-vants could provide much, if they were barred from practically every chamber.

⌇

I crossed the threshold of the breakfast chamber and fulfilled Nancy's prediction. I was the last guest. Mr. Macy and the gentlemen rose in unison. I stepped forward to greet him, but with a slight shake of his head, he reminded me that in public, we were casual acquaintances, at best. He'd had even less sleep than I, but he showed no sign of fatigue.

"Miss Elliston, I'm pleased you've finally decided to make an appearance. I'll have to ask you not to be late again. I find it rude." His eyes twinkling, he pulled out a chair for me.

I wanted to say something amusing, but a witty comment eluded me. Even Lady Foxmore seemed to expect it. She hovered her fork over her hard-boiled egg, waiting. When I remained silent, she looked at Mr. Macy, shaking her head. He didn't seem amused.

It was impossible not to glance at Elizabeth and Henry to gauge matters between us. Arms crossed, Elizabeth refused to look in my direction as she spoke to Henry. It seemed to me she avoided looking at me, but Henry cast me a dark look.

I returned it with one of my own, not particularly enjoying his company either, now that I believed him traitor to Elizabeth.

Directly across the table, Mr. Forrester glared at me with suspicion.

My temper plus my lack of sleep got the better of me. I was tired of the treatment I'd received thus far and scorned his look with one of my own, not caring that Mr. Macy watched our exchange as he sipped coffee.

"Gentlemen, what say you of a hunt today?" Mr. Macy set his cup aside.

Rooke dropped his fork. "Whatever for?"

Mr. Greenham shifted his eyes to Mr. Macy and studied him a second. "I'd welcome it."

"And you, Mr. Auburn?" Mr. Macy smiled at Henry.

Henry stabbed his eggs, glanced at me, then gave a curt nod. Whether he approved or despised the idea was impossible to read, even for me.

"Robert?" Mr. Macy turned fully in his direction and paused before asking, "What say you? Will you exchange picking my locks for something more honorable?"

With a menacing look, Mr. Forrester shrank against his seat.

"Good. We'll hunt," Mr. Macy concluded.

⁓

As soon as breakfast ended, the gentlemen excused themselves to change. Mr. Macy rose and bowed to Mrs. Windham. "How do you ladies plan to spend your day?"

Before anyone could speak, Lady Foxmore held up an authoritative hand and announced, "The light in this breakfast room is excellent for embroidering. We shall sew here."

My face fell at the prospect.

Mr. Macy gave me an amused look before nodding his consent and bowing from the room.

Servants were summoned to run and fetch our baskets. Lady Foxmore ordered that a larger, more comfortable chair be brought into the chamber; then, with the air of a martyr, Mrs. Windham declared herself to have a headache and to be in need of a better chair. Lady Foxmore wanted to sit in the sun; Mrs. Windham declared her eyesight failing and herself in need of sun, despite her headache.

It was no easy task to settle into the wooden chair placed between the two ladies to sew. Lady Foxmore demanded I stay put while Mrs. Windham declared it was a pity her ladyship hadn't chosen Elizabeth as her companion as she would better suit her ladyship.

Warmed by the sun, her ladyship lost no time in napping, but Mrs. Windham lost no time in lecturing me. As she plied her needle, she plied her tongue about my ingratitude.

Her words gnawed at me. All I wanted was to escape, to work out my thoughts, to puzzle over Mr. Macy. I wanted to consider Mama's death and how to avenge her. I desired to find a moment alone with Elizabeth to tell her about Henry. Being at Eastbourne only deepened my impatience. Commonplace things, such as hours bent over sewing, are tiresome enough under ordinary circumstances, but when surrounded by the mystery and intrigue of Eastbourne, the task was tedious.

Thus, when Reynolds entered the room and threaded his way to me, I felt relief.

"I beg your pardon, miss," he said, bowing, "but there seems to be a slight miscommunication with your maid's schedule. If I might borrow you to unlock your door."

I stared at him, knowing perfectly well he had a key to my chamber, but then realized what he was doing. I stood, dropping my sewing, which I quickly bent to collect. "Oh yes. Yes, of course."

"I shouldn't wonder," Mrs. Windham said beneath her breath, "the schedules got mixed up. The poor child would make a terrible housekeeper, simply terrible. Elizabeth manages our household like clockwork. You would do well to communicate that to your master."

Reynolds ignored her, then escorted me into the hall and around the corner, where Mr. Macy took my elbow and chuckled, cornering me. His eyes sparkled with amusement. "Pray, Reynolds, that I am never a sick man."

"That I already do, sir," Reynolds said.

"What?" Mr. Macy turned. "Are you a praying man?"

"As was your father," came Reynolds's staunch reply.

"Yes, but we both know that my father was a fool," Mr. Macy said softly, before turning to me. "Though now I've seen what a mean little nurse our Miss Elliston would make in a sickroom, I am most grateful for your troubles on my behalf. I thought her about to cry when she found out she'd be trapped sewing."

"I should imagine, sir, Miss Elliston would feel quite differently, were she attending a sickbed."

"There we disagree," Mr. Macy said smiling, tracing a finger down the side of my face. "Especially if it is my sickbed, for I intend to pursue this young lady into marriage. Don't you think most wives would be most grateful for an opportunity to be rid of their husbands if there's enough wealth on hand to sustain them?"

"There you are wrong, sir." Reynolds gave his master a chiding look as I bent my head, color filling my cheeks.

"Think you I can trust her, then?" Mr. Macy chucked my chin. "But see for yourself how silent she is on this subject, though I must say, she blushes beautifully."

"I hope her too sensible to respond to such nonsense. If I may make bold, sir, you promised your land agent you'd return straightaway, and that was nearly a quarter of an hour ago."

Mr. Macy made a noise of disgust. "Yes, business. Even now, as I try to woo myself a wife, business. What? Shall I hand you the task of courting her?"

"Certainly not!"

Mr. Macy gave a good-pleasured laugh, as if amused his servant took him seriously. "Yet you might, Reynolds; you still might. What say you, little one?" He turned his focus back on me. "Now that I've rescued you, how shall you redeem your time? I daresay Mrs. Windham seems to be in one of her finer sulks. If I may recommend it, avoid her for the rest of today, lest you are returned to your cage."

His presence was like stepping into the warm sun after a dark winter night. Some sort of rarity in him buoyed my spirits.

"Well?" he coaxed. "An entire day lies before you, and I wish to know how my freed captive will spend it."

"Are you not hunting, then?" I asked, recalling breakfast.

"I haven't even yet asked for her hand," Mr. Macy said, showing his teeth in a smile to Reynolds, "but look how she practices tracking my schedule. You may have an ally." Then to me, "Yes, little one! I shall hunt soon. Business came up and I promised the men I'd join them within the hour. In the meantime I have done you the favor of freeing you from her ladyship, Forrester, and our dear Mrs. Windham in one fell swoop. Reward me by telling me how you shall bide your time."

All at once, I saw my opportunity to gain the information about Mr. Macy that not even Nancy could gain. "Will you allow me to explore Eastbourne?"

"Explore Eastbourne?" Mr. Macy acted insulted, but his eyes betrayed pleasure. "There you see, Reynolds, I told you. You'll woo her for me regardless. She wishes to inspect my prospects. No, do not blush again, Miss Elliston. You wouldn't be female if you weren't itching to see my estate. Here, Reynolds, you may testify on my behalf." He removed a key ring from his waistcoat. "My personal keys, Miss Elliston. The only complete set which will open every lock and every door."

Reynolds visibly startled as Mr. Macy pressed the metal ring into my hands.

"I want you to swear to me," Mr. Macy continued in a stern tone, "you will not touch my papers or any other personal matters. Do not enter the study we were in the other night, either. Do you understand?"

I started to nod, but his face hardened. "Verbal agreement, Miss Elliston."

"Y-yes, I swear."

He lifted my chin in an unrelenting grasp. "No one other than you touches these keys. Not John, not Reynolds. Understand?"

"Yes," I whispered.

His stance loosened, though he continued to lift my face upwards. His eyes lingered on my mouth with an expression that suggested he had all but resolved to ignore our witness. Then all at once he released me. "Reynolds, escort her today."

"A third generation of lifelong service," Reynolds said as Mr. Macy departed, his eyes fastened on the key ring, "and he has yet to pay me that honor."

The keys were as heavy as a small weight, yet I marvelled at the level of trust and confidence Mr. Macy had placed in me. I couldn't remember anyone ever having placed that much faith in me.

"Might I suggest you begin with the library?" Reynolds's tone was soft, as if gently reminding me he was present.

I nodded, so touched that I was tempted to press the keys against my heart. I forced back emotion and gave Reynolds a shy smile, knowing he couldn't possibly understand the rush of emotion flowing through me, then picked up my skirts and made ready to follow him.

I am told that little more than a year later, men in powdered wigs debated vehemently for hours about the significance of my having the keys and my exploration of Eastbourne—as if that had any legal bearing on the matter. That, however, is another story for another time.

～

Reynolds unlocked one of the large doors and opened it with a pleased air. "I shall wait outside."

If the former heart of Eastbourne was a monastery, its new center was its library. The chamber felt as ancient as a forest, as stuffy as an attic, but rich with life. Above me the ceiling, as large as a train station's, vaulted into a stained-glass dome. Weak light backed it, so it did not cast down flecks of colors, but in the full sun I had no doubt there would be pools of colors.

It was a library, yes, for books lined shelves, which lined walls, which went up three stories with carved stairs and heavy banisters. Yet it was also a museum, an apothecary shop, a classroom.

Through a glass cabinet displaying exotic birds, I spied an open drawer containing rows of eggs, their shades and colors so beautiful and dull it made my heart ache. Through the wavy glass I saw one leathery sample labelled *Alligator*.

I turned from it to a furniture grouping before the large hearth. Tables, long and large enough to belong to a chemist, were stacked with papers and inkwells. Mr. Macy had said to leave his papers alone, but I chanced to see what sort of things he wrote about. The tang of cigars greeted my nose as I approached and lifted a few sheets. To my disappointment, his notes were in Latin.

Another table was crowded with apothecary jars and various potted plants preserved in liquid. A book lay open, a dried plant segment tucked in its spine. Its seeds and flowers had been affixed to the pages alongside handwritten notes telling of its medicinal values. Next to it, butterflies were in the process of being mounted.

I looked over my shoulder, amazed at the sheer number of volumes in the room. Nearby maps and display cases called for exploration, and beyond those, smaller rooms with more treasure.

I left the table, deciding I would beg Mr. Macy tomorrow to explore his library at leisure, knowing I could spend three or four afternoons here without boredom.

I retreated to the door and exited.

Reynolds gave me a surprised frown. "Was it not to your liking?"

"Oh yes!" I shared my rapture and was rewarded by the glow of pride that lit his face.

"May I see the ballroom?" I asked, recalling Lady Foxmore's statement that Macy withdrew from society on a night when he was throwing a ball.

A shadow passed over Reynolds's face as he wet his lips. "Well, Mr. Macy did give you his keys." He looked down a dark passage. "Very well, though I must warn you, it's been unopened for fifteen years."

Reynolds had no key to this room, and it took me several attempts to unlock the bolt. When the doors finally moaned open, I refused to enter. The decayed chamber lay in shambles. Dust-coated cobwebs hung in crooked angles. Velvet draperies, partly disintegrated from years of hanging in the damp, hung on their rods like rags on a beggar. The mirrors lining the upper half of the room were either cracked or lying in shards on the floor. Broken chairs and overturned tables were scattered about demolished instruments.

I stared at the space, wondering what sort of man would utterly ruin his own ballroom.

"Perhaps—" Reynolds stepped forward, shut the doors, and motioned for me to relock them—"you'll allow me to show you the card room. That too hasn't been used in over a decade, but I think you'll find it more suitable."

I nodded agreement, glad to leave whatever memory disturbed that chamber.

There is little point to describing all that I saw in Eastbourne that day. Were I to spend a month exploring, I scarcely would have acquainted myself with the estate. A museum in London could not have held more wonder, nor a haunted palace more mystique.

I declined lunch, still filled enough from our late breakfast, but as the day stretched late into afternoon, my stomach grumbled.

"Shall you take tea now?" Reynolds asked.

I held back my annoyance at my need for food. In every chamber we'd entered, every gallery I'd explored, I'd cut short the time, denying my desire to explore every nook and cranny. I wanted to see all of Eastbourne, and daylight was fading.

"Which room is that?" I asked, pointing to a grand-looking door.

"Mr. Macy's personal billiards room."

I lifted my brow. There had been two other billiards rooms. "His personal one? Does he use it often?"

Reynolds smiled. "Yes, I should say so."

"One more room," I begged of Reynolds, heading toward it. "I want to see it."

Like the other rooms favored by Mr. Macy, it also bore the scent of cigar in addition to the lingering scent of his pomade. Indentations in the leather chairs suggested frequent use. A dressing gown, similar to the one I'd worn, was slung over the table that needed refelting. I resisted the urge to scoop it up to smell.

I ran my fingers over the billiards table, picturing Mr. Macy, coat off, collar unbuttoned, calculating his next move. Over the

bar, paintings of horses were grouped in mismatched frames—
some round, some oval, and others rectangular.

It was only as I turned to leave the room that I spotted the
green coffee set with carved dragons. All warmth left my body
as I knelt before the occasional table to study it.

Once more I saw the broken cup.

The very devil himself was engraved on my father's features
as he lifted his fist.

I remembered Mama's screams as she threw herself before
me, the crimson blood that spotted her gown.

Long-forgotten words rang from the past. *"Priceless.
Irreplaceable. Only one in existence."*

I tasted the fear I'd experienced that day, as my finger
plucked the air, counting the settings. Five. It lacked a setting to
be a complete set. Mentally I roamed the house. It had been so
long, I couldn't even recall what room it had once sat in.

"Miss Elliston?" Reynolds asked in a concerned voice from
the doorway.

I tore my eyes from the set and somehow rushed from the
room.

"Are you ill?" Reynolds took my side as I bent over.

I wanted to shake my head, to laugh at the frightened look on
his face, but I felt too numb. That memory had long been buried, but now I remembered Mama's cries each time my father's
fist fell.

A dent formed between Reynolds's brows, but before he
could speak, I shook off his touch. "Reynolds, I wish to retire.
Would you kindly direct me to my chambers?"

"Shall I take—?"

"No." I nearly screamed the word; any second I felt ready to
cry. "Just tell me which direction."

He didn't hesitate. "If you turn left at the end of this hall, I
believe you shall find your way quite easily. Shall I bring a tea
tray to your room?"

I shook my head, leaving. The hall led me to the arch, and from there I reached my room a few minutes later. Yet instead of entering it, I leaned against the door, breathing hard. Part of me longed to return to the billiards room and examine the coffee set again—to make sure it really had been ours. Only there was no need to. I knew the set was unique. I felt sick with the knowledge it would be hours before I could seek explanation.

I bent my head toward the dark stairwell that wound up to Mr. Macy's chambers. That's when my heart slowed as a plan formulated. Here, I realized, was probably the best opportunity I would ever have to truly judge what manner of man Mr. Macy was. Was not one's bedchamber his most intimate space?

Before I could change my mind, I bounded up the stairs. One locked door waited at the top. Kneeling, I tried every key, but to no avail. Only then did I recall Mr. Macy's statement that our chambers were identical.

I drew out the ribbon that hung around my neck and inserted my key. The lock clicked.

Sixteen

꘎

COLD AIR, carrying the reek of tobacco, streamed from the chamber. I clutched the door handle, stunned. His chamber was a paradox. Though it was the exact size of my chambers, it was stark and open, undivided by walls. His bed was a cot with a coarse woollen blanket stretched over it. Armoires stood like wardens between pegs filled with his clothing. Near the fireplace, a sea of ash and cigar stubs surrounded a leather chair. I felt nervous viewing the space and turned to leave. There seemed little point in remaining. A glance took in its oddity.

And yet, as I stepped away, I spied a glint of white beneath the bed.

It is no easy thing to intrude on a man's bedchamber, much less peruse papers he'd forbidden me to touch, but reasoning I'd come this far, I completed the treachery. With one swift movement, I crossed the room and knelt. My skirt stirred the floor dust as I took up the sheet.

There, drawn in smudged charcoal, was a sketch of me—the type a travelling artist might render. My likeness had been taken after my father's death, for I recognized the mourning bonnet. I traced my fingers over the rendering of my face, touched. If this gentle and despondent image was the one Macy believed, no wonder he'd become attached. Even I desired to rescue me.

Keeping the paper in hand, I stood, wondering why he'd had it commissioned, then took in the room. This time I ached with a protective nature. How could anyone look upon this gaping scar of isolation and remain unmoved? My exploration had formed a picture of his daily practices. He spent time in the billiards room, library, and personal study. The rest of his house he neglected, attending to some unknown business. Yet, somehow, I'd become endeared to him. I was the first outreach he had made beyond these walls in years. Only why?

I replaced the page, careful to make it look exactly as it had. Before exiting, I shook my skirts free of dust. I locked the door and checked it twice before trudging downstairs with a new sobriety. I had found the future I sought—someone older and wiser than Edward. Not a father, but someone with the steadfastness that we associate with age. I had not been alone after Mama's death, after all. Unbeknownst to me, Mr. Macy had been there all these months too.

∽

When Nancy knocked on my chamber door, my emotions still had not settled. I'd alternately paced and sat before the hearth, trying to reason what to do next. I unlocked the door, deciding to trust her.

"Come." I pulled her inside. "I need you."

"Aye," she agreed, frowning over my appearance, "that you do."

"No, listen." I drew her close. "I want Mr. Macy. Make me eye-catching tonight, better work than you've ever done—please."

She gave a strange grimace but dusted off her hands. "Aye, I'll do it, if that's what thou *truly* wants."

I wet my lips, surprised at my sudden resistance to my own

scheme. I struggled to find words to soothe Nancy, but it was needless. She was already tearing through my wardrobe.

By the time Reynolds rapped on the door, Nancy's face was flushed. Red curls had worked their way free and stuck out in tufts. She'd been silent, but now she wiped the back of her brow with her hand. "Well?"

I turned and considered my reflection. Despite Nancy's position, her skills were exceptional. She'd coiled my ebony hair high, in rolls that shone with every turn of my head. Mama's pearls felt cool against my neck. I touched them, recognizing the wisdom. Since pearls were unsuitable for young girls, by wearing them I asserted my commencement to womanhood.

I nodded approval as Reynolds knocked a second time. After opening the door, Nancy bobbed. "By your leave, miss." Keeping a wary eye on Reynolds, she tiptoed around him and then rushed away.

"How did you manage her?" I smiled, sweeping my trailing skirt from the door. "For weeks I've tried to coerce her into proper behavior."

His eyes warmed. "Managing servants is part of my occupation. Are you recovered, Miss Elliston?"

The coffee set flashed to mind, but I nodded.

"Mr. Macy shall be most pleased to hear it. He was quite anxious to learn you'd retired early. Shall I take you to the dining room?"

I extended my arm so he could accompany me as a gentleman, rather than a servant. Delight spread over his features.

⁓

That evening, a chill hung in the hall like a damp blanket, so when Reynolds shuffled with stiff movements to open the doors for me, I suspected rheumatism. Though he took pains to look nonchalant, tiny wrinkles about his eyes bespoke his suffering. A surge of affection welled as I considered how painstakingly

... the

he'd cared for me since my arrival. Though it wasn't proper, I placed my hand on his shoulder. "Reynolds, thank you."

His eyes, so galvanizing they nearly hurt, turned on me with surprise. "Why, you're quite welcome, Miss Elliston. Quite welcome, indeed."

Unused to this sort of tenderness, I flushed with embarrassment, ducked inside the chamber, and stared at my surroundings. Once again, I was the first arrival. I eyed the dazzling display, aware that if I succeeded, no more would I be an orphan, cast aside and unloved. My future would be just as dazzling as this room.

I was so riveted by my thoughts that I only registered the next arrival when the door banged. Hoping it was Mr. Macy, I spun toward the newcomer, taking no care to hide my rapturous delight.

To my surprise, Lady Foxmore's painted face hovered just above view of the table. Behind her, the towering form of Mr. Greenham entered.

Anger twisted her face as she marked me. "Tell me," she intoned to Mr. Greenham, "*tell me* he was not alone with her all day today."

Like a henpecked husband, Mr. Greenham half lowered his eyelids as he went to the drink trolley. "How should I know where she, or anyone, was today? I was hunting, remember?"

"This was not part of the agreement, John!" Lady Foxmore grew shrill. "She is under my direct care! *I* am her chaperone now. I gave no permission for him to . . . Just look at her! How dare he! I expressly told him—"

"Peace, Adelia," Mr. Macy commanded from the threshold.

The tone of his voice alone cast a pall over the room, but as he entered, his presence seemed to crowd out the four walls. Mr. Greenham averted his gaze, bowing his head, acknowledging Mr. Macy's mastery.

Anger, however, continued to cloud Lady Foxmore's face.

Mr. Macy lifted an eyebrow at her, but she did not back down. Beneath her white powder, her face was scarlet with anger.

Mr. Macy gave me a slight nod of welcome, then looked over his shoulder. "Ah, Miss Windham, Mr. Auburn, welcome."

Elizabeth was quick to read the mood and shot me a questioning look as she curtsied. "I pray you will excuse Mama. She's retired with a slight headache."

Henry likewise sensed the tension. His shoulders squared, he scanned the room. He eyed my dress, his mouth slanting down, before giving Mr. Macy an unhappy look. He did not return Mr. Macy's greetings.

"Welcome," Mr. Macy announced as Mr. Rooke and Mr. Forrester joined us. "Please, take your seats."

There was far less confusion this time as everyone resumed their usual seats. Mr. Macy seated me, then went to aid her ladyship. She, however, refused. "John!" Her mouth twisted as she batted away Mr. Macy's hand. "Where's your sense of decency? I'm an old woman. Help me to my chair."

Mr. Greenham rose and, with a weary sigh, obeyed.

Lady Foxmore's face contorted with wrath as she sat opposite me.

"Such a scowl, Adelia," Macy said, signalling for the footmen to begin. "It is not like you to behave so unbecomingly."

"How can I not?" She waved away the servant who attempted to fill her glass. "I wagered a fortune that once you met that . . . that . . . scarecrow, this madness would end."

Mr. Macy's eyes narrowed. "Then next time, I suggest, don't wager against me."

"How could I not? How could you be serious? She, 'to term in gross, is an unlesson'd girl, unschool'd, unpracticed.' And I? Am I expected to stand idle and watch as you make a gross fool of yourself?"

As she gestured at me, Henry nailed me with an accusing stare.

I could not have been redder if I had unscrewed a jar of her ladyship's rouge and smeared it over my face.

"Mind your tongue." Mr. Macy's voice was subdued, but nonetheless as abrasive as a winter wind. "As far as I'm concerned, your standing with me rests entirely in her hands. Make no mistake: should she tire of your company, I shall oblige her."

"Oh, ho, ho. What?" Lady Foxmore scoffed. "Will you suddenly refuse my invitations that you've declined for the last fifteen years? How frightening! Or shall you send me packing home? You forget, I am the child's chaperone. If I leave, she leaves."

A soft chuckle escaped Mr. Macy. "Adelia, I have no quarrel with you, nor do I wish one."

"Satisfy me with this much. Why here? Why that skinny, milk-faced girl when I can secure you a countess or even a duchess?"

"Nobility?" His voice was flat as he faced her. "Is that what you think I lack?"

"You lack far more than that if you're serious about pursuing this child. Never, in the whole of my life, have I seen a more disadvantageous match."

"Nor a more outrageous fee."

Lady Foxmore looked amused. "So she told you? Good. Know that I intend to collect full payment for this travesty. For I have never been more ill-used. But in all earnestness, what is this girl to you? Whatever it is you seek to gain by her, I can guarantee you, you won't find it."

Lady Foxmore handled the truth like it was a sword, sparing no one. Each word cut, making it difficult to keep my seat. I longed to retaliate with every black rumor I'd ever heard about her. I realized now her offer to find me a husband was betrayal. Somehow she'd gotten pulled into Mr. Macy's attempts to defy my guardian, while all along she'd planned to thwart any such marriage. Beneath the table, Mr. Macy placed his hand over mine, which gripped the arm of my chair.

"I readily admit," said Mr. Macy, his voice tight, "that my past is not what it should be. And yes, I deserve no such succor as sits here. Yet you and John both know how greatly I have struggled to be free of my mistakes. What is it to you if I wish to seek mercy at her feet?"

Lady Foxmore gave a cough into her wineglass and was obliged to cover her mouth with a napkin. Red bled through as she coughed up the wine she'd wrongly swallowed.

Until then, the others had tried their best to ignore the grumbling conversation at our end of the table, but as Lady Foxmore expelled the remainder of her wine, all attempts at feeble conversation ceased and silence reigned.

I shifted my gaze to Elizabeth and Henry. Both leaned against the backs of their chairs, watching me like accusing members of a jury.

Mr. Forrester leaned forward like a bird dog pointing to its game. "We all know you're arguing over that girl there. My servant tells me she absented herself from the others all day today." He censured me with his look. "If you don't mind my asking, where were you?"

I have since learned that there are those who try to make others feel guilty simply by acting as though they are culpable.

I was particularly susceptible, as my household had suffered from angry and violent outbursts. Afterwards, Sarah would shush and chide me for crying over such trifling matters. I realized much later, of course, her goal was to keep my father from another rampage, but as a child, I believed my emotions were wrong. Thus I learned to doubt my perceptions. People like Mr. Forrester wreaked havoc on my life until I learned to identify them.

So when Mr. Forrester accused me, my mouth felt too dry to answer. I felt as though I had done something unpardonable.

"Ah yes, that reminds me." Mr. Macy patted his pockets.

"I believe you retain my keys, Miss Elliston, from your earlier exploration. May I trouble you for them?"

I knew from the small smile that Mr. Macy offered me that all was well and I could ignore Mr. Forrester. Feeling all eyes on me, I produced his key ring from my handbag.

It had the most profound effect on Mr. Forrester. He stiffened with an expression usually reserved for wives viewing the village trull.

Mr. Greenham gave a gasp before he set down his glass and stared at Mr. Macy. "Those are . . . *your* keys?"

Mr. Macy inclined his head once as an answer but kept his focus on the keys in his hand, as if mentally counting them.

All at once, Mr. Forrester straightened and an evil look of glee crossed his face. He smirked at Mr. Macy with the air of someone about to checkmate his opponent. "Miss Elliston, please, this is very important. I need to know if, during your tour, you saw a small ivory box." He cupped his hands to indicate an object about the size of Mama's sewing kit. "It would have stood on four small legs, and—"

"I beg your pardon, Mr. Forrester." The surge of protectiveness I felt over Mr. Macy surprised even me. "But I am not inclined to speak of what I saw."

Mr. Forrester looked affronted, but Mr. Macy's eyes sparkled as he turned to Lady Foxmore. "And that," he said, his voice full of pride, "is why I will trust my own judgment over your duchesses."

෴

When dinner ended, Mr. Greenham approached and spoke in Mr. Macy's ear, while he tapped an index finger on the table. Mr. Macy's gaze flickered in my direction with regret before he nodded and sighed. "Gentlemen," he announced, "let us retire for brandy in the billiards room."

I watched the gentlemen leave with a shadow cast over my

own mood. Though Mr. Macy had managed to carry the dinner conversation after our horrid start, I still felt acutely embarrassed. Nothing had gone the way I'd hoped. I had yet to steal a moment with Mr. Macy, though I'd spent hours dressing, and mention of the billiards room brought back to mind the coffee set.

Wanting no part of her ladyship's biting tongue, I retired to the darkest corner of the drawing room and tucked my feet beneath me. I even attempted to withdraw from Elizabeth, but within a half hour, she and Lady Foxmore found me.

Her ladyship gave a slight shake of her head, as if my hiding had managed to further deepen her disappointment in me.

Elizabeth, however, went to me and motioned for me to make room for her on the settee.

Grudgingly, I met her gaze but did not move my feet.

"Don't make me sit on you," she threatened. "I will."

I grimaced at her, considering refusing to let her join me. Doubtlessly she felt it her duty to point out her concerns about my behavior. The fact that I couldn't defend any of my actions made me irritable. With a sinking feeling, I realized that I was also duty bound. I still needed to tell her about Henry. I removed my feet.

"Juls?" Her face still bore the marks of exhaustion as she sat.

"I know what you're going to say," I said. "I'm begging you, please don't. You don't understand this."

"Think about what you're doing," she finally said. "Think of all that we planned."

I did not respond immediately, for her words opened a door I thought I had shut. Grief, however, comes in cycles and will not be ignored when it knocks. Unwillingly, I plunged anew into the heartache I felt over Edward.

Though it was folly to even consider Elizabeth's plea, I gave a last fleeting look at our beautiful plans. Edward was supposed to

become a barrister, and when Henry came into his full inheritance, we'd join him and Elizabeth at Auburn Manor.

The four of us had planned that our children would grow up
together and play in the same fields we had. How many pledges
had we sworn to continue to live as wild and as free as we were
then? How many times had I daydreamed about the first time
the four of us would sit down to dine, each wearing a grin
because we'd know we had won—that despite society, despite the
obstacles, our foursome's bond had remained intact.

I took a breath against the rising ache. Like a wave's retreating after hitting shore, the cycle of grief ended, leaving me
strangely numb. Such thoughts were pointless now.

Having lived with her mother, Elizabeth had an uncanny
sense of when to speak and when not to. Thus, she'd held her
peace while I'd entertained the vision, but when I shook my
head, tears filled her eyes. "How can you give up? Not now.
Fight. Would you really trade what we four share, even for
something as grand as this?" She waved her hand over the hall
with its intricate ceilings, ornate moldings, and rich furnishings. "Edward will recover from this madness in time. I know
he will."

I reined in my emotions before answering. "It was a dream,
Elizabeth. A silly, childish, nonsensical dream. It is far time we
outgrew it anyway." I placed my fingertips on her arm. "Not just
me, but you, too. I don't think it's coming true for either of us."

She gave a snort at that idea. "How can you turn your back on
us now, after all we swore to each other?"

"What if it's not just Edward and me parting ways? What if
it's you and Henry too?"

Confusion lit her eyes as she cocked her head.

I wet my lips, uncertain how hard she'd take the news.
"Dearest, I overheard a rumor . . . about . . . Henry being
engaged."

Instead of the dismay I expected, she looked a trifle annoyed, then took up my hands. "Never mind that. Henry and I are fully capable of handling that matter."

I felt my eyebrows lift, even as my blood ran cold. "Elizabeth! You mean you know?"

"It's not us you should worry about." She started to say more, but the door opened, revealing the missing gentlemen. Henry looked first for Elizabeth, who rose and went to greet him. Mr. Greenham claimed a seat in the corner, looking more plagued than ever.

Mr. Macy's probing glance looked for me, and when he found me, he offered an encouraging smile. He patted Henry's shoulder as Elizabeth joined them, made a pretense of getting coffee, and then, to my relief, he joined me.

"Have you ever played billiards, Miss Elliston?" He presented a cup, speaking loud enough for all to hear.

"I have not."

"I've always wondered how a lady would play the game."

"What an odd notion," Lady Foxmore called. "I doubt a true lady would enjoy it. So perhaps you are in luck, Chance."

"I don't know if I'd play with her," Henry said, frowning at me. "I warrant she'd cheat."

"Do you enjoy reading?" Mr. Macy ignored them by facing me and crossing one leg over the other. I looked up, realizing he was trying to undo the damage from dinner.

Feeling heartened, I turned from Henry too. "I do, very much."

"Not novels, I hope."

I fingered the edge of my saucer, feeling juvenile. "I have no objections to them."

"I'll never understand why a delicate, blushing lady enjoys reading harrowing tales of distress."

The clever comment that eluded me at breakfast finally presented itself. "You seem very aware of their contents. How many have you read?"

His hearty laugh rang out. "I have been caught! Yes, it does not hurt for a gentleman to read a novel or two. Especially the ones written by women. I advise it to anyone desiring to learn the art of seduction."

A shocked hush fell over the room. His statement scandalized, and his eyes shone for it. Mr. Greenham stood and retreated to the window. Henry glared at me before turning his baleful stare on Mr. Macy.

Mr. Macy inclined his head as though submitting to Henry's decorum, then leaned to my ear. "Shall it please you to learn I've ordered countless novels for my library? I hoped you'd have a penchant for them."

I blushed and the silence deepened. "Sir, we're alarming the room."

"And you're enjoying it as much as I am. Your eyes fairly dance with amusement."

I couldn't hide my smile.

"Shall we shock them completely?" He leaned still nearer. "Shall I kiss you here and now?"

"No. Do not!" I cried out before realizing he was jesting.

Heads swivelled in our direction. Henry started to rise, but Mr. Greenham approached first. "Chance, I don't approve."

Mr. Macy slowly raised his eyes, allowing an uncomfortable pause. "John," he eventually said, "we have known each other a long time, and your friendship is more valuable to me than any other. Therefore I would consider it abhorrent should anything—" his eyes indicated me—"come between us. You of all people ought to know I would never act improperly toward Miss Elliston."

"May we speak privately?" Mr. Greenham asked.

"Not tonight." Though Mr. Macy returned his gaze in my direction, I doubted he saw me. "I'm uneasy in my mind about you. Perhaps in the morning, after I've had opportunity to think."

After a stiff bow, Mr. Greenham returned to his chair. While everyone tried to ignore the obvious tension, Mr. Forrester rose, his eyes darting between Mr. Macy and Mr. Greenham's slumped form.

The carefree mood was not restored. Lady Foxmore eventually declared she was tired and needed Henry's arm. Elizabeth offered her help, likely looking for an excuse to steal a moment alone with Henry. I watched, calculating the length of time before Henry and Elizabeth would return. When ten minutes had passed and Mr. Macy remained submerged in thought, I placed a hand on his arm. "Shall I also retire?"

He stirred and looked around, returning his gaze to me with tenderness. "Not unless you feel fatigued. I've waited all day to have you to myself."

Mr. Greenham stood.

"John, wait." Mr. Macy left his chair and followed him from the room. Rooke looked up from his book, and taking interest, joined them.

Mr. Forrester alone remained. He peered into the hall before turning his unabashed gaze on me. "Quickly now, are Macy and Greenham fighting?"

My heart fluttering, I picked up my untouched coffee with the air of not having heard.

"You're the only one privy to their conversation." He took Mr. Macy's seat and placed his hand over the top of my coffee, preventing me from taking a sip. "Tell me what they said."

I twisted my mouth, giving him a hateful glare.

"Don't tell me you're half-witted enough to trust him over me."

"I trust him with my life." I enunciated my words, growing angry.

"What if I told you I had information that would change your mind?"

"Then I should hope you had hard proof," Mr. Macy answered

from the door with Mr. Greenham looming behind him. "She already knows you're here to blackmail me. I've had enough of your game. I'm calling your bluff. If you have something devastating, let's hear it. Now."

Mr. Forrester gritted his teeth.

"I thought as much," Mr. Macy said. "You may continue your visit, but for now, I'll thank you for ridding me of your presence."

With his hands clenched, Mr. Forrester ducked his head and left.

"Are you all right, Miss Elliston?" Mr. Greenham brushed past Mr. Macy and hurried to my side.

I nodded but said to Mr. Macy, "Why are you allowing him to stay?"

"Because if he's here, he's not with your guardian, causing more havoc." Mr. Macy poured himself a brandy. "John, I promised Julia a walk in my hothouses tonight. You're welcome to join us."

Mr. Greenham shook his head. "No, but satisfy me this. Now that you've met her, are your intentions the same?"

"They are," Mr. Macy said. "There is a genuine attachment on both sides."

Mr. Greenham bowed and left the room.

"Well, at least that much is out of the way," Mr. Macy said once the door closed. He softened, seeing my distress. "Come." He pulled me from the chair and wrapped his arm around me. "John will be fine. All day, I've anticipated this time. There's something I'd like to show you."

Seventeen

THE MOONLIGHT that blanketed the grounds that night made every blade of frosted grass glitter, giving the landscape a celestial appearance. I clutched Mr. Macy's sleeve, wondering what he planned. At the crest of the far hill, another great house stood, barely lit with stars blinking above it. As I stared at the apparently empty house, I shivered, my skirts billowing in the wind.

"The conservatory will be warm," Mr. Macy promised.

Having crossed the great lawn, he steered us back to the gravel paths passing the kitchen gardens, enclosed in glass frames. At the hothouse, he released me to select a key. I rubbed my arms, viewing the glass, fuzzy with frost. A breath of humidity was expelled when the door opened to reveal a narrow stone path stretched between high beds of scarlet geraniums. I gasped with wonder. After thirty feet, the conservatory expanded into a spacious glasshouse filled with tall palms and flowering creepers.

I entered, hands over heart, breathing the rich scent. Mr. Macy's mouth twisted in amusement as he locked the door behind us.

I turned. "This is my favorite place in Eastbourne."

"This?" He seemed further entertained as he gathered me. "There are matters I wish to discuss tonight. Only first, tell me of your day."

As we brushed past, geranium petals scattered over the walkway. Smaller conservatories connected to the main hothouse, each brimming with green. Mr. Macy indicated for me to sit beneath an orange tree, then crouched on his heels near the bench, enfolding my hands in his. "Tell me everything."

As I spoke about the rooms and artifacts that interested me, he plucked an orange blossom and tucked it into my hair.

"There was one room . . ." I faltered, hesitant to mention the coffee set.

His smile tightened. "You didn't wander into my ballroom, did you?"

"Not the ballroom, the billiards room."

"The billiards room!" He laughed. "Whatever is the matter with it?"

I moistened my lips. "Well, there's a coffee set . . ."

"The coffee set." He sat hard on the ground, still staring at my hands in his. "Yes, I'd rather forgotten that." An empty, soulless look filled his eyes as he aged the span of years in seconds. He appeared so weary, my heart wrung. "You want an explanation, no doubt."

At that time, I was young and immature enough to wish I'd never brought up the wretched coffee set. I was used to apologizing in the face of my father's swift temper, and I feared to upset Mr. Macy. Whatever the explanation, I reasoned, it couldn't be worse than beginning my life as a servant in Scotland. "No," I said. "No explanations."

Fingers dug into the flesh of my upper arm and I was yanked to my feet. I hadn't even felt him stand. I gasped in pain, turning toward him. He towered over me, malice fixed on his features. "What do you mean, no? Who sent you?" He shook me. "Bradshawl? O'Connor?"

"I . . . I . . ." A tear escaped as I stared at him, bewildered.

He loosened his grip, but his stare bored into me. "You what?"

"I don't care about the set because . . . I . . . I love you." The words tumbled from me without permission, but I sensed they were the right ones.

His eyes narrowed but he tipped up my chin, forcing me to look him in the eye. A shadow flitted across his countenance, a desperate look. He released me and turned, pinching the bridge of his nose. After several seconds, he came back and gently took my elbow. "Here, come. Sit."

My arms ached where his fingers had dug into them. I tried to resume my seat, but I was trembling so much, I missed the edge of the bench. He caught me and placed me securely on the seat.

"I'm going to take full advantage of your statement." He knelt before me, drawing my hands to his chest. "Are you willing to enter into an engagement with me here, now, tonight?"

I stared in disbelief. Did he actually think I would accept him when he had just shown himself capable of violence toward me?

Yet he seemed to, for he watched my rising doubt and panic without offering one word or look of comfort. I faltered as I studied his complete self-possession; here was a personality unlike any I'd ever encountered.

"I need a moment," I said.

"Take your time."

My arms smarted, but feeling the strength of his fingers as they gripped mine, I realized he'd restrained himself from causing real injury. But I couldn't forget the malevolence that had gnarled his features. Had it been to frighten an honest answer from me? I searched his eyes, looking for a hint of his thoughts, but they held depths I didn't comprehend.

Who was Mr. Macy? I wondered, as he held my hands, waiting.

Thoughts of his bedchamber flooded me with empathy. No matter what the reason for this strange behavior, it didn't change the fact I'd fallen in love. His hand tightened around mine, giving the impression I was the only light in his dark world. Only if that was so, I couldn't understand why he continued to wait patiently, his expression concealing all emotion. I wanted him to reason with me, to explain.

I swallowed. From the day of Mama's burial I'd determined to wed. Had I not spent months struggling to escape my fate? Was I so weak that I wouldn't dare to reach out and take what I wanted?

I lowered my gaze. My heart felt like an overwound music box.

Then, even more than now, marriages were business arrangements. The upper crust had always been sustained by the economy of matrimony. Two days was scarcely enough time to gauge my future, yet how many marriages were contracted reckoning only on properties and funds? The balance was in my favor. Nonetheless, I felt the chains of becoming the legal property of someone other than Edward.

"Yes." I lowered my gaze. "I'll enter an engagement."

"You took some time coming to that answer. Are you certain?"

I nodded, feeling tears well. "Yes, only I'm frightened."

His low chuckle filled me with assurance as he lifted my chin. "I swear, never again shall you feel a rough hand laid upon you. Mine or any other. I am a man of my word. You have nothing to fear."

I nodded again and again, wiping away tears before he slid next to me and gathered me in his arms. "What were your thoughts toward the end of your discourse?" he asked. "I couldn't follow their sudden twist."

"You followed the others?"

He wiped my wet cheek with his thumb. "You are very transparent, dear, especially to one skilled in reading people. Now answer."

"I was thinking of the way *wife* and *servant* are synonymous."

He turned my face with one hand, grinning. "So you read seventeenth-century poetry, do you? Leave Lady Chudleigh on the shelf, for she never married me. I do not intend to lord it over you." He paused, regarding me. "I'm going to explain the coffee set, so later nothing comes between us."

"Nothing could."

He laughed and kissed my forehead. "You are a study, dearest. But come. Let's return to the house. This is no longer the proper setting for us."

⁓

Mr. Macy locked the study, tossed his keys on the desk, and added kindling to the embers. I remained by the door while he coaxed the fire. He seemed to have composed himself since leaving the greenhouse, but I hadn't. Only after flames curled around the cedar log did he take notice of me.

"Sweetheart." He grabbed his housecoat and drew me into the room. "Here, wear this. It will warm you until the fire catches."

I pressed the satin against my face, yearning for his comforting smell. Reynolds must have laundered the robe, for only lye tingled my nose. While I donned it, Mr. Macy selected a cigar. He faced the hearth, smoking, while I settled in one of the couches. His internal debate seemed to end the same moment he grew weary of his cigar, flicking it into the fire.

"Last night," he said, turning, "you informed me you required no knowledge of my past. Though gratified, I knew keeping it was an impossibility." He leaned against the mantel and bit his thumb with an expression of discontentment. "I've grown so suspicious over the years, I never imagined you'd

require no explanation when confronted with your first hurdle."
He laughed once and rubbed his jaw. "I feared you were a trap.
A clever, clever trap."

When he joined me on the couch, I scooted toward him,
knowing the warmth of his arms would remove the sinking feeling in my heart. I didn't want to know his past. I feared it.

"No, remain there," he said. "I wish to observe you, lest
I reveal too much and you regret your troth."

"Then tell me nothing. For all I care, you could have stolen
the set like a common gypsy."

His hand angled, and he studied me so long I feared I'd displeased him. Eventually, he stood and sauntered to the drink
table. "I would rather spare you this knowledge as well." He
poured two brandies. "Yet you need to know. Not only for an
explanation of the coffee set, but your own protection requires
it." He handed me a drink with a wry smile. "I wonder whether
you'll find my account better or worse than the theory that I
stole it." He slouched in the couch opposite me, taking slow sips
of brandy.

Uncomfortable, I drew my legs up and wrapped my arms
around my knees. "Then tell me, and hurry. Had I known
tonight would be like this, I never would have mentioned the
horrid set."

"Would you not?" He placed his brandy aside. "That's
scarcely better, darling. The unknown is always more threatening than the known. I shouldn't like to see you brooding and
pacing Eastbourne. Better to come early for explanations."

I hugged myself tighter.

He opened his cigar case and withdrew another cheroot.
When a line of smoke spun idly over his head, he studied the
fire, saying, "Tonight, I planned on asking you to marry me. At
best, I hoped you would accept for your protection. You've taken
me by surprise with your declaration of love." He took a swig of
brandy, then stared at the empty tumbler. "I think you've known

me long enough to understand I have ways of finding valuable information. Call it an uncanny knack, if you like."

He rose, refilled his glass, then settled himself at my feet. "In my youth, I used this ability for gain and, perhaps, amusement. Years ago, I sold information to both your father and your guardian, enabling them to blackmail each other. The coffee set was a payment from your father."

"My father?" I couldn't muster surprise. It sounded like him.

Mr. Macy rubbed his forehead. "They hated each other, bitterly. Had I known how far they would take it . . . I will not reveal the particulars, but eventually your father and I had a falling out. In anger, I gave your guardian information that ruined your father, and as it turns out, your mother also."

I sifted through Mr. Macy's words, but they were too vague to help me make sense of the situation. "Why is he my guardian, then?"

"Perhaps we ought to end this discussion. I only desired for you to learn why I reacted as I—"

"Tell me."

"No." He rose to join me on the couch. "He's a dangerous man who fears his misdeeds coming to light. The last thing I intend to do is further endanger you by revealing them."

I opened my mouth to argue, but Mr. Macy's countenance stopped me. Frustrated, I crossed my arms. "Why were you involved in their battle, then?"

"I used to hire myself out for extortion and blackmail. They both sought my aid, and to my deep regret, I betrayed them both to each other."

During this speech, I had been looking at my hands, but now I raised my gaze. How could anyone sound so matter-of-fact about such things?

"And now you know some small part of my past." He tilted his head, keeping his acute gaze on me. "I've spent my life paying for the mistakes of my youth. It's why I live in isolation. Why

I was suspicious of you tonight." He crossed his arms. "Do you regret your promise to wed me now?"

I felt as Mr. Greenham must have during dinner, outside of Mr. Macy's pleasure. Did he expect me to repent of our engagement and beg out of it? His cold gaze certainly gave that impression. My illusion of him was splintered, but not my love. My voice came out unsteady. "But why are you angry with me?"

Warm arms surrounded me, but before I could bury myself in his chest, Mr. Macy kissed my forehead. "Sweetheart, I've never been further from anger in my life."

"But you're acting so cold."

He swept loose strands of hair from my shoulder. "Because you've not yet considered what I've disclosed, or considered how you view me in light of the knowledge."

"It doesn't matter. Not one bit of it."

He lifted my chin. "There's more, dearest. I need you to pay attention. I've damaged very powerful people. There are those who seek revenge. It's why I trust no one, never become attached to anyone—"

Fear coiled in my stomach. "Does that mean that you don't . . . you aren't . . . ?"

"That I don't what, dearest?"

I felt as if I'd been sinking into a miry bog because I'd followed will-o'-the-wisps. My eyes filled. "You are only marrying me to redress a wrong?"

His laugh was hearty before he kissed the side of my face. "I spoke too carelessly. Forgive me. Do you think I'm incapable of protecting you unless we are married? But so you have no doubts, allow me to state it plainly: my heart is solely yours." He kissed my forehead. "I ought to warn you, though—" he wiped my cheeks—"tears have no effect on me. I'll allow them tonight, but must ask you refrain in the future. In return, I'll give you nothing to cry over." I nodded, trying to abate them. He laughed softly. "Now you understand. Our attachment leaves me vulnerable, Julia. There are many who wish me harm. I need your trust if I'm to keep us safe. Do you understand this?"

I nodded.

"No, it's plain to see you're far too innocent to comprehend any of this. But why should you? As my wife, you'll never have anything to fear." He stood, took my glass, and refreshed the brandy. "You have far more right to question me than I you, but my curiosity demands to be satiated. What caused your sudden sentiment in the hothouse?"

I tugged on the cuffs of his dressing gown. "I went into your bedroom today."

The decanter dropped to the table with a crack. "You didn't have the key."

"It's the same as mine."

"Clever." It was spoken in a near whisper through gritted teeth as he rammed the stopper back into the bottle. "And how, pray tell, did viewing my room evoke that emotion?"

"I saw your loneliness."

His mouth slanted downwards as his eyes became haunted. "Do not explore areas of my life that you know I want left alone. It's for your sake. I've only told you the smallest bit of my past, only a fraction of the part involving you. Do not seek to learn more than I disclose. Otherwise, you shall have no happiness as my wife."

"Is . . . is there more, then?"

"Yes, and far, far worse than I've told you." He slipped his arm behind me, bringing comfort and assurance. "There, I've frightened you again. Rest assured, dearest—" his nose nuzzled my hair—"I am a different man than I was in the past. Now you must have your own questions."

Mr. Macy may have been adept at switching from shocking topics to bewildering situations, but I was not. The heavy ticking of the clock filled the room as I tried to sort through my mind to find the right inquiries to make.

"Did my guardian . . . Was Mama a threat to him, like my father was?"

"Not to my knowledge, but your guardian probably wasn't chancing it." Mr. Macy moved away, so he could view me.

"Did my mother know of your past?"

"Not to my knowledge."

I nodded, tallying his words. She wouldn't have agreed to a match otherwise. "What will happen when my guardian learns of our marriage?"

He grinned and sipped his brandy. "Blind rage might be an apt description. Certainly, he'll wonder why I married you." He laughed as though he hoped that would be the result. When I dropped my gaze, I heard him set his drink down. "Julia, it's my concern how he responds, and I daresay, I'm far better at this game than he is. Forgive my amusement, but I'm rather looking forward to his learning of our alliance. At least I won't have to tolerate his presence any longer."

"Then you still have . . . contact?"

"Yes, I've tolerated his evil for years, keeping tabs on his doings. All for the sake of keeping an eye on your family, especially after your father's death."

"Tell me his name."

"No."

"When we marry?"

"No. Why keep asking when you know I'll not reveal more?"

I felt my brow furrow, knowing it would not be wise to tell him that I wanted revenge for Mama's death. As if sensing my need for comfort, he drew me close and kissed the nape of my neck. "I'd make a sorry protector if I failed to keep you safe. That's all you need to know. Enough about him."

I shut my eyes, leaning into his kisses.

Pulling aside the dressing robe, he let his lips travel along my collarbone. With two fingers, he traced my face, then turned me toward him to study the effect of his advances. A smile played over his lips before he covered my mouth and deepened his brandy-laced kisses. My tears dried as I forgot all else. There, as he crushed me against him, nothing else mattered; his past ceased to exist. His hand took hold of my hair before his thumb traversed down my neck, raising gooseflesh over my entire body.

I obeyed his touch, surrendering to his will, allowing him to lay me down. I did nothing to halt his fingers from removing the combs from my hair one by one.

After a lingering kiss, Mr. Macy withdrew slightly and looked down at me stretched out over the couch alongside him. The heat of his hand still tingled on my skin. I stared up, out of breath, scarcely cognizant of how we'd gotten into that scandalous position.

He traced the neckline of my gown, running his fingertips just beneath the ruffled lace. His head bent nearer mine. "Finally, a conversation more worthy of our time. Shall we broaden the scope of our topic?"

I stared up, battling my desire to nod. Pride took over his countenance as he viewed me. I wonder now how I must have looked to him, desire smoldering in my eyes, scarcely able to catch my breath.

Suddenly, without warning, he leapt to his knees and snatched a revolver from the closed box on the side table near us.

"Very sorry, sir," came Reynolds's voice from the door. "I assumed you were in the hothouse and was delivering this."

Mr. Macy uttered a low oath as he replaced the firearm, but his face filled with relief before he rested his forehead on his empty hand. "Knock, regardless."

Free from its combs, my hair tumbled about my shoulders as I sat, trying to hide my face.

"I debated whether to fetch you." Reynolds continued as if not seeing me. "It's from London."

"London?" Mr. Macy stiffened. "Who delivered it?"

"Snyder, sir."

Mr. Macy glanced at the door. "Has he left?"

"Yes, sir."

Mr. Macy eyed the leather pouch tucked beneath Reynolds's arm. "All right, set it on my desk, then leave us."

As Reynolds crossed the threshold, Mr. Macy laced his fingers in my hair and leaned over to kiss my neck, but I buried myself in his chest, heat emanating from my face.

"It's only Reynolds," Mr. Macy said, but I refused to budge until the door banged closed and the lock scraped. "Perhaps it's time you overcame your demureness," he said, viewing me. "A blush or two is alluring, darling, but you do take it beyond the normal limits." His gaze wandered to the package and then the clock. "Do you think you could sleep here?"

"Sleep?" I sat up, feeling as though I'd been doused with cold water. "What? Now?"

He tucked my hair behind my ear, still viewing the desk. "Yes, the letter is undoubtedly urgent, but I loathe leaving you."

I frowned, wondering what one did with all the cravings he'd set loose. "I can try."

He finally returned his attention to me and bestowed a knowing smile before kissing my forehead. All too soon, he rose and fetched a blanket, which I punched into a pillow.

At the desk, he opened the pouch, which contained a large number of parchments. From the moment he started to read, I knew I'd been displaced from his thoughts. Biting his thumb, he sat with his eyes moving across the first page. The longer he read, the more his frown deepened. Eventually, I settled down and stared at the blue-green part of the fire near the logs.

Until now, I'd shunned all thought, all memory, of Edward. Yet as I lay tangled in Mr. Macy's dressing robe, the feel of his touch still fresh, my thoughts finally turned back to the path I'd declined.

I shut my eyes and saw Edward's boyish face grinning as it had right after our first kiss. That day, the sun had filtered through the green canopy of leaves, accenting the honey color of Edward's curls. Nearby, a rushing brook had gushed through mossy rocks, its happy gurgle blending with our laughing voices.

Heartsick, I hugged myself tighter and opened my eyes to stare at the crackling fire fighting the frigid air. I stifled regret and worked to commit new sensations to memory—the smoky fragrance of the fire, the scent of brandy.

I turned over, listening to the susurration of Mr. Macy's papers. Though I feigned sleep, memories of Edward, one shadowing another, haunted me late into the night.

I woke to find additional blankets covering me and the fire smoldering. Remnants of a dream involving Mr. Greenham sheltering me beneath an umbrella clung to my consciousness. Mr. Macy still sat at his desk, looking over documents, his attention fully absorbed. I watched as he'd read a paragraph or sentence and then leaf through dozens of other papers, comparing them, shaking his head. Finally, an impish grin tugged his mouth and relief softened his face.

I sat up.

He noted me immediately and closed the portfolio, his good mood seemingly secured. "I must hurry you to your room. It's after six."

"Who is Mr. Greenham?" My voice was coated with sleep. I sipped the brandy still sitting out to rid my mouth of its ill taste.

"John?" He set down his pen and stretched, grinning. "Of all the people to wake up wondering about. Next to you, he's my most trusted friend. Only I can rely on him better. He neither cries nor explores my chambers." Mr. Macy rose and knelt at my side, smiling.

I placed my arms around his neck. At that moment, he meant more to me than anyone. He was all I had. I breathed in his musk, knowing the scent would soon mean I was in my husband's arms.

Mr. Macy kissed my cheek. "Are you ready? Every passing minute increases the danger of being seen."

I stood, grateful his strong arm steadied me. He removed his dressing robe, then unlocked the door, allowing in cool gusts of morning air. "What made you think of John?"

"I dreamed of him holding an umbrella over me."

Mr. Macy shook his head, chuckling. "Endeavor to become fast friends with him. You shall often find yourself in his company for protection. He's been in one of his slumps recently. Just ignore it. He experiences them every so often."

Eighteen

THE BRUSH CAUGHT a snarl of my hair, wrenching my head back. In the oval mirror, I watched Nancy dip her head in apology. Too benumbed to care, I rubbed my eyes. Everything felt blurred, and sitting motionless only increased the leaden feeling.

My eyes evidenced tears, and on my neck there were two blotches that resembled bruises. I frowned, touching one. There wasn't pain when I pressed it.

"No one will sees them but mysell." Nancy flitted me a nervous look. "Scented oil will cover th' cigar scent till thou hast bathed." She held a section of my hair, indicating what had exuded the smell.

I groaned and buried my head in my arms, feeling no inclination to explain myself to a common scullery girl. Why should I care? I was engaged, wasn't I? I smiled at the thought. Any reasonable person would doubt my sensibilities. Who else would betroth herself to a man who admitted to shameful secrets? It was madness, but I was firm in my decision.

If Mama's death taught me how drastically life could change in one moment, Mr. Macy taught me how one's perspective could change in one cycle of the clock.

Nancy disappeared into one of the side chambers and reappeared with a dark bottle. She uncorked it, and the fresh scent of hyssop filled the room. Her deft fingers kneaded the oil into my hair, giving it a glossy appearance. With pins held between pressed lips, she carefully coiled my braids, then pinned them at the nape of my neck, hiding the marks. At Reynolds's smart rap on the door, she twisted an imaginary key over her closed lips.

⁓

Upon my entering the breakfast chamber, Mr. Greenham rose and studied my appearance. With an annoyed flick of his hand, he threw his napkin on the chair and approached.

Except for Lady Foxmore's glance, everyone else remained in private worlds. Rooke scanned the newspaper. Henry, sporting a swollen eye, conversed with the Windhams. The table lacked only Mr. Forrester.

"Where shall I seat you?" Mr. Greenham touched his eyelids with a tired air.

I studied him. If he was Macy's trusted friend, then he was mine. "Next to you, please."

Mr. Greenham cast me a fatigued look, but obliged before ensconcing himself in his own seat.

"Greetings." Macy's voice carried from near the door. He strolled through the breakfast room as various salutations were returned. He smiled seeing Mr. Greenham with me and squeezed his shoulder. Macy winked at me, pulling out his chair. "I trust everyone is rested."

I unrolled my napkin, wondering how he managed to appear invigorated when he'd slept less than I had, then with gratitude I saw the benefit in that it kept suspicion from us.

Footmen arrived, filling the room with the scent of eggs, anchovy toast, and headcheese. Too exhausted to eat, I leaned back in my chair, using Mr. Greenham's form to block me from being seen by the others. Silverware clinked against porcelain over the sounds of tea being sipped. Mr. Macy gave me a concerned look, but before he could inquire, the butler entered with a post for him.

Here I finally found occupation. I studied the stationery with interest. It was expensive, and the gold seal looked like a family crest. I gathered the sender was pompous, for the insignia was at least the size of a shilling, wasting precious wax.

Mr. Macy brushed crumbs from his hand and took up the missive. The paper was thick; the sunlight did not bleed the words through the page as he read.

"John." Mr. Macy's tone held a new sobriety as he passed the note to Mr. Greenham.

I craned my neck to peek, but Mr. Macy tapped my slippers with his foot and shook his head. I complied but couldn't resist gauging Mr. Greenham's response. Perspiration dotted his forehead as he read the note, and his skin turned sallow.

"I fear John and I have an unexpected matter to clear up. We must leave immediately." Mr. Macy stood, placing his napkin over his plate.

I stiffened, feeling as though all breath had been knocked from me.

"Henry," Mr. Macy continued, "will you pledge to remain here while I'm away?"

Henry tilted his head, squinting.

"Chance, of all the nonsense." Lady Foxmore set down her utensils. "It's at your insistence we're even here. Don't you dare even think of it."

"Perhaps our party constricts you." Mrs. Windham shielded her eyes from the sun behind Mr. Macy. "Indeed, I shouldn't mind being amongst my own rooms again. We could leave."

"I assure you, madam—" Mr. Macy touched the crown of my head—"it is your party that makes me anticipate my return."

The touch, though improper, had been so brief and so affectionate no one dared to object, though Henry glowered with his one good eye.

"Am I required?" Rooke asked.

"Yes, here. Now if you'll excuse us."

Having been sandwiched between them, when they rose and left, I felt exposed and then emptied as their footsteps departed.

Elizabeth says I transformed during that breakfast. My face grew haggard and my eyes filled with the terror worn by young mothers losing their first babe. Once when I asked her why she didn't say anything, she replied, "I didn't dare. Not while you wore that numb, bereaved expression."

It is true, though, is it not? People leave grief well enough alone, lest the dark spirit rise and turn its ruthless gaze in their direction.

But did my expression deserve Elizabeth's censure? I know not, for I passed no looking glasses for the rest of the day. I do, however, recall my thoughts. Outside the Windhams, I had no one: no grandparents, no aunts or uncles, no friends. My entire existence was enclosed within this one sphere.

Who, I wondered, would believe the precariousness of my situation? Like as naught, Mrs. Windham would think me brainsick if I suddenly declared my guardian murderous and that I had become engaged to the most elusive bachelor in England for protection.

Betrothal, I realized, offered no sanctuary. Only marriage did.

That day I also absorbed the true meaning of *alone*. What I did not understand then was that it is the plight of every human, part of the curse, though most seem blithely unaware. I remained with our party. I occupied a chair in the corner of the drawing room. I looked over my book, a silent observer, watching while the others bantered and played cards—there were genuine smiles and comradery, while I only felt the pull of emptiness.

❧

That night, the past haunted me.

In a dream, I revisited arriving home after Mama's burial, dragging my heavy skirts over the threshold. Once more I stood with numb indifference and watched as mud, caked to the hem of my skirt, fell in clumps and blended with rainwater. With tingling familiarity, I dreamed of Sarah's wizened face peeking around the corner, of her pointing with hands raw from scrubbing to the drawing room, declaring the vicar was here.

I knew my lines, for this was a dream and I'd once played my part. But now, as I tugged at the knot of my bonnet with chilled fingers, I wanted to wake. Anger shrieked. Why should I listen to him rant about my coming damnation for a second time?

It was Reynolds's voice that recalled me to the land of the living.

"Miss Elliston." A hand tapped my shoulder. "Miss Elliston."

I woke with a start, surprised to find I was crying.

Reynolds leaned over me, the light of his candle casting a strange sheen over his face. "I beg your pardon, miss. Only there's . . . a situation."

I stared, too dazed to answer. Then as I shut my eyes, the genuine pieces of my day fell into place. Macy and Greenham's departure, listlessly following the party from room to room, my inability to eat, the endless hours of whist.

"The time?" My stomach revolted from fatigue as I sat up.

"You retired an hour ago," Reynolds said. "I am truly sorry to wake you, only there's a gentleman at the gate."

I waited.

With the patience of a nursemaid teaching a toddler, he gave a bow. "What shall I do with him?"

"Do?"

"Yes. Mr. Macy placed you in charge of Eastbourne during his absence. He informed me of your felicitous tidings this morning."

"I'm in charge?" This news sobered me. "What would you normally do?"

"Set the dogs on the rascal, only he insists Mr. Greenham invited him."

"Who is it?"

Reynolds patted his vest, then withdrew a rain-spotted, cheap grade of card. I knew even before I touched it. With warbling emotions, I turned over the card and stared at Edward's name, caught between guilt and joy.

"Do you recognize the name, then?"

I clutched the card to my chest, uncertain whether to laugh or cry at Reynolds's question. My voice came out unsteady. "Yes. He . . . he's a very dear friend. Have a room prepared. I'll greet him." I stood, but my head spun.

Reynolds caught my arm. "Might I suggest you remain abed? Perhaps you'd rather greet him in the morning?"

I shook my head, picturing Edward standing in the pelting rain refusing to leave the gate. Any other sensible person would go to the inn and send a letter up in the morning. But not Edward. "No. I'll greet him tonight."

With a glint of surprise, Reynolds bowed and left.

Alone, I slid from the bed and quickly donned my dress, then looked in the mirror. An apparition greeted me. When I'd climbed into bed, I'd allowed the pent-up fears over Mr. Macy's departure to vent in the form of tears. My eyes were puffy, encircled in dark shadows. A wrinkled dress framed the macabre appearance. My throat tightened at the thought of Edward seeing me like this, but there wasn't anything to be done.

Taking a candle from a wall sconce, I hastened toward the entrance of Eastbourne. Compared to my bedchamber, the air was frigid. Here reason finally settled. I touched the places where Mr. Macy's kisses and hands had wandered—my temples, the hollow of my neck and collarbone. My sudden rush of emotion over Edward's arrival was madness, I realized. I was engaged to another man.

I leaned against a cold pillar, biting my nails, imagining what Edward would say if he knew about the manner in which I had become engaged to Mr. Macy. The tender way in which Edward asked for my hand had been nothing like the scene in the green-house. It had been gloaming when Edward came up the hill near Am Meer and joined me where I sat reading under the ancient oak. At eighteen, he seemed so grown, so handsome. Carmine oak leaves were adrift in the air as he approached. One caught in his curls, which I plucked as he knelt beside me. How marvelous I thought it that a member of the peerage should look upon me with such love in his eyes.

I bit my nail so hard it drew blood, forcing my attention back to Eastbourne. I slid that hand behind my back. Why, I wondered, did that memory surface right now?

"Marry me."

Edward's words, neither command nor question, had been husky with emotion.

I shut my eyes and laid my cheek against the icy pillar as I recalled the chaste kiss we had shared. It brought to mind how very dissimilar Mr. Macy's touch was. The very nature of that hunger was different. The desire that welled from within was base and carnal. The forbidden ebbed and flowed at the merest shimmer of Mr. Macy's touch. He summoned an appetite that could never be sated, and he alone commanded every unchaste desire within me. I welcomed him.

But Edward . . . I frowned, disliking the strange bemingling of emotions. What was it I sought from him? He had blotted himself from my story—so why was I here and waiting in the middle of the night for him? And why did I ache so much?

I rubbed the nape of my neck, realizing how much matters were complicated by Edward's arrival.

As the jingle of harnesses and the thumping of hooves approached, I rose from my thoughts as one awakens from the watery layers of slumber and hugged my arms tight against myself.

Men's voices yelled instructions outside as someone threw open the front door. Edward entered with a sober, even grim look.

Heartache pierced me as he paused in the doorway, taking in the hall, which did not gleam as it had upon my arrival. Rain made his boots and coat slick, as well as tightening his curls, something he hated. I felt a rush of affection as I recalled the rare occasions on which he'd grudgingly allowed me to extend one curl with my index finger so I could watch it re-form.

I chuckled, recalling the day Henry had called him goldilocks, and in a fit of temper, Edward tackled his brother, causing them both to fall into the creek.

Edward's head jerked in my direction and he squinted into the dark. "Julia?"

Not trusting my voice, I stepped forward. No twist of fate could have been crueller than that moment, for the man who met my gaze was my Edward—not the vicar I'd met in the Windham drawing room or at his parents' dinner—but my Edward, matured and beautiful.

Seeing him was so unexpected I couldn't speak.

He ran his gaze over my features, resting longest on my eyes.

"What . . . ?" I had to swallow the lump in my throat as I pulled my arms tighter against my stomach. "What are you doing here?"

Goodwill marked his features. His eyes were filled with expectation. His apology, his love, his chagrin were all wrapped in that hopeful smile.

"I couldn't do it," he said in a low voice. "I couldn't live with myself if you went away and I never saw you again. I couldn't live with that."

Speech was impossible.

He gently tugged me a step closer to him and touched his forehead to mine. "I don't know what we're going to do, Juls, but I swear, we'll find a solution. All right? I swear on my life."

Tears formed, which I did my best to contain. This I had not envisioned.

With a caring expression, he pulled back and studied my features. "I don't blame you if you never want to speak to me again. But please, I beg you, talk this out with me. I think we've both been operating under an enormous misunderstanding." He shook his head. "I think—no, I am certain—Henry and Elizabeth only compounded it. I am so sorry, Juls. So sorry."

Pulling my shawl tighter, I gazed up at Edward, undergoing a thawing sensation—only I refused its balm. He'd ended our engagement and now I was betrothed to another man. How could I begin to explain this to him, to untangle this mess?

Worse still, I felt like a blind fool. How could I have thought for even a moment he wouldn't come? Even Henry and Elizabeth knew this moment was coming.

How could I have not?

Behind me, Reynolds cleared his throat, then stepped into view. I tore my gaze from Edward, feeling heat flush up my cheeks.

"The gentleman's key." Reynolds's lips pressed into a white line as he extended it to me. His face was hooded by the dark, giving the impression he had sockets instead of eyes.

My fingers fumbled, and the key landed on the floor with a loud brattle.

"Here." I retrieved it, then pressed it into Edward's hand. "I—I . . . I should warn you, our host is very particular about keys. He—he . . ."

Edward's hand fisted around the key as his eyes slid to Reynolds.

"You are to keep it with you at all times," Reynolds finished with a clipped tone. "No one is to possess it except yourself."

Edward stared down Reynolds for a full half minute before finally giving the valet his back. Edward removed his coat and draped it over me. His lingering warmth soothed, but his hand was tense as it clamped my shoulder. "Juls, allow me to greet Mr. Macy, then let me escort you to your bedchamber."

With Edward's back to him, Reynolds shot me an accusatory look.

My hands felt so numb I could scarcely fold my fingers. "You can't. He left."

Edward frowned, looking puzzled. "All right then, which way to your room?"

I weakly gestured to the passage and we started toward it. Edward stiffened when the sharp click of Reynolds's shoes sounded behind us. None of us spoke as we passed through the various corridors of the estate. When we passed the archway, however, Edward paused long enough to brush the walls with his fingertips, afterwards rubbing his thumb and forefinger together. At my chamber door, he exhaled, looking at the empty hall.

"Are the Windhams up there?" He climbed up two steps of the murky stairwell. "You're not alone in this section of the house, are you?"

"No one is permitted on those stairs." Reynolds's tone was fierce, stopping Edward's progress, though he continued to peer up the narrow stairs.

"Fine, but I want Miss Elliston moved."

"You may take up the matter with Mr. Macy when he returns."

"I would—" Edward slid off the step, wiping his hands—"but this part of the house is damp, and I fear she's ailing."

"I am not in the habit of moving guests without permission. I assure you, her room is not damp."

"Yes, it is exceedingly comfortable." I laid my hand over Edward's arm, then to cover the gesture, quickly removed his coat and offered it back. "I assure you."

Edward took his coat, still eyeing the stairwell. "Do you not sense it, then? Let me take you to the Windhams. I'm certain Elizabeth would let you sleep with her."

I shook my head, certain that by morning Henry would have filled him in on my doings. "No, I shouldn't fancy that. Besides, she kicks in her sleep. Really, my room is fine."

Edward seemed to debate internally a moment, then pressed my hand in his. "All right, sleep well." And lowering his voice, "Tomorrow let's finally talk about our predicament."

"Allow me to show you to your room, sir." The anger in Reynolds's voice was dim compared to the fury in his eyes.

As they retreated, I placed my palm on the door handle, glad Edward hadn't insisted on seeing my room. I waited until they disappeared, then unlocked my door. Before the hearth, I sank into one of the chairs and tried to collect my thoughts.

Our predicament, I thought.

Edward had no idea. Feeling a headache forming, I rubbed my temples, wondering if that meant that Edward still considered us betrothed. Why that thought gave me the mad desire to cry, I no longer cared to explore.

Yet something that was a cross between a sob and a laugh escaped in disbelief that Edward, my Edward, had come—now that it was too late.

Nineteen

❦

WHEN I AWOKE, weak daylight seeped through my bedchamber as memory of Edward's arrival crashed upon me. Uttering an oath, frustrated that Nancy hadn't awoken me, I consulted the mantel clock. Its hands marked an hour far past lunch, nearer to tea.

The previous night, my emotions had been a wild tangle, but now, like a deft seamstress sorting through her mending basket, slumber had restored my sensibilities. She'd darned the fears, hemmed up confusion, and ironed out my faculties. Without anxiety ruling me, I was in a better position to handle my quandary.

Two men had good reason to consider themselves engaged to me.

One of them, and I knew which one, needed to be disappointed.

Desirous of fresh air, I faltered to my feet and cracked open the window casement and leaned out. At some point, the constant drizzle had ceased, leaving the air sodden. Lichen, made more visible by the damp bark, clung to trees the patina of aged copper. Above, dun-colored clouds layered the skies, promising rain despite the current respite. I ran my fingers through my tangled hair and then turned.

My chambers, at least, offered a cheerier outlook. Fresh roses, arranged amidst sprigs of holly and boxwood, nodded in the cool breeze. I touched their velvety petals, amazed Reynolds had still bothered after what he'd witnessed last night. It wasn't difficult to imagine the report he'd make to Mr. Macy as to what had transpired during his absence. And by now, I reasoned looking at the clock, Henry had likewise given Edward an earful. Best to go face him, I decided, and have it over with now.

Not wishing to hear Nancy's opinion on top of everything else, I pulled and shook out the first dress I found. Thankfully Mama and I had lived without a lady's maid, so I was accustomed to donning my own attire. Afterwards, I brushed and arranged my hair. Satisfied with my simple toilette, I hastened from my bedchamber.

In the main entrance hall, maids and menservants measured oil for sconces and replaced spent candles. My presence brought panic, for they scurried the moment my shoe clacked against the marble floor. Inside the dining room, the maids unfurling table linens nudged each other to look at me as I passed.

Mrs. Windham's loud voice echoed from the conservatory, indicating where to find those of my own station. Drawing a fortifying breath, I braced myself to see Edward and entered.

Mrs. Windham looked up from her knitting. It looked as though she'd been babbling to Henry and Elizabeth, who seemed to be concentrating on a game of chess. From the back of the room, Lady Foxmore held Reynolds captive as she instructed him in low tones. Edward sat in a high-back chair. The moment I met his gaze, he rose, tucking a book beneath his arm.

It hurt to meet his eyes, so I dropped my gaze.

"Ah, here she finally is." Mrs. Windham set her knitting in

her lap. "How can you say she is ill, Edward? All that ado and Julia looks perfectly healthy to me."

With eyebrow arched, Lady Foxmore turned. Merriment abounded in her expression, calling to mind the scandalous stories involving her. My current situation was the exact sort of amusement she was rumored to feast upon.

Edward sidestepped a chair, approaching me. He broke into a smile. "Yes, you do appear much better, for which I'm thankful." Reaching my side, he kissed my cheek.

His mouth thinning, Reynolds tugged at his collar, and Henry exchanged a sly glance with Elizabeth as he moved his queen.

I froze, mentally trying to adjust my opinion as to what Edward had—and had not—been told. Apparently not much.

Only later did I learn of Henry's reunion with Edward—how Henry had whooped and nearly dove over the table when he found Edward sitting wan, crouched over a breakfast plate, his lips pressed tight.

I did not see Edward shove off Henry's salutations, nor witness Edward dragging him into the hall to admonish him over his utter lack of care for me. Those events were only added to my repertoire of knowledge years later—years too late to matter.

All I had at that moment was a cold, needling sensation that for reasons of his own Henry had decided against telling Edward about Mr. Macy, just as he and Elizabeth had conspired to keep knowledge of Edward's ordination from me. Judging from Lady Foxmore's mirth, she'd gone right along with them.

"Yes, yes, we've all been aflutter with disagreements over whether you've been eating." Mrs. Windham's voice pulled my horrified gaze from her ladyship back to her. She beckoned me to come assist her so she could wind her yarn about my hands. "No one could remember, which annoyed Edward to no end."

Her edict gave me the excuse I needed to escape. Twisting my left ring finger with my right hand, I dropped into the chair she'd indicated.

Mrs. Windham gestured for me to spread my hands apart, then started winding mohair yarn about them. "Edward claims you've lost weight. Such nonsense! As if you didn't arrive on my doorstep looking more starved and beaten than a drunkard's wife. I'll thank you, missy, not to go wandering about Eastbourne in the dead of night, too. Indeed, you should have heard the lecture I endured for allowing your chambers to be so distant from mine." She puckered at Edward.

"What's this?" Lady Foxmore's cane tapped the floor. "I had not heard of this."

"Had you breakfasted with us," Mrs. Windham continued, "you would have witnessed your vicar lecturing me most dreadfully. My poor heart has not yet recovered. It appears last night Edward found Julia wandering about the estate in the dark."

Lady Foxmore chortled. "And here we assumed you safely abed, child. Tell me, has this happened before?"

My chest constricted as I met her eye. I felt the spasm of muscles twitching in my cheek. Lady Foxmore shook her head, shaking with silent laughter.

"Leave Julia in peace." Edward appeared with tea and a filigree plate containing delicate finger sandwiches. He still recalled my favorite foods.

I paused, stunned at the depth of feeling awakening in me. I'd been so angry with him after discovering he'd become a vicar that I hadn't properly grieved him. Thus emotions I thought dead flickered to life.

I gritted my teeth, determined not to feel anything.

Kneeling at my side, Edward slid his hands into the skein of yarn to take over for me. When our hands grazed, his hazel eyes met mine. With our own silent language, he communicated for me to remain silent in present company.

Head bent, I ate a few bites of the refreshments. Between Henry, Elizabeth, Lady Foxmore, and Reynolds, I was an actress on stage with critics waiting to peck apart the performance.

"You missed a note from Chance while you slept," Lady Foxmore said after I'd forced down a few bites. "Only I can't seem to recall it now." She snapped her fingers at Reynolds.

He stepped forward. "Yes, Mr. Macy sent a note stating he hopes his guests remain comfortable and anticipates resuming his visit. To memory, he cannot recount ever having spent such pleasant nights."

Nothing except the perfect lilt, the complete boredom in which Reynolds said it could have saved me. As it was, only Henry and Elizabeth's accusatory eyes lifted from their ivory-and-ebony chessboard toward me. The lemon bread turned to sand in my mouth, but I could not afford to choke.

Mrs. Windham cast on with a snort. "Well, someone ought to inform him Julia is not enjoying pleasant evenings, wandering about Eastbourne when the rest of us think she's abed. The very idea."

Lady Foxmore smirked. "Yes, I daresay Chance would be rather punctured to discover she is not enjoying her evenings as much as he is."

"Well, he has no one to blame but himself," Mrs. Windham said, bringing a full blush to my cheeks. "I tried to tell him to situate her near me."

"There we disagree, Edith—" Lady Foxmore's merry gaze did not shift from me—"for I have it on the best authority she's been extended the very best the man has to offer."

"Untrue." Edward's voice was dark. "I was at her bedchamber last night and found that section of the house most unsatisfactory."

"Her bedchamber?" Lady Foxmore slowly turned her head, giving Edward a smug smile. "How positively indecent."

I coughed, then gagged on the pastry.

Teeth clenched, Edward sloughed the yarn from his hands and stood. I covered my mouth with my napkin. My eyes were wet as I sputtered into the cloth.

"Here." Edward took my plate and set it aside, then seized Mrs. Windham's shawl, which had been piled near her feet, to drape over my shoulders. To Mrs. Windham he asked, "Have you any objection if I take Julia for a walk?"

"By no means. Take her," Mrs. Windham said. "I insist upon it. She looks very ill indeed. Fresh air is the very cure."

"Henry." Fist clenched, Edward ordered his brother, "Chaperone us."

"As if Julia's reputation could be tarnished in your hands!" Mrs. Windham waved him away. "Leave Henry and Elizabeth by the fire. There promises to be a chill in the air tonight. I'll not have Elizabeth breathing in the vile stuff."

Edward's knuckles turned white. "Henry. Now."

"Coming, coming." Henry moved his king, then stood.

Elizabeth cast him a look, which seemed to ask whether he still thought their plan a good idea.

Mrs. Windham's mouth twisted as Henry chucked Elizabeth's chin, then in a tart voice she said, "Elizabeth, of all the laziness to just sit there. Join Master Henry on his walk, for heaven's sake."

Elizabeth jumped to her feet and raced from the room, managing to make it to the hall before the pendulum of her mother's opinion swayed yet again.

～

I felt under surveillance as Edward and I waded through the ankle-deep leaves strewn over the grounds. Though Reynolds remained silent as Edward ushered me outdoors, the way he slipped into the hall behind us and the manner in which the blues of his eyes followed us effectively communicated he planned to keep me under watch.

"Give me a minute, Juls." Edward clutched my hand in a tight clasp. With alacrity he plowed through the damp, thick carpet of leaves. "That someone should affront your character like that, that it should be a lady, *my patron*, of all things!"

I eyed the roiling clouds above. Any minute they would burst. I prayed fervently that they wouldn't, not yet. Ahead of us, Elizabeth screamed with laughter as Henry urged her to run through a pile of leaves.

Not everyone will understand why on that first walk I did not put Edward on his guard. It wasn't that I didn't consider it. The thought weighed heavily upon me with each step we took.

Mama's death had taught me too well how rarely we are given back those jewel-toned moments we most wish to live again. For three years I had lived for this very culmination—the hour I was reunited with Edward.

Those who have undergone the death of a loved one know how we wish for another day, hour, even just one last look from our departed. To me, the day I learned Edward had become a vicar was the day he'd died. My wishes were no different in the wake of that loss.

It was a miracle of miracles that my Edward was there. I didn't care what had happened beforehand, nor what I knew was forthcoming. I wanted this hour, this day, and I dared not break the spell.

And perhaps, if I'm honest, I still hoped against hope that things might work out as I'd planned after all.

We turned a corner to the sight of Henry, on the ground, shovelling great piles of leaves on top of Elizabeth as she tried to claw her way free, laughing too hard to make much progress.

Edward frowned, but as he watched, his temper was doused, for laughter sprung just beneath the surface of his eyes. After a few more silent seconds of watching their behavior, he chuckled. "Do you recall the time Elizabeth was caught after we stoned Farmer Ruben's bee colony? How the good man locked her in his pantry while he fetched Mrs. Windham? I honestly think Henry would have smashed the windows had we not stopped him."

I nudged my toe into a pile of the brackish leaves. "I recall you whispering that Henry was a fool to stand by. That had it been me, nothing would have stopped you."

Edward tipped his head back and laughed. With its sound, a thousand memories of summer nights rushed back. "I'd forgotten I'd said that."

Elizabeth found her feet, and after shaking the debris from her hair and dress, raced after Henry, who'd managed to steal her glove, which he dangled just beyond her grasp.

Though I knew the longer I remained silent, the deeper my betrayal of Edward became, I valued the precious, dying hours more than transparency; besides, I hadn't yet worked out how to say it. My face must have betrayed my thoughts, for Edward studied me a moment, then looked at the labyrinth where tall hedgerows cast long shadows over the turf.

"You know—" he tucked my arm beneath his, drawing me to his side as he slowed us to an amble—"I'm fairly certain we're still not forgiven for the stings Ruben received that day. You should see the evil eye he gives me as I preach."

I forced a smile.

Edward sensed that it wasn't honest and went straight to the heart of the matter. "I wrote that letter in the heat of my emotions. Forgive me it. Shortly after I handed it to Caleb, her ladyship summoned me and sent me to another parish to assist them. I had a lot of time to think during my absence and deeply regretted sending that."

I ducked my head. "Then why didn't you send word?"

"I wanted to do this in person. When I returned I found you had left with her ladyship. I kept thinking how you said that it was your mother who kept you away from Am Meer. All those years I thought you stopped visiting because I became a vicar. Did you even know?"

I kicked a pebble on the walk. "I had no idea you'd taken orders."

"When did you first learn of it?"

"That morning you called."

He gave a disbelieving laugh—one touched with annoyance, yet mingled with relief. "Well, that explains your look of fury. No wonder you acted so . . . And here I thought . . ." He trailed off, apparently deciding against telling me that part.

For several minutes only the rustle of leaves filled the air.

"When you stopped visiting Am Meer, I kept hoping you'd forgive me for changing our plans. So all that time, you still considered us betrothed? Did you not wonder at my long silence?"

Bewildered, I met his gaze, realizing he had not been the one to send those coded messages that had been tucked into the letters that came from Am Meer.

Shrieks of Elizabeth's laughter carried through the gloaming, followed by Henry's shouts.

I shut my eyes, seeing the full picture. Not only had Henry and Elizabeth hidden Edward's ordination from me, but they themselves had added those snippets to Elizabeth's letters. No wonder I received so many oak leaves. Edward would have been more original.

My vision blurred as I realized how much we'd lost over a simple misunderstanding. I have found that those who try to shield us from the truth, regardless of the reason, end up doing the greatest harm. Truth alone sets you free, not lies and omissions.

Edward's brows drew together with a look of concern, and I realized I had not yet answered his question. I tightened my shawl. "There was no silence. Henry and Elizabeth must have taken it upon themselves to make it look like you were sending mementos."

Tendons rose along Edward's neck as he jerked his head in the direction of their voices. I saw his Adam's apple rise above his cravat as he swallowed to control his anger. But when he returned to me, pain lined his face.

"So when you arrived at Am Meer," he finally said, "you were still of the mind-set we were engaged, while I thought you despised me, but were visiting because your mother had died and you had nowhere else to go."

"You could have come by and spoken with me."

"I was trying to make matters easier for you by staying clear of Am Meer." He shoved his hands in his pockets. "Then, when you wrote and spoke of your grief and asked if I would consent to join you when you dined with her ladyship . . ." His cheek dimpled. "I couldn't sleep or eat for two days, I was so excited. I had a chance to redeem myself, to explain."

I folded my arms yet closer to my body, saying nothing, feeling every imaginable emotion. No reaction, I thought, was my best choice. Yet despite my decision, I felt a rushing desire to cry. That same thawing feeling I felt the night Nancy polished my shoes returned, only in far greater measure—like a great sheet of ice shifting on a lake, its rifle shot shattering the calm winter silence, riving apart the shores. I'd survived my father's drunken rages, Mama's death, and months of bone-chilling isolation by mentally clinging to the happy ending I believed I'd have with Edward. Until that moment, I'd shunned the worst of my heartache—needing to survive.

But now the pain suddenly rose up, seizing me. It was safe to cry. It had been real.

My devastation and sorrow were perhaps most acute at that moment. For until then, I scoffed at those who claimed they were conflicted in love. Secretly, I judged them as being shallow or trite. Furthermore, I deemed them woefully mistaken. It wasn't possible, I thought, for anyone who'd found her Edward to be in such a dilemma. The fact that one was torn meant she'd not found her true soul mate.

Yet here I was, caught in just such a way. While my feelings for Mr. Macy were still burgeoning, I was betrothed to him—and I didn't regret it. In a matter of days, he'd gained entrance to the same level and position in my heart that Edward had held for so many years.

"I'm here now," Edward said after a few minutes of walking. "I'd like to make amends and start anew. I have been puzzling over our dilemma of faith. Do I have your promise you'll hear me out until the very end?"

I frowned. Church and my lack of religious beliefs were about to enter our conversation. "You know I will. When have I ever not?"

Despite the seriousness of our situation, his eyes crinkled with mirth. "Oh, I don't know. I seem to recall a few conversations you left rather abruptly."

I shifted my arm, which was tucked beneath his.

Grinning, he looked askance at me. "Now that I think of it, I ought to require a promise that you'll not pitch an apple at my head if my idea doesn't suit you."

Suddenly, it was just us again, and I gave an odd-sounding laugh, the kind that relieves stress. I buried my face against his shoulder, giggling at the horrible memory. I'd only meant to demonstrate how frustrated I was with his teasing. I'd no intention of actually hitting him. The apple, however, intended otherwise. It struck him square in the eye. He had cursed, kicking a nearby tree. From above, a second apple fell atop his head with a sickening thud. While Henry and Elizabeth roared with laughter, I'd turned and fled.

"Are you finished yet?" Edward asked with mock annoyance as my giggles continued.

My own merriment sounded strange to my ears. It had been ages since I'd laughed, yet my laughter was contaminated.

Edward must have noticed its tremulous tones, for he stopped and drew me into his arms. "Come to think of it, I'm not sure I recall your apologizing for that yet. I walked around with an eye swollen shut for nearly a fortnight, unable to give a satisfactory reason for it."

I allowed myself to be pulled close. As my forehead came to rest against the starched white collar fastened about his neck, tears wet my cheeks. There was room for both. I still fit. While the clerical mark wasn't comfortable, but stiff and unyielding, I could tolerate it.

Looking up proved to be my undoing. The weak light made his face appear hale and darkened his flaxen curls. The rapture of his gaze caught my breath. How was it, I wondered, that I had become engaged to Mr. Macy?

Without thought, against all rationale, I rose on my tiptoes, tilting my lips to Edward's.

No other invitation was needed. He cupped my face with rough, calloused hands and kissed my forehead, cheeks, and eyes. I buried my fingers in his hair, allowing his hands to slide to my waist.

In such moments, there is only a sensation of falling, a sense of warmth. There is only eternity, stretching in both directions.

It was Edward who broke the embrace, his body tense as he disentangled from my arms.

Panting, I followed the direction of his gaze.

Rooke and Mr. Forrester observed us a short distance away. Their hard eyes glittered.

Mr. Forrester opened his mouth to speak, but before he could say a word, Rooke gripped his arm, and with a low oath, nodded toward Eastbourne. With a violent shake of his arm, Mr. Forrester threw off Rooke, but trudged toward the estate. Twice, he looked over his shoulder and sent stabbing looks of hatred at me.

As Rooke retreated, I covered my mouth. My knees felt so weak, they started to buckle.

"Never mind them," Edward said, supporting my elbow. "They have no knowledge of our betrothal. However, if that tall one looks back one more time, I shall take it upon myself to teach him manners."

Twenty

CONDENSATION CLUNG to my gown as we entered Eastbourne. My steps felt weighted as we shed the gloom of night. *No Catherine Howard,* I thought, condemning myself as I eyed the shining marble. Yet here I had acted just as foolish, without even Lady Rochford to blame.

My hands were so clammy, I couldn't manage the simple clasp on Mrs. Windham's shawl.

"Here." Edward stepped before me and unhooked the shawl. It snagged on his calloused palm as he slid it from my shoulders. I must have looked as shaken as I felt, for he then wrapped his warm hands around mine. "There's no need to feel guilty because of those two."

"Might I remind you of the time?" Reynolds's crisp tone preceded his stepping out from a shadowed corner.

I was so startled, I jumped. Feeling like a child caught with her finger in the sugar bowl, I faced him, feeling my face flush.

Reynolds's blue eyes met mine with a glint of disapproval, but I detected no sign that he'd heard the worst yet. "As it stands, there's scarcely enough time to dress before dinner."

Flustered, I moved my hands behind my back, but Edward placed a hand on my shoulder and drew me to him, then handed Reynolds my shawl. "I am poor and have no need to pretend otherwise. What say you, Julia? Shall we go as we are?"

I forced a smile, praying Reynolds would understand.

His silver brows rose. "If it is your whim, Miss Elliston, to dine as a pauper, it is none of my business. If I may be excused."

Inside the dining room, hundreds of candles flickered within the sparkling chandeliers. Their light spilled onto the table below so that its snowy linens were the color of honey. Mr. Macy had remembered that I read the language of flowers, for bridal roses and lilacs were tucked inside a bed of holly amassed on the center of the table. The fragrance of spiced wine filled the air, and I turned and found one of the sideboards held thick crystal goblets surrounding a steaming pitcher.

I detached myself from Edward. It was clear to me what was happening. Despite what Reynolds had witnessed, he was still following Mr. Macy's instruction—to oversee my stay, to woo his future bride. Even from a distance, Mr. Macy was tending my needs, pampering me, and sending notes with hidden messages, while I trampled on his grace and kindness.

The sharp crack of Lady Foxmore's walking stick ended my brooding. Ostrich feathers bobbed from her headdress as she entered. She studied us a moment, then declared, "Well, boy, you've managed better than I thought. Had I wagered money, I'd have predicted you would have waned, not our Miss Elliston."

Edward bowed, acknowledging her statement but not taking the bait to ask why.

I tightened my fist over my stomach, trying to look indifferent, though I knew I failed.

Lady Foxmore eyed me, giving a low chuckle, then hobbled into the room. To my astonishment, Edward did not offer to assist her, but rather crossed his hands behind his back, making it clear he would not be of service.

"When you were a boy, Edward," she rasped, struggling to walk, "you climbed the highest tree in my orchard and fell when the bough couldn't support your weight. I had hoped you'd learned your lesson in picking the wrong apple."

"That was Henry."

Lady Foxmore pulled herself up to her full height. "Then learn from your brother. I have a personal investment in the child. I'll not tolerate your interference. Am I clear?"

Edward turned toward her with a smile. "Henry claimed it the best apple he'd ever eaten, worth breaking a leg over as well."

Lady Foxmore gave a raspy laugh as she returned to hobbling toward the table. "And you were fool enough to believe him?"

Edward bowed. "I believe anything snatched from your care is a deed well done."

The challenging looks they exchanged went far deeper than my situation.

Their animosity was thick.

Whatever it was that Edward silently accused her of, it changed her disposition. No longer did her eyes sparkle. Rather she became venomous. Leaning on her walking stick, she hobbled to the table.

Mrs. Windham crashed into the room, nearly upsetting the drink tray. Her gaze darted about the room. "Where's Elizabeth?" Her voice quavered.

Edward looked to me, but I shook my head. I'd not seen them after their escapade in the leaves.

Edward gave a slight cough. "We last saw them by the labyrinth."

Lady Foxmore rubbed her forehead. "Tell me your brother did not take her in."

"The labyrinth?" Mrs. Windham fluttered to the window, though the maze lay on the other side of the house.

"Come, sit." Edward ushered her from the window. "Henry shall tend her."

"Yes, I daresay he shall." Lady Foxmore's rings glittered in the candlelight as she placed her hands on the table. "Your parents best hope they find their way out before dawn, lest Edith demand an engagement."

Mrs. Windham perked her head. "Is it a very complex maze?"

"I know not," Edward said.

"You are my witness." Mrs. Windham fluttered her lace at him. "See how my hand trembles." She exhibited her hand and purposefully shook it. "You may be called on to testify if they do not come out soon."

"Yes, yes, come on." Edward urged her to the table.

Mr. Forrester and Rooke entered together; neither looked particularly pleased. Mr. Forrester sneered, catching sight of me, then went straight to Edward and grabbed his arm. "Sit with me. I need to talk to you."

Edward frowned at his lack of manners, but after a second, acquiesced. I watched, helpless, as they took seats together. Eyeing me with displeasure, Rooke took the empty chair next to me.

That evening, Mr. Forrester turned his nose at every course, choosing instead to question Edward. What he searched for, I couldn't guess. He queried Edward's heritage, schooling, theology, vocation, why he chose church over law, and so on. Every time he nodded approval to one of Edward's answers, he'd reword it, as though trying to unearth inconsistencies.

"I forgot to inquire, Edward," Lady Foxmore said as the topic turned toward the new laws regarding tithe, "did you ever manage to collect from Robert White?"

Edward paused and looked down, his hand tightening over his spoon. "Yes, of sorts."

"Tell me you refused the sow. You know I do not want that filthy swine."

A faint tinge of red crept up Edward's neck. "You know he lacks the monies—"

"Then I want a new tenant in his stead, one who pays his corn rent."

"With a new babe?" Edward met Lady Foxmore with vengeance. "You'd evict him before winter? You know his leg crippled him, not to mention the untimely frost."

Lady Foxmore looked smug as she folded her hands on the table. "I could perhaps be persuaded to bargain." With a smile, she gave me a slight nod. "I take the swine in trade, you return home. Tonight."

Edward's face remained like stone, but his chest heaved.

"Oh no, not Robbie's swine!" Mrs. Windham wrinkled her nose. "You must not accept that one. For I have it on the best authority last month he fed it moldy oats, and the thing had dysentery for weeks. I should not think it would taste good. There would scarcely be any cracklings, besides. Now if you want a good pig—"

"I am reminded—" Edward's voice was terse—"Robert did manage to pay using his meadow silver. You shall have your precious money."

Lady Foxmore's eyes grew excited. "Honestly. How on earth do you plan to cover for them all, especially with the newly appointed tithe commissioners demanding full records? What of Mrs. Beaton and her chickens? And Harley Crumbwell's elderberry wine? Not to mention those pitiful cottagers near your parents' house with their six birdlike mouths? Are you going to tell me *all* my tenants have paid *in full*? Go home, Edward. If you won't leave for your own good, do it for theirs."

Edward's hand fisted, but he said nothing.

Lady Foxmore circled the rim of her wineglass with her finger. "Yes, consider carefully between that child and your flock. For I swear to you, every night you spend beneath this roof, one family loses my philanthropy."

I sat speechless. Though part of me longed to rise up and decry her underhanded tactics, the other part of me knew that the best possible outcome would be for Edward to go home. It had been a mistake to admit him to Eastbourne in the first place.

Edward slid his eyes to me, as if weighing the matter.

Mr. Forrester scoffed, digging his hand through the nut dish. "Allow me to be of service, if you're talking about that piece of work." He popped nuts into his mouth, gesturing toward me.

Edward darkened. "Mind your tone, sir."

"That girl—" Mr. Forrester ignored him, crunching between words—"is trifling with your affections. Do not allow her to befool you. She is an unchaste coquette—"

Edward flew to his feet and grabbed Mr. Forrester by the collar, choking off the remainder of the statement, then dragged him from the room before anyone else could react.

For the length of five seconds, anger and shock circulated through me, while Lady Foxmore tilted back her head and laughed, clapping her hands.

For the only time in memory, Rooke allowed something to come between him and his dinner. He caught my wrist as I jumped from my chair. "No. Leave Forrester to Macy."

"Hurry!" Lady Foxmore wiped her eyes, calling to the footmen. "Bring the child something stronger than claret. Brandy, I should imagine, by this point."

⌁

"Such a thing would never have happened in my day." Mrs. Windham collapsed onto a tufted chair, waving a fan over her face. "Indeed, I should like the opportunity to contend with him now. Unchaste coquette! Did he corner you in some dark hall and make advances, which you spurned, Julia? There are some who will do that—ruin your reputation in their anger. Indeed, if he wished to court you, he should have come to me. I would have cordially welcomed him, though I shall do no such thing now. No, indeed. No matter what his fortune."

I fingered my lace cuffs, saying nothing.

Edward rose from the desk-like table, poured coffee from the nearby service, and handed it to Mrs. Windham. "Taste it. Is it hot?"

His attempt to quiet her failed, for she bustled her skirt, looking at me. "I hope you slapped him when he kissed you. Such an ill-bred man. Coquette, indeed. As if you've ever dallied with anyone's affections."

I stared at my hands. Guilt dampened any outrage I may have otherwise felt. All I wanted was Mr. Macy's return. Somehow, I knew he could set this all right. Edward gave a frustrated sigh before reseating himself behind the pile of books and sermon notes.

"You're going about it all wrong," Lady Foxmore said to him. Then, with eyelids half-closed, she turned to Mrs. Windham. "The temperature seems to be falling. Let us hope Elizabeth's constitution is strong. I knew a girl who died in similar circumstances."

Mrs. Windham touched her lips, turning to the window.

"There," Lady Foxmore said to Edward. "Now we shall have calm."

Edward threw down his pen. "I promise, Henry will properly care for her." He rested his eyes on me, seemingly disturbed in his thoughts.

"Just where exactly is Miss Windham?" Rooke looked up from where he sat on the hearthstone cleaning his pipe.

"In the labyrinth with Mr. Auburn," Lady Foxmore said.

He laid a sooty rag next to his brandy. "What the Jupiter are they doing in there?"

Lady Foxmore arched her eyebrows. "Exactly what you're assuming."

"They're lost!" Edward glared at her, but she only shrugged and sipped her coffee.

Rooke scowled. "There's a promise of rain in the air, if not sleet. Go, fetch them." When we all stared, he stood. "Are all of you honestly that helpless?" He grabbed his jacket slung over a chair and shoved his arms through the sleeves. He looked at me. "Stay in this room. I'll return in a moment."

He swept from the room, swearing as he buttoned his coat.

Lady Foxmore's gaze followed his retreating form. "Of all the uncouth people. We can all sleep better if that one never finds his way out again."

"Why. What's wrong with him?" Mrs. Windham asked.

Lady Foxmore set her coffee aside. "Chance has a ghastly habit of finding and befriending vagrants. I am told he picked that one off the streets of London. Rumor has it he was acquitted of thuggery on a mere technicality, although—"

Mrs. Windham dropped the teacup in her hands.

"Nonsense." Edward placed a paperweight over his notes. "There's been more than enough gossip tonight. We'll not cast down a man on rumor." With a grimace, he rose, then cast himself on the settee I occupied.

For several minutes I picked at my lace cuff. All I wanted was for the evening to end so I could retreat to my own room.

"Is Mrs. Windham correct?" Edward eventually said in a low, angry voice. "Did that man attempt to kiss you? Is that why he glared when he found us, and why he said that during dinner?"

My stomach sickened, a mingling of fear and guilt. I shook my head.

His left hand gathered into a fist. "Has anyone else here tried to kiss you?"

It is no pleasant sensation to feel yourself pale. Cold tingling begins at your scalp and prickles its way down to the pit of your stomach.

Thankfully the door clicked open and Henry entered hand in hand with Elizabeth, followed by Rooke. Henry's jacket cloaked Elizabeth's shoulders. Her damp hair lay limp, but her cheeks were rosy as she clutched the coat for warmth.

"I have been most abominably used!" Mrs. Windham

tottered to her feet, tears instantly in her eyes. "Henry, I shall not tolerate such behavior from you. You have ruined my only daughter, ruined her virtue and her only chances of securing herself a good marriage."

"Mama, hush." Elizabeth pulled the coat tighter, her eyes mischievous.

Henry laid a hand on her shoulder and woodenly said, "Please, accept my apology—"

"No, indeed I shall not!" Mrs. Windham's mouth screwed before her voice pitched to a shriek. "The only apology I'll accept is an engagement. You've kept her out the entire night." Her eyes fluttered, full of tears. "And without a chaperone."

Lady Foxmore glowered at the clock. "It's scarcely after nine, Edith. And for my part, I swear never to breathe a word of it."

"Edward!" Mrs. Windham's shrill shout in our direction caused us both to jump. "You must write your father about this outrage this very minute."

I watched as Henry gave Elizabeth a grin on the sly, telling me they had planned for this all along. I crossed my arms over my stomach, praying this wasn't their plan to ensure their future together.

Mrs. Windham stretched her hands in a plea to Edward. "You must insist he do his duty to my Elizabeth and force Henry to wed her."

For a moment, Edward appeared ready to refuse, but after studying his brother, he gave a tight-lipped nod and rose.

To my surprise, Rooke immediately filled his vacant seat. Using the light emanating from the whale-oil lamp, he scraped the inside of his pipe bowl with a penknife. "Just remember Macy runs a very tight ship." He indicated Edward with a nod.

I felt my throat thicken. "Must Mr. Macy learn about it?"

Rooke laughed. "You've a better chance keeping a draft from your house during a gale storm. Makes little difference whether I say anything or not. Mark my words, Macy'll know within ten minutes of being home. I get the feeling summat bigger is behind the scenes in your case." He screwed the mouthpiece back in and tapped the pipe in his palm. "So, for what it's worth, leave the vicar be. I happen to like him."

He left the seat as abruptly as he'd taken it.

From the corner, Mrs. Windham stopped her hysterical weeping long enough to correct Edward's spelling while he attempted to write a letter with three people instructing him all at the same time on what to say.

I wiped the residue that had landed on my dress, as apprehension danced along my nerves. A glance in Edward's direction, as Henry, Elizabeth, and Mrs. Windham argued over word choice, was enough to smite my conscience. Rooke was right. Something bigger was happening, and the longer I kept Edward in the dark, the more endangered everyone would become. For there was no doubt Henry and Elizabeth would feel duty bound too. They didn't deserve to find themselves dealing with someone as dangerous as my guardian.

I stood, overwrought.

Edward noticed and sheathed the pen in the inkwell. "Julia?"

Desperate to escape without being questioned, I squeezed the layers of my dress through a tiny space between chairs, in an attempt to reach the door before Edward did. I wanted time alone to think. Edward wended his way to the door, then placed his arm before it, preventing my leaving. "What did that man just say to you, to make you afraid?"

"Afraid?"

Annoyance flickered over his face. "Do not deny it. I encounter that expression every time I pay an unexpected visit to a cottager who has stopped attending church. What did he say?"

I gave a slight shake of my head.

"Something is happening here." Edward's voice lowered. "I don't pretend to understand what—"

"Were I you, Edward—" Lady Foxmore lowered her teacup as

she interrupted—"I would focus my energies on leaving before midnight. For I was not in jest over what I spoke during dinner."

Edward's mouth hardened.

Survival exists deep within each of us, though often at great cost to our soul. I steadied my breathing, imbibing my own pain. The last twenty-four hours had been pure folly, and I knew it. It was time to end this.

"Go home, Edward." I placed my hand on his arm. "This was a mistake. You shouldn't have come."

Instead of the barb I intended, Edward studied me with a keen look. "I know you, Juls. You can't lie to me. Are you going to stand there and say you have no desire to try to find a solution?"

I met his eyes with the coldest look I could muster. "You forget, I have. Her ladyship is finding me a husband."

Intensity marked his features, an expression that promised he'd brook no rival. But then, with the air of one willing himself to calm, he placed a hand on his hip and studied me. Dissatisfaction sculpted his features.

"How do I know," he asked Lady Foxmore, looking over his shoulder, "that if I leave tonight, you'll not change your mind about rents again? If this is going to become a card you play every time we disagree, I'd rather call your bluff now."

She laughed. "I have little need to bluff, but so you have it, I give you my sworn word."

"Yes, yes," Mrs. Windham added. "It is the very thing! Take the letter to your father in person and tell him I am near fainting. You must convince him of his duty to amend this situation immediately!"

The muffled jingle of coins sounded from Edward's pocket as he checked his funds. Once more he turned toward me, but I refused to meet his eye. I knew him. The jut of his jaw told me he wasn't leaving.

"Henry," he said in a quiet voice, "will you see me out?"

Henry's entire body swelled like a bullfrog's, but Elizabeth redirected him with a whispered word. Henry frowned at whatever she said, but then after studying Edward a moment, joined him.

I stepped aside, allowing the brothers to pass. Once they turned the corner, I shut the door and sagged against the wall and covered my mouth to hide my sob.

Reynolds stepped from a dark corner, his face soft.

I hastily wiped my eyes and straightened. "I—I didn't see you. Were you there the entire time?"

"I was waiting for you." His tone was sympathetic as he offered his arm. "Are you ready for bed?"

Reading his offer for a truce, I took his arm.

"Was he a former suitor, then?" Reynolds asked gently.

"Yes." My voice came out thick. "Once I thought I would marry him."

"Ah." Reynolds gave my hand a pat before he removed a candle from a wall sconce. A ring of light illuminated the passage we threaded.

A few silent minutes slipped by before I gained the ability to ask, "How good a friend is Rooke to Mr. Macy?"

Reynolds shot me a chiding look. "I never inquire about Mr. Macy's guests. Nor do I comment on them."

"Oh." My disappointment echoed through the stone hall.

He smiled. "Neither do I comment on former suitors, though I imagine Mr. Macy will have his own way of learning what passed between the two of you. Your chambers, Miss Elliston." He opened my door.

Alone, I stripped off my dress and wrapped myself in bed, curling my fingers into the downy pillow. Rooke's statement continued to unsettle me. Of course, I realized, Mr. Macy kept his household under surveillance. He had enemies. I had been childish and naive. Why had I instructed Reynolds to allow Edward to come in at all?

Why couldn't I have foreseen that it served no purpose except to further hurt us?

I turned on my stomach, appalled that I'd allowed matters to go so far. It was one thing to allow Mr. Macy to assume risk by marrying me—but quite another to pull those I loved most into the intrigue.

Twenty-One

"WAKE, MISS! Please wake." Nancy's frantic shaking pulled me from my slumber. Beneath her freckles, her face was pale. Sun streamed through her red hair, which was still unbound.

I propped myself on my elbows. "What?"

"That servant." She panted for breath. "He telled everyone that thou is sharing Mr. Macy's bed."

"Wait, wait." I clutched the sheet, sitting. "What?"

"Mr. Forrester's manservant. Before breakfast he announced to th' staff that thou were spending thy nights in Macy's bed."

"Are you certain that's what he said?"

"I heard it with me own ears."

I rubbed my fingers over my forehead, nausea souring my stomach. The mantel clock marked an hour before breakfast. My various thoughts channelled into a stream of agreement. I needed to be the first to breakfast in order to defend myself.

"Hurry, dress me." I motioned her to move out of my way. While Nancy gathered my things, I paced. The hardest thing to reconcile was the fact I *had* been spending my nights with Mr. Macy. Impossible to rectify.

Nancy wasted no time. With deft fingers she buttoned, tucked, and smoothed my gown. My world felt shaken, but the steady way she twisted and pinned my hair in place gave me a measure of surety.

To my relief, Reynolds waited outside my door. He bowed. "Did you sleep well?"

I closed my door, but my fingers shook too much to lock it. He obliged.

"Reynolds," I said as he pocketed his key, "there seems to be a rumor circulating amongst the servants."

"Ah, so you heard." He tucked my arm under his with a pat. "Act natural. If it's mentioned, which I highly doubt, act bothered that your time was wasted."

Somehow, I hadn't anticipated that advice. "How did the rumor start?"

"Mr. Forrester's manservant."

"How did he know?"

"Know what, Miss Elliston?" He cocked his head toward me. "Unless Mr. Macy reminds me of something I forgot, as his personal valet, I'm with him every night. A most ridiculous notion if you ask me."

His response was so unexpected, I held my peace as he guided me.

Near the pillared hall, I asked, "Did Reverend Auburn leave last night?"

Reynolds did not betray even a flicker of emotion. "Yes, just before midnight." It was at least one gain. Edward wouldn't be on hand when the scandal broke. I dismissed Reynolds with a nod, lest our being seen together confirm the reports.

Footmen stood in the breakfast chamber polishing silver and rubbing flannel over the crystal goblets. The way they ceased their banter upon spotting me in the doorway served to confirm my belief they'd heard the rumor. I backed into the hall.

Away from their view, I leaned against one of the cold pillars and slowly slid down until I was seated. The scent of soaplees and turpentine rose from the recently scrubbed floor. I buried my eyes in the palms of my hands.

I drew my knees to my chest, then folded my arms over them, ignoring the strain on my stays. I tried to imagine what Mama would tell me to do, but could only hear her telling me to be safe. It was what she said every time I left the house.

Well, she'd have her wish. I would be safe. Hopefully Mr. Macy might never learn about Edward's visit. With such a scandal circulating, I couldn't risk Mr. Macy not marrying me now.

"Julia?"

I opened my eyes to find Elizabeth bending over me. Concern etched her brow as she stooped and placed her cool fingers in mine.

"Will you promise me something?" I asked.

Her fingers gripped mine. "Yes. What?"

It was hard to speak through the tears. "Do not be angry with me today, no matter what you learn about me, or I won't be able to bear it."

"Learn what, dearest?"

Tears blurred my vision but I could not tell her.

"I swear," Elizabeth said, tightening her fingers over mine. "I'll keep Henry in line too. And you know Edward will stand by you."

I blinked. "Edward?"

Her eyes sparkled. "Goose! Her ladyship only said he couldn't spend a night under *this* roof. So he and Henry sought out a local clergyman, and Edward spent the night in his barn."

I felt horrified. "And what about that pig farmer, Robbie . . . Robbie . . ."

"White," Elizabeth finished for me. "He doesn't breed pigs,

thank goodness! Mama is right. I wouldn't want his swine on my table either." Then seeing my expression, she grinned. "Don't worry about her ladyship. The fact that Edward bested her will only delight, not anger her. You disapprove, but wait; you'll see I'm right."

Before I could argue, a pair of booted feet raced nearby. A tousled-looking Henry turned the corner. He greeted Elizabeth with a grin, then scowled at me, pulling on his coat. "No more of your nonsense," he ordered. "I've kept Edward from learning about your flirtation with . . ." He jerked his head, indicating our surroundings, as if Mr. Macy and Eastbourne were one. He lowered his head and his tone. "I've about had it with Edward and you! Don't expect me to keep interfering on your behalf."

He turned and stomped through the entrance hall and outdoors before I could retort. I allowed my head to sink against the pillar. "Elizabeth, can you stop him?"

Frowning, she crossed her arms.

I gave a laugh, realizing the folly of my request. Nothing stopped Henry once he set his mind to something. Elizabeth was equally mulish. Together they were tempestuous; few could stand against them.

Edward and I had always managed, though.

I rubbed my temples. There was no utilizing his help. Besides the fact that I suspected his intentions aligned with theirs, I needed to place distance between us today. When Mr. Macy learned about the kiss we'd shared, at the very least I wanted to be able to show him that I had spurned all contact with Edward afterwards.

I shut my eyes, realizing that day would be amongst the hardest in my life. Besides balancing a scandal that could make me unmarriageable against one of Henry and Elizabeth's mad schemes, I needed to break my own heart by ending my relationship with Edward, firmly enough so he'd go home, but hopefully not so harshly that he'd hate me for the rest of his life—for that I could not bear.

My thoughts came in quick succession, and I made my resolutions just as quickly, so that by the time I held out my hands, asking for Elizabeth to help pull me to my feet, scarcely a few seconds had passed.

"You know as well as I do," she answered my question about stopping Henry, "it's for your own good." She laced her fingers in mine. "Come on, let's go eat some breakfast. I'll tell you about the labyrinth. You and Edward really ought to explore it."

Elizabeth paid the footmen no mind as we entered the breakfast chamber and chatted about how Henry had wooed her last night, as if they weren't present.

I helped myself to a cup of coffee and then, stirring it, considered the staff. Daily, I realized, they witnessed our secret lives, guessed at the ghosts in our past, and carried the ability to ruin us with a single word.

The thought was a stunning one. My entire life I'd lamented the fact we only had Sarah and, before my father's death, doddering old Luther. Elizabeth and I used to roll our eyes whenever Henry and Edward would meet us beneath the ancient oak and inform us we were lucky as they stripped off shoes, stockings, stiff frock coats and then ran their fingers through their hair that had been waxed in place, in order to play.

I scraped the bottom of my cup with my spoon, for the first time understanding them. Whereas Elizabeth and I had always been free to run from Am Meer barefoot—as neither Sarah nor Hannah could manage more than a short dash—the boys had to face an army of face-washings, spoonfuls of cod-liver oil, and lectures not to ruin their polished shoes before breaking their way outdoors.

As the footmen continued to set up the buffet, pretending not to hear Elizabeth laughing over the bad verse Henry had written and shared, I considered the idea that if I wed Mr. Macy my every movement would be known, especially given the way he managed his household.

I set my spoon aside, ignoring the tightening in my stomach. With a sip of coffee, I realized Edward and I were switching places. He'd finally broken free—throwing off all conventions in this mad attempt to live out his ideals, which I knew from my father's example would make him a pariah. Whereas I had left that horrible circle and now moved toward the glittering lights of society—but at the cost of confinement.

I wasn't certain if Edward would like his new circumstances, but I was determined to enjoy mine. That was, if I survived the obstacles until Macy returned.

⁓

By midmorning, I had harrowed my heart over forty times. Edward could not approach me without receiving a bedamning glare. He could not please, could say nothing which I did not spurn. I accepted none of his tender ministrations. If he offered a chair, I went to the window. If he fixed a plate, I wrinkled my nose. If he asked to speak, I expressed my need of solitude. Each time he lifted his eyes with hurt confusion, anguish lit through me. But I could not relent. I suppose some might wonder why I did not just confess my full situation to my friends, rather than driving them away with my actions. But I knew them well enough to know if they learned about my guardian, they'd act, exposing themselves to this person's wrath. The very fact they were intruding upon my trip to find a husband proved it.

Better, I reasoned, to inflict pain on them myself, if in the end it meant sparing them greater hurt.

By early afternoon, Edward ceased trying to engage my attention and retreated from the room. Only Elizabeth seemed to suspect I was breaking my own heart. With hurt confusion she watched me as I continued to play faro with her and Lady Foxmore, as if not caring.

Glaring at me, Henry stalked after Edward. Only then did the hurt rise, and did my throat tighten. Could I really just force Edward to leave me alone by ignoring him? My remaining bets slipped from my fingers onto the green felt.

"If you'll excuse me," I whispered to Lady Foxmore, unable to stand it.

"Sit, child." She nodded to the ace I'd backed after drawing the queen as the loser. "You're only doing what you must. 'Tis good practice for you. He shouldn't even be here, and we both know it. Besides, I suspect you have a rather good reason for remaining."

Elizabeth paused, her heavy breathing emphasizing her collarbones. It seemed to me she was praying I would shove aside all bets and seek out Edward. Instead, I sank against my chair and waited for her to draw the next card.

"King wins," Lady Foxmore said. "Place your new bets."

I slid four halfpence back to the ace and looked toward the window, where grey clouds gathered.

Throughout that long day, I carefully studied each face, servants' and masters', trying to gauge who heard the gossip. I wasn't sure how much longer I could operate under such strain and continue to act normal. The thought makes me laugh now, for I've since learned the immense amount of stress beneath which the elite not only endure, but also perform.

⌇

Maintaining our nightly custom, we met in the drawing room after dinner. Though she appeared weary of my company, I affixed myself to Elizabeth, resting my head on her shoulder, watching the rain rattle the windows.

Henry recited poetry to Elizabeth, thankfully from a book, while Edward worked on a sermon, his eye travelling between the clock and myself, as if to ensure a midnight departure. More than once, he tried to meet my eye, but I refused.

Rooke remained nearby, pretending to nap, but I had the impression he was keeping watch.

It was well past ten when Reynolds entered. My body felt thick as honey as sleepiness weighted my limbs.

He returned a book to the shelf and collected dishes. I shot him a questioning look. He retrieved a carved wooden box with a dome lid and opened it, revealing cigars. He tucked the item under his arm and left the room.

Understanding his meaning, I sat straight. Mr. Macy had returned.

I jumped from my seat and started toward the door.

"My heavens, Julia, are you suddenly ill?" Mrs. Windham asked.

"I'm fine. It's only that I am tired and can hardly keep my eyes open." I dipped to her ladyship, then left the chamber before Edward could rise from his chair, and hurried after Reynolds.

Twenty-Two

REYNOLDS TAPPED the study door and then stepped away. It burst open and Mr. Macy's eyes roamed the darkness until they settled on me. With a nod to Reynolds, he pulled me inside and slammed the door. The first night we'd met, he'd been Morpheus, the god of dreams, once more giving his bad tidings to mortals. That night, however, he could have passed for a highwayman. Muddy boots lay in a corner. A dripping, but expensive, frock coat was slung over the desk chair. His evening shirt was soaked and clung to his chest.

He pulled me close and buried his face in my neck. His unshaven chin rasped my skin. Breathing in the scent of my hair, he enclosed me in his arms. "Julia."

Though a chill clung to his wet clothing, permeating my dress, I sank against him, relieved. My grief over Edward had created a niggling fear that I might no longer feel an attraction toward Mr. Macy. That fear was vain.

He was as captivating as ever, and as his mouth met mine, all shyness left. Here I found the assurance I sought. I grasped his sleeves as his arms slid around my waist; then, grateful he wasn't angry, I ran fingers through his dripping hair.

"What's this?" He chuckled, withdrawing. His forelock fell over his eye, adding to his appeal. "No blushes?" He kissed my shoulder, moving downwards. "How far will you allow my advances?"

Here, I pushed away.

"Somehow, I doubted you had lost your demureness that easily. No retreating." But with a chuckle, he released and went to the fire where he added a log. "I've thought of little else except you for these three days. I rode hours ahead of John, nearly breaking my neck. You can't possibly fathom my pleasure in seeing you."

Unable to ascertain whether he'd learned Edward was here or not, I moved to the couch and stiffly sat on its arm.

He turned, studying me. "Most men fear that if they wed, their wives will never cease their chatter." He joined me, then pulled me from my perch into his lap. "I've yet to hear a word from you."

Having no desire to speak, I curled against him.

He accepted me and twirled a lock of my hair between his fingers. "I wish I had more leisure, dearest, but I've never allowed this much time to pass before learning what happened during my absence." With a swift movement, he pushed me from his lap and faced me. "Let's set a new precedent. I'll hear from you first."

I settled against the couch. So he didn't know about Edward. I drew up my feet and searched the room as though an answer would be written on the wall for me.

"Uh-oh. There's a guilty look if I've ever seen one." He reached for the brandy behind us. "Did you break something, darling? You needn't feel alarmed."

A sickening feeling rushed over my stomach as I imagined him hearing of Edward's and my kiss.

He dropped the glass stopper back in the bottle's neck. "What? What happened?"

"Well . . ." I entwined my fingers, knowing the only way out of this mess was straight through it. "First, Edward arrived—"

"Edward? I know scores of Edwards. Be specific."

"I meant Reverend Auburn."

He elevated his eyebrows. "Ahh. Look at me, dear." When I did, he sank against the corner of the couch with a ghost of a smile, laying his arm over the top. "Is this Adelia's vicar, the one you might have met *once or twice*?"

Though I wanted to nod to confirm it, my body felt frozen.

"Never mind. Everything about your countenance confirms it. Well, how did he take the news of our attachment?"

I dropped my gaze and studied the pattern on the rug as intently as I'd ever studied a carpet.

"You know, dearest, you are a very easy read. Tell me?"

I swallowed. "I think he came because of me."

He inclined forward and raised my chin with his finger. "No, there's more than that lurking in your expression. What else?"

Wildly, I sought for something half-truthful. "Well . . . I allowed him to kiss me."

He leaned until his head rested on my shoulder, then shook it with a laugh. "Sweetheart, that's cruel. You only give him false hope."

"You're not upset?"

"No, darling." He tangled his fingers in my hair. "Though I'm less inclined to leave you unattended in the future. With all your blushes, you didn't strike me as one to take amusement in sporting with someone's affections, much less a vicar." He backed away and considered me. "Was I selfish with my timing? Perhaps you need to break a heart or two in order to be content in marriage."

I started to explain, but he drew my wrist to his lips and kissed it.

"No words are necessary. Disappoint him gently if you wish, but not so gently that it never gets accomplished. If you lose control of the situation, alert me and I'll assist. Did anything else happen?"

I tried not to look as amazed as I felt. Was that all he was going to say? Yet I knew Rooke might still make a nuisance. He'd witnessed it and knew it had been far more than an innocent peck. "Rooke took it upon himself to follow me today, to keep watch."

"Rooke?" Macy poured a brandy. "I'll speak with him. Is that all, then?"

I shook my head at how easily my duplicity had been skipped over. "Mr. Forrester insulted me."

Mr. Macy rose menacingly. "He did what?"

"He told Edward I was—" I blushed in light of our previous conversation—"I was an unchaste coquette."

His lips thinned. "I swear to you, he'll rue the slur. Who stood up for you?"

I dropped my eyes. "Edward. I believe he boxed him, for his lip is injured. Edward wouldn't allow him to rejoin our party until he apologized."

"Does that mean Robert actually apologized?" Mr. Macy sounded incredulous as he dropped into his seat. "How long did it take?"

I shrugged. "A full day." During dinner that evening, Forrester had entered with a cut and swollen lip. With his back turned toward Edward, he bowed to me, his face sneering. When he'd apologized, he looked over his shoulder and asked if Edward was satisfied.

Mr. Macy laughed and shook his head. "Well, at least you prey on deserving men. I'll take care of Robert, too, though I'll spare you the details. Is there anything else?"

"Yes." I felt sullen and looked away.

"Is there no end? I'm beginning to wish for a wife who will talk my ear off, have it out at once. What else, darling?"

"The servants are gossiping about us spending our nights together."

He appeared too stunned to speak.

"Except they're not saying we're meeting. . . . They're saying . . ." I closed my eyes, too flustered to say the word *bed*, uncertain what other terms there were for it. "Mr. Forrester's servant started the rumor."

"How the devil does he know?"

I shivered at the fury in Mr. Macy's voice. "Could it have been Reynolds—?"

"No, that much I am certain of." He pulled a cheroot from the box. Near the hearth, he lit it. Several minutes passed as he considered the news.

"Should I leave, perhaps?" I finally asked, feeling lost.

He broke from his thoughts and tossed his cigar into the fire. "Did you think I'd forgotten you?" He smiled. "Sorry, dearest. It's good I returned. It seems there's a deficiency in my household." He walked over and pulled me to my feet. "I think it's best to end our time early. I need to talk to others. I'm taking you to your room. Do not leave it tonight, under any circumstances."

"Allow me to remain with you instead?"

His face softened. "No, you wouldn't enjoy my methods of shaking my household. I need to learn how far the rumor has circulated. If it reached the village, your guard—" He stopped when I clutched him, then ushered me to the door. "Turn from fear. You are under my care."

With a firm grip and swift pace, he escorted me to my chamber. Inside my room, he closed every shutter and checked the locks on every casement, then inspected the hinges on my door.

"There's no need for alarm," he said when he'd finished, wiping his hands. "I'm just not taking any chances." At the door, he kissed me with a succession of small kisses until I'd almost forgotten he was leaving. "Later," he promised. Using his own key, he locked me inside.

I sat on the hearth and allowed the cool, hard stones to sober me from the inebriety his touch had caused. I hugged myself, amazed that everything had just been solved. My full confidence in Mr. Macy was restored and unwavering.

He was enthralling not only because of his uncommon appearance, but because he held his fate in his own hands. It is only upon meeting a man who rules his own destiny that one realizes how rare such men are.

Mr. Macy was my first and last.

How shall mankind, which is lost and stumbling, not be drawn to someone who knows his path? Who understands his way, without questions but with decisiveness?

What had I to fear from my guardian? Or from my future?

My only dread now was the moment when Edward would learn of our betrothal. The notion of writing him a letter appealed to me; that way I could word it exactly right. But my earlier anxiety left me feeling spent, and though I doubted I could sleep, my head felt too weighted to write. I stretched out over the grouping of furniture nearest the fire and closed my eyes, listening to the fire hiss and pop.

~

I awoke in a cold sweat on the settee, still tormented by clinging visions of Mama. Reynolds was bending over the grate with his back toward me, holding a poker. I threw my feet over the settee, feeling ill.

"Where's Macy?"

I must have startled Reynolds, for he bumped his head on the mantel. He rubbed the spot. "In his study."

I rose on unsteady feet. "Take me to him."

"It's not a good time. Besides, he made it very clear he is not—"

"Take me, now. I'm ordering you." I sniffled back a tear, feeling frantic for comfort.

His stiffened his shoulders and assumed a bland look. "Very well, miss."

Though we saw no one, the estate pulsated with life. Footsteps echoed through corridors, and light glimmered from various passages. Reynolds ignored them all, holding his candle high as we passed. When we reached the study, he tugged on his waistcoat. "I hope you appreciate this." He gave the door two sound raps.

"I said no disturbances!" The door flew open. Mr. Macy glared at Reynolds with clenched teeth, then spotted me. "Julia, what in the world?"

"She insisted on being led to you, sir."

Mr. Macy studied me. "Sweetheart?"

I prayed he'd see my need. If I tried to speak of my nightmares, I'd weep.

He held out an arm, and I threw myself at him. "Reynolds, you may leave. Thank you for bringing her." He drew me close, and I stifled a sob. He placed a comforting arm around me. "Did I frighten you by checking your room? Forgive me."

Tears wet his shirt as I burrowed deeper into his chest. "No. I had nightmares about Mama's murder."

The sharp crack of glass caused me to jump. Mr. Greenham stood near the fire, observing us. Atop the mantel, brandy sloshed in its tumbler.

"Problem, John?" Mr. Macy stopped stroking my hair and wiped my cheeks.

Mr. Greenham bridled, but like a defiant schoolboy ignoring his tutor, he crossed his arms and refused to answer.

"John, I am in no mood for this."

Mr. Greenham snapped up his head. "Do not speak to me of moods. You swore! You swore not to do this."

"And what is that?"

"Nightmares? Really. She's known you less than a week. We agreed—" his voice rose a pitch—"*we agreed* nothing more than her current danger. Then Forrester. Have you any idea the condition I found her in the other morning? Do you even care? And now, on top of everything else, a scandal!"

"Ah, so the truth emerges. Do you really think it's better to allow her to continue believing her mother committed suicide?" Mr. Macy's iron-sharp tone made my flesh tingle. "If we're going to tiptoe around frightening her, why not just state her guardian bears a slight grudge? Or better yet, we fear the air in Scotland might disagree with her constitution. That certainly is less alarming."

Mr. Greenham glared, flexing his jaw.

"Or perhaps you think you'd make a better protector. Is this your bid to take full charge of the situation?"

Darkness filled the hollows of Mr. Greenham's eyes as they shifted away.

"So I thought." Mr. Macy crossed the chamber and opened the door. "Unless you're willing to risk your estate and your family by taking her in and hiding her, do not question my methods. She's hazarding as much as we are, and I'll not leave her ignorant of matters."

Mr. Greenham picked up his glass and smashed it against the wall. Chest heaving, he stormed past us and slammed the door, causing papers on the desk to sail to the floor.

Wide-eyed, I grasped Mr. Macy's sleeve.

"John and I always have disagreements." Mr. Macy's tone was light as he tucked my hair behind my ear. He frowned at the streak of brandy running down the wall. "Though he'll lament this one if glass embeds itself in your foot. Come, sweetheart, let me return you to your room. I'll sit with you until you sleep."

Knowing I'd never sleep after that display, I shook my head.

He gave a rueful chuckle. "Stay, then, if you insist."

On the couch, he cradled me in his arms. The blaze cast a scarlet hue over the room. In the quivering light, Mr. Macy's face was half-veiled. He fixed his gaze on the flames in such a way that I knew his thoughts fell into dark places I was barred from following. Like Mr. Greenham, his ruminations seemed tangled with disturbing thoughts, only Mr. Macy seemed to have mastered them. For his features were determined rather than morose.

Yet I sensed his melancholy as I settled against his chest, for every so often he'd pull me closer and press his face into my hair, though I did not believe he remembered I was present.

It seemed to me that he needed me far more than anyone else ever would. I encircled his neck with my arms, wanting to communicate that he owned my love and his cryptic past didn't matter, but grew shy when his gaze focused on me.

He nodded as though he read my thoughts. "Go to sleep, sweetheart. I shouldn't even be indulging your night fears." His eyes centered on the fire, but he gathered me near again.

I closed my eyes, listening to the steady beat of his heart, until my breathing grew deeper and I surrendered to sleep.

Twenty-Three

THE INSISTENT CHURRING of a warbler woke me. I turned on my stomach and stretched, catching sight of a note and a small key ring atop the bedside table. I groaned with the realization Mr. Macy must have carried me back to my room and tucked me into bed. I threw off my covers and then opened the draperies. During the night, the storm had passed, leaving a washed landscape. I pushed open the shutters and allowed the breath of morning to clean the room. Taking a seat on the bed, I slid a hatpin under the wax seal.

> *Darling,*
> *I had planned on spending the day with you. None-theless, several things require my attention. To help keep you amused, here are your own keys. I shall join the party at dinner. Know my thoughts remain with you.*
>
> *Chance*

I smiled, reading his name. It was hard to imagine feeling intimate enough to call him Chance, even after we were wed.

Mr. Macy suited him better. I tucked the note in my stationery box, then studied the keys. They were labelled, and along with each of the formal rooms, he'd included a key to the hothouse.

Nancy banged on my door, calling my name. I closed the stationery box and locked the lid, considering it strange how some mornings Reynolds let her in and other mornings she knocked.

"Hold on," I said, trying to locate my key as she kept banging.

"I gat news. Hurry."

I frowned, doubting I wanted to hear it.

The moment the bolt unlocked, she rushed through the door and nearly toppled me. "He's gone!"

"Who is?"

"Who does thou think? That manservant. Th' one who started th' rumor. Naught one word has been spoken about how thou spends thy nights. In fact, not a one of his servants are even talking."

"Has Mr. Forrester likewise departed?"

"Nay." Her nose creased, looking over my wrinkled dress, but she started on the first button. "He's been up before dawn searching for his servant."

I stood still, trying to absorb the news, then smiled. What it must have been like for that servant to have wakened to an angry Mr. Macy or Reynolds and been escorted from the grounds in the storm. I shook my arms free of the sleeves and stepped from the dress. I felt no pity for the manservant, nor his master.

"What was Mr. Forrester doing awake before dawn to notice that his servant had left?"

Nancy shrugged and unfurled a petticoat. "Master Henry is leavin' this morn too. He gats a letter from home. Miss Lizbeth 'tis upset."

This was news! I pulled the strap of my petticoat over my shoulder, mentally calculating that it was too soon for Henry to have been summoned home because of the escapade involving the labyrinth. I hoped, for Elizabeth's sake, it didn't involve the engagement Mr. Forrester had spoken about my first night here.

I watched Nancy ready my outfit. It was glorious to have her back to her normal chatter. In one night, Mr. Macy had managed to sweep away my ruination. Even Nancy, who knew I'd spent my nights with him, seemed to have dismissed the report with the vanishing of its source.

❦

"Eh, ain't that a relief." Nancy poked her head out the door, looking at the empty spot where Reynolds usually stood. She shifted the basket of laundry on her hip, following me into the hall. "He was flitting 'bout th' house last night, waking servants one by one to gan somewheres. I wouldn't mind learnin' what he said to 'em."

"One should think you'd be glad to have been spared a lecture," I said.

"Aye, but I can't help wondering how they managed to stop th' gossip and all."

I locked the door and pocketed my key, considering Nancy as she retreated. I'd speak to Mr. Macy about employing her as soon as we were wed.

I found the passages I needed to take, but before reaching the main hall, I spotted Rooke leaning against the wall.

"There you are," he said. "Are you always late?"

"Are you waiting for me?"

"When Macy returns and finds a rival, I don't care to have him asking me why I didn't prevent it."

It was my turn to act coy. Clasping my hands behind my back, I shrugged as if I thought him melodramatic. "Mr. Macy didn't appear concerned about it last night."

Rooke pushed himself upright and unfolded his arms with a smug smile. "So you are spending your nights with him?"

My blush betrayed me before I could deny it.

"I daresay that's none of your business, Rooke," Mr. Macy said behind me. His steady arm enclosed my shoulders, and he tugged me against him, pressing his cheek against my head. "Did you find my note, sweetheart?"

Still embarrassed, I nodded.

"Good. I'll see you at dinner, then." His tone growled as he addressed Rooke. "I'd better not hear another complaint about your badgering her. Understood?"

Rooke opened his mouth and started to protest but thought better of it and gave a stiff nod.

"Tonight, then." Mr. Macy kissed my temple, then turned out of sight.

For a half second, we both stood there, then with a triumphant smirk, I left, allowing my skirts to swish around the corner.

When I entered the breakfast room, only two gentlemen were present: Edward and Mr. Greenham. Both stood in greeting, but Edward stepped forward.

Wordlessly, he offered his arm, then waited to see if I'd take it.

I dropped my gaze, touched that despite my treatment of him yesterday, he'd not given up hope. When I accepted his arm, the relief filling his body was unmistakable.

Edward pulled out a chair, placing me between himself and Mr. Greenham, who watched us without displaying emotion.

"Did you sleep well?" Edward set tea and an assortment of foods before me.

I hated the ardor for him that swelled within me. "Very well, thank you." Then, recalling that Mr. Greenham knew of my nightmares, I added, "Most of the night, anyway."

"I'm heartened to see someone concerned over Miss Elliston," Mr. Greenham said in a bored tone, adding cream to his coffee. "I've noted that no one else seems to inquire after her well-being. I rather believe you are good for her, Reverend." He met my eyes with the same bizarre gaze he so often fixed upon me.

Frustrated, I shook my head. I understood so many looks and gestures, but not the meaning behind that pensive gaze.

Edward wrapped his fingers around his cup and leaned back, considering Mr. Greenham. After a thoughtful pause, he asked, "Sir, what can you tell me about that Rooke fellow?"

"Rooke?" Mr. Greenham wrinkled his nose with disgust. "What of him?"

Edward frowned. "I don't know exactly, only he said something to Miss Elliston the other night, and ever since then, her behavior has been—"

"Rooke is no one." Mr. Greenham's statement had finality about it. As though the door on all further conversation about Rooke was closed, then locked.

Alarmed, I shifted my gaze to the uneaten novelties spread over the table. Edward knew, I realized. Unlike Elizabeth or Henry, he'd pieced together that something was wrong. Very wrong. And he was mentally trying to work out the mystery.

Though I was withholding information, Edward wasn't. He turned from Mr. Greenham, perhaps sensing the pointlessness of asking about Rooke, and faced me. "You should know," he said, "Henry's leaving today."

"Yes." I tore off a corner of a currant bun, hoping to keep Edward on this topic. "My lady's maid informed me this morning."

Edward cocked his head, looking pleased. "Don't tell me that Sarah's here too!"

I nearly smiled, recalling our shared terror of my nursemaid. Mama tended to take long afternoon naps while at Am Meer, leaving Sarah in charge. She suspected us too. Every time I slipped away, she hunted for hours until she found me—always hoping that just once she could catch me with Edward and prove her suspicion. It was all we could do to keep a step ahead of her. Once, she'd found me beneath the ancient oak and lambasted me for a quarter hour, trying to make me confess I'd not been alone. Had she only looked up, she'd have seen Edward grinning down from the branch above her.

"No." I shunned the thought of Sarah. "My guardian sent her away."

"Your *what*?"

Shock tingled through me as I lifted my gaze to Edward and realized my mistake. A look of satisfaction played over Mr. Greenham's features as he sipped his brew.

Edward leaned forward. "You have a guardian? Whom?"

I widened my eyes, then made a point to stare at Mr. Greenham. Edward must have understood I had no desire to speak with him present, for he moved his hands to his hips in an impatient gesture.

He sat for a few seconds, frowning, then declared, "Well, if Sarah's not here, are you and Elizabeth sharing Hannah?"

I bit the insides of my cheeks, hating that I had to admit my fortunes had fallen so low as to needing to borrow a servant from the Windhams. "If you must know," I said in a clipped tone, "I have a girl named Nancy now."

"Nancy!" Edward exclaimed.

I felt a blush spread through my cheeks. Of course he knew Nancy. His parish was small.

Then he laughed outright, but to my surprise he clapped his hands with delight. "Good for you, Juls! I never imagined her in the role of a lady's maid, but I'm glad you're managing to keep her out of the workhouse."

I didn't deserve his praise, for in truth, I had yet to ask Nancy about her past. Yet at the same time, I suddenly wished I were the kind of person Edward believed me to be, making me wonder if I once had been.

"What say you to a walk in the garden after breakfast?" Edward asked.

"I think taking air should be very beneficial to Miss Elliston," said Mr. Greenham. "Why wait for breakfast to end? It's apparent you two have no appetite but much to talk about."

Once more I gave him a disbelieving stare while Edward gave me a hopeful look.

I sighed, knowing there would never be a good time to disillusion him.

Nodding, I pushed my plate away. With luck, when Henry left later today, Edward would go with him.

~~~

That morning Edward and I remained on the gravel pathways, as the ground was soft. The morning breeze scattered a few leaves that floated lazily before us. Walking over the path, hearing the robins' shrill chirps, I found it difficult to believe my circumstances. I fingered the cashmere fringe of my shawl, viewing Eastbourne. Windows shimmered with sunlight and I wondered which one Mr. Macy was behind.

In order to explain my difficulty, it is necessary to recount a story about Edward from his youth. The summer he was fifteen, on a particularly hot afternoon in July, his tutor lost patience with the brothers' continual inattention. As punishment, he instructed them to write an additional essay about the virtues of the Corn Laws before dismissal. Henry scrawled out an essay, repeating his teacher's views, and hurried outdoors. But Edward outright refused on the grounds he didn't agree there were virtues to be found in the laws.

His stubbornness incensed his tutor, who first beat the back of Edward's hand with a ruler until scarlet welts swelled over its surface. Then he threatened that Edward would not leave the schoolroom until the assignment was complete. Edward spent the night in the dark, sitting at his desk, refusing to write.

When I learned of the incident, I was incensed. Any fool could see that external pressure would never work with Edward. Either one changed his mind, or one changed the context. Had the tutor simply rephrased the assignment—say, asked for an essay on *what the gentry considered* the virtues of the Corn Laws— Edward would have turned it in within an hour.

Thus, as we strolled through Mr. Macy's garden, I endeavored to disappoint Edward in a manner he would accept. Only what could I say? I was forbidden to speak of my guardian and Mama's murder, although letting Edward learn that I was in danger would not help me to attain my goal. I couldn't live with myself if I allowed Edward to believe another man had replaced him in my affections.

Eventually, I came to the conclusion that I needed to utilize our most poignant difference—God.

While I mulled on how to approach the topic, Edward dug his hands deep into his pockets, then stated, "You're not going to like what I have to say. But will you at least promise to hear my plan and give it a full day's thought before rejecting it?"

"Depends," I answered.

"On what?"

Like a wrestler assuming his position before a fight, I fixed my gaze on the horizon. "It depends upon whether your plan involves church or God. If it does, I can tell you right now, I reject it."

"And if I want to discuss it anyway?" His tone darkened.

"Then our walk is over. And so are we."

Edward caught my arm, stopping me. "Every time God is mentioned, you take flight. Well, you're going to finish at least one of these conversations. And it's this one."

I tried to twist from his grip. "What? You're going to force me!"

"Yes. I've waited two days to say this, and you're going to listen."

"No, I won't! Because no matter what you say, it won't change my mind."

"What are you so frightened of, Julia? If your beliefs are as well-founded as you pretend, then why do you fear this discussion? Are you afraid I'll prove my point? Are you afraid to discover that maybe your father didn't know everything?"

I felt my chin jut as I stared up at him, breathing heavily. He knew, *he knew* I hated it when people treated my beliefs and my father's as one. Our fight began in earnest.

Edward lifted an eyebrow, as if sensing my change.

"No." I ground out each word, wrangling to be free. "Because even if your God is real, then he's earned my disobedience. Hear me, Edward. I will never follow him!"

Edward's face twisted in disbelief.

"So prove him if you can!" I yanked my arm as hard as I could. "But mark my words, even if you do, it makes no difference."

"But that's not fair, Julia. You're not even considering me!"

"Fair?" I yelled, not caring who heard us. "You want fair? Well, guess what? So do I! But I'm never going to have it! You haven't an inkling of what I've endured! And I won't meet the demands of a God who idly watched it happen. How dare you argue fairness with me! Were you considering me when you took your vows?"

His jaw tight, Edward shifted his gaze from me, drawing deep breaths as if willing himself to remain calm.

This rankled me further. In the past, he would have argued back without censoring himself. Unable to wrench my hand free, I stomped on his foot in a childish display of temper. Shocked, Edward finally released me. Picking up my skirts, I marched as fast as my legs could carry me.

Edward was immediately at my side, gravel crunching beneath his boots. "You're going to hear me out."

In response, I picked up my skirts and hied faster toward Eastbourne.

By the time I reached the pathways near the estate, I couldn't breathe. Nancy had done her job too well. My stays were so tight, I could scarcely gasp for air. I placed a hand on my side, where a cramp had started.

Edward, who'd kept pace, took my elbow and directed me to a bench, tangled amidst ivy. "Sit."

Unable to do anything else, I obeyed, narrowing my eyes.

"It's not my fault you've matured and graduated to stays," he said, reading my silent accusation. He removed his handkerchief and handed it to me. "What are we doing?" Edward asked quietly.

I bunched the handkerchief beneath my nose. "There's just so much that you don't know. So much I can't tell you."

"Then listen, for a change." Edward crouched and sat on the heels of his boots. "Last year, Father gave Henry some land as an early inheritance. There's an abandoned house on it, which Henry gave to me after you arrived at Am Meer." His cheeks reddened. "It isn't much, Julia. You know my prospects are not what they once were when my ambition was law. Nonetheless, I know I am doing what God called me to do. I know I've made the right choices."

"You should have discussed with me or at least made me aware."

"How, Juls? How?"

I scowled, wanting to argue but knowing there was nothing to say. Because it was improper for Edward to write me, Elizabeth had always been our only possible contact.

"I don't blame you for disliking that I've become a vicar. But don't, in your anger, chain yourself to the likes of Lady Foxmore. She is a wandering star and will lead you to ruin. Have I ever steered you wrong? Have I ever placed care of myself above care of you?"

Edward paused, as if to give me space to consider it. My throat thickened, for to memory, he never had.

"Here's what I propose. Allow me to fix up Henry's house. Stay in my parish. Remain with those of us who love you. I know that you'll flourish given time with Henry, Elizabeth, and me every day. My parish is filled with good people. They'll accept you. Yes, I have to insist you attend church. But it will be me who is your vicar—not that man. Not the man who did that to your family. One year. That's all I'm asking. If at the end of that year, you want to continue, then fine; nothing will change. I have always been willing to wait for you. If you want to leave, then I'll do my best to help you find a good situation." His hands tightened over mine. "If you find that you can join the church and we can marry, and you still want me, then we'll wed."

Doubtlessly I looked as though my soul were made of stone, for I simply stared, betraying no emotion. But within, it felt as if my heart had stopped. Of course Edward had found a solution, given the little knowledge of my situation that he had. I easily envisioned his plan—the carefree days he wanted to gift me with. I pictured an entire year in his parish. Attending harvest parties, dinners, and balls. Helping Elizabeth and Mrs. Windham can their goods for winter. Lazy winter afternoons, knitting before the fire while Henry read aloud. Long, rambling walks with Edward in the countryside, talking over his sermons. Strawberry picnics in white gowns, playing croquet over Am Meer's lawn.

The images became so real, I grew heartsick. All at once, I knew I couldn't do this to him. I wouldn't do this to him. If he was still fighting for me, I would fight for him too.

My hands felt clammy as I met his gaze and whispered, "There isn't time."

Edward's eyes sharpened.

I wanted to say that there wasn't hope for us unless he ran away with me, right then. But even those words died on my tongue. Edward's posture warned me of that impossibility. In order to act, Edward needed to understand the context. And that I was sworn to keep secret. But I was not under oath to keep prior knowledge from Edward.

"I'm scheduled to leave for Scotland," I said quietly.

He joined me on the bench, his brow furrowed.

I proceeded to tell him about my guardian and the strange

requirements he placed on me, and that ultimately I'd been ordered to Scotland.

"I'm not going," I told him. "Hear me. I will do whatever it takes, even marrying her ladyship's choice for me."

Edward's expression upon hearing those words is hard to describe. He half closed his eyes and stared blankly at the ground. "Well," he said, "that certainly changes the plan a bit, doesn't it?"

"What plan, Edward? We have no plan."

"It's only three years until you attain the status of *femme sole*," he said, plowing forward. "One of my father's cousins lives in Scotland. Surely I could visit him at least once during that time."

I shook my head, feeling as though my life were an aberrant waltz, playing minor chords when major chords were needed. My inability to wield Edward in conversations like I used to frustrated me. Bluntness, I decided, would serve me better.

I glanced around, catching only the pleasant sound of voices that carried on the breeze in the stable yard and the coo of doves as they searched for feed. At least as far as I could tell, no one was overhearing us.

I leaned forward, feeling like a traitress to Mr. Macy, then whispered, "You don't understand. I am not going to Scotland. That's why I hired Lady Foxmore. Either you marry me now or it will never happen."

Edward's brows pulled together as he also inclined. "Or," he said, "I take the third option. I wait for God's timing. Why are you suddenly whispering? And why this sudden rush to marry? There's something more that you're not telling me, Julia. It's as obvious as the nose on your face."

Wide-eyed, I stared. I felt much as a scullery maid would, having snuck upstairs in the dead of night only to find the housekeeper waiting there in the dark with hands on hips.

"Something fearful is perching on your soul," Edward continued, rising. "And what I don't understand is why you're attempting to handle it by managing me. Well, it won't work. I won't make decisions that affect the rest of our lives based on partial information. What's really happening here, Juls?"

Had someone poured a pitcher of water from a frozen stream over my head, I could not have felt more chilled. I stood.

Edward planted his hands on his hips as I took a stumbling step backwards. My legs were so weak I felt like I was wading through a pool of honey that suctioned my feet to the ground.

I am not sure how matters would have ended. But at that precise moment, the sound of a horseman screaming at his mount rent the air. Mr. Forrester rode into view, his frothing horse tearing up the turf. Mud-covered, Mr. Forrester slid from the mount in the stable yard. Like a man intoxicated, he screamed curses at the stablemen while he beat a bucket of feed with his whip. When one of the stable hands rushed out, Mr. Forrester lashed him with his riding crop.

Edward bolted toward them, and Henry Auburn appeared from the side of the stable. A struggle ensued, during which Mr. Forrester noted me, watching, stunned, a short distance away.

"You!" he screamed, pointing toward me.

Henry shoved his chest, forcing him backwards a step or two, shouting, "You dare point at a lady, sir!"

Anguish and fury seared over Mr. Forrester's face. Using his entire body, he tried to pummel past Edward and Henry. "That . . . !" he screamed, losing energy when he couldn't break free of the Auburns. He started sobbing. "That is no lady! That is . . ." He sank to his knees. "Is no . . ."

Edward caught my eye, and with a jerk of his head indicated his desire for me to retreat indoors.

❧

A pale ghost, I slipped inside the library and then locked the door behind me. I checked and rechecked the lock before backing away, steadying my breath.

When I entered Eastbourne, I'd felt so panicked by Mr. Forrester's accusation that I spun in a circle twice, trying to determine which direction to take. I decided against one of the nearby common rooms left unlocked for our use, not wanting to risk meeting her ladyship or the Windhams. I likewise spurned heading toward my chambers, as Edward knew where they were located.

Luckily, I had my set of keys. Recalling that the largest and most ornate key belonged to the library, I had set off in search of it. Within a few minutes I made my way inside the vast chamber; its multiple entrances and central location helped me to find it quickly.

Inside, a fire invited me from the other end of the gallery. Fighting back tears, I crossed the room and climbed into an oversized chair that had been positioned at an angle to enjoy the hearth. I took up a camel-colored blanket that lay crumpled over the ottoman.

I was still stunned. The morning had not gone at all as I'd planned. Here I had thought I could manipulate Edward. But he'd not only called my bluff; he'd outright demanded I be truthful with him.

I drew my feet onto the oversized cushion, gathering the blanket against my chest. The scent of cigars and sandalwood did little to untangle my overwrought nerves. How could I have been so stupid as to complicate matters even further by asking Edward to elope with me? What would I have done if he'd said yes? Exposed him to my guardian's wrath?

I gave a hysterical laugh, half desiring to cry, as I imagined what Mr. Forrester might be saying to Henry and Edward at that very moment. Like a ninny, the moment I was accused, I'd fled.

"What a fool I am," I said to myself. "How will I ever be able to explain that away?"

"There's always a way, darling," Mr. Macy said from the corner behind me.

The blanket tangled in my feet as I sprang up from the chair. Mr. Macy reached and steadied me from behind, before I managed to kick it off.

"Sweetheart." He chuckled, then kissed my forehead. "It wasn't my intent to frighten you. Are you hurt?"

Heat rushed over my face. "You were there the entire time!"

"Well, I didn't just appear out of the air. I saw you were in no mood for disturbances." His voice comforted, even as he sounded amused. "Yet it would have been heartless to leave you alone, when you were so obviously disturbed. I thought it best to wait it out. Someday I hope you'll return the courtesy." He refreshed a half glass of brandy sitting out and handed me the tumbler. "Care to disclose what is so unexplainable?"

The guilt staining my soul now stained my cheeks. "Mr. Forrester just arrived in the stable yard and was . . . rather angry."

Mr. Macy grinned. "Yes, I rather imagined he would feel put out. What else?"

"When he turned his crop on one of the stable hands, Edward . . ." I froze, realizing I'd used his first name.

"Go on," Mr. Macy encouraged.

While Mr. Macy lit a cigarette, I told him about the scene Mr. Forrester had caused, and how I'd run away when he started accusing me. Mr. Macy frowned as he listened, but with a fluid movement stamped out his cig, disturbing the thin blue line of smoke that wavered from it.

His brow knit as he crushed the paper into the ash. "You've nothing to worry about. I guarantee you Robert was restrained from saying more after you'd left."

I studied him, wondering how he could be so certain. He reclined against the back of his seat and smiled. "Reynolds informed me you went walking with Reverend Auburn. How did that go? Better than yesterday?"

His forthrightness put me at ease. "No. He thinks I'm going to Scotland and wants to visit me there."

Mr. Macy's laughter was genuine. "No, that's scarcely better, is it, darling? Do you really think it wise to discuss the topic of your guardian with him? Are you certain he won't start poking around for answers?"

I looked away, realizing I hadn't considered that.

"Perhaps John's assessment is correct." Mr. Macy steepled his fingers, studying me a moment. "Maybe the sooner we amend this, the better. Besides, it's high time you had stability. Let's marry before this week closes. I daresay, I can afford time away. No business, I promise. We'll spend an entire month in my London home. Shop, theatre, opera, whatever you wish." He leaned forward and searched my face.

For a second, as I thought about Edward, I wanted to stall Mr. Macy, but instead I nodded acceptance of his plan.

"Can we steal away at night?" I asked. "Marry, then go to London? Let Reynolds see Ed—everyone out of Eastbourne. Please."

Mr. Macy cocked his head. "Don't you think that's rather unkind to Reverend Auburn?" Instead of sounding annoyed, his voice softened. "All right, if that is your wish. Though I hope you have better sense than to attempt something like that with me." He twisted the ring on his pinkie. "You do realize eloping with a hermit twice your age will cause a sensation. Are you ready to handle the gossip?"

To show indifference, I arched an eyebrow.

He laughed. "Yes, I believe you are. That's my girl. Would you like to spend the day with me? I have work that needs my concentration, but your presence would not disturb. Your novels haven't arrived, yet I should be able to locate something useful to read, though perhaps less interesting."

I desired to remain, but I sensed a reluctance behind the offer. Unwillingly, I shook my head. "No. Henry leaves this afternoon, and I should say good-bye to him."

He rose and offered a hand. He pulled me to him and kissed

along the side of my face. "I'll see you later tonight," he promised, whispering into my hair. When he stepped back, his eye
settled on a glass cabinet near us. "Here." He strode to it. "I have
something that ought to amuse you."

He unlocked the case and with both hands lifted a book. I
joined him, curious, then tried to hide disappointment, seeing
an engraving of Shakespeare on the front paper.

"The first folio of his works ever published." He handed it to
me. "It's priceless. Not even Reynolds is permitted to touch it."

I stood but placed my hands behind my back. "I fear tearing it."

"Small cost for keeping you amused." He extended it. "Take it."

I obliged, but once in my chambers I placed the folio on my
writing desk. Feeling tired enough to sleep, I did.

Henry left late that afternoon, when the front lawns were
dappled with shadows of branches flecking the lawn. Reynolds
alerted me in time to see Henry and his manservant leading saddled horses to where Mrs. Windham, Elizabeth, and
Edward waited to say good-bye. I strolled toward their grouping
as Henry whispered privately to Elizabeth, aware Edward was
keenly studying me.

Mrs. Windham wobbled and grabbed hold of my arm as I
approached. "These partings are too much to bear. Lend me
your arm. My strength is quite gone, I assure you. All these
comings and goings, indeed, are very disagreeable. 'Tis more
than a soul can bear."

"Here," Edward joined her other side and tried to catch my
attention. "Take my arm."

Mrs. Windham staggered against him. "My head spins, and
my heart is having such spasms every time I think upon dear
Henry's journey. Indeed, tonight I shall be worse. You promise
to comfort me, though I fear that shall be no easy task."

Smiling, Henry approached us.

"Oh, my dear boy!" Mrs. Windham flung against Henry with such force he nearly stumbled. "My dear, dear boy. You must take care not to fall from your horse and injure your head. Do not risk becoming chilled. If it rains, you must remain at an inn. If anything happens to you, Elizabeth and I would have no one except ourselves."

Henry cast his brother a weary look.

"Here, allow me to seat you, Mrs. Windham." Edward steered her toward a bench.

Within two strides, Henry crushed me in a hug, lifting me from my feet. "Fare thee well, Julia. I've done my part. Now all that's left is for you two to stop acting like children."

It was so *Henry* that I laughed, then hugged his neck tight, giving a sob.

"No crying, now. I'm only going home to pick up Devon and then to school."

"Take good care of Elizabeth," I replied in a choking manner as he set me down. "Or so help me—"

He gave me an odd look, but as he rarely understood Edward or me, he brushed off the statement. "You'd do better to warn her to take care of me."

With that, he laughed, then swung into his saddle. He took the reins from his manservant, instructing, "Take the main road. I'll meet you there." Then, clucking his tongue, he dug his knees into the steed and sprinted over the turf, his cape streaming behind him.

Horrified, I watched as he urged his horse toward an insurmountable wall. In a sylphlike movement, the horse sailed over the obstacle and disappeared under forlorn pines.

"Here—" Edward collected both Mrs. Windham and Elizabeth—"have no fear for Henry. Do you remember, Elizabeth, the time he took a counterfeit tumble in order to lose a bet?"

Elizabeth laughed, sounding weepy.

Edward tried to meet my eyes, but once more I shunned him.

"Well, thank the good heavens for Henry," Mrs. Windham continued, but then suddenly reached out and batted Elizabeth. "And to think, missy, of the frenzy you went into when you learned that we were going to visit Mr. Macy. Indeed, Elizabeth, had you followed my counsel, we could have been spared this entire trip. The very idea of such comings and goings for no reason at—"

"How quickly you change opinions, madam," Elizabeth said. "I seem to recall you were anxious to come and very keen to marry Julia to Mr. Greenham."

"Greenham?" Edward looked over his shoulder at me, confused.

"Such nonsense." Mrs. Windham looked up at the rustling ivy that covered the stonework. "Mr. Greenham is too tall to marry her, and I always said so. It was you who insisted and needled our way on this trip."

Elizabeth rolled her eyes at me.

Thankfully, when we entered the drawing room, Lady Foxmore sat writing correspondences. I was summoned with a wave to join her. She said nothing, but gave me a new stack of letters to place wafers upon.

⁓

Shades of evening darkened the landscape that night as I turned from the looking glass and peered outdoors. Clouds enshrouded the sky, dimming the stars and moon with their murky wisps.

I recall Nancy walking on her knees, tugging the petticoats under my green taffeta dress. The pains she took were astonishing. The first time I sat, I mused, the dress would crease and her labor would be ruined. Nonetheless, I turned to the looking glass, pleased with the glittering emeralds at my throat and in my hair. They emphasized my green eyes and called attention to my thick ebony braids, where jewelled combs held a bewitching style. I touched an earring, thinking it strange that Mama had never worn them.

"Nancy," I asked, "would you like to work for me?"

She finally stood. "As thy lady's maid?"

"Of course." I turned sideways and viewed the back of my dress. "I shall not live with the Windhams very long. I . . . I . . . might have to leave you first." I faced her and gave her my full trust. "I'm going to elope with Mr. Macy, but I shall send a servant to collect you during my honeymoon."

Joy flooded her features. "Think on!" She looked around my chambers. "Me, a lady's maid for the mistress of this house."

Reynolds's signature knock sounded on my door, and I placed a finger over my lips. "You mustn't tell a soul. Are you willing to work for me then?"

"Aye, but what about Reverend Auburn? Does he know?"

The wall of denial I'd carefully constructed during the day tumbled.

"What of him?" I smacked her hand as she went to adjust my sash. "He has nothing to offer me. No more talk. Open the door."

"Is Miss Elliston ready?" I heard Reynolds ask.

I cast a doubtful gaze at the darkening sky, but shook off my fears and joined Reynolds. His familiar face filled me with warmth.

"It's good to see you," I said. "I worried when you weren't outside my door this morning."

He tugged his white gloves tighter. "My apologies, Miss Elliston. There was a ghastly problem with the servants last night. I fear I overslept." Reynolds looked over my elaborate dress. "Will you wait here a moment?"

When I agreed, he bounded up the stairs with a youthfulness that surprised me.

"Shall I ga or stay?" Nancy asked.

"You're dismissed. Tomorrow we'll discuss the terms of your employment."

She curtsied and scampered down the hall. My thoughts turned to my own house. What would Mr. Macy choose to do with it? I also wondered if I could find Sarah. Surely Eastbourne could find something for an elderly servant to do.

Hearing footsteps, I turned to find Mr. Macy appraising me with a self-satisfied air. All day doubts had cobwebbed my mind, but like a maid with a broom, his presence cleared every one.

"Turn about," he ordered.

I complied but blushed.

As he sauntered down the last few steps, his gaze rambled over my body. "Reynolds spoke correctly. You do need a proper escort to dinner." He enfolded me in his arms. "Though my appetite is no longer for dinner." He nuzzled my neck, then glanced toward my chambers with such dissatisfaction that I drew in a sharp breath of fear. His mouth curved in a sardonic smile. "It seems the adage of a blushing bride on my wedding night shall come true for me." He circled my waist with his arm. "Come along, you. We'll resume the conversation later, with far better results, I daresay."

❧

Mr. Macy opened the doors and escorted me into the dining room as if I were the queen herself. Heads swivelled in our direction. Seeing the first course under way, I almost retreated, but Mr. Macy kept a firm grip on my elbow, forcing me to stand.

Lady Foxmore placed her spoon down with a knowing chuckle. "I say, this is quite a surprise."

"We . . . we . . ." Mrs. Windham stared, wide-eyed.

"We assumed you weren't joining dinner." Elizabeth squeezed her napkin. "And Julia, since you missed tea, we thought you had a headache."

Mr. Macy laughed and nodded to his footmen, who looked

more nervous than the party. "You did well to begin." He stepped away from me, holding my hand up. "It was just as well that I lost track of time. Look at the seraph I found wandering my halls, lost."

Mr. Forrester snorted.

Lady Foxmore's voice rang through the room. "You must have paid her some handsome compliments, Chance. You should have toned the adulation down. The child is positively crimson."

"Call her Miss Elliston," corrected Mr. Macy.

Edward, who had risen with the other gentlemen, now approached and removed my hand from Mr. Macy's. "It's ill-bred to make a spectacle of a lady."

"I am thoroughly rebuked." Mr. Macy bowed, then nodded permission for me to go with him. "Miss Elliston, please accept my apology."

Edward stiffly bowed, but after holding out my chair, he sat with fist still clenched. "Of all the men to find you alone. Did he say something improper?"

There was no doubt Edward would consider improper most of what Mr. Macy had whispered between kisses on the way to the dining room. I smoothed my skirt, feeling certain all eyes were on me.

"I'll address him tonight," Edward promised, glaring in Mr. Macy's direction.

I focused on the bowl of gingered-carrot soup placed before me, my stomach tightening.

"Where did you go after Henry left?" Edward asked.

Just looking at him, I found myself aching. "Lady Foxmore needed assistance."

Edward frowned, looking in her direction, but returned his focus to me. Quietly, he said, "I spent the afternoon in prayer, and I have a proposition."

I dipped the tip of my spoon into my soup, afraid to breathe.

"Go to Scotland, Juls. Let this be your first step of faith. Go with the belief that God will reveal himself to you there. Drop this nonsense about Lady Foxmore finding you a husband."

I eyed him, ready to argue that impossibility when Edward stunned me with "You won't go alone, either. I'm going with you. I'll lower my status and find work as a curate. If the church is overburdened there, then surely some great house nearby will have need of a valet or footman."

At first, I didn't think I had heard him correctly. I thought it one of those rare occasions when your mind twists what you've heard into something you've wished for, but when you clarify, you feel like a fool.

Yet the manner in which Edward met my eye told me I hadn't misheard him.

"I say," Lady Foxmore called. "What are you two being so secretive about? If your conversation is worth having, share it with the table. We lack on this end."

"We are speaking about God." Edward placed his hand along the back of my chair. "Perhaps from amongst all my parishioners, you ought to join us."

With a laugh, Mr. Macy turned from his conversation with Mr. Greenham. His eyes rested on Edward's hand, then shifted to face us. "I agree with Adelia. The conversation is dull. I've heard fascinating things about you, Vicar." He folded his hands on the table and leaned forward. "May I pose a few questions about your work?"

"You may."

Mr. Macy proceeded to ask about Edward's daily duties, drawing the questions repeatedly to the hours he worked and how it affected his social calendar. "It will help when you wed someone, will it not? Tell me, Edward—" Mr. Macy gave me a mischievous glance as he used Edward's first name—"What sort of requirements must your wife meet?"

I felt Edward stiffen. "Sir, I cannot see the point of your question."

"Yet I think you do." Mr. Macy began to slice a joint of roast beef with his knife. "Does not your religion teach not to undertake a task without counting the cost? Why are you dissembling it?"

Edward made no reply but stared.

"Your wife must be confirmed in the church; am I correct?"

Edward still made no reply.

"I imagine it must be trying to be a vicar's wife." Mr. Macy placed the cuts of meat on a platter for his footman to distribute. "Will your wife attend the sick? The curate's wife in this parish spends most days going between her duties at home and those who are ailing."

Silence.

"However, I commend the woman," continued Mr. Macy. "It's not easy to stand side by side with grief. She's always spending nights with women who've lost husband or child. I've been informed she's required to spend an hour a day reading Scripture, since women seek her out with questions they are too embarrassed to bring her husband."

Edward did not remove his eyes from the table.

"Adelia, this will interest you." Mr. Macy turned toward her. "Recently, the curate purchased his wife a new bonnet. The thing caused an uproar. Apparently, members of the church thought her vain." He laughed. "The poor woman isn't even allowed one luxury, lest she cause unrest amongst the congregation."

I signalled for my soup to be removed, too stressed to eat.

"I, for one," said Mr. Forrester in a wry voice, "wonder why you're so intimately acquainted with the details of the curate's wife."

Mr. Macy smirked in his direction. "Don't assume I'm entirely without religion, Robert."

Mr. Forrester waved his wineglass in my direction as if to

make a comment, but when he locked eyes with me, he choked. Red wine spewed from his mouth over the tablecloth. He coughed into his napkin, shoving his chair from the table. He stared at me with such a look of disbelief, I laid hold of Edward's arm.

Mr. Macy stood. "Something bothering you, Robert?"

Trembling, Mr. Forrester glanced at the door, then at Mr. Macy. "I'm leaving. Don't try to stop me." He reached into his waistcoat.

In unison, Mr. Greenham and Mr. Rooke rose.

Mr. Forrester pulled out a revolver with shaking hands and pointed it toward Mr. Macy, then glanced at me. "If anyone moves, I'll shoot."

Mr. Greenham pushed back his chair.

A gunshot rent the air. Edward dove under the table, pulling me with him. My ears rang from the sound of the shot, and the sharp scent of gun smoke filled the air. Clutching Edward, I watched muddy boots backing toward the door until Mr. Forrester himself came into view. When he reached the door, he opened it with his hand behind his back, then spun and pounded down the hall.

Footmen were the first to recover movement, and Mrs. Windham sound. Her wailing voice crowned the uproar of noises.

The tablecloth lifted, and Mr. Macy knelt into view. I sobbed with relief and stretched out my arms. He slid me toward him and enfolded me in his arms.

"I'm all right, sweetheart." He pressed the side of his head against mine. "Can you explain what just happened?"

"I—I don't know. He was looking at me, and . . . and then . . ."

Mr. Macy sighed, then craned his neck. "John, come," and when the gentleman arrived, "Forrester guessed and has gone to fetch her guardian."

"I told you—" began Mr. Greenham.

"Take everyone to the art room." Mr. Macy withdrew a key from his pocket. "Lock them inside. No one leaves until I say, understood?" He pulled me closer, his voice like one trying to calm a spooked horse. "Julia, shhh. I need you to gather your wits. I swear, nothing will harm you as long as I own breath."

I shook my head. We both knew that legally my guardian owned me. There was no course of action we could take.

"I'm not leaving!" Edward shouted behind me. "Get your hands off me."

I cringed, recalling his presence, then peeked in his direction.

He looked as though he'd been pierced, his face as white as chalk as he watched Mr. Macy cradle me. His eyes pleaded for answers.

I couldn't bear to look longer. Mr. Macy, however, stared with a calculating expression. "John, allow him to remain." Mr. Macy placed a hand on my head. "She'll need the protection he can offer. Send Reynolds to me as well. Quickly."

I looked toward the guests. With the help of the footmen, they were being ushered to the hall. Mrs. Windham must have finally fainted for the first time in her life. She clung to a servant, who kept putting smelling salts under her nose. I surveyed the room, looking at the place where Mr. Macy had stood, and saw how close he'd come to death. Mr. Forrester couldn't have missed by much. A chunk of plaster was missing from the damaged wall.

I lifted my head in amazement. How could Mr. Macy be so calm in the face of death?

"There you are," Mr. Macy said. "You're regaining color, which means you recover from shock easily. Good. This is going to be a trying night for you. Are you listening?"

I avoided looking in Edward's direction, where he now loomed above us.

"Give me your full trust tonight," Mr. Macy requested. "Obey everything, the moment I ask it. Understood?"

I nodded, too frightened to speak.

Reynolds entered, and Mr. Macy rose and strode across the room to him. Forsaken, I finally looked at Edward. He'd been waiting. His face was constricted with anger and pain.

"What's going on, Julia?" He knelt on one knee beside me. "Who is Mr. Macy to you?"

I buried my face in my hands for a second, with the mad idea that if I just stopped looking, none of this would be true. "He's protecting me from my guardian."

Edward glanced at Mr. Macy and shuddered. "No. Not that man." He placed a hand on my shoulder, and I felt anger and betrayal coursing through him. "Why did you not confide in me if you needed help?"

"I couldn't tell you." I looked toward Mr. Macy. "I was sworn by oath."

Mr. Macy finished with Reynolds and looked in our direction. Showing no emotion, he made his way back to us and extended his hands.

"Is my guardian coming here?" I asked, being pulled to my feet.

He wrapped me in his arms and kissed the crown of my head. "Yes. I believe so."

"Remove your hands from her," Edward demanded. "She may be naive enough to trust you, but I'm not."

"You lack understanding, Reverend Auburn." Mr. Macy said. There was something in his languid voice that soothed and assured. "It greatly pains me to make this request, but I fear you need to marry us tonight. I've obtained a special license."

I buried my face against Mr. Macy's chest. "No, not Edward. Not him."

"There isn't time to go to anyone else." Mr. Macy drew me close, speaking into my hair. "Your guardian lives in the house that crests the hill. He will arrive any moment."

Panic made it hard to breathe.

"I'm not marrying the two of you." Edward's voice filled with ridicule.

My world closed in with terror. I slid my arms around Mr. Macy's waist and clung to him. "Please, Edward. You must. I'm begging you."

"She's in grave danger," Mr. Macy said. "If you've ever loved her, then do what's right by her. She's confessed her flirting with you since the night of our engagement. I know you're not ready to hear this, but I love her. You're incapable of offering the protection she needs. Her guardian is a powerful—and dangerous—man."

"I'll not marry the woman I love to another man." Edward yanked me from Mr. Macy's grip and forced me to face him. "Nothing will induce me to marry you to him. You've scarcely been here a week. You have no knowledge of him, nor the woman who matched you to him. We're going to wait for your guardian and let come what may."

"Don't be a fool, Edward." Mr. Macy gathered my long curls to one side of my neck. "She's spent every night with me since her arrival. It would be to her great benefit to solemnize our union."

There was such a long silence, I finally dared to look at Edward. He stared at my neck with loathing, and I realized the fading marks had been exposed.

"Who is her guardian?" Edward took a seat, looking nauseated, and pressed the heel of his hand into his forehead. "I'm required to make certain she has permission to wed."

Mr. Macy moved me aside and went to the drink table. "He destroyed her family and seeks her life. He killed her mother." Mr. Macy poured brandy, which Edward accepted. "Reynolds is bringing the license. As you'll see, the archbishop granted us dispensation from the law. I know you care for her. I promise to make her a worthy husband."

"A man without honor cannot make a worthy husband, sir." Edward placed his drink aside. "The only reason I'm marrying you is to cover her shame. If she's with child, no one will be able to prove it was formed out of wedlock. Though God knows what sort of life I give her."

The misunderstanding was more than I could bear. "Edward—"

He silenced me with a look.

Mr. Macy likewise gave me a warning look. "Will you marry us now, then? Time is important."

Reynolds entered with a footman, holding a document. Mr. Macy pointed at Edward. "Give him the license."

My legs felt made of sand instead of flesh and bone. I sank into a chair while Edward perused the paper, surprised to find tears running down my cheeks.

"Get up!" Edward tossed the parchment on the table, then forced me to my feet. "Do not sit and weep. How dare you? It's my heart that's been trampled on, not yours." His voice lowered to a hiss. "Does your future husband know how far you allowed my advances?"

I cried harder.

"Just because you have lost interest in the girl—" Mr. Macy sauntered to my rescue and removed Edward's hand from my arm—"doesn't mean I have."

Edward glowered a moment longer. "Kneel. I want this over with."

Sailors say to capsize in arctic water is the worst of all deaths, for when one is plunged into the shocking temperatures he is immediately disoriented and breath is driven from his body. Icy fingers and limbs make it impossible to grasp wood or ropes, or even to climb aboard wreckage. Invisible needles pierce every part of the body, driving back all rationality, all sanity. The only hope of survival is for another to reach down and pluck one out from such a fate.

That night, as Mr. Macy pressed my hands between his, I felt as callous as a person sitting in a lifeboat watching another drown—for no one struggling in arctic water could have appeared more frantic than Edward.

His face was whiter than parchment as he worked to keep composure. "I require and charge you both that if either of you know any impediment as to why you should not be lawfully joined together in matrimony, do now confess it."

As Edward recited the vows to Mr. Macy, I studied Edward's face, wondering whether he would have refused to marry us if I had confessed everything to him. An intense desire to transfer my care from Mr. Macy to Edward overtook me.

"Wilt thou have this man—" Edward turned toward me—"to thy wedded husband, to live together after God's ordinances in the holy estate of matrimony? Wilt thou obey him; love, honor, and keep him in sickness and in health; and forsaking all others, keep thee only unto him, so long as ye both shall live?"

When I made no reply, Edward frowned. I prayed he understood my plea to give me another chance. His expression became haunted; then his features hardened.

Mr. Macy's hand tightened around mine.

"I will take this man," I whispered.

"Who gives this woman away in marriage?"

"I do, sir." Reynolds stepped forward and placed his hand on my shoulder.

Edward finished the ceremony without looking at me, then placed a hand over each of our heads. "Eternal God, send thy blessing upon this man and this woman, whom we bless in thy name; that, as Isaac and Rebecca lived faithfully together, so these persons may surely perform and keep the vow and covenant between them made—"

Mr. Macy shook Edward off and gathered me to his chest. "Reynolds, get the paperwork. I want it signed immediately."

Edward followed Reynolds and wrote the necessary information, then sat at the table with his head resting on his arms while the footman and Reynolds added their names.

Reynolds brought the inkwell to us, and Mr. Macy added his signature with a flourish, then pulled me to him when I avoided his gaze. "Sweetheart. There was no choice. I had to remove you from the legal care of your guardian."

My hand shook as I added my name. "Tell Edward, then. This is more than I can bear. He has to know."

Mr. Macy gave Edward a doubtful look. "I fear you don't know what you're requesting. He isn't going to take the news well." When I pleaded again, he nodded and rose, brushing his hands alongside his coat. "Edward, my wife refuses to rest unless I inform you that she's still a maiden."

Edward lifted his head. Every tendon in his neck rose as he pivoted his head in my direction. Then, like a fire moving from the kindling to the log, his eye blazed on Mr. Macy. He stood. Yet before he could advance, Mr. Forrester and six clamoring men bustled in. All wore tailcoats, one with a napkin tucked in his collar. The man next to Mr. Forrester halted midstride and viewed me with a wince.

I instinctively knew him, though I'd never laid eyes on him before. Middle-aged, he stood at a good height, with greying hair near his temples.

He glared at Mr. Macy. "Why is my daughter here? What is it you hope to gain?"

I lost my ability to breathe. I had his features. My eyes, my hair—they matched his. I covered my mouth and almost lost my stomach, only Edward's hand gripped my elbow before I could.

"Your father?" he whispered, kneeling beside me. "Lord, forgive me; oh, God, what have I done?"

Unable to take my eyes off the man, I couldn't respond. My breath came in short gasps.

"I think you mean my wife, Roy." Mr. Macy lit a cigar he'd withdrawn from his waistcoat.

Twenty-Four

❦

THE MAN STANDING before us appeared too angry to find his voice. He made choking noises, while red splotches spread over his neck. Every feature gnarled in his face.

Mr. Macy glanced over his shoulder and realized I'd sunk to the floor. He set down his cigar and knelt before me, placing his hands on my shoulders. "Julia, are you all right? Your support is still necessary. I never intended for you to learn he was your father. Do not lose faith in me now."

Edward backed from us, his mouth twisting with grief. "Sir—" his voice shook as he addressed my guardian—"I've wronged you. I joined them in marriage just now."

My guardian glowered at Mr. Macy. "I forbid it. As her legal guardian, I forbid it."

"Are you able to sit if I bring a chair?" Mr. Macy addressed me, ignoring everything else. He held my gaze with a steadying look. "Rooke, fetch my wife a seat."

I silently pleaded for explanation as the walls seemed to close in upon me.

Rooke appeared, lugging one of the heavy chairs from the table. He hovered, apparently waiting for further directions, but was waved away.

Mr. Macy lifted me and placed me on the cushion. Reaching behind me, he poured a brandy.

My guardian gripped his walking stick like a weapon, eyeing Mr. Macy. "Step away from my daughter."

Mr. Macy pressed the glass in my hand. "Sir, I grow weary of repeating this. We are speaking of my wife, my legal wife."

"What is it you want?" My guardian's voice sounded flat.

"Want?" Mr. Macy looked over his shoulder. "What do I want? You charge into my estate, then dare ask that! For the moment, I want time alone with my wife. It is our wedding night, after all."

Edward clenched his fist and started toward us, but one of the men grabbed him.

"Stop playing, Macy, and give your demands."

"I've had enough." Mr. Macy took my arm and lifted me from the chair. Despite the tension, his touch was gentle and caring. "We're leaving."

I clutched his sleeve as we passed the gawking men. My guardian—for I still could not call him my father—slid both hands to the bottom of his walking stick and held it over one shoulder, ready to strike. "I forbid you to take one more step," he screamed. Spittle landed on my cheek.

I clutched Mr. Macy's dinner jacket in terror.

"What the devil are you trying to do, Roy?" Mr. Macy pulled me close, shielding me. "Don't you know anything about the fairer sex? Are you trying to scare my wife witless, approaching her like that?"

"Take him captive," my guardian said. "I want this marriage investigated."

Two men approached Mr. Macy. They exchanged glances that dared each other to be the first to seize us. When a stout man finally gripped Mr. Macy's arm, Rooke reached inside his waistcoat.

"No, Rooke," Mr. Macy warned. "This one's mine."

My guardian approached, looking ready to yank me from Mr. Macy, but I shrieked and clung tighter to my husband.

Mr. Macy wrapped his free arm around me and gave me an assuring squeeze. "Reverend, would you be so kind as to look after my wife while I'm occupied? I believe these gentlemen alarm her."

For a moment, it did not look as though Edward would comply, but as he studied the faces surrounding us, he stepped forward and grudgingly offered his hand. Mr. Macy nudged me in his direction.

"Who are you?" my guardian asked as Edward wrapped his arm around my back. "How do you know her?"

"She is no one to me." Edward sounded worn.

"Then leave. You've done enough damage."

"Not until I'm convinced she's safe," Edward said, leading me to a chair.

My guardian narrowed his eyes but turned toward Mr. Macy. "I demand to see the marriage license."

With a careless gesture, Mr. Macy reached into his frock coat and retrieved the document. "I think you'll find everything in order."

The paper crackled as my guardian shook it. The longer he stared at the paper, the more human he became, even glancing up once with an expression akin to pain.

"Instruct Isaac to oversee the guests from the house," my guardian ordered someone. "Have him make any excuse he sees proper. Then ask him to go to my library and find every clandestine marriage that's been questioned since the Marriage Act of '53." He paused and looked at me over the page again. "Tell him I want every ecclesiastical exception he can find, every common law that has been upheld or broken in the courts, even if it takes all night."

"Rooke," Mr. Macy said, "tell Reynolds to have our guests packed and sent home within the hour. As soon as everyone has safely left, tell John to fetch the magistrate."

⌒

No servant entered the chamber after the commotion began, so Mr. Macy's lavish second course remained on the table. For what felt like an eternity I watched as the candle on the sideboard dripped to a waxen mound. By the time someone returned, the fire had burned to ash, leaving the air chilled.

A man entered with a stack of handwritten papers, which he gave to my guardian, who moved near the wall sconce. In the dim light, he squinted. I leaned as far as my lacings allowed, catching a glimpse of Mr. Macy. He stood between captors but gave me a slight nod that I did not return. My fear had played itself out, leaving me numb.

My guardian noticed. "Sit up straight, and act like a young lady." His eyes constricted. "Why aren't you in mourning for your mother? When did you discard it?"

I cringed.

"When I ask a question, you answer me."

Edward gave a dark chuckle, rubbing his forehead at the thought of anyone handling me, before answering for me. "She stopped wearing it about a week ago."

"You're her vicar? You allowed it?"

Edward accused me with his stare. "She knew of my disapproval."

Mr. Greenham slipped into the room that moment with a man whose shirt hung open at the top, revealing a flabby chest, and whose red boots didn't match his attire. He blinked at Mr. Macy, then rubbed his eyes. "'Ere now, what's happening?"

My guardian finished glaring at Edward, then stood with a

scowl. "There's been a marriage. She's been stolen from her legal guardian and forced to wed."

"Lord Pierson?" The sleepy stupor left the man's expression and he fumbled with his mismatched trouser buttons. He turned toward me, tucking in his shirt. "That so, miss?"

I denied it with a shake of my head.

"I'm the one who called you, Harry," Mr. Macy said. "These men have forced their way into my home, and as you can see, are holding my wife and me captive."

"You married Mr. Macy?" The amazement in the magistrate's voice washed me with fear. He shook out a purple handkerchief and mopped his brow. "Blimey."

Mr. Macy gestured to the men holding him hostage and the magistrate recovered.

"This is Mr. Macy's residence, isn't it? You can't hold a man hostage in his own home. Release him."

"Thank you, my good man." Mr. Macy rubbed his arms where he'd been held.

"No one leaves this room without my permission." My guardian spoke while keeping his attention on the papers.

"I fear you're not going to find this as cut-and-dried as you hope, Roy." Mr. Macy strolled to his drink table and poured an amber drink, which he handed to the magistrate. "Scotch is your preference, I believe. For the record, no force was involved. That ravishing creature you see there came to my home under the protection of a mutual friend. She married me for protection from Lord Pierson. I also would like to defame the notion that he's her legal guardian. After the death of her mother, he forged papers and illegally assumed that role."

My guardian stumbled backwards, as if he'd suffered a blow.

Mr. Macy lifted his glass. "In the future, pay more attention to whom you hire to forge documents."

I buried my trembling hands in my skirt, knowing my face looked wry.

To my surprise, Edward rose and took a protective stance behind me.

Mr. Macy also looked over and frowned. "John, take my wife from the room. There's no reason she needs to be subjected to any more of this."

"She remains," my guardian replied, still flipping through papers.

Mr. Macy and my guardian resumed arguing, but I could no longer distinguish the words. My stays felt so tight I wondered if I were going to faint.

"Miss Elliston?" Mr. Greenham's kind voice penetrated through the mist.

I focused and found his face near mine. Dully, I nodded.

"Sir!" Mr. Greenham trapped my hand between his. "I'm taking her outside to recover. Look at her pallor."

"Take her." The magistrate waved us away before anyone else could speak. "It will give me time to straighten things out here."

"Come. Fresh air will help." Mr. Greenham hoisted me to my feet and looked at Edward. "You as well. We need to talk."

Mr. Macy nodded his gratitude as we passed and mouthed, *Take her to her chamber.*

Mr. Greenham's boots rang in the entrance hall as the doors clanged shut. Keeping a hand on my shoulder, he studied the space with fierceness.

"Well, sir?" Edward asked.

"Outside." Mr. Greenham prodded me toward the front door.

I stepped into the dark night, grateful for the strong winds that revived me. A chalky smell promised rain, and piling clouds obscured the moon. Resting against a stone lion, I drew drafts of night air into my lungs. Here, at least I could think. While Mr. Greenham studied the sky, Edward removed his jacket and draped it around my shoulders.

"Edward—" I touched his hand and he recoiled.

"Do not speak to me."

Mr. Greenham tapped me. "Miss Elliston."

"She's Mrs. Macy."

Ignoring Edward, Mr. Greenham signalled me to follow him. "Walk me to the stables."

In comparison to the tempest brewing inside the house, the coming storm felt serene. Desperate for answers, I descended the stairs and tried to keep pace with Mr. Greenham, who took them two at a time. "Is that man . . . my father?" I asked.

"He is," Mr. Greenham said.

Few value just how fragile a person's psyche is. All those pieces, both the good and bad, the values, the lessons, the beliefs that construct us—they're all woven into the fabric of our being. Once you start pulling out the first thread, the entire person is in danger of unravelling.

So it was that night. Instead of asking how such a thing was possible, my mind rejected further questions in that direction. I concentrated on my highest concern. "Is he dangerous?"

Mr. Greenham leaned against the wind, steering us toward the stable. Before he opened the door, he peered into the darkened grounds and whistled to someone, receiving a whistle back. Then, opening the top half of the door, he said, "Have Night Owl saddled with enough rations for a week and funds for six months."

"Sir?" The groom shot a doubtful look toward the house.

"That's a direct order."

The groom bowed. "What about Cosmo?"

Mr. Greenham nodded. "Macy didn't say, but have him saddled as well."

Taking a lantern from inside the stable, Mr. Greenham gathered my arm, then led us to the edge of the garden path. He looked at Edward, the light casting a strange shadow over his features as he lifted his face to the wind. I now suspect a sort of begrudging cheer—like a plant covered in frost, who knows the morning sun will kill it but can't help but eagerly wait for the first rays of light.

"Sir—" he returned his attention to us, to Edward more specifically—"I charge you with her safekeeping. See her out of this estate." He moved the lantern toward me and studied me by its gleam. "She's not strong enough to endure this marriage. If you are a man of God, you will see to it."

Edward braced my shoulders with his hands and shouted over the wind, "She's his wife now. What can you possibly expect me to do?"

Mr. Greenham indicated with a nod that grooms were approaching and that we must be silent. In the relentless wind, leaves cycloned around us, cackling like hags. Mr. Greenham accepted the reins of both horses—a black and a grey stallion— and a leather satchel.

When the grooms ran back to their other duties, Mr. Greenham checked the buckles and saddle of the grey horse. He removed a cape from a saddlebag and donned it. Drawing the collar up to conceal the lower half of his face, he turned to us.

"I don't care how you manage. Only be forewarned, Macy takes special interest in her." He stuck his foot in the stirrup and swung his leg over the mount. The horse pranced, tufts of its mane lifting in the wind. Mr. Greenham gripped the reins tight with one hand, giving the night a challenging look, before turning his feral gaze our way. "I murdered her mother for Macy when she got in the way. So be sure to use caution."

I jerked my head up, but it was too late for questions. Digging his boots deep into the steed's rib cage, Mr. Greenham took off, leading the other stallion by the reins. They melted into darkness.

Once, when I'd scrambled up a hayloft after Elizabeth, the ladder had tipped backwards, taking me with it. I felt the same sensation that night, only without the comfort that a haystack waited to cushion my fall.

I faced Edward, unable to mask my sheer panic and confusion. I shook my head in disbelief. *It can't be,* my mind said over and over. I dropped to my knees. I didn't want to believe it. I wouldn't believe it. Nonetheless, I sank to the ground and emptied my stomach until there was nothing left but dry heaves. Edward knelt beside me and wiped my mouth with his handkerchief.

"Lord, I need wisdom." He gathered me in one arm. "God, please help me. Guide me. I don't know what to do now. Forgive me."

New waves of sickness gripped my stomach, and I choked anew. When I turned toward Edward, pleading for help, he watched me helplessly. Then all at once his face hardened. He stood and with clenched fists strode toward Eastbourne. Fearing separation from him, I stumbled after him.

He never looked back as he entered the great hall and charged to the dining room. When the doors bashed open, the men looked over in surprise.

Edward headed straight toward Mr. Macy and swung at his face. Blood gushed from Mr. Macy's nose as his head thwacked the wall behind him. Before Edward could tackle him, three men contained Edward, though he struggled against them.

On the floor, Mr. Macy appraised Edward as he stanched blood with his sleeve.

"Julia." Edward stopped struggling and held his hand out to me. "Come here. I want a witness to confirm what Mr. Greenham just said."

Mr. Macy's eyes slit with an expression that made me feel as though a hand of cold terror had gripped my soul. The storm outside erupted, pounding the windows. Water trickled down the panes.

Edward grew tired of waiting and turned to the magistrate. "Mr. Greenham confessed to killing her mother for Mr. Macy."

Mr. Macy relaxed and leaned against the wall with a relieved-sounding chuckle.

"Her mother died of natural causes," my guardian said to

Edward, but he cast a questioning gaze to Mr. Forrester. "I especially checked that point."

"What do you know of her death?" Mr. Forrester asked me.

The memory of our village apothecary's merciful face thundered back to me, and the way he explained to me the law about suicide. If it became known that Mama had killed herself, all her possessions would belong to the Crown. He and his family were near starvation themselves, yet he'd taken pity on me and broken the law so I wouldn't lose Mama's dowry to the Crown.

"Well?" my guardian demanded.

I clutched my stomach, knowing if I told the truth it would launch an investigation. Mr. Hollis, the apothecary, would be jailed. His wife and children would go to the poorhouse. And for what, I wondered. Would they even find anything at this point, if they unearthed Mama's body? Yet if I said nothing, would it allow Mama's murder to go unpunished?

"I don't know what Mr. Greenham meant." My voice quavered as I lied. "My mother died of natural causes. I was there."

Mr. Macy lifted his head and stared at me with surprise.

Edward likewise gaped, then shook his head. "But outside, you . . . What is it you fear telling these men? You believed Mr. Greenham. I saw that you did."

"You mistook me, sir." I buried my face in my hands. Only I didn't want to cry. I never wanted to cry again. A few hours ago, I sat in this very room, eating dinner, talking to Edward. Now I was Mrs. Macy, and Mr. Greenham had killed my mother, possibly upon the orders of my husband. My entire life had been a lie. I didn't even know my own father. Surely I would wake soon from this nightmare.

"Julia, look at me."

I obeyed Mr. Macy's command.

Without shifting or blinking, he met my gaze. "What John said has no truth."

Our eyes locked in unspoken conversation, but I couldn't understand the language, so I reburied my face.

"I want to speak to my daughter alone," my guardian said. "Colonel, will you be so kind as to fetch some papers for me. Simmons knows where they are."

I heard the jangling of keys and murmuring.

"You'll have to forgive me," Mr. Macy said, "but I feel my wife has experienced enough for one night. I'm not going to allow a private talk with you on top of everything else."

"I've had enough," my guardian replied. "I'm ending this marriage."

There were gasps, and I looked up in time to see flames devouring our marriage license.

"You know I respect your position in government, Roy," Mr. Macy drawled. "However, we both know your authority doesn't carry that far. Burning it will make no difference."

He strode to me and offered his hand. Blood smeared his palm and fingers. Blood likewise covered his face and white shirt.

I pressed against the wall, unable to remove my sight from the red caking his hands.

"Sweetheart," he whispered. "You mustn't believe what John said." He stepped closer, but cringed when I shrank from his touch. He wiped his hand over his trousers, looking miserable. When he knelt, his nose trickled blood again. "Rooke, keep my wife safe. I'm going to change." Then to me, in the kindest of voices, "Nothing will happen to you in my absence."

As the doors swung shut, I caught a glimpse of him giving instructions to Reynolds.

I hugged myself. I felt weary, wearier than I'd ever been. I rubbed my throbbing forehead with my fingertips, listening to the low hum of whispering. The doors opened, but instead of Mr. Macy, a middle-aged man entered with a leather satchel. He handed the bag to my guardian, who looked in my direction.

"Can you drink this?" Edward knelt with a glass of claret. His tone was kinder.

Shame kept me from looking at him.

"Juls," Edward said softly.

I heard him, but the words were far away, as if he were speaking into an ear horn on the other side of the chamber. I blinked, trying to focus. My layers of skirts shifted as he knelt upon them.

"Jane Canton's wedding?" He whispered urgently. "Think hard. Do you remember our conversation in the hay field?"

I faced him. My life had crumbled, and he wanted me to remember something that happened over a decade ago when we had spied on a wedding? Yet even as I resisted that idea, images of a young bride came to mind—a thick garland of orange buckthorn berries atop her head, the way afternoon sun touched her yellow gown, making it glow. Yet it wasn't her beauty that stood out; it was her red-rimmed eyes, her pale face, and the whiteness of her lips as she approached the church. It was clear, even from our vantage, that the marriage was a great tragedy.

"Why doesn't she run?" Elizabeth had whispered, looking at Henry.

We all turned toward him. In our youth, Henry, the oldest, was expected to explain the unexplainable. He scowled, pressing his lips together as the young bride's brother ran up the steps and obediently held open the door.

It was impossible not to see there was something haunting about her poise and grace as she accepted the inevitable. No heroine staring at the scaffold could have been statelier.

"Run," Elizabeth whispered, clutching fistfuls of grass, using her toes to push herself forward. "Don't just stand there," she urged the bride. "Take flight!"

Like me, Henry must have scanned the faces of those surrounding her. Anger glinted in their eyes and hardness formed the downward slant of their mouths.

336 BORN OF PERSUASION

"She can't," Henry finally concluded for us, turning on his back, as if disgusted. "There isn't anyone to help her."

Even as I looked at Edward that night in Eastbourne, I felt the same stirring I'd encountered in the sanctuary. Edward waited, silently, willing me to remember.

Gooseflesh rose along my arms as I understood what Edward was communicating. It wasn't practical and the odds were too astronomical to believe, but we'd already planned for this very event. The four of us had spent that entire afternoon imagining how to escape a wedding.

The idea birthed swiftly, like a mother's sixth babe, born while the midwife's back is turned. I only had time to meet Edward's gaze and nod—I understood. I wanted to flee.

"My things?" I whispered as my guardian broke from the men.

Edward gave a slight shake of his head.

To leave behind all of one's possessions is a more difficult task than one envisions. The moment one detects the smell of smoke in the house, most people do not dutifully exit, but quickly rummage through desk drawers and jewelry boxes, saving the irreplaceable. With the tips of my fingers, I touched the cold emeralds encrusting my necklace, cognizant that Mama's locket was in my bedchamber. It contained my only portrait of her.

While I adjusted, my guardian's shoes appeared in my view. "I wish to speak with you. What I have to say doesn't concern others. You may leave now, Reverend Auburn." To me, "Can you recommend a place for our conversation?"

Edward nodded for me to comply, but the green of his eyes slid across the dining room, in the direction of the stables, telling me where he'd be.

I gave him a nod, telling him I understood, then pointed to the chamber where her ladyship had taken me my first night. "There's a small room off the hall. We can talk there."

The chamber looked much as it had the night of my arrival. Heavy beams combined with the ancient weapons made it appear spartan. My guardian moved with disgust toward the stiff leather and horsehair chairs lined before the stone mantel.

"I despise Eastbourne." My guardian's gaze roamed over the pockmarked weapons. "You never can tell what really belongs to him or what's been extorted."

I collapsed into a chair, feeling cheeks burning. Though Mr. Macy admitted he'd blackmailed, until then I'd paid no heed as to how the riches of my future home had been achieved.

"I wondered if you had the capacity of blushing." My guardian took a seat. "Never have I seen such a nauseating show from a lass in my entire life. What sort of creature did Lucy raise?"

I leaned against the chair, hardening my emotions at the mention of Mama's first name.

"Only the memory of your mother stays my hand of wrath." My guardian growled out each word. "It would serve you right if I gave you no means to live apart from Macy."

My guardian pulled out a folded paper and slammed it on the seat next to him. "When your mother married William, I agreed to give you one of my emerald mines. You wear stones from it tonight. Here is the paperwork."

I gazed at the vivid green ring upon my finger, recalling how I'd once overheard Mama state she didn't dare wear the stones; the distinct color was too recognizable. Understanding grew as to how Mr. Forrester had guessed my identity.

"There's also a handsome living left to you from my mother." He pounded another paper over the first. "She learned of your existence and took pity. I'm glad she died, sparing herself the knowledge of how shameless you are."

I met his cold look. I detested him, as much as if he had killed my mother. "How would you know what I am?"

"Macy claims you've spent your nights with him. Did you?"

His question stunned me as I realized he thought me brazen. Later, I decided, much later, I would evaluate this situation. "Yes, I did."

My guardian looked about to strike me, only instead he flexed his hands. "There's some money I've put aside over the years, as well as your father's living and estate, though I confess, I'm surprised at how poorly your father managed his money."

"William is not my father."

"Neither am I." My guardian returned my stony gaze with one of granite. "As far as I am concerned, you are dead."

I crossed my arms and legs, then kicked my foot in small circles. My eyes stung, my throat closed, but I would never give this man the satisfaction of seeing me wounded.

"I'm leaving." He rose and wiped his hands together. "I suggest you hire someone to handle your finances. The account is yours. I will keep a falsified name on it, giving you the means to live apart from Macy, if need be. Though now that he's accomplished his goal of injuring me, I doubt he will bother you."

"Good riddance." At least my voice didn't betray my pain. I gritted my teeth until they hurt. "Had I known that was his goal, I would have helped more."

My guardian stared at me as though repulsed. "Never show your face to me again."

When the door slammed, I gasped for breath and stared at the door. Panic needled my veins. I needed to locate Edward before Macy found me.

At least I had the presence of mind to scoop up the papers and deposit them into the satchel. My guardian must have stalked straight from the chamber, through the dining room, and out the door, for the men were all gone. The room was empty.

I stepped over the threshold of the dining room and paused, too shaky to continue. Footsteps rang through the entrance hall.

Certain it must be Macy, for the count of several seconds, I registered only fear.

I sobbed relief when a rain-soaked Edward appeared at the door on the other side of the room. Upon spotting me, he placed a finger to his lips, then signalled me to approach.

Had Mr. Macy arrived first, I am uncertain how I would have reacted. It is devastating enough to lose trust in a person—but to have placed myself in the hands of Mama's murderer was more than I could handle.

Edward likewise was on edge as he pulled me against his chest and backed us toward the door. His nostrils flared as he glared toward the darkened part of Eastbourne.

It wasn't until Mr. Macy sauntered into the light from a dark passage that I realized he was there. He wore a clean white shirt, untucked. His face had been washed and his wet hair combed back.

"Really now, Edward," he said, his tone tranquil. "I would have expected better from you than to steal another man's wife."

I squeezed my eyes shut, turning my face against Edward's chest.

"Julia," Mr. Macy's voice soothed. "Are you now afraid? Have I not sworn my protection over you? Come to me. No harm will come to you. We need to talk."

I tugged on the lapels of Edward's frock coat, begging him to remove us.

"Sweetheart," Mr. Macy coaxed. I opened my eyes in time to see him extend his hand. "Have I ever given you reason to doubt my love? What did your father say?"

Edward let out an angry laugh, taking a step backwards. "Never mind what was discussed. Back away! She's coming with me!"

Mr. Macy paid no attention to Edward. His singular gaze was fixed on me. His expression was a mixture of concern and pity. "Is it your desire to leave Eastbourne?"

I nodded once.

Mr. Macy held up both hands and, with the gentlest of movements, stepped forward. "All right. I'll wait until you're ready to talk. I promise you this: whatever Roy said was tainted. We've been enemies for years now. And John—"

"Don't you dare speak to us!" Edward yelled, taking us another step back.

"I don't think you've quite grasped the dynamics of this yet," Mr. Macy said quietly, turning his head to view Edward. "Allow me to make this plain. I'm tolerating you, Edward, because I fear it might unhinge my wife to rive the two of you apart, just yet. But do not mistake my mercy as permission to take part in our conversations. This is between Julia and me."

His words stole my breath.

Edward almost crushed me as he wrapped his arm around my shoulder. "We're leaving now. Make no attempt to follow us."

My feet barely touched the floor as Edward hurried me from the room. With a firm grip on my arm, he led me through numerous passages. In his other hand, he gripped the leather satchel of papers my guardian had given me.

Five minutes later found me in the stable yard, with rain racing down my hair and dripping off my chin. I ran my tongue over my lip, unable to taste the saltiness of my tears. The water cascading from the roofline made the orders Edward shouted to the coachman impossible to hear.

I stood numb in the mud. Edward glanced back at me every few seconds, damp hair sticking to his forehead, as if he feared I'd disappear.

"Come on!" Edward shouted over the percussion, sloshing through the puddles to fetch me. "We've got to hurry. I don't trust him."

Cold water streamed down my neck and into my bodice as Edward braced my upper arm, leading me to the carriage. I climbed in and collapsed on the velvet seat, staining the upholstery and dripping puddles on the floor, representing one more thing I'd ruined that night.

The vehicle swayed as Edward grabbed the bars and swung in. He sat opposite me and silently watched me cry. Whether it was with pity or apathy, I could not discern.

Twenty-Five

⚜

WE ARRIVED at our destination the following day before noon. My eyes burned with weariness as I studied the homestead where Edward had taken us. The frost that had glittered over the landscape earlier that morning had dissolved, leaving behind piebald patches of mud and dead grass.

Behind a wooden fence, a russet-colored cottage waited, enshrouded in a thick, brown fog. Smoke curled lazily from its chimney.

Edward alighted from the carriage, leaving the door open. He looked in the direction of the house, then all at once sank to the ground, as though he'd used the last of his energy. He placed his elbows on his knees and buried his head in his hands.

Inside, dark-green draperies parted and someone peeked out before snapping them shut.

A moment later, Henry emerged from the cottage, pulling on his frock coat. A young man with fiery-red hair followed.

"Edward?" Henry ran to his brother.

Upon reaching us, his face wrinkled with confusion. As his

gaze moved over the mud-stained carriage, I noted that one of the wheels was bent at an odd angle. He frowned but said nothing. He faced me and his eyes sharpened.

For a moment, I nearly lost my resolve not to cry, but then forced aside all emotion.

"Edward, what on earth?" Henry demanded.

Edward rubbed the heels of his hands deep into his eyes. His shoulders expanded as he drew in deep drafts of breath. "I married her, Henry. I married her."

The redheaded man burst into laughter. "I'm sorry," he said as Henry turned and glared at him. "It's just that judging by the state of their arrival, I don't know whether to congratulate them or pay them my condolences."

Grey swam before my eyes, adding to my dizziness. To keep from losing consciousness, I propped my hand against the carriage for support.

Edward clasped Henry's upper arm, regaining his brother's attention. "I married her to Macy."

Henry shook his head. "That's not possible. I only left yesterday. The banns couldn't have been started."

Edward's knuckles whitened. "He had a special license from the archbishop. It just happened, and then I panicked. I wasn't even sure you'd still be here. I just . . . came."

Henry's brows scrunched. "I don't understand."

"I," screamed Edward, emphasizing each word, struggling to rise, *"married—her—to—Mister—Macy!"* He swiped his sleeve beneath his nose, his voice growing anguished. "And that's not all. She's Lord Pierson's daughter. All this time, I've been wooing his daughter. Lord *blooming* Pierson's daughter!"

Henry cast me a wild look, one that asked if Edward had gone mad.

"Wh-ha-ha-what?" Henry's companion tipped backwards, holding his stomach. "You expect us to believe that? She married *the* Mr. Macy, and oh yes, did we forget to mention whose daughter she is? Go somewhere else, Edward. I know an Auburn prank when I meet one."

"Oh, you're just brilliant, Devon!" Edward flung his arms open, looking truly dangerous. "Yes, this is all a grand joke because we've nothing better to do than ride through the night, risking our lives and reputations, so we can fool you. Ha-ha. We made you think Julia is Lord Pierson's daughter." He spun toward his older brother, gesturing toward me. "Henry, I couldn't just leave her there. You've got to help us!"

Henry, however, didn't answer. He just looked at me.

I felt too numb to do more than return his stare. My only thought was that I wanted to bury my head in a pillow and sleep, to return to dreams, to abstraction—anything to be free of reality.

Though I had spent many summers in Henry's company, at that time, I had yet to fully understand his nature or appreci-ate his mind-set. To him, I was already a sister, cherished and beloved. Grief is an apt description for the emotions that delin-eated Henry's face. For a full minute, he seemed uncertain what to do. But then in three steps, he strode to me and crushed me in his arms.

It was so improper and so ridiculous. He knew better. Nevertheless, I buried my face in his chest and finally felt able to give a sob.

"You idiot!" he screamed at Edward. "Have you any idea what you've just done!"

"Do not yell at me!" Edward matched his tone. "Don't you dare! You cannot understand the agony I am suffering."

"Agony! You want agony!" Henry's upper lip curled as he left me and pummelled Edward. In the next moment, they became a wrestling blur of fists and jabs as they grappled with each other on the ground.

"You mustn't fight," the redheaded man pleaded, circling them. "All right, all right, I believe you!"

It was perhaps the first time someone outside of Elizabeth or me witnessed one of their *pas d'armes*. Since boyhood, Henry and Edward had settled more arguments this way than I care to recount—with Edward usually the loser.

Less than five minutes later, both lay panting on the ground with no clear winner.

Leaves and twigs stuck in Edward's hair as he stretched his arms on either side and stared up where trees, black from damp, stretched elongated fingers toward the dun-colored sky.

Once more I felt that sweeping rush of dizziness and slouched against the carriage in hopes of warding it off. Henry sat up from the ground and motioned his friend to aid me.

Edward groaned, turning on his side.

"Come on, get up." Henry stood and stretched out his hand to his brother. "We're not accomplishing anything right now. We'll delay further talk until the two of you rest. Devon, have you got a bed Julia can use?"

When my eyes fluttered open, the first thing I saw was a chamber pot, shelved directly above my head. Rosy light rounded the white enamelware side as it caught the rays of the fading sun. I squinted at it, then turned on my side and viewed the space, trying to place myself.

Piles of paper trays held shabby clothing. A new tallow candle waited upon the table. I saw no matchbox.

On my first attempt to stand, the bulky layers of my wrinkled dress arrested my progress, but with renewed efforts, I escaped the sagging mattress.

"Hello?" I called.

The only response was the plunk of water dripping in a pot. Above it, the yellow stain had spread so that it now discolored the wall, too. My voice felt swallowed, and for one fearsome moment, I was reminded of the weeks after Mama's death.

Edward tells me I made a tragic figure when I entered the kitchen. I have little memory of how I found my seat or ended up wearing Edward's frock coat.

I do, however, recall the remains of a primitive tea: a brown teapot, honey, butter, and oatcakes. My hand moved over my stomach as the thought of eating knotted my throat.

The redheaded man pushed a plate of oatcakes toward me, smiling. "Well, give us an introduction already, Ed!"

"Julia—" Edward's tone was flat—"this is Henry's best mate, Devon Addams."

"Well, I can't very well call her Julia." Mr. Addams frowned like an impatient child.

I looked up, suddenly uncertain of my own name. The thought of being called Mrs. Macy sickened me. Edward likewise paled.

Henry patched the awkward pause. "Call her Miss Elliston."

"Huzza! There's a name to be likened with. Elliston? Like the reprobate William Elliston?"

Both Henry and Edward stiffened, ready to defend my honor.

But in a strange way, the tug of anger was what I needed. It centered me. I needed something to dislike in that hour. I angled my head, giving him my coldest look. "Am I to assume you are acquainted with my father's work, then?"

"Your father?" Mr. Addams gasped. "But I thought your father was—"

I felt my face burn with the realization I apparently had neither name nor father. I was no longer certain of anything.

Edward glared at Mr. Addams, moving the teapot nearer me. "Here, Juls, eat if you can."

The fare was simple, plainer even than the meager foods Mama and I survived on after we were left alone. Yet surprisingly, the oatcakes weren't hard, but soft and infused with spices and chopped fruit. With relish, Mr. Addams explained his process of soaking both the apples and raisins in brandy before adding bitters into the mix with the sliced ginger. Edward listened, with one incredulous brow cocked that this was our topic of conversation, but when he saw me relax and eat, he grudgingly approved.

During that meal, I learned the uniqueness of our circumstances. Henry always visited his friend's family before school started—later I learned he did so in order to be on hand so he could pick up Mr. Addams's travel fare, knowing of the family's hardship.

Henry's visit was a sort of holiday for their household. The entire clan scrimped and saved in order to see the youngest member, Devon, educated. The fact that he was at university and that his friends now included the landed gentry was an accomplishment the entire family celebrated. Proud that the son of a viscount annually spent a night beneath their roof, the older siblings descended upon the crowded cottage, bringing their best dishes, making a feast of the event.

But apparently that year, while Mr. Macy and I were kneeling before Edward, one of the older Addams sons broke his leg, which sent his panicked wife into labor. It being the first grandchild, the entire family had moved the gathering to celebrate the birth and offer assistance.

"I can't believe they're missing this!" Mr. Addams said as he placed another cake on his plate. "Tea with Lord Pierson's daughter!" He looked at Henry. "This is unbelievable. Incredible, really."

"You wouldn't have thought so, had you met him," Edward said, frowning.

"Oh, wouldn't I!" Mr. Addams smeared honey over his cake. "Have you any idea how much power that man wields? In Parliament alone, it's extraordinary, but combine his influence with his wealth!" He bit into the scone, pointing at my ears with his butter knife. "Da is gonna be mad he missed his chance to see that man's daughter, lemme tell you."

"Who is he?" I asked Edward quietly.

"Da? Oh, you'd like him—"

"She means Lord Pierson," Henry said.

Mr. Addams looked all astonishment and stopped chewing to swallow. "Do you not know? He's our country's greatest hope." When I gave a small shake of my head, he prodded, "London's Lion? Oh, come now! Have you never opened a newspaper in your life?"

I hadn't. But Mama had.

My heart pounded with the memory of how anguished she'd always appeared as she'd waited for my father to finish the *Times*. Most days, he'd sneer at her before tossing the paper into the fire, but occasionally, when he forgot, Mama would tiptoe to his seat and anxiously scan the columns before his manservant entered to burn it.

Confused, I twisted my napkin beneath the table, wondering if Mama had loved that man. The thought seemed monstrous.

Yet as I shifted in my seat, I recalled that he had referred to Mama by her first name. Was it possible that he'd had feelings for her?

Placing the oatcake aside, I shunned the idea. It led to a door that I had no wish to open. Whatever had happened between Mama and that man felt too painful to explore. I had my own worries.

"And what is Lord Pierson to us?" Henry's thoughts matched my own. He faced Mr. Addams. "It's not like you can mention this." Then, speaking to Edward, "We've got to move quickly. It'll look suspicious if Devon and I aren't back on time for school. If we're going to get you two safely to Scotland—"

"Scotland!" I gave Edward a confused look, wondering what they'd discussed while I was still slumbering.

He winced, looking at his hands, which twisted and untwisted his napkin on the table before him. "We're not eloping, Henry. She's married!"

Henry made a scoffing noise. "Yes, well, when you *steal* another man's wife, generally one assumes that's not a point you've taken issue with. What else are you planning on doing if not assuming new identities and disappearing?"

Edward crossed his arms. "It wasn't like I had a plan."

"Maybe we're missing the obvious here." Mr. Addams said. "Maybe there's nothing to do except wait. I mean, consider it. All evidence suggests that this brute gained her affections in order to strike a blow at Pierson. You said the license was burned. How is he even going to manage to get the marriage recorded in the parish books? Besides, what other husband allows his wife to leave on their wedding night? Obviously, he's opened the door to gain grounds for divorce or annulment."

"Which means—" Henry's voice waned—"he could sue Ed for damages."

Edward frowned and dropped the napkin in order to stick his hands in his pockets. "Let him. It was worth the risk getting her out of there."

"Nonetheless, I wouldn't fancy spending the rest of my life in debtor's prison. You could, you know, if he suddenly takes offense."

"No, I don't think so," Edward said. "It doesn't strike me like that. I almost have the feeling he didn't care that I took her—like the legal marriage was all he was after. I think that's what Greenham was trying to tell us. That Macy murdered Mrs. Elliston to achieve that end."

Mr. Addams gestured to me. "Yes, but didn't she deny the fellow's claim?"

"Yes, I've been waiting to ask you about that," Edward said.

I glanced at Mr. Addams, uncertain what to say before him.

"You can trust him with anything," Henry said.

I studied the young man in question again, not certain what to make of him. Next to him, Edward gave me a slight nod.

"I feared I'd send Mama's apothecary to jail," I finally admitted.

"How's that?" Henry asked.

I briefly sketched the circumstances of Mama's death and how Sarah and I hid what we thought was her suicide. I told them how Mr. Macy had pointed out the inconsistencies, confirming the idea that she had been murdered, but also why I'd publicly denied the possibility.

"Well, that's one mystery explained, at any rate." Henry leaned back in his chair. "And for what it's worth, I'd have done similar, Julia. You're right; by now all evidence would be gone and a decent-sounding chap would be in prison, while the murderer strolls about free."

Mr. Addams gave a nervous laugh, holding up his hands. "Whoa-ho. We don't even know that there's been a murder for certain, and here we've already convicted the man and kidnapped his wife. Can we slow down a bit, please?"

"He's a murderer," Edward said. "I know it in my bone of bones."

"Well, hurrah for you, but the law demands a little more than your hunch."

"What I want to know," Henry said, "is why would anyone kill Mrs. Elliston? I mean, she hardly ever spoke, and from what I gather, she hardly ever left the house. Why kill her?"

I flinched, hearing his uncensored assessment of Mama.

"Because she got in the way," was Edward's testy reply. "Greenham said so."

"Yes, but what does that mean?"

"Well, hold up," Mr. Addams said, pointing up a finger. "Perhaps in an attempt to injure Lord Pierson, Macy planned to wed Julia, but then her mother caught scent of it and forbade it. Thus, 'she got in the way.'"

I rubbed my forehead, disliking the cold pit expanding in my stomach. "No. That doesn't fit. Mama gave her permission for our union. I saw the letter myself. There was no doubt she wrote it."

"So what do we know, then? Anything?" Henry asked, reining in the conversation. "Any other theories as to why he would murder Julia's mother?"

Silence met him.

I dully sat back in my chair, feeling my throat tighten. Edward drew me closer to him and buried his nose in my hair.

"All righty, then." Henry folded his fingers together and placed them on the table. "If we can't answer the 'why' of the matter, let's discuss our options." When no one spoke, he held up his index finger. "Option one, and it has my vote: Edward elopes with Julia and they assume new identities."

"I'll not cozen the law to steal another man's wife," Edward warned.

"Oh, that's rich, now that you've already taken her."

"I'll not add to my crime by lying and pretending I have any right to wed her. It's dishonorable." Edward's voice was cold as iron. "What is our next option?"

Outdoors, the bleating of sheep carried in the wind. I turned a weary gaze toward the window.

Mr. Addams held up two fingers. "Seek legal help. See if there's some ambiguity, some odd phrase in the law you can take advantage of."

Edward gave a curt shake of his head, showing his doubt. "Maybe."

"Three," Henry said. "We seek Lord Pierson's help."

Edward stood and strode to the far end of the chamber, as if the suggestion were more than he could bear. "No. You haven't met the man, Henry. That door is closed."

"Well—" Henry threw his hands up—"there you have it. I'm out of ideas."

Mr. Addams smiled. "Four. Maybe we'll get lucky. Perhaps this Mr. Macy will take no further pains. And she can pretend it never happened and move on with her life." He twisted to face me. "If he doesn't register your marriage in the parish records and enough time passes, you could even remarry. Just don't tell the vicar."

Edward half turned and glowered over his shoulder.

"It's growing dark." Henry glanced toward the window. "And I don't fancy spending an extra day here, just waiting. You two need to make a decision." He turned toward me. "Julia?"

Edward frowned as I was singled out. Henry's motives were obvious. Of the two of us, I was the more likely to elect the plan Henry favored, saddling Edward with the additional burden of disappointing me if he disagreed.

"I vote Scotland." I frowned at the irony.

"Ed?"

Edward turned back to the window and stared hard into the night.

"The law," he said after a long silence. "I want Churchill's opinion."

Twenty-Six

I COUNT THE NEXT TWO DAYS as amongst the most precious of my life. That first night, Edward and I talked into the wee hours. Once Henry and Mr. Addams retired, all encumbrances were gone and we spoke freely, rediscovering each other's traits and joys.

Alone with Edward, I unburdened myself of every detail about Mama's death. I told of our certainty that it was self-inflicted, and how the apothecary and I had determined that there was no other option but to conceal it. I explained again how Mr. Macy's questions had caused me to revisit the scene, this time drawing a different conclusion. And I begged Edward's forgiveness for failing to confirm Mr. Greenham's claim. Then, as dawn began to lighten the sky, Edward told me about his decision to become a vicar.

That part was difficult. During his first year at university, he'd fallen in with chums who were dedicated to prayer and revival. It lit a fire in Edward, who had always believed in Christ but had never made the connection that a person could be a full-fledged disciple and not just someone who observed the rites of the church. While at home, he found a mentor, the man whom he wanted to consult for legal advice in regards to me. It was Churchill who first convinced Edward he had to be willing to risk losing me to truly be a follower of Jesus. He had taught Edward that one must be willing to forsake all—mother, father, even future wife.

At first, anger swelled in me at Edward's willingness to forsake me in his pursuit of God. The thought incensed me. He had held my hands while he spoke about it, and I longed to twist free and refuse to ever speak with him again.

Yet I held my peace for two reasons. First, Sarah was wont to tell me that my performance could shame a banshee when I was aroused; therefore I refused to speak until I regained a measure of control. Second, I had no right to speak. I had not forsaken Edward, but I'd actually married another man. Furthermore, I knew my reasons for doing so were nowhere near as noble as Edward's. He wanted to change the world at cost to himself, whereas I only wanted to feel safe, regardless of anyone else.

So I listened as Edward shared his faith. To my surprise, despite his belief that I might never return, he had faithfully read my father's entire collection, studied it, and was ready to present me with counterthoughts. Arguments that were so natural and unadorned, I feared their simplicity.

Somewhere during that long night, I allowed myself to tentatively consider Edward's faith. Most attractive of all was the mind-set under which Edward operated—that he'd never be left or forsaken by God. It brought to mind my first night in Eastbourne, when I wondered if anything was constant in this world.

Yet so much had changed in my life in the last forty-eight hours that the idea I might lose yet another part of my identity was too overwhelming to consider. I already felt stretched to the point of breaking. Thankfully Edward was not like others

I'd encountered. He did not press his suit. He did not watch me with eyes full of hope. Instead, he encouraged me to go to bed and sleep.

The next day was Sunday. While we waited to have the carriage fixed, Edward did not pressure me to attend church. Instead, he tiptoed out of the cottage on his own, leaving me a note in case I woke.

That afternoon, Henry and Mr. Addams pored over the Addamses' scanty library, hoping to find something of help to me. Edward and I sat before the fire with a deck of cards, playing scabby queen.

I know now he'd purposefully chosen a game that required little thought. In those quiet, empty hours, I recognized my foolishness at believing I loved Mr. Macy. In just two days on the road with Edward, I'd once again gained sight of the girl I'd been, the girl I thought I'd forever lost.

Thus when we arrived at the smithy's yard the following morning, I was unprepared. As we emerged from the carriage, the young apprentice's eyes widened at the sight of my gown, but not with respect for my station. Rather, it bordered on disbelief.

While Henry pointed out the bent wheel, the apprentice's gaze kept shifting to Edward's collar.

"You a vicar?" he asked when Henry stopped speaking.

"I am."

The apprentice's eyes shifted to Mr. Addams. "These friends of yours, Dev?"

Mr. Addams gave a curt nod. "Yes. Why?"

Wiping his hands with a rag, the apprentice's eyes shifted back to me.

"Something wrong, Abe?" Mr. Addams asked.

The apprentice eyed me, his one hand flexing, as if making an urgent decision. "Get her back in the carriage," he whispered. "Get her and the vicar back inside it. Then go find a newspaper. You'll see what I mean."

"I'm sorry," Henry said, "but do what—and why?"

The apprentice approached Mr. Addams and bent his head, lowering his voice. "It's funny, is all. Last night I kept waking up in a cold sweat, dreaming 'bout Burns and that hunting pup. Remember that? Dream after dream, one after 'nother, until finally, after midnight, I figured it were an omen." He gave Edward a quick apologetic nod. "Not that I actually believe in that sort of stuff. But then looking at the paper this morning—it struck me summat was off, you know, 'bout that reward. And now, here these two are."

"Reward?" Mr. Addams asked.

The apprentice retreated to a small, dark office, then emerged with a newspaper that fluttered in the wind. "Take it."

"Oh, of all the absurdity," Mr. Addams said.

Edward, however, took the paper from the apprentice and searched his face. "Thank you."

The man flushed, doubtless pleased and embarrassed to have an obvious member of the gentry addressing him so frankly.

The wind refused to allow Henry to open the newspaper. It blew tightly against his fists, refusing to stay open. In desperation, we climbed back into the carriage to have a look.

News of my marriage had already reached the gossip columns. Only the story was twisted. It said I had seduced Mr. Macy in order to secure my position in society. It was reported that I was illegitimate and had blackmailed my father into giving me funds to run away with my lover, a vicar. Mr. Macy had also placed an advertisement, begging for my return. He described my dress in detail, as well as a general account of my looks. Of course, later, he published several of these pleas and I learned that all across England, women gathered weekly in parties, in order to read his heart-wrenching notices and then weep together.

But most stunning of all was the offer of five thousand pounds for my safe return.

"By George," Henry whispered beneath his breath.

The vast amount brought me the first tingles of awakening. Who in his right mind paid five thousand pounds for the return of his wife?

I stared at Edward, trying to comprehend.

His eyes looked feverish, even as he pulled me tight against himself. He buried his nose in my hair. He clutched me tight, the way a child holds his most precious possession when fearing it will be snatched away.

I pressed against him too, feeling the hardness of his muscles beneath his suit.

"Flee," Henry said. "Flee now."

Edward looked coldly upon him. "And how do you propose I do that, Henry? Without money, with her in that gown, and with everyone on the lookout for her?"

Henry frowned at me. "Haven't you anything else to wear?"

"No," I said. "My clothing is at Eastbourne."

It was obvious what Henry thought next, for he pinched his shirt at his waist, looking at me as if mentally measuring our difference. He scowled, looked at Edward, then skipped to Mr. Addams, who was the slenderest. "What about belting her into one of Devon's suits?"

"And then what?" Edward sounded surlier. "Don't you think it will raise questions the first time we enter a dressmaker's wearing Devon's clothing? Not that I have money to buy her a wardrobe. You don't think questions will be raised about us? Because surely in Scotland no one cares about five thousand pounds! It's nothing short of a miracle that smith is letting us escape!"

Mr. Addams visibly started and then blanched.

"What?" Henry demanded of him.

Before he could respond, the apprentice knocked on the carriage door, having finished his inspection. Henry scowled and climbed out. Mr. Addams pulled the curtains, as if fearing

Edward and I would be spotted, before exiting and shutting the door.

"What am I going to do?" I whispered to Edward.

"We," Edward said. "What are *we* going to do? This is our problem. Not yours alone." He cupped my face to view me. "Do you understand?"

Swallowing tears, I nodded.

"Hear me, Juls. I am going to fix this."

I placed my right hand over one of his, savoring the feel of him.

His hands were already cupping my face; therefore it only took the slightest motion, just a tilt of my head, the lowering of my lashes, to unleash the torrent that had always existed between us.

I scarcely was cognizant of the first kiss—it was hardly a kiss, but more of an affirmation. I was Julia. He was Edward. Nothing could change that. We were still us. Regardless of what passed.

From there it only grew. Every pent-up fear, every desperate hope, every lonely hour we'd lost—all somehow found their way into that moment. It was as though each touch healed, as though Edward were pulling me from the frozen ice in which I'd been encased—and I were doing the same for him.

The carriage door opened, bringing with it a cool swirl of air.

I felt Edward's body stiffen before he slowly turned to acknowledge Henry and Mr. Addams. I wiped my lips, turning away from their horrified expressions. To my embarrassment, my gaze landed upon the newspaper on the opposite seat that declared me brazen.

"Not one word, Henry," Edward said in a tone that not even Mama in her most obstinate mood would have disobeyed. "Not one!"

I straightened in my seat, tucking my hair back into place, feeling my cheeks turn scarlet.

Henry's face was granite, and he stepped into the carriage.

Seething, he faced Edward. "This—" he wagged his index finger between us—"I will not tolerate. So help me, Edward, man up and elope with her." Henry's nostrils flared as he leaned right into Edward's face and spoke through clenched teeth. "If I ever catch you acting like that again, while refusing to take the nobler action, I will not hesitate to call you out!"

"What?" Edward still breathed heavily as he pinched the bridge of his nose. "You think I intended for that to happen?"

Henry yanked him by his lapels and shook him.

"Henry, stop!" I grabbed one of his hands and tried to remove it from Edward, but he was too strong. "Please, stop!"

All at once, Henry released him and Edward jerked his arm away. The brothers sat panting heavily across from each other.

"Come on. Let's go," Mr. Addams said, climbing in. His face matched his hair as he avoided looking at me.

"I'm taking us home, so you can talk to your precious Churchill," Henry said. "And then I'm leaving you to your conscience. All your pretty speeches, Edward, all your exhortations to follow the gospel, and this—" he pointed between us—"this is the summation? Do not ever attempt to speak to me again about what is noble. You've lost that right."

Once I had seen the vicar back home caught in a lie. When cornered, he grew stately and dignified, and he glared at his accuser with such coldness that even I, from a distance, squirmed.

Edward's reaction couldn't have been more different. Pain flushed his eyes before he looked down with anguish at his hands. He could not have seemed more horrified by his actions if he discovered he had strangled someone.

His face contorted as he shut his eyes and faced the window.

I threw out my hand in order to balance myself as the carriage swayed into motion. Edward's reaction staggered me more than Henry's rebuke. It was the first time I realized the depth of Edward's convictions.

Dread prickled along the back of my neck. In the past, Henry had never grown angry when we'd made mistakes. He used to be the first to brush the dust from our clothing and congratulate us after a mischievous prank—no matter the outcome.

The Henry I remembered couldn't care less if Edward married and then stole me.

Unease filled me, and I gave Henry a keen look, trying to reason this. Only a month ago, he and Elizabeth were firm in their belief that I could lure Edward away from his religious craze.

So why did Henry now fear that his brother would hazard my future and then abandon me to it?

❧

When we stopped before a row of slate-roofed buildings with mullioned windows, Henry hopped out first and began his inspection of the carriage. Edward assisted me, then turned to Henry, who knelt in the dirt with the driver.

"Are you coming with us?" Edward asked him.

Henry frowned, measuring the angle the wheel was bent at with his hand. "Yes, I'm coming." To his driver, "Take it to Wilson and Sons. I'll be there as quick as I can."

Edward directed me to a building trimmed in blue. The hanging sign read, *Mr. Winthrop Lydon Churchill. Solicitor.*

A shop bell announced our entrance as heat rushed from the building. Scents of caraway and ginger diffused outside. Inside, an elderly man slept by the fire. He reminded me of Luther, our old manservant, except that when he awoke, he wore a friendly smile.

"Edward, my dear boy." Aged hands gripped the ends of the rocking chair as the man pulled himself to a stand with rheumatic movements. "I thought you had gone visiting."

Henry and Mr. Addams entered and doffed their hats.

The old man stopped in his tracks as he looked in my

direction. He tugged on his ear, considering me. His gaze lingered longest on my gown.

Wrinkled from head to toe, I imagined I looked like Mr. Forrester. My green taffeta gown would never be the same. Some of the lace along the bottom had ripped and hung in a frayed loop. My hair, at least, was pulled back in a plain style and my emeralds were safely tucked inside Edward's satchel. I returned the frank stare, wondering if he'd read the paper.

The old man gave a heavy sigh. "When you've been in this business as long as I have, you learn that visages like yours never bear good news. Come in. Bad news will keep until there's tea in hand. That is, provided you have the time."

Henry frowned. "No, we'd much rather get this over with as soon as possible. We've a lot of preparations to make."

"We have time." Edward glared at him.

The elderly man nodded, shuffling back to his seat. "Very well, then. Edward, will you fetch the service? Hot water is on the stove."

Edward pulled one of the armchairs away from the overbearing blaze and directed me to it. Then to his brother and his friend, "Henry, Devon, don't touch anything. Please, just sit."

Henry snapped down the lid on a box he'd been peering into.

While the gentlemen settled, I tucked my feet beneath the chair, then smoothed my skirts in hopes that a few wrinkles would uncrease and clasped my hands over my lap. Every nook and cranny was stuffed with small curios, instruments, aged papers, and antiquated pens. Shadows from the fire flickered on both dusty and polished surfaces. Scents of bergamot and orange mixed with the ginger and caraway. Condensation on the windows offered privacy from passersby. *What a strange place,* I thought with dismay, *for my future to be decided.*

After five minutes, Edward appeared carrying a tea tray. While Mr. Addams moved a pile of books, making place for the tray, Henry went to the oversized desk and procured the wooden chair for Edward's use.

Mr. Churchill served tea. My cup was so ancient it lacked a handle and was overrun with hairline cracks, rivalling the spiderlike veins that crisscrossed its owner's hands. When the last cup had been served, the elderly gentleman faced Edward. "So, boy, why have you brought me Macy's lost bride? There's no need to look surprised. One only has to look at her to realize who she is."

Edward leaned forward as his brows drew together. "I need to know how to assist her. I rashly married the two of them. She left Macy, and I want to maintain her ability to stay away from him. There are things about him—" Edward's voice was so strained it closed on itself—"abhorrent, unspeakable things. Depravity she cannot possibly fathom. Do you remember telling me once about a case you worked on years ago? His name was Adolphus, I think. Her husband, he is similar to this man. Maybe worse."

Mr. Churchill recoiled with a shudder. "Edward, to repeat that name is to invite death. I am disappointed in you, boy. I told you about that client in confidence."

"Forgive me." Edward rubbed the bridge of his nose. "I've not slept well. But that is the level of evil we're dealing with."

"Have you proof? That's a grave accusation."

"You won't like my answer, but I know because I sense it." Edward sat straight. "I'm absolutely convinced he's evil, though I lack proof."

Mr. Churchill shut his eyes, seemingly too overwhelmed by our ignorance to know where to begin. Every time he looked like he was about to say something, he'd give his head another slight shake. "Edward, I credit you enough to not explain the obvious. But hear me, boy. Even if you had proof, what do you expect me to do?"

"Surely there must be some action she can take. Can she sue for separation? On grounds of cruelty, perhaps?"

Tugging his earlobe, Mr. Churchill studied me. "Are you in danger?"

"Yes," Edward answered for me.

"Let the girl speak for herself." Then to me, "Be truthful. Do you fear your master?"

To this point, I'd listened, unable to think. With a frown, I recalled Edward's irritability when Lady Foxmore had tried to gossip about Rooke. It wasn't in Edward's character to accuse anyone, much less to the degree he had accused my husband. I stared at him, wondering what he'd heard that he couldn't repeat or admit he knew. Had he learned that Mr. Macy had once been a blackmailer? Or, I wondered, had he heard something worse?

"Is she incapable of speaking?" Mr. Churchill asked Edward, sounding earnest.

Edward turned to me. "No. She's exceedingly shy. It's all right, Julia. I've known Churchill my entire life. He will not steer us wrong. You can answer him. Has Macy ever hurt you?"

"He . . . Mr. Macy . . ." I felt the sting of tears, uncertain why I felt compelled to cry.

"Has he injured you?" Mr. Churchill asked with concern threading his voice.

I shook my head and swiped a tear.

"There's hope," Mr. Churchill said to Edward. "If he had, and she forgave the behavior, she would have lost the legal right to plead her case. But if he hasn't threatened her life or limb, she has no grounds to sue for separation."

"There must be some action she can take."

Mr. Churchill removed his spectacles and folded them over his lap. With a weary look, he rubbed tired eyes. "He's her husband. He has full legal custody of her. Not only can he sue for the restitution of conjugal rights, but also, lawfully, he may force his way into any house and carry her away. Edward, what do you seek from me? I'll credit her husband this much: at least he seems very concerned. I've read his public letter to her. Its very tone is forgiveness and understanding for her youth."

"Well, then, maybe she can contest the marriage. It's never been consummated. Even Henry and his friend agree she may have argument, since they lied to me so I'd wed them."

"What did they lie about? Did they hide a legal impediment, or their true identity?"

"No." Edward's strained expression told me he would not reveal how the marriage was brought about. "It was nothing of that sort."

"Did you solemnize their vows?"

"Yes."

"Then, being a vicar, you know the law on this. She's married."

Tugging at his collar, Edward strode to the window. He cleared a small spot with his sleeve and peered through the wavy glass.

"Are you even certain she's in danger?" Mr. Churchill asked after several minutes of silence. "She does not impress me as frightened."

Disliking the keen look with which he studied me, I shifted my gaze, wondering what these men would think of the fact that I'd married Mr. Macy fully cognizant that his past held dark secrets.

"He has kept his true self from her," Edward said.

I shifted my feet, wishing that statement were true. I felt too ashamed to correct him.

"Then she may be perfectly safe. I read the man's entreaty and thought him quite anxious over her to offer such a sum. Besides, she must have felt some degree of affection for him. How did she come to leave him? How did this matter even fall into your hands?"

"I stole her after the ceremony." Edward faced us and ignored Mr. Churchill's shock. "I do not confess to know what he experiences toward her, but it's not love or respect. If it were, he wouldn't have enticed, manipulated, and then ruined her."

I tucked the various wisps of hair that had escaped my chignon behind my ears as if unmoved by their speech. Nonetheless my throat swelled. At that time, I did not understand that Macy had manipulated me. For had I not willingly agreed to our arrangement? Thus I only felt shame upon hearing Edward's assessment.

"Surely," Edward continued, "you know of some safe haven, someplace I can take her."

Mr. Churchill looked at me as he rocked to one side as though his hip disturbed his comfort. When he spoke again, he looked only at Edward. His voice was lowered. "Edward, why are you still with her? You know what you must do."

"A good shepherd seeks out his lost sheep."

"When the other ninety-nine are in safe pasture, not scattered abroad. Have you any idea what will happen to your parish? Have you no better sense than to covet the wife of another man? Has all I've taught you been for naught?"

Edward let out a tired-sounding laugh. "I'm not coveting; I'm protecting. Do you have any idea how trying it is to watch someone twist and manipulate the person you love? Tell me where to take her."

"There is nothing you can do for her. Step aside. Allow the man to collect his wife."

"Surrender her to a ruthless man?"

"Have you any choice? By law, she's his property. Of far more consequence, you cannot both follow God and keep another man's wife. You must choose. If she's called, God will see to her. If she's not, then allow the dead to bury the dead. What can she be, except an instrument of death to you as well? Remember, Edward, 'to deliver thee from the strange woman, which forsaketh the guide of her youth. For her house inclineth unto death.'"

I had felt shame before, but now anger birthed, spreading sparks through my body. I lifted my gaze and pierced Mr. Churchill with a cold stare.

"Do not quote Scripture to me." Edward sounded fierce. "She's not seducing me. If you want me freed, give me options. I cannot surrender her to *that* man. Assist me; do not lecture me."

"Cannot or will not? She looks no more than eighteen, nineteen, and is obviously a gentlewoman. Therefore, she must be someone's ward. Let that person offer her protection. At least he'd not be neglecting his parish and risking his soul."

"She has no one except me." Edward laughed bitterly, running his fingers through his hair. "I'm not abandoning her."

"You cannot possibly feel justified before God."

"Evil does not begin to describe her husband. Surely I'm justified in—"

"Are you arguing with me, or with your conscience?"

"You expect me to just hand her over, knowing he will destroy her? No wonder Greenham told me she wasn't strong enough for the marriage. Who could endure such a marriage?"

"Whether she can endure it or not is moot. This may be the means by which God is breaking her, bringing her to himself. It only remains for you to stand aside. What is done is done. Allow it to play out."

It was not my first brush with such reasoning. I was used to such judgments; therefore Churchill's speech had no effect on me. It was, however, the first time Edward witnessed it. Therefore, it was Edward I silently studied.

He looked unable to speak as he backed toward the door, shaking his head. He exited, the bell jangling sharply.

Henry's chair creaked as he rose and reached inside his coat. "Thank you. How much do we owe you?"

Mr. Churchill waved away the thought of a fee. "Henry, I would that you and your friend step outside. I want a moment alone with the girl."

Henry's warm hand clamped my shoulder while Mr. Addams deposited his teacup to the tray. "Let's go check on the carriage, Devon."

He patted my shoulder one last time as he departed. My chest tightened in anticipation, much as it used to during an encounter with the vicar back home.

Mr. Churchill waited until Henry and Mr. Addams had stepped outdoors before fastening his watery blue eyes on me. His tone came out stern and accusing. "What kind of girl are you?"

Having no other recourse, I stonewalled my emotions and gave him my blankest stare.

"Have you any idea the damage you're causing with your brash behavior?" He snorted through his nose, sitting straight. "Running away from your husband! Endangering Edward's reputation with your folly."

For one fearsome second, I pictured the reverend from my village, gnawing on a poultry bone as he condemned me with a full mouth. How well I saw his wagging chin and pouchy cheeks ballooning like a bullfrog's.

I levelled my gaze at Mr. Churchill, knowing I could handle hours of this sort of attack. I'd learned early how to harden my heart against it.

But Mr. Churchill's next words penetrated my armor. "Had you a shred of love for Edward, you would release him. Only the most selfish sort of person drags someone else down with him as he drowns. Cut Edward loose, if you have any pity left in your heart."

Truth spoken without compassion is perhaps the most devastating of all blows. It leaves one condemned of his faults without a ray of hope to cling to, or a door of change to exit.

I stared, staggered by the truth of Mr. Churchill's argument.

I was the one who had gambled all and lost. Not Edward. Not Henry. I'd stretched my every resource—financial, emotional, physical—in an attempt to secure myself.

I'd exhausted all that I had—and now in desperation, I was on the verge of devouring the resources of those dearest to me.

I stared at Mr. Churchill, surprised by the physical throbbing of pain in my chest that accompanied the realization:

This wasn't who I wanted to be.

❧

I stumbled from the shop with the feeling that I stood on the precipice overlooking a vast canyon. All I could see at that moment was the loss—like a landscape scarred after a battlefield.

"Juls?" Edward placed his hand on my forearm.

I stared up at him, knowing the inevitable had come. We were lost to each other.

Something of my thoughts must have been plain, for Edward shifted his gaze and peered through the shop window. "What on earth did he say to you?"

"That was scarcely legal advice." Mr. Addams approached, wrapping a red muffler about his neck. "I was thinking something more along the lines of *Bright v. Clark* or something, some obscure precedent. Ah well. Don't choke it off to a full loss, Edward. At least we can save ourselves the trouble of visiting a bishop next. Your solicitor saw fit to play both roles."

"What did he say?" Edward's gaze remained unbroken.

"Fancy that old man actually thinking Adolphus exists," Mr. Addams continued. "And that he's met him, of all things!"

"You're coming with me!" Edward slipped his fingers through mine.

"I'm not going back in there," I protested, finding my voice.

His teeth clenched, and he looked once more inside the shop. "Nor would I ask you to. We're going to my house. I'm going to seek my father's advice."

"What about Henry?" Mr. Addams asked. "He's still with the carriage."

"Tell him where we're going."

Mr. Addams trotted after us. "Do you really think it wise for the two of you to be alone?"

Edward quickened our pace, his arm tense.

Blusterous winds whipped the layers of skirt between my legs and swirled around my ankles. I welcomed the cold sensation and took deep breaths of stinging air, welcoming the change from the overheated shop.

For a mile I stumbled alongside Edward, too stunned to cry, too bruised to speak. By the time we reached the crab apple tree planted at the edge of town, I wanted to rant against the lot I'd been given.

As a child, I determined I would be loved. I would never be like Mama, despised by her own husband and aloof from nearly everyone. I had Edward, Henry, and Elizabeth as proof. I planned to embrace my father's ideals, only with a kinder and gentler demeanor, which would allow me to be more persuasive. I planned to succeed where he had failed.

Yet despite my best efforts, only days after my wedding I was estranged from my husband, had disgraced the name of Elliston, and was confronted with the truth that if I truly loved Edward, I must banish myself from him, too.

I picked up a rotting crab apple and threw it with all my might against the tree. And then another, and another, and another. I screamed my frustration in the wind, then, having nothing left to do, sank to the ground beside the gnarled tree and buried my head in my arms.

Edward's hand came to rest on my shoulder.

"Why me?" I sobbed at him, turning. "Why? What did I do to deserve this? Why am I the only one who keeps losing everything and everyone over and over again?"

Pain knit his face. "Everyone suffers, Juls."

I gave a bitter laugh that was mixed with tears. Then, catching sight of a cottager hoeing his field in the distance, I pointed. "Not that man! Tomorrow he'll rise and live the same day over.

You can't tell me that he's about to discover that the person he married is a murderer. Or that his father isn't really his father after all. Or that the man who claims to be his father denies his existence. Or that his name is being circulated in the papers with lies attached to it!"

Edward studied the man for a long moment, as if considering my argument. When he spoke, his voice was gentle. "Perhaps not, and perhaps all of Jacob Turner's tomorrows are the same—but how do you know if that day is worth living again and again? Do you see his stiffness as he moves? He has rheumatism, and some days he tells me that it feels as though his joints are no more than bone scraping against bone. Each step is agony, but he must work or starve. Most days his food is little more than a thin gruel, and he's been saving months to buy a new blanket before winter sets in."

I dried my eyes with the sleeve of Edward's frock coat, and I studied the cottager anew. Edward had spoken truthfully about the man's afflictions. Each time he lifted his hoe, he hesitated, then squared his shoulders as if willing himself to strike the earth. Each clod of dirt was hard-won. Yet he continued.

Could I do less?

I knew what needed to be done. Churchill had seen to that. In order to protect the ones I loved, I needed to embrace the very isolation I had sought to avoid.

"How can you believe in a God who is so cruel?" I asked.

Edward's countenance took on an aching look. He did not have to ask what I meant. Though the ground was cold and wet, he joined me. And because he did not rush to answer, because he took the time to consider my viewpoint, I listened when he finally began to speak.

"Imagine the kindest, gentlest man you can. A man who reaches out to the most wretched and works to restore the undeserving. No injustice is tolerated, no snobbery, no bickering."

I eyed Jacob Turner, predicting where Edward was going.

"Now imagine him a general," Edward continued, "and off to war. During this time, all sorts of horrible rumors and distressing reports have reached his home country and his family's ears. And while these reports may be true, those who know and love him best can only tell others to keep faith. There are explanations; surely there are a myriad of reasons that have not yet been revealed." He pointed at the cottager. "Men like him are like that family. He keeps faith that this isn't the full story."

I cocked an eyebrow at him.

"Wait for the ending," Edward said.

At that moment, though, the only ending I could envision was Macy collecting me as his wife, which drew my thoughts in a new direction.

"Who is Adolphus?" I asked, recalling the name Edward had used to communicate how evil Mr. Macy was.

Edward made no comment on my seemingly erratic switching of topics, though his brows knit, and an emotion I could not name settled over his features.

"It's . . . it's . . ." Edward sighed through his nose, as if searching for a way to explain this. "It's a name. A sort of countersign to London's criminal lot—a collected body of the worst rabble you can imagine. The problem is the name is so legendary, no one knows what's what anymore. Some say there is a mastermind, others that he never existed. An MP is murdered, a priceless jewel is misplaced, and people right away start whispering this was no ordinary crime and this imaginary figure is credited."

I wrinkled my nose. "And what has this legend to do with Churchill, then?"

"Years ago, when Churchill still worked in London, he met a man who hired his services. Rather than give his name, the man told him to call him Adolphus. That was years before rumors of this crime syndicate started."

I hugged my knees tight against my chest, thinking that Edward had chosen an apt comparison. As I mentally reviewed some of the priceless treasures of Eastbourne, I resisted the urge to give a bitter chuckle. How easy it would have been for people to pay off Mr. Macy with a priceless heirloom, and then blame the item's disappearance on this mysterious Adolphus.

Mr. Macy had been up front about his blackguard past, but nothing could excuse him from his lies to me or Mr. Greenham's accusation of murder.

But how to escape a husband?

I shut my eyes, calculating the task ahead of me. Lord Pierson had furnished me with papers to financially provide for me. I needed to access the funds. I also needed clothing. My mind flew to the ragbag at Am Meer, where I'd left my mourning garb.

Edward disturbed my thoughts by slipping my hand in his. "Come on. Let's go talk to my father."

My throat tightened. I wanted to argue against the pointless-ness of asking Lord Auburn for help, but I realized this was a necessary step for Edward. It would haunt him to his dying day if he didn't feel he'd done everything possible to rectify the situation.

For his sake, I nodded and allowed his help in regaining my feet.

I cast one last look at Jacob Turner struggling to etch out his survival in that plot of earth. After Auburn Manor, I deter-mined to visit Am Meer. I wasn't sure how to convince Henry and Edward to back away or how to access my funds yet, but at the very least I could get out of this outlandish gown.

❧

By the time we arrived at Auburn Manor, my hair was wind-blown and my already-wrinkled dress was smeared with rotted crab apples.

I glanced at Edward, wondering if he still thought this a good idea. Apparently he'd been waiting for some time for me to acknowledge him, rather than breaking into my thoughts.

"Let me present you," he instructed as we marched up the steps. "Be forewarned, I'm going to disclose everything—our secret betrothal, Eastbourne, that I've broken the law."

I nodded. This would be worse than the time Mrs. Windham found a spider crawling amongst her petticoats.

"If my father is very angry, I'll remove you. Only promise to let me handle the speaking, even if he addresses you."

I nodded again, wishing we were already in the future and this trial passed.

He pulled me down the hall and opened the second door on the left. "That's odd. They're usually here, unless . . ." He looked further down the hall. Keeping a firm grasp on my hand, he opened a door to a different parlor.

Lord and Lady Auburn looked up from their tea, their mouths parted in surprise. Across from them, Mr. Macy sat on a settee. He raised an eyebrow, looking at my hand firmly clasped in Edward's. I dropped it.

Mr. Macy set down his teacup and gestured toward me. "Ah, here she is now. May I present my wife, Mrs. Chance Macy."

Lord Auburn rose and glared at his son. "Edward, come with me to the library. Now."

Edward placed an arm around my shoulder, pulling me to him. "No."

Lady Auburn covered her mouth, slowly closing her eyes.

"*Now*, Edward." Lord Auburn swung open the door.

Edward looked toward his mother. "Will you promise to remain with Julia until I return?"

"Go with your father, Edward," she said, sounding weak, stirring from her seat.

Mr. Macy moved his gaze from me to Edward. The air pulsated with animosity.

"Do not leave this room," Edward whispered to me. "I'll fetch you the moment I finish." He released me, and his retreating footsteps pounded down the hall.

Lady Auburn took my hand, but her eyes followed Edward with a look of alarm. "Come," she said in a soft voice, pulling me toward Mr. Macy and gesturing for me to take my place next to him. "Your husband is an exceedingly understanding man. You have nothing to fear."

I watched in fascinated horror as she bypassed Edward's request, crossed the room, and left, shutting the door behind her.

Twenty-Seven

I SANK INTO MY SEAT, staring at Mr. Macy. His tapered fingers reached into his brocade waistcoat and retrieved a gold cigar case. With the air of a chiding husband assessing his wife's account books, he viewed my dress, over which I still wore Edward's coat, while lighting a cheroot. He reclined, blowing long streams of blue smoke into the air, never removing his gaze from me.

After several long moments, I found it difficult to match his scrutiny. How, I wondered, could he continue to sit there and say nothing? In an attempt to appear unaffected, I gave him a withering stare.

The corners of his mouth tugged up as he lazily blew his next stream of smoke.

Strangely, my fear subsided and anger took its place. I raised my chin, meeting his gaze. He would learn I was not the same girl he'd seduced. His smile increased as he settled further back into the couch, waiting.

I slid one arm from Edward's frock coat. "I believe it's customary to offer me tea."

"Of course, darling. How unforgivable of me." He leaned over the silver service. With an elegance I could never hope to attain, he poured a cup. "I must beg you excuse me, but tea isn't our usual fare. How does my wife take it?"

I laid Edward's coat aside, my fingers quaking at having been called his wife. "With sugar."

He presented my cup with an exaggerated bow. "Well, at least we are speaking again. Dare I hope you've passed through the unreasonable fear stage?"

Knowing my voice would betray my anxiety, I swallowed the brew, scorching my throat.

Mr. Macy crossed one leg over his knee and took another draw from his cigar before studying it. "Julia," he pressed in a smooth, even voice, and then met my eye, "did I not request that you come to me personally if you heard disturbing reports regarding me?" He stabbed out his cigar. "Tell me what your guardian said. Ever since you spoke with him, something has severed your affections."

"Nothing he said stands between us."

"Is it because I hid the fact that he was your father?" Mr. Macy's voice sounded soft and repentant.

I struggled to remain composed at the mention of the man, hating that a wound whose existence I still denied suddenly throbbed.

"I confess it was underhanded." He reached over and picked a piece of meadow grass from my gown. "Now that you've met, perhaps you understand why I concealed his identity. Tell me, what did you make of him?"

Though I did my best, it was impossible to hide the hurt.

"He's disclaimed you, hasn't he?" Mr. Macy sat back with a snort of disgust. "Knowing Roy, I shouldn't feel surprise. Though, I confess, my wrath is provoked that he left you at my mercy, especially when he only remembers me as the man from my past."

I eyed him, amazed at his ability. It wasn't coincidence, I realized, he'd turned the topic to my father. He'd found and exploited a trauma I'd only recently discovered myself.

"How did you find me?" I asked.

"Sweetheart." He shook his head. "We only have a few minutes, and you waste them on a question like that. If you are going to insist we play this game, then it's essential you have better tactics. Try again."

His statement twisted my emotions in a new direction. I stared, realizing he truly meant it. Then, angry, I gritted my teeth and decided to switch the tables on him. He'd used my father to throw me off balance, therefore I would use Mama to throw him off his.

"I believed Mr. Greenham when he said he killed my mother."

"Well, if John says he did, he did."

"He also said you took part in it." My hands shook so badly the china cup slipped from its saucer and cracked on the floor. Tea spread out over the hardwood floor. I stared at his polished boots and cringed, waiting for his coming wrath over my accusation.

Mr. Macy picked up the broken cup and placed it on the saucer, which he removed from my hands and set aside. His fingers enfolded mine. "Julia, look me in the eye. I swear to you, I believed your guardian had killed her."

Truth was plainly written across his features. His hands were warm. He didn't blink or shift his eyes. If he was lying, then he believed himself.

Doubt chiseled at my resistance. Not knowing what to think, I looked up at the ceiling to hide the tears that welled.

He chuckled, removing a white handkerchief, and wiped my eyes. "I fear your maneuver didn't work very well, dear heart. Instead of dismantling me, you appear to have dismantled yourself. Shall I let you have another go?"

I stared, knowing I was at the losing end of a game of tug-of-war. How was it possible to feel both panic and relief? "I think you are lying. Those horrible rumors in the paper prove it. How could you publish those things about me?"

He held his head at an angle, like a haggler in a marketplace weighing an offer. "Next time, darling, don't say 'I think'—it sounds weak. Outright accuse. It will pinion half of your opponents." He crossed one foot over the other in a lazy motion. "As far as your accusation, has not my own name been smeared alongside yours? Do you think I enjoy playing the role of cuckold? It was Forrester's paper that started the nonsense. All I did was advertise a reward. Which, if you consider it, was the best thing I could have done. Would you rather I'd acted like a scorned husband?"

"Forrester?"

"It appears he's found his revenge on me after all." Straightening, he withdrew his cigar case, which he tapped against the heel of his palm. "Now, before I begin my inquiries, have you anything else to accuse me of, darling?"

I stared, not certain what to say. Talking to him was like trying to walk on the ocean. Every step, every word shifted. The fact that Mr. Forrester had published the scandal shattered the framework again. Every time I thought I understood something, it changed.

"No?" His voice hardened. "That's good, because I have questions for you." He set his gold case on the tea table. "I am only going to ask this once, so make no attempt to deceive me."

I stiffened, waiting for him to question me about my improprieties with Edward.

"Why," he asked, lacing his fingers together, "did you seek out Churchill?"

Sensing his humor was strange, I blinked, uncertain. Yet I felt compelled to answer him—to appease him, even. "We . . . we sought legal counsel."

"Why—" his tone sent gooseflesh over me as he leaned forward—"Churchill?"

I swallowed the sour taste in my mouth.

"Just tell me the truth, dearest," Mr. Macy said. "I swear my anger shall not touch you."

I tried to swallow, but my mouth had dried. His eyes wore an intense light, and before I could determine the meaning of his fierceness, I tried to explain.

Once I started, however, it became impossible to stop the flow of words. I confessed all—going to Mr. Addams's house, how we'd discussed our options, which one I had voted for, the blacksmith's apprentice, and finally our discussion with Churchill.

At first, Mr. Macy listened with confusion, showing only surprise, and then a glint of humor when I told him I'd voted for Scotland.

For several seconds after I finished, the clock's ticking filled the chamber.

"Is that all?" he asked, his voice stern.

"What else is there?"

He studied me, frowning. Then, like a mighty gale sweeping away the storm of anger, his eyes crinkled.

He laughed, but sympathy replaced his smile. "Did you truly vote for Scotland, darling?"

Heat rose through my face.

"Shall I call him out, then?" He laughed, rubbing his forehead. "It might make me the first man in history to duel someone for *not* running away with my wife. I fear it won't reflect well on you, dear heart. People will wonder."

The dizzying rate at which he changed topics was more than I could handle. Though all trace of his anger was gone, my stomach continued to cramp.

"All right, dearest, I can see you're in no mood for banter, so I'll cut straight to the point. We're leaving this afternoon for London."

I looked toward the door, wondering how much longer until Edward would return for me.

"I'm sorry, dearest. It wasn't my intention to barge in on your little holiday for another week or so, but some rather pressing business has come up."

"Business—" I forced myself to look back at him—"or blackmail?"

His expression never flickered. "If you insist on knowing, our marital problems have created a rather interesting consequence. I've been informed that a more disagreeable sort of person is seeking you. He believes he's found my vulnerability and intends to use it."

"Do you really think I'll fall for that again?" I asked. "That I'm in danger and I need you to protect me?"

"Whether you believe me or not is of no consequence. You haven't any say in the matter. I'm sorry, darling, but as a precaution, I'm removing you to her ladyship's residence immediately until we can be ready to leave."

I stared, refusing to comprehend. To me, the idea that he could collect me while I was inside Edward's house was an impossibility. Then, with a start, I realized I had no recourse. Legally, I was this man's property.

He rose and retrieved his riding whip, hat, and gloves.

"Sweetheart." His voice chided as he approached. "You have nothing to fear. You've been perfectly safe this entire time. I've had one of my men keeping watch. I'll never allow you to be in a situation over which I don't have full control."

I stared at him, harrowed at the idea that I might have been watched the entire time.

When he held out his hand, I did not take it.

"There's nothing to fear, Julia." His voice tranquillized. "When we wed, did you doubt I'd make a devoted husband?"

I fastened my gaze on the door that Edward had not yet come back through. "No."

He gripped my arm and pulled me to my feet, leaving me no choice but to comply. "I am the same man you married. Besides—" he grinned—"after paying Adelia her two thousand pounds, I can't run the risk of losing another five."

～～

Mr. Macy's fingers pressed into my back as he ushered me into Lady Foxmore's antechamber. He handed my wrap to the butler. "Inform her ladyship and Snyder of our arrival. My wife is fatigued and most likely famished—"

The sound of Lady Foxmore's walking stick interrupted him. "Chance?" Ire tinted her voice. "What on earth do you think you're doing, forbidding my servants to step foot off the property? I have errands I need—"

She moved the portiere out of her path. Her eyebrows elevated. "I thought you said you weren't going to take possession of her yet. Has something happened? That's hardly fair! I hope this means you've conceded your bet."

Mr. Macy cast her an annoyed look as he threw off his cape. "I haven't time. Julia and I are leaving as soon as possible. I desire time alone with her before we absent ourselves." He turned to the butler. "Have a full tea prepared and brought to the library. Have one of my men run to fetch my wife's trunk. Give him directions to Am Meer." He looked at me and explained, "I had clothing waiting there for you, darling, as a precaution."

I avoided looking directly at Lady Foxmore's suggestive face as Mr. Macy led me to the library. Gloom coated the chamber upon our arrival. Mr. Macy strode to the window and opened moss-colored draperies. Weak light seeped through the dusk. He gestured with an out-turned palm for me to remain, then left.

Feeling at a loss, I sank into the settee and touched my face and neck, as if to ascertain I were in one piece. I swallowed, wondering where Edward was and what he was doing. Surely by now he'd at least located Henry.

I wiped my cold palms over the skirt of my dress, wondering if they'd know to seek me at her ladyship's. When we'd left Auburn Manor, Mr. Macy hadn't told anyone where we were headed.

The butler rolled a tea cart into the room, then set a round table. Mr. Macy returned as the last dish was placed.

"Send Snyder to me," he instructed, waving the manservant from the room. Mr. Macy observed me for a few minutes, turning only when footsteps pounded down the hall.

A man with angular features appeared.

"Have you news?" Mr. Macy asked.

The man's nod toward me questioned whether Mr. Macy wanted him to speak in my presence.

"She's my wife. You may speak, provided you mind your tongue."

The contempt left the man's features, and he nodded apologetically as he held out two posts. "Rooke came while you were gone."

"Remain on the grounds." Mr. Macy snatched the letters from his hand and closed the door. Turning to me, he waved at the spread. "Go on, dearest, eat. I have business." He glanced at his watch. "If we leave in the next two hours, we'll reach my London house sometime after nightfall. We'll not be stopping at an inn, so this will be your last meal of the day."

I sat feeling as displaced as a rag doll that had been dunked in the laundry and wrung out, but not returned to her little mistress. I stared at the tea, but my stomach felt envenomed with panic, making it impossible to eat. I glanced at Mr. Macy.

He sat at the desk and inspected the letters for evidence of tampering before he broke the gold seal of the first one. Though I felt no appetite, I obediently poured tea while I studied my husband. This was no ordinary business that occupied his mind. Something terrible was afoot. My hands grew cold, and I turned from my speculations. It was best not to dwell upon it. I didn't want to know more about Mr. Macy's world. All I wanted to do was stay calm. It was only a matter of time until Henry or Edward arrived.

I stared at my tea, forcing myself to believe they would come. They simply had to. They wouldn't leave me like this.

Mr. Macy crumpled the first letter and with gritted teeth hurled it into the cold grate. When he ripped open the next post, he stopped breathing.

He slid the note into his trouser pocket, went to the stocked trolley, and poured a brandy. Not following protocol, he took a slice of cold roast beef and wrapped a piping-hot roll around it. While he chewed, a hunted look spread over his features, and his glance kept returning to the window. "Stay here." He rose, tossing his uneaten portion upon a platter of grapes. He yanked the draperies shut, filling the room with gloom. He lit a lamp but it did little to dispel the semidarkness. With a kiss on my forehead, he removed my teacup from my hands. "If you're not hungry, sleep before our journey. You're tired. Excuse me; I'll return in a moment."

I rested my head upon the arm of the velvet couch until he left; then I went to the window and parted the draperies. A gloomy mist enfolded the landscape.

I shivered and glanced at the hearth, wishing for fire. The white, crumpled paper Mr. Macy had tossed there still lay in the grate.

Edward's words surfaced to memory. *"I'm absolutely convinced he's evil, though I lack proof."*

Would it help, I wondered, if I found evidence? I tiptoed across the room and knelt. The house was still and silent, so I retrieved the letter and smoothed out the wrinkles.

Have checked from Lombard Street to the Thames. There is no sign of him. Will search Lothbury next.

I balled it back into a crumpled sphere and started to replace it, but a hand snatched mine.

"What the blazes do you think you are doing?" Mr. Macy asked.

I flinched and met his penetrating gaze. An admonition rose from within, warning me not to lie. "I was reading this."

"Why?"

Surprised by the domination in his tone, I felt the impulse to lie but resisted it. "To . . . to see if it was extortion."

His grip loosened, and the cold edge left his eyes. "Well, at least you're an honest sneak. If you must know, I'm searching for John. Someday I intend to see him writhe at your feet for making that assertion. In the meantime, you need to make a decision, Julia, and I expect you to make it now. Decide what sort of marriage we're going to have. I'm not releasing you from our union. You can either be a token wife, and after securing an heir, I'll see that your needs will be provided and leave you to your tea circles and dinner parties. Or you can stop asking questions and accept me as I am. Which shall it be?"

I tried to withdraw my hand from his, but he held my wrist like a vise.

"Do you think I wish a cold marriage, outside your affections?" I whispered.

"Then for your own happiness, leave my papers alone." He threw my hand down and rubbed his creased forehead. "I'm sorry, dearest. Today is not a day to test me." He smiled, but it seemed forced. Worry lingered in his eyes. He bent over me, and with slow, provocative movement ran his fingers along the nape of my neck; then he kissed me near my ear. "Can you sit tight? Finish your tea; read a book."

His movements felt mechanical, and his eyes kept returning to the door so that each caress was tainted. I met his gaze. "How much peril are we in?"

His body loosened. "I would not place you in danger, but

thank you for considering mine your own. Can you make your-self happy here? Just now, I'm not able to entertain you, though I intend to give you my full attention tonight."

"Who is after you?" I insisted, suspecting he'd purposefully tried to embarrass me from further questions.

There was a loud thump in the hall. Mr. Macy gave me a warning look to remain and crept to the door.

He peered through the crack before closing it. "I swear that maid drops more things than she can possibly be worth." He strode to me and offered his hand. When he pulled me to my feet, he pressed his nose into my hair, then kissed the tip of my ear. He led me to the couch, randomly selecting a book along the way. "My estates are secure. When we reach my house, you may wander freely. For now, read this. I'll return shortly."

Once the door closed, I flopped on the couch and stared at the volume in my hands, amazed that he expected me to just sit there reading like a good wife. I opened the calfskin book, unable to concentrate on the black print.

I shut my eyes and tried to picture describing this moment to the others. I tried to imagine what sort of questions they would ask, to see if I'd tried every manner of escape. All at once, I could imagine Henry's sarcastic voice saying, "Please tell me you at least checked the windows."

Shutting the book, I made my way to the glass panes that lined the wall. Her ladyship's house was high off the ground, but I was willing to risk the drop. If I managed to make it outside, I decided, I would head for Edward's and my oak. I would climb to the highest branch and wait. Eventually, if he knew I was miss-ing, he'd look there for me.

I unlocked the latch and pushed, but the window did not budge. For five minutes, I jostled and shoved each window, try-ing to see if I could free one of them from whatever bound them shut.

Frustrated, I returned to the couch. Breaking the window

wasn't an option either. The individual panes were too small to crawl through.

Knowing Elizabeth would ask whether I'd tried picking the lock with a hairpin, I slid one loose and tiptoed to the door. Though I angled and poked it several ways, the lock did not give. I pictured Elizabeth frowning as I retreated to the couch.

For the next several hours, I kept rising and looking out the window, hoping to see Henry or Edward in the distance, but each time the landscape was empty.

❧

"What!" Mr. Macy's harsh voice carried through the door, waking me from my shallow slumber.

The cushion sank beneath my hands as I pushed myself up. Mr. Macy swung the door open, and behind him stood the man I'd seen earlier.

"I'm sorry; were you sleeping?" Mr. Macy paused, I believed, to temper the anger in his voice. "Your lady's maid has not packed for you yet. I sent my carriage to have your belongings loaded. She sent word that she decided to line your trunk with new paper and hasn't finished. Apparently, she lost the key to the trunk after emptying it and scraping off the old paper."

I realized he could only be speaking of Nancy. My heart pounded with some measure of hope. If Mr. Macy had sent a carriage to Am Meer, then Edward must know where I was.

Even if he didn't, there was a small hope that Nancy would join me—and that brought relief. All at once, the events of the last few days compounded into a need for release, and I fought the urge to giggle.

"She has a stubborn streak." I laughed with rising panic. Even to my ears, my laughter sounded freakish. "Only Reynolds can handle her." Then, to keep Mr. Macy from suspecting Nancy's ruse, I added, "This is her way of objecting that we didn't ask her to come along. Send a note, telling her she's to join us later." My laughter died into a sob just as Lady Foxmore appeared in the doorway.

"Problems with your wife, Chance?" she asked.

"Her nerves are overwrought," he said, waving her silent. "Adelia, we're going to spend the night. Prepare a new room. It'll scarcely do to keep Julia in the one I've been occupying. There's ash everywhere."

"Are you going to require I obtain every key to this room from my servants as well?" Lady Foxmore asked.

"You know I am. Just humor me, Adelia. I'm in no mood for banter."

❧

"You disappointed me, child," Lady Foxmore said as her footman placed oyster soup before her. "I'd had hopes you'd evade Chance longer, give him a taste of how it feels to be loved and spurned. After all those seductions, I cannot tell you the satisfaction it gave me to watch him on the receiving end." She wagged a silver spoon at Mr. Macy. "Now you know how Lady Caroline felt the time you—"

"Be quiet, Adelia." Mr. Macy gave her a black look. "Sweetheart, is your soup not warm enough? Send it back."

I dipped my spoon into the dish, taking his hint not to give Lady Foxmore the satisfaction her jibe intended but feeling displaced anyway.

"Does your wife know you've requested the bishop to arrive tomorrow, to investigate whether her lover should be permitted to keep his church?"

My spoon clattered into my soup. "Edward's going to lose his living!"

"He's not losing his church, Julia," Mr. Macy said. "I'll make certain of it. Adelia, with your permission, I prefer silence."

Lady Foxmore smirked and slowly turned her head from him

to me. "Did you at least punish him for sending notice to auction off your house and furnishings?"

Confused, I looked across the table at Mr. Macy.

Mr. Macy sank back in his chair with a weary look. "Sweetheart, my intention was to limit the places you could hide." He gave Lady Foxmore a deadly look. "I'm in no mood, Adelia. You're setting foot on perilous ground."

Lady Foxmore only smirked in reply as I gripped the arms of my chair, feeling the helplessness of being a wife. Had my house been sold, then?

"You can't do this." Tears of indignation sprang to my eyes as I threw my napkin on the table. "What gives you the right? What are you trying to do? What about my furniture, and—?"

Lady Foxmore rapped her wineglass with her spoon until the tinging stopped me. "Child, he cannot answer more than one question at a time."

Mr. Macy leaned over the table, rubbing his forehead. "Julia, just tell me what I need to do for an expedient recovery. I have no wish for argument between us. Now that you've returned I can reclaim it, or you can list the items you want. I'm not denying you anything or taking anything. I'll have Reynolds send a carriage to collect them."

Lady Foxmore laughed. "Listen to you, sounding like a husband bribing his wife for favors. I refuse to believe you are suddenly incapable of charming your way around this. Why are you gratifying the child? She's a mere girl. You, the man who once—"

"Adelia, not another word."

His sinister tone made Lady Foxmore clamp her mouth shut.

"Excuse us." Mr. Macy rose and walked around the table to collect me. "My wife and I shall retire now."

When the footman shut the dining room doors behind us, Mr. Macy started down the hall with the air of someone containing his wrath. I stumbled alongside him, suffocating on my objections and anger. Yet I held my complaints. He was nothing like his former self. He seemed completely occupied by some abstruse problem, and I had no desire to draw his attention to myself.

He guided me down a corridor and up a heavy staircase with an ornate banister. Before a door at the top, he withdrew a key from his waistcoat, then unlocked the chamber. The scent of cigar blanketed the stifling air. I leaned against the threshold, trying to smother the anger that had surfaced during dinner, and surveyed the room. It had the same effect that his bedroom in Eastbourne had on me, tugging at my sympathy. Only now I steeled myself against that better emotion. I had not forgotten Edward's sentiments about Macy in Churchill's office.

The chamber lacked a servant's care, and I recalled that Macy alone possessed the key. How could Mr. Macy be this distrustful of everyone? On my left, an ivory-handled razor lay across an enamelware basin filled with cloudy water. Next to it, a leather shaving kit hung open, containing lotions and various bottles— most uncorked. The sheets on his bed were twisted in knots, evidence that he thrashed in his sleep.

Leaving me, he stepped over cigar ash and stubs, removed his jacket and waistcoat, and cast them upon the unmade bed. After unfastening the collar buttons of his linen shirt, he slipped it over his head.

Embarrassed by the ease with which he undressed before another person, I averted my eyes, heat filling my face, but when he left his trousers on, I looked up again. During summertime, I'd often seen bare-chested peasants working, their shirts tied about their waists. Mr. Macy was as fit as any of them. Sinews moved over his chest and arms as he gathered apparel and underclothing, which he shoved into saddlebags. He turned to collect papers fanned over a nightstand. A deep, jagged scar ran across the right side of his back.

I stared at it with aversion. The marred part of his body cor-roborated the sinister rumors surrounding him. No gentleman would be someplace where he could be stabbed. I marvelled that he'd even survived such a wound. Like Edward's calluses, it branded him as someone who had transcended his calling as a gentleman into an entity of his own choosing. Unable to refrain, I stepped forward and touched the defect.

Fingers crushed mine before I'd barely brushed the surface. Mr. Macy cursed, but his voice was grieved. He released me and then inspected my hand with a repentant face. "Julia, my word, are you injured? When I'm not facing you, you must always call out my name before you touch me. *Always.* Is that understood?"

I nodded but then, unable to take more, shook my head. His bare skin felt feverish as he wrapped me in his arms. "Now is not the time to panic. Today is over. Abate your tears. Forgive my brooding. There has been much on my mind tonight, but perhaps it's time I turn my attention to my reckless young wife."

He grabbed a white silk shirt folded over the towel rail of his washstand, slid it on leaving it untucked, then added an oriental banyan, which fell to his knees. He closed his shaving kit and cast it outside the door, then piled saddlebags atop it. Lastly, he threw frock coats and linen shirts into the hall.

"This isn't the way I envisioned gathering you to me," he said, surveying the dim hall with a shake of his head. "I ought to require Adelia's head on a platter for that display during dinner." He kissed my temple, then guided me down the hall, continuing to soothe with his voice. "Let us at least see what sort of room she arranged first."

My feet turned to clay, but he intertwined his fingers in mine and led me further down the corridor. My legs quivered but carried me. When he stopped before a door and unlocked it, Mr. Greenham's accusation that Mr. Macy was responsible for Mama's death wormed its way back into my consciousness. Though I'd forced it from my thoughts, it now hurtled back to consciousness and sent stabs of icy fear through my limbs.

The chamber contained sitting and sleeping areas divided by

pillars. A cheerful fire lit the room, a respite from the autumn air permeating the walls of the estate. Glass lamps decorated with prisms shimmered as they spread an inviting light. Elaborate bouquets adorned tables and nightstands.

Mr. Macy nodded approval and, placing his hand on the small of my back, started to enter. Every qualm, every dark speculation about Mr. Macy filled me with a distrust that fluttered through my body, and I broke into a cold sweat. When I refused to take another step, unable to keep the agony from showing on my face, he turned his head and surprise registered on his features.

"Don't tell me you fear your wifely duties," he said with a tilt of his head, but his tone held no jest, only astonishment. "You never used to fear me."

I cupped both hands over my eyes, and Mr. Macy drew me to him, allowing me to shield my face in his nightshirt. This was more than I could bear. As much as I had felt attracted to him before, I now felt only trepidation at the thought of consummating our marriage. It wasn't just his touch I dreaded, but the finality of the act.

"Do not feel embarrassed, sweetheart." He held me a moment, then placed distance between us. "Have I ever hurt you?"

Unable to answer, I shifted and looked down. With a steadying gaze, he ushered me into the room, then locked the door.

"Darling." His tapered fingers ran along my neck, and then he kissed the places still tingling from his touch. "Had I not been neglectful toward you today, I daresay, we could have avoided this. Allow me to assure you of my devotion." He removed the pins holding my hairstyle, unwinding one coil of hair after another. He lifted my hair and gave tantalizing kisses along the nape of my neck.

Every sensation was heightened due to my uncertainty, and my mouth became so dry I could scarcely swallow. Instead of leading me to the bed, he lowered me upon the couch.

"Dismiss from your mind everything Adelia said. I swear to you, I shall make amends. Fear of living without you drove me to those measures." He lowered himself beside me, interlaced his fingers in the back of my hair, and turned me toward him.

He kissed the hollow of my throat with slow, caressing kisses, all the while pulling me to him until I was breathless. I closed my eyes, trying to shut out the chaos, having no choice but to accept that this man was my husband. He tasted like wine, and the scent of cigars pervaded my senses. A brief yearning for Mama rose and ebbed.

When he drew back, strands of my dark hair clung to his hair and shirt, webbing us in. His fingers slid under me, and he unbuttoned the back of my dress. I closed my eyes, but when he slid my gown off my shoulder, new uncertainty swept through my body, and my eyes fluttered open to meet his dark gaze.

It was in his eyes. Something dark and unexplainable was rooted in his soul. Cold. Hard. Ruthless. Yet intermingled with it was pride that I was his wife. He remained poised over me, as though reading my thoughts and desiring to see where my private discourse would take me. My body grew cold.

He was capable of great cruelty. How I knew, I was uncertain, but I did, in the same way I knew I was outside that part of him, that he would never harm me. I was his wife, one with him. Or would be. The thought that I was about to unite with something poisonous petrified me. I swallowed and looked toward the door.

"Let's not do that again." Disappointment flickered across his countenance, but then he cradled my hand against his face, kissing the wrist. "You are my wife. Would I harm that which I love most?"

I stared at him. How could he have known my thoughts? His words sounded true, yet rang false, and I couldn't yet discern which sense was right. Every emotion conflicted. His every action, his every word and movement cried devotion.

Could he be as evil as Edward believed and still love me? I needed to deliberate, but the force of his presence only increased my confusion.

"You still resist me?" Amusement coursed through his velvet tones. "Such a curious wife I have chosen. You've no idea the number of women who wished to be my bride, and yet here you are, your heart beating with fear, though you've never been safer."

Someone banged on our door. Mr. Macy's body stiffened. "What?"

"I beg your pardon, sir, but your wife's maid has arrived and insists upon seeing her mistress."

The tension in Mr. Macy's body ebbed, and the momentary fear that had lit his eyes disappeared. "I'm perfectly capable of tending to my wife. Send the girl back to Am Meer," he called over his shoulder; then adjusted me in his arms.

"She's my servant." I struggled against him to sit, feeling able to breathe again. I needed to see Nancy. I prayed her arrival meant that Edward was here too. "She's mine. Have that man fetch her and keep her here."

He caressed the tips of my fingers between his. "I plan on spending the entire night with you. I'll tend you in the morning."

"You keep saying I'll have liberties. Prove it. I want her."

He studied me, indecision lurking in his eyes; then, with an annoyed slight shake of his head, he rose and unlatched the door. "Wait, come back," he commanded, but before anything more was said, a second set of footsteps came flying from another direction.

"Excuse me, sir," a man said, "but—"

"What now?" Frustration tinged Mr. Macy's voice as he spun in that direction.

"A Mr. Magnus Bradshawl just arrived. He's requesting an audience with you. He said you would want to know he was here."

The matter pressing upon Mr. Macy's mind had come—I

could practically taste it—but instead of alarming him, it revived him. The atmosphere ignited with friction, and snap returned to his eyes as determination replaced the hunted look.

"Here?" Mr. Macy asked with a laugh. "The fool. Where?"

"The antechamber, sir."

The angular man arrived, giving Mr. Macy a worried look as he panted to catch his breath.

"Stay and guard this room." Mr. Macy glanced over his shoulder at me. "I don't want my wife stepping foot outside it."

"But—"

"I know who's here," Mr. Macy said in a venomous tone, "and I want my wife guarded." He snapped his fingers at the butler. "Send her lady's maid to tend to her during my absence." Then to the man nearest him, "Give me your revolver."

He shut the door and locked me in the bedchamber without glancing at me. Urgent conversation came to me in muffled tones before feet rushed away. When all was silent, I crept to the door and pressed my ear against it. A man coughed on the other side.

Too stunned to do more, I sat on the hearth and nervously wrung my skirt. I was lost. Mama would have known what to do. I pressed my lips, starting to cry, but forced myself to stop, desiring to be a self-governing woman. Only what could I do locked inside a bedchamber?

The bolt on my door clicked open. Nancy entered, her eyes round. A large, ugly bonnet framed her sharp face. She looked at me—near weeping, half-dressed—and her face paled. I knew what she thought and pulled my dress over my chemise before wiping my tears.

She knelt beside me, tearing at the knot under her chin. "Reverend Auburn is outside, waiting for thee. Thou mustn't waste time. Make haste. Don my dress."

I gave a shaky laugh.

She slid my dress from me. "Does thou has to asks why?

Thou knows as well as I do." After removing my dress, her fingers flew, unbuttoning hers. "He sent me to tell thee he'll wait in th' orchard as long as it takes. He bids thee to find a way of escape. Here, takes me dress."

I could scarcely think straight as I pulled on the brown garment.

"Hurry, miss." Nancy shook her dress, only halfway on me, rushing me.

The coarse twill irritated my skin. With yanking tugs, she buttoned me, then wound my hair into a bun and wrapped a scarf over it. After tucking my hair from sight, she added the hideous bonnet.

Nancy slid the peasant clogs from her feet and slipped them onto mine. They felt warm and moist, but I ignored it.

"Art thou ready?" she whispered, struggling into my dress.

"What will happen to you?"

Her eyes begged for compliance. "I'll blame it on thee and tells him thou ordered me to hand over my clothing and snuck out."

I shook my head, imagining the wrath Mr. Macy would direct toward Nancy. "I can't leave you here."

Before I could protest, she called through the door in an attempt to speak without her northern accent. "My lady's maid forgot something. Open the door."

Swearing was followed by the jangle of keys. Nancy shoved me outside the moment it opened and tugged the door shut behind me.

My heart raced in my throat as the man cast me a quick glance, relocking my chambers. Tension claimed his features as he returned his attention to the hall swallowed in darkness. I chose the first passage away from his sight.

Twenty-Eight

I TURNED THE FIRST CORNER and slipped Nancy's clogs from my feet. Using the bonnet to shield my face, I crept to the grand staircase and tiptoed down.

When my foot touched the bottom step, Mr. Macy's voice carried from the end of the corridor, where an open door spilled a rectangle of yellow light onto the hall floor. His words were indistinguishable, but his soothing voice possessed a hypnotic quality, both sinister and alluring. I gripped the banister and paused, imagining him sprawled in a chair, fingers steepled before his nose, eyes fixed on his victim as he foretold in his seductive voice the coming horrors.

The ruthlessness I sensed behind his tender kisses moments ago now lurked behind the beauty of his voice. The incantation kept me transfixed, casting a finespun spell, making it impossible to move. *Dare I stir his wrath?* I wondered. *Last time, I had permission to leave.*

During our childhood, Edward had once caught a robin and handed it to me to hold. Its heart thumped so rapidly against its breast, I thought it should die of fright. The beating in my own

chest could have matched it as I slipped down the passage leading to the front door.

Outdoors, wisps of fog writhed around my dress in serpen-
tine coils. A raw wind stirred the rolling brume, making the
estate an island amidst a boiling cauldron. On tiptoe, I strained
to see past the ring of light surrounding the house. Darkness
and shadow reigned.

Chest tight with fear, I peered into the gloom but discerned
no shapes that resembled trees. Hadn't Nancy said Edward
would wait for me in the orchard?

I merged into the darkness, folding my arms for warmth.
The moist air seeped through Nancy's gown. I headed toward the
back of the estate, concentrating to keep myself lower than the
hedges. As my eyes adjusted, I detected the dark outline of trees.
A light winked through branches—a wavering hope.

I cried with joy and love for Edward. Forcing my legs forward,
I stumbled toward the glimpses of light. Now damp, my dress was
plastered to my skin, but not even that slowed my movements.
When my hand grasped the first tree, I nearly sobbed with relief.

"Edward?" I softly called into the night.

There was no answer.

"Edward, please." I raised my voice. "Edward. Answer me!"

"Here!" he called, but his voice was strangely thick.

Branches snapped and leaves crunched nearby. The mist
roiled as I clung to the tree, waiting. Dressed in his cassock,
Edward walked toward me, but he staggered.

"I feared you wouldn't be able to find me," I said, hastening
toward him.

"I'm here." Grief filled his voice. "Here."

He removed the familiar brown woollen coat and draped it
over my shoulders.

It provided a barrier between Nancy's homespun and the
wintry air. The lantern swung as he pointed into the night. "We
must make haste."

A wind blew from the east, filled with the scent of wood fire and fir. Pine needles chafed when we turned from the woodlet into a thicket. Beneath our feet, soft mossy turf sank as we passed. Though his arm guided me, there was no embrace in it.

It was Edward, but a strange Edward. His eyes blazed with an intensity I'd never seen before. He supported me as we clambered up a steep bank, pebbles clattering behind us.

"Here, sir." Henry's driver peeked over the top of the bank, holding a lantern. He stretched out his hand.

Edward's strong arm girded me as he accepted the help and scrambled to the top.

Finally able to pause, I turned to study Edward. I saw him, although nebulously. Damp curls rested against his pale face and his eyes were rimmed with red.

He untied Nancy's bonnet, carefully searching my face. With a look of desperation, his gaze darted between the carriage and me. "Did he hurt you?" Before I could respond, he demanded louder, "Did he hurt you?"

I shook my head.

Edward sagged in relief, then handed me into the carriage. Stepping up behind me, he called out, "Drive!"

"'Tis no ordinary fog." The driver's voice sounded from the box seat. "Sure you want to risk it?"

Edward peered into the swirling mass. The murk had grown so thick it crept into the carriage, blanketing my feet. The lantern cast a shadow over the cleft of his chin as he stared at the mist.

"Yes," he said in a hoarse voice. "We've no choice. Give the horses leave to find the path. Pray they can find their way through this mess. Head north."

Edward climbed through the open door. I gripped his coat, pulling it around me, struggling to comprehend his mood.

"What's wrong?" I asked. "What happened?"

He emitted a harsh choking noise, and for a minute, I feared he couldn't speak. "Churchill . . ." A sob rent him as he reached for me and buried his face in my neck. His shoulders shook, and his breath was hot on my skin.

I clutched him, too bewildered to speak.

Before I could inquire, Edward asked, "Who would murder such a kind old man?"

It was only this afternoon that I'd sat across from him, having tea.

"Who would beat a feeble old man to death?"

I drew a sharp breath, recalling how carefully Mr. Macy had questioned me about Churchill. I shook my head, wanting to deny my own thought. Surely it was a coincidence. It couldn't be linked to the man's murder. It couldn't be.

All at once, I realized how trying today must have been for Edward. He'd lost track of me, learned his mentor was murdered, and had probably spent the remainder of his time trying to piece together a rescue plan.

"Where's Henry?" I asked.

Edward sat back, wiping his eyes with his sleeve. "Forgive me," he said. "I am overwrought."

My ears rang as I realized I was missing something. Something horribly awry, horribly wrong. A vague feeling of terror crept over me as I tried to think of what. Then all at once I knew. I'd left Nancy locked in a room waiting for Mr. Macy.

The thought was so monstrous, I felt both hot and cold.

"Stop the carriage." I raised my voice to a scream. "Stop the carriage."

The driver obeyed, and I stumbled into the cottony wisps. Edward hopped down after me and grabbed my hand.

"Let me go. Let me go!" I tore from his grasp so violently, I lost balance and fell to the road. Pebbles embedded in my hands. I covered my mouth, trying to hold on to the last shreds of sanity.

"Juls?" Edward knelt beside me.

"I've got to go back. I've got to. You don't understand." And then I told Edward about my time with Mr. Macy and how intimidated I'd felt as he questioned me about Churchill.

Arms wrapped me from behind as Edward knelt, gathering me from the marshy ground to settle me against his chest. "We can't go back," his voice lulled as he cradled me. "By now she's probably been discovered and it will do no good. We need to get you away from here."

I clutched the back of his cassock as I sobbed into his sinewy chest. His clothing smelled like smoke, not the sooty scent of a coal fire, but of burning wood. How many times had he smelled of campfire when we were younger? I clung to him, wanting to go back, wanting to be twelve again, when my only worry was that Mama or Sarah might find us.

"Come on." Edward helped me to my feet. "We haven't time. We've got to move."

I gave a bitter laugh. "Where do you think we can go?"

"As far north in Scotland as we can get," he replied.

"He'll find us," I said. "I've already told him about my vote to go there."

When his brows knit together, I held up a hand for silence. "Please, let me think."

In quick succession, I combed my mind for other possibilities. We couldn't stay in Edward's parish any longer. I considered using the papers my guardian had given me to withdraw a tidy sum. But I'd have to go to Mr. Graves, and that would delay us—besides, I feared I was now a bane to everyone I touched.

With a slow movement, I turned and looked at Edward.

The slant of his shoulders made him appear worn and weary. The desperation in his eyes worried me.

All at once, I realized I'd won the battle—when forced to choose between his faith and me, Edward had chosen me. But I felt no victory.

"It won't work, Edward, and you know it. We have no living, no money, and would live every day of our lives in fear of discovery. We'd be starting with nothing, without friendship or support. Besides, we both know you'd be miserable. You can't go against your convictions without it destroying you."

"I'm not leaving you alone in this."

I tucked my knees to my chest and wrapped my arms about them, knowing he'd be stubborn. I considered using his parish as an argument, which made me wonder how many unseen lives hung in the balance of the decisions we were making. How many souls depended upon Edward?

Churchill's rebuke came fresh to my mind, strengthening my resolve. *"Had you a shred of love for Edward, you would release him. Only the most selfish sort of person drags someone else down with him as he drowns."*

My throat ached as I acknowledged that the only noble thing to do was to release Edward.

I took a deep breath to quell my despair. How, after a lifetime of being ostracized, had I found myself here again? Especially when all I had tried to do was escape this fate? I gave a disbelieving laugh. I didn't even have family left.

Yet that thought wasn't true, and I knew it. There was still Lord Pierson.

My next idea went against all rationale, all prior experiences. Every fiber of my body rose up with a strong cry that there might be one more chance. One more chance to be free of Mr. Macy.

I clutched Edward's sleeve, scarcely able to believe what I was considering. "How powerful is my father?"

Edward blinked with confusion. "Your father? You mean Lord Pierson?"

I nodded, recalling Mr. Addams's descriptions. "Do you think, if he chose to, he'd be able to protect me from Mr. Macy?"

"He's powerful enough to." Edward's answer was measured. "His reputation is that of being one of the most fair and upstanding members in the House of Lords. Why?"

"Take me to him."

Twenty-Nine

TWO NIGHTS LATER, well past midnight, we arrived at my father's estate. Maplecroft sat under the watery light of the moon. The estate looked every bit as august as Eastbourne, only instead of sprawling with centuries of architecture, it was a fortress of perfect geometric precision. The end towers rose in defiance against the night sky. Twenty or more chimneys rose above the roof, putting me in mind of sentries guarding a castle.

Edward climbed out first and studied it with trepidation, but when he reached back and offered me his hand, he gave me a smile of encouragement. "You know, I've been thinking," he said as my feet hit the ground, "no one's anger would be as kindled as his was that night at Eastbourne, if he hadn't lost something precious to him."

I clutched my stomach, wanting to believe him but not quite able to.

"It's going to be okay, Juls," he said. "If anyone has the persistence to win him over, it's you."

I took a deep breath and faced the estate in slight wonderment that the man who had fathered me lived in such magnificence. "Edward, what if his wife doesn't know about me?"

He looked surprised that I asked the question, and then said, "I don't think that's going to be a problem. The papers always like to remind the public that he puts England first because he has no one else. I believe he's been a widower for many years."

His words birthed a new hope in me as I took in the estate anew.

He too was alone. Perhaps my task wasn't impossible.

We stood another minute, hand in hand, too daunted to approach. Edward gained courage first. "Come on."

Keeping our fingers locked, we marched to the front door. Edward hesitated before lifting the massive knocker and striking it against the door. On my right, engraved on a polished brass plaque, the word *Maplecroft* gleamed in the moonlight.

Wind stirred my skirts, and I looked over my shoulder, surprised to find the outline of Eastbourne visible at the bottom of the ravine. A lone light was visible in the vast estate. Seeing that watery light made me tighten my hold on Edward's hand.

The scraping sounds of bolts turned my thoughts.

"Remember," Edward whispered, slipping his arm in mine, pulling me tight, "allow me to reason with him. Let me act as mediator."

I nodded as the door swung inward, revealing a man in a green satin robe, clutching a candle as thick as his forearm. The flickering light revealed hooded eyes.

Edward bowed. "We request an audience with the master of the house on urgent business."

With an arrogant snort, the man started to shut us out.

Edward wedged his foot in the door. "We will not quit this property until we have seen him."

"Lord Pierson is away and not expected back for another fortnight."

"Then we need to know where he's gone," Edward insisted.

"It is Lord Pierson's daughter who asks. She is seeking his protection."

The nameless man's gaze wandered to me. "Stand in the archway, by the door. Touch nothing."

I nodded, and he shut the door behind us. The flame wavered as he crossed the foyer and ascended the staircase. At the top he turned right, disappearing down a passage, leaving us in near darkness. Three stories above us, a domed skylight showed passing clouds illuminated by the moon.

The monotone ticking of clocks from various rooms blended into dissonance. My breathing sounded loud, and I squeezed the folds of my skirt, shifting my weight. Above, the sound of a door closing was followed by solitary footsteps.

Instead of Lord Pierson, however, a young man appeared at the top of the stairs, wearing a rich dressing gown and carrying a candle. The dour-looking servant followed him.

Edward and I kept our hands entwined as we listened to the cadence of their descending footsteps.

The young man reached us first and studied me with an incredulous look. "That's astounding," he said. "You look just like her." He laughed, a warm, golden laugh, then sobered.

He inclined, looking between Edward and myself with wonderment. "Forgive me my unorthodox greeting. Here, let us adjourn to the drawing room." He indicated a room on his right.

He faced the servant. "Simmons, have James woken. I want him to serve us."

With a scowl, the older man obeyed. I watched his retreating form, recalling the ridiculous argument Mrs. Windham and Elizabeth had about whether his name was Simmons or Simon. How unimportant it seemed now.

"Here, this way," the gentleman said. "Please."

We entered a room cloaked in darkness. The gentleman lit several lamps, then kindled a fire. He tugged on a bell pull and then turned. "Forgive me." He gestured to a chair. "I forget my manners. I'm—" he shook his head—"I'm shocked that you're actually here. Lord Pierson was expecting you. He left instructions for your arrival."

I cast an uncertain look at Edward.

"I'm sorry," Edward finally said, "but you are . . . ?"

"Lord Dalry," the young man stated, "but please, call me Isaac."

"Lord Dalry!" Edward took a step back in astonishment before giving him a slight bow. "Good heavens, forgive me. I had no idea."

The young man frowned, as though embarrassed. "Please, call me Isaac. Have a seat."

Strictness pervaded the drawing room we occupied. The ceilings were high and papered, the windows layered in brocade and silks. A grand pianoforte sat at the far end.

I stared at the books arranged in perfect order on the shelves. Footstools sat equidistant from the chairs, as if they'd been measured and lives depended upon keeping them perfect. There were no indentations in the carpet to suggest anything ever moved.

A footman arrived, freshly awoken as evidenced by his mis-buttoned shirt and wetted hair. "Simmons said you requested me, sir?"

"Thank you, James. We've guests. Please bring a light tea," Lord Dalry ordered.

The footman gave him an incredulous look. "In the drawing room at three in the morning?"

Lord Dalry grinned. "Oh yes, in the drawing room!" He rubbed his hands together. "We're going to bend all sorts of rules tonight. And I don't fancy doing so on an empty stomach."

The footman bowed and retreated.

"Now to business," Lord Dalry said. "I'm authorized to extend Lord Pierson's protection, and from what I understand, I need to extend his apology as well." His smile looked practiced as he faced me. "Had your father shown you any mercy that night, Macy would have injured you further, as a means of further exploiting him. It was for your own protection that he acted as such."

I lowered my gaze, not wanting him to see the effect his words had on me.

"Where is Lord Pierson?" Edward asked.

"He's with a group of men who are working to do something regarding Macy." Lord Dalry tapped his fingertips together twice, as if considering how much more to say. Lowering his tone, he decided upon, "They're very close to proving that Macy is Adolphus."

I sank against the back of my chair, amazed at how hated that name already was. I glanced at Edward to see how he took the information. During the last two days, I'd learned that Churchill had been like a father to him.

The footman returned with a large tray, which he placed on the table.

"Please." Lord Dalry gestured to the spread. "Help yourself."

"Are you hungry, Juls?" Edward asked, ready to fix me a plate.

I shook my head, suddenly desirous of being alone.

Lord Dalry rose. "Forgive me. I imagine you both must be very fatigued. Lord Pierson believed you'd only come here as a last resort, in desperation, if you will." He looked at my dress, as if noticing it for the first time. "Perhaps I was too eager in my greeting. I warrant the both of you would prefer to sleep first. Have you luggage?"

Edward shot him a vexed look as he also stood and grasped my arm. "She has nothing."

Lord Dalry remained unruffled by Edward's demeanor. "James," he said over his shoulder, "please fetch Simmons and let him know that our guests are ready for bed." Then to us, "Perhaps explanations can wait until morning."

A few minutes later, Simmons reappeared.

"Take the girl to Lady Pierson's room," Lord Dalry instructed. "I'll show the reverend to the guest chamber nearest mine."

Simmons grabbed a candle and made motion for me to follow him. He returned through the main hall, then trudged up the stairs, never looking behind. I followed, glancing once at Edward.

At the top, Simmons turned left and opened the door at the end of the corridor. The candlelight illuminated an ornate four-poster bed. Excessive draperies adorned the windows. They looked tawdry, even in the dark.

"The late Lady Pierson's room," Simmons said, a sour note in his voice.

I gave him a nod of thanks, then crawled into the bed.

⁓

I awoke later that morning to the scent of lavender and jasmine. When I opened my eyes, I found myself in a room smothered with gold-textured silks and gaudy furniture. Sun poured through heavy lace covering the window and moved in waves amongst the intricate patterns over the carpet.

I slid from the massive bed and walked to the window. Eastbourne sat at the bottom of a steep ravine. From where I stood, it no longer looked like a grand estate in the process of repair but like something once lovely, now decaying. With quiet dismay, I scanned the protruding architecture and gargoyles, then yanked the lace panel back in place and turned to face the room again.

A washstand stood behind an elaborately embroidered silk screen. Though it was stocked with tooth and nail brushes, towels, and soaps, there was no water in the porcelain basin. I searched the chamber for a bell pull but was unable to locate it amongst the lavish decoration.

I had tended myself for too many years to feel dismay.

I shed Nancy's coarse dress and placed it on the silken

bedclothes. My throat smarted as I wondered what had happened to her. I swallowed, hoping I could give Edward a message to relay to her.

I gathered and pulled my hair over my shoulder, then opened the wardrobe. The scent of heavy perfume stung my nose as I looked through the late Lady Pierson's dresses. She must have been stout, for nothing looked like it would fit me. I envisioned Nancy frowning at what little there was to work with.

A knock on the door was followed by the entrance of a middle-aged woman, who was no taller than my shoulder. Behind her, two maids followed. She bobbed, and the maids bobbed.

"I'm Mrs. Coleman, the housekeeper," she announced. She stared at Nancy's dress spread over the bed. The wrinkles around her mouth tightened as she viewed the empty fire grate.

I drew in a breath, knowing I looked beggarly. Then, recalling Edward's refusal to put on airs, I straightened. I eyed the girls behind Mrs. Coleman, deciding their dresses were suitable enough for me. "Good morning," I said. "As you can see, I have no belongings. I wonder if perhaps there is someone my size on staff, someone willing to lend me a dress? I fear nothing here fits me."

Mrs. Coleman blinked four times before finding her voice. "I grant you," she said, entering the chamber, "you're more petite than your mother, but we can manage." She proceeded around me and pulled a billowing, ivory brocade dress from the wardrobe.

It took both maids and the housekeeper to lower the grand dress over my head. With deft fingers, they made tucks and pinned them, then removed the gown. One of the maids bundled it in her arms, and with her chin to her chest, scurried from the room. When she exited, two more maids entered with steaming pitchers, which they carried into the room before giving me half curtsies and leaving.

For an excruciating length of time, Mrs. Coleman washed my arms and legs. The remaining maid brushed and oiled my hair and then styled braids that looped and interwove into each other. The dress arrived while Mrs. Coleman was perfuming and powdering me. When she opened a large jewelry box, I noticed the majority were emeralds. She selected an expensive set, including combs encrusted with diamonds.

"Won't Lord Pierson—I mean, my father—object?" I asked when the maid shoved them into my hairstyle.

Mrs. Coleman cast the maids a warning look when they expressed surprise, then primly responded, "Perhaps the vicar at your school stressed the importance of humility, but now you're a reflection of your father's status."

Her response astonished me to speechlessness, but there wasn't time to inquire. When they finished, I rose, nodding my thanks, surprised at the weight of the gown.

Outside my door, more maids stood with fresh linens. They bobbed as I sailed past them. When they entered my room, I raced down the hall toward the grand staircase.

I found what I sought immediately. At the bottom of the stairs, Edward waited beneath life-size portraits, leaning over his Bible. He failed to notice me at first as he sat, legs crossed, his brow furrowed.

Above, light poured through the vaulted ceiling's dome. Marble floors, azure-colored walls, and white baroque trim greeted my eyes. The huge staircase curved at the bottom. Portraits lined the lower hall and steps.

My heart felt like it would burst as I pattered down the stairs to him.

Before I reached him, however, I was arrested by the sight of one portrait in particular. She could have been me, except that her attire belonged to the last century. The resemblance was uncanny. Peculiarly, she wore the exact set of emeralds that I had inherited from Mama—every piece, excepting the headdress.

I stared a moment, recalling how much I'd longed for family the night I observed Mrs. Windham and Elizabeth reading in the hall by candlelight. Apparently I did resemble someone—and rather strongly too. That moment marked the first time I truly accepted the idea that Lord Pierson had fathered me. It birthed a desire in me, or rather a fierce longing to gain back some of what I had lost.

Seeing me study the painting, Edward said, "I fear our Mr. Forrester isn't very sharp if it took him an entire week to figure out who you were."

I laughed, then when Edward opened his arms to me, flung myself into them. He held me tight a minute; then he whispered, "Can you fetch a shawl? There's something I want to show you. Only make haste. I have a feeling when it's discovered that you're awake, we haven't a chance in all the world to talk privately."

I pulled away from him but took up his calloused palm and kissed it before running up the stairs.

When I arrived breathless in the chamber, I learned I had broken protocol; all the maids froze with horror.

"I just need a shawl," I explained, heading toward the wardrobe, starting confusion anew, for one girl stepped forward to fetch it for me, but then seeing I made motion to help myself, stepped back.

"Can you find it?" I asked her, knowing it would be quicker.

"Yes, miss." She dipped. She selected a watered silk that matched my dress, but I shook my head.

"Something very warm, if you please."

The girl shot another maid a nervous glance, and I knew that Edward and I would have to run for it. My father's staff clearly did not know what to think about my wanting to go outdoors. Nevertheless, she returned with a thick, fringed cashmere shawl.

I nodded my thanks, turned, and took flight.

"We've got to hurry," I told Edward, holding the shawl above my head in order to wrap it around me as I hied down the stairs.

He nodded and held out his hand.

We burst onto the frost-covered grounds that dazzled beneath the rising sun. Our breath curled above us, dancing in a song of thanksgiving as we hastened around a garden path.

"Here," Edward said, releasing me. "We mustn't be seen holding hands. I'm not certain how it started, but the staff thinks I'm your teacher. I'll pull out my Bible and read aloud; you follow. Keep your head bent. That way if any servants look out the window, they'll assume we're keeping the school's morning routine. They won't like our school very much, nor will they think us proper, but nonetheless . . ."

As long as we remained in sight of the house, Edward held his Bible before his face, reading—a psalm, I think—waving his free hand as if preaching, too.

I followed, thinking us ridiculous, but I didn't care. It was so like the old days. I imagined Henry and Elizabeth laughing in Am Meer's drawing room when Edward recounted our escape from my father's house.

Once we were free from view, Edward slowed and caught pace with me. Hand in hand we walked in silence, tromping across ground from which an early mist rose.

I shoved aside heartache, knowing that later I would drown in it. But for now, for that moment, I was determined to savor every minute with Edward.

"This is what I wanted to show you," Edward said as we entered a pasture. "I found it this morning, during my prayer walk."

By this time, I was breathing hard and my body was a strange mixture of temperatures—cold nose, ears, and toes, but warm elsewhere. I lifted my gaze to an ancient oak that stood near the entrance of the pasture.

A few rays of morning sun broke through the clouds and fell

aslant on the tree. I pressed a hand against my chest, feeling tears rise. "How can this be?" I asked. "How is it possible?"

"I have a theory," Edward said in a quiet voice next to me, "but you won't like it."

My breath curled in the frosty air as I laughed. Were it not impossible, I would swear that this was our ancient oak. It was identical in nearly every way.

Moss clumped over its massive trunk and up the centuries-old divide of its first two boughs. Straggles of leaves still clung to its twisting, meandering branches. Below, their fallen comrades carpeted the ground, looking as dry and as pitiful as corn husks. I covered my mouth, laughing at the bittersweet feeling, then grew teary. Just like our tree, one massive root still pulled up violently from the ground, as if the tree once took a mind to change locations but couldn't manage it.

I felt the release of more tension than I thought possible. How many times during the past three years had I daydreamed I was at the ancient oak? Then I laughed for the sheer absurdity of life. How could I have married Mama's murderer and yet still receive a gift like this moment? No jewel, no vase, no painting inside the halls of Eastbourne could ever compete.

Edward kept his fingers twined in mine, not speaking.

And somehow, illogical though it may be, the joy of that moment unlocked the pain. I covered my mouth and tried to stifle a sob. Embarrassed, I turned from Edward, not wanting him to hear. Not if this was our last time together. But it was for this reason he'd brought me here.

"Here." He tugged on my fingertips.

He led me to the tree, and then, taking a giant step up, he hoisted himself onto the lowest recumbent ledge. I gave him my hands, and with a shake of my head recalled how the soles of my shoes always slipped over the moss. Thankfully I found a knotty hole that the toe of my shoe could fit into. The initials *BD + EG* were carved next to it.

The next moment found us cradled in the massive bough, stretched out over the cushions of moss, looking up at the rambling crown of the tree. I settled my head against Edward's chest and shut my eyes, content just to be there, to be held.

For a half hour, we spoke no words—not needing to.

"I don't think Henry and Elizabeth are going to believe you," I eventually said as a flock of crows passed, "when you tell them about this tree."

A laugh rumbled in his chest, filling me with an unspeakable happiness. It had been so long since I'd heard it. "Hmm, I don't think they're going to believe me when I tell them I took tea with Lord Dalry at three in the morning and spent the night in Lord Pierson's estate."

I groaned, recalling the debonair gentleman. "Who is he, anyway?"

I felt Edward move, as if he were shaking his head. "A lord I've read about in the paper multiple times, though I don't think he's taken his seat yet."

I frowned, wondering when Edward had taken an interest in politics, but then realized it must have started after he gained a parish. How many of those laws directly affected him now?

Silence followed, but now that a reminder of reality had cropped up, I disliked it.

I twisted my head to view him. "What are you thinking about?"

Again he chuckled. "Well, I'm thinking that we just had—at least, I hope we just had—our worst fight. It was bad. You ended up married to someone else, and I broke the law and ruined Henry's carriage."

I laughed at his description. My thoughts turned toward my first morning at Am Meer and how different he'd acted, so I said, "You're a horrible vicar, you know."

His breath curled in the air, he laughed so heartily. "Thank you. I cannot tell you how much I appreciate that from someone who has never heard me preach. Admittedly, I do have one parishioner who causes me more problems than you can imagine. Her family was somewhat famous—"

"Her ladyship?" I said, smiling, as I squirmed to become comfortable.

"Hmm, make that two parishioners, then. No, this particular one comes from a family that is known for its animosity toward the church. But fear not." Edward shifted his arm, allowing him to touch the top of my head. "I think I've made some progress with her. The last time I spoke to her about God, she neither pitched an apple at me, shoved me in a creek, nor made a most unladylike display of herself by screaming and running away."

I laughed, turning on my side, ignoring the fact that I was wearing ivory and lying on moss. I wanted to see Edward's face.

"I'm not so certain," I said. "I have it on good authority she convinced her vicar to elope with her, even though she was already a woman of scandal."

Edward said nothing, but the laughter faded from his eyes.

"What made you decide to risk your faith by taking me to Scotland?" I asked him.

He shifted position, turning to place his back on the opposite branch. When he spoke, his voice was thicker. "I don't fully know. I've been told on multiple occasions that I needed to take care with Churchill, that he was a bit on the legalistic side. Henry was so certain what I needed to do." He frowned. "Juls, I really would like to know. What did Churchill say to you?"

"He told me only the most selfish person pulls someone else down with him as he drowns, that I needed to release you."

Edward frowned, a deep sadness filling his eyes. His jaw tightened as he looked at me anew. "I feel as though I'm responsible for Churchill's death, somehow. On the day he told me about Adolphus, he forbade me to repeat that name. He said something terrible would happen if his association with the man became known."

"Don't blame yourself," I said. "It wouldn't have made a difference. Macy knew we'd been to Churchill's office."

Edward shut his eyes, as if pained. "Yes, well, that was my grand idea too."

Knowing the best way to shift Edward from this mood wasn't to give him comfort, I said, "If Macy is this Adolphus, what on earth do you think he wants with me?"

Edward smiled. "Well, for starters, your father is the most powerful man in all of England, and it looks like he's been actively fighting this crime syndicate."

I tried to reconcile the dark rumors with what I'd experienced under Macy's care. Every emotion twisted.

"For starters?" I asked, wondering what else Edward suspected.

He grinned. "Well, I can't argue with his tastes."

I furrowed my brow, not understanding at first, but then laughed. "So what happens to us now?"

"We wait, just as we always have."

I cast him a curious look.

"If Macy is connected to even a fraction of the crimes associated with Adolphus, then it's only a matter of time before justice catches up with him." His voice sobered and grew tender, even. "He'll be hanged, Juls. I want you to be prepared. There may be some infamy connected to being the wife of such a famous criminal."

I smile now at the irony of Edward's words, though his guess was as good as any other as to what would happen.

That day, however, I folded my hands and tried to mentally adjust to the possibility that I might see Mr. Macy dangling from a scaffold. Only once had I witnessed a man being publicly executed, and I had no wish to ever repeat the experience.

Edward took my hands in his, pulling my thoughts from such a gruesome possibility back to him. "Hear me, Juls; really hear me. Let this sink deep into your memory. I am coming back for you. No matter what happens, no matter how long this takes. I swear it."

I nodded, feeling my throat thicken. "But what are we going to do about the difference in our beliefs?"

Edward laughed. "How different are they at this moment? Are you at least willing to admit perhaps there's more?"

I swallowed, considering his question. Everything in me twisted anew at the idea of having to admit I might have wrong beliefs. I considered the sensation I'd felt in Eastbourne's chapel and the impossibility of all that had happened. My fingers took in the carpet-like moss and rough texture of the bark.

How strange, I thought, *to base faith on a tree.*

But I laughed at the happy and foolish idea. "Yes, perhaps I can concede *that* much."

Grinning, Edward slipped down from the tree. Strong hands grasped my waist, and a second later I joined him on the ground.

"What happens next?" I asked.

"I leave this afternoon." He tucked my arm beneath his. "My parish needs me, especially in light of Churchill's death. I can only imagine how anxious Henry and Elizabeth are."

"I forgot to tell you," I said, lowering my voice. "Mr. Macy had asked the bishop to come to determine if you should be allowed to remain in the church. I should have told you last night."

Edward shrugged. "I'll figure out something to tell him."

"Or maybe you can allow Henry to explain it."

He smiled at my jest. "No. I think not."

We fell silent as Maplecroft loomed into view. Edward stood, his rebellious curls dishevelled over his forehead as his vestments undulated in the autumn wind.

"It doesn't look any less imposing in daylight, does it?" Edward asked. His hand tightened over mine. "You can do this, you know."

I nodded. I had family again. A father. And apparently a father who wasn't as unfeeling as he first appeared. That would take some getting used to. And I had so many questions—questions about Mama, how they'd met, the circumstances surrounding my birth, why she had married the notorious William Elliston, and if it had been Lord Pierson writing to Mama in those final months. My throat ached as I acknowledged my truest wish. "Do you think I can make him love me?"

Edward grinned. "All I know is, Lord help the man."

I squeezed his hand as tightly as I could, never wanting to let go. Yet I knew if I didn't, I would never discover the other side of love.

I took my first step of faith.

In a society where truth is elusive and knowledge deadly, Julia Elliston must learn to watch her step.

Turn the page for an exciting preview of

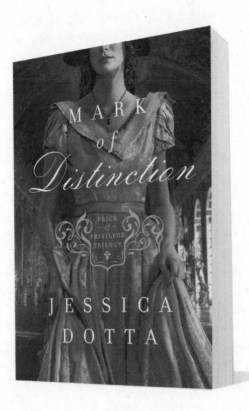

Available summer 2014 in bookstores and online.

TYNDALE
FICTION

www.tyndalefiction.com

THE EIGHT MONTHS that followed my arrival at Maplecroft have been called one of the greatest cozenages of our age. My father and I have endured endless speculation as to the amount of hours poured into its plan and execution.

Truth comprised of bare facts is rarely more flattering than legend. In reality, our sham was little more than a mad-dash scramble, composed of one improvisation after another. Events kept unfolding, forcing us to take new action, making it impossible to steer from collision.

I am an old woman now. Ancient some days. I had no idea my story would cause such an uproar. When I first penned it, my only intent was to address the rumors of how the entire affair started. I was weary of hearing how *I* seduced Mr. Macy. As if *I*, or anyone, could. The very idea is laughable. Long life has its advantages. One's perception grows clearer, even if sight does not. I now better understand how shocked the infamous Lady Foxmore must have felt during our presentation. Her pretension was unequalled. Yet there I stood, a pale, scrawny girl in rags, chosen by one of the most illustrious men in her circle to be wed to him. It is no wonder she thought it a grand jest. How could she, or anyone who knew Macy intimately, have guessed just how resolute he was upon marrying me?

Since my story's publication I have been accused of deceit, of besmirching the innocent by fabricating my story in order to gain public sympathy. Some have pointed out that I unfairly suggest that Mr. Macy is responsible for the murder of Churchill, Edward's solicitor. They remind me of the documented fact that the culprit was apprehended, and he was little more than an unstable man—and that it's merely coincidence that his death occurred on the same day that Mr. Macy collected me.

Others state that if I were truly innocent, then how is it my story escalated to treason, and how could it have ended so tragically?

It is this last challenge that causes me unrest. I cannot recount the mornings I've stood before my window, debating whether it is best to allow the matter to rest or to persevere and tell the tale in its entirety. I've wrestled with my conscience, wondering what good it will do to reveal all. Shall I so easily expose the sins of my father? Like Ham, shall I peel back the tent flap and expose his naked shame to the world? Will it bring back the dead? Or change anything?

It was only this morning, as I turned to retreat to my favorite chair, that I decided. I caught sight of my paternal grandmother, Lady Josephine, watching me. She is ageless, of course, forever capturing the bloom of our youth. It is curious to me now that I did not consider myself pretty then. Youth is its own beauty, and I wasted mine wishing I were other—more fair, more statuesque. But of no mind! As I paused and studied her painting, my great-grandchildren rushed past my window, tripping on their own merry shrieks. They fell in a muddle, and then just for the glory of it, lay on their backs, spread their arms, and laughed.

I chuckled, imagining their incredulousness to learn my frolics were once as madcap as theirs. Lady Josephine also watched with her ever-present coy smile. For some reason it brought to mind how her portrait gave me strength during those long months with my father. Something about her smile used to assure me that her anecdotes were no less mischievous than those I shared with Henry, Edward, and Elizabeth. I regret that I will never learn about them.

It is this thought that decided me.

I will for my grandchildren and great-grandchildren to know me.

Not the version they'll find archived in the newspapers. Heaven forbid they search there! I care not to contemplate the opinions they'd form. No, I will write this wrong. Let them at least judge me by truth, though it is hard to say whether it makes me less of a culprit. Let the world think what it will. I am much too old to care, anyway. I have aged past the point of cowing to opinions.

It all began, of course, with my father.

Not my stepfather, William Elliston, whom I believed begot me up until that devastating night that I wed Mr. Macy.

But Lord Pierson himself.

❧

A narrow sliver of light streamed through the dark hall as I pushed the library door open ever so slightly. Careful not to be heard, I took measured, tiny steps forward, fearing the door might creak and give me away.

"What did you expect I'd do?" My father's was the first voice I heard.

"Even if she's not placed here by Macy," Mr. Forrester shouted, "this will ruin you! They may forgive you for having an ill-begotten child, but to lie about it is committing political suicide. You can't honestly think you can hide her identity from that lot!"

Holding my breath, I leaned forward and finally took my first glimpse. Inside, a roaring fire cracked and hissed, casting a glow on the heavily polished wood. At the hearth, Mr. Forrester spread the tails of his frock coat apart as he warmed his backside.

My father sat, bent over his desk, carefully writing out a document before him.

"She doesn't even resemble your wife." Mr. Forrester dropped his tails. "Nor does she possess grace or manners. How are you going to convince anyone she's lived her life in a finishing school? What school produces something like her?"

The uncomfortable look that passed over my father's face as he dipped his pen told me he secretly agreed with the assessment. "You can keep wasting your breath," my father said, "but I shall move forward with this. Either help me or leave."

"Of all the stupidity, Roy. Tell them it was a misprint. Or send her to a real finishing school."

My father picked up the document and perused it. "No."

Mr. Forrester hit the oak mantel with his fist. "What about marrying her off?"

To my dismay, my father chuckled. "Is that an offer, Robert?"

Mr. Forrester sneered before slumping into a nearby chair. "No, absolutely not." He paused a moment, as if winding up again. "And what are you planning to do when it's time to present her at court?"

My father dipped his pen, ignoring him.

"Who do you think is going to sponsor her? Have you even thought of that?"

Still my father didn't answer.

"What? Are you just going to sit there and ignore me now?" Mr. Forrester asked. "You haven't a clue, have you?"

"If necessary, she'll come out this season and take her place."

There was a derisive snort. "As what? Mrs. Macy?"

"She's no more his wife than I am. And you know it."

"I know nothing of the sort." As if at wit's end, Mr. Forrester grabbed his hair and held it in his fist for a second. "She'll be the ruin of you. She's mannerless, rude, short-tempered. One morning I found her whiskey-slinging before breakfast! No one is going to believe the story you've concocted."

"Isaac met with her before determining how to handle this. He thought her capable enough."

I frowned, not certain who Isaac was, but then recalled Lord

Dalry, the gentleman who'd greeted Edward and me the night we arrived.

Mr. Forrester scrambled to his feet, knocking over a nearby glass. "After all he's sacrificed for you, you're destroying his career along with yours. Have you even considered how selfish you're being?"

My father's features hardened before he retrieved his pen, dipped it in ink, and started to write again. "I'm not doing anything to anyone. He and I discussed this possibility before I left, and he chose to take it."

Mr. Forrester's mouth pulled downward as his jaw jutted. "I wish I'd never laid eyes on your daughter. Had I known any of this would happen, I never would have fetched you that night."

Instead of a reply, my father considered Mr. Forrester. "Would I better gain your support, Robert, if you knew that this measure thwarted Macy?"

Mr. Forrester huffed. "How do you mean?"

Sighing, my father leaned back and opened a bottom drawer of his desk. "Look over some correspondences between her mother and myself. Simmons collected all documentation after her death, so you'll find my letters in there as well. You'll see that Macy has been planning to collect Julia for some time now." He slid a black portfolio across the desk.

I gasped, but thankfully it went unheard.

Mr. Forrester snorted and sprawled himself into one of the teak chairs planted before the desk, leaving his arms and legs dangling. "It makes no difference. Even if Macy planned this years ago, your daughter is his strumpet now. Her loyalty sleeps with him."

Nevertheless, he opened the portfolio with a flip of his hand and withdrew a sheaf.

Sight of that first letter tortured me. After Mama's death, I'd spent months searching for the mysterious correspondences that frightened her. I'd emptied her desk, torn apart her wardrobe, dumped out every drawer, and overturned her mattress. The passion seized me one afternoon after I'd been staring at the endless circles the rain formed in puddles. Like a feebleminded woman, I went from despondent to frantic. Believing Mama had taken her own life because of a series of correspondences, I wanted answers. And I would not be put off. I had searched and searched until Sarah finally found me sitting in the middle of a wrecked room and begged me to cease.

Even from my distance, I recognized sheaves of Mama's stationery and had to resist the urge to rush into the library and snatch up the file.

I couldn't see Mr. Forrester's face, but he made quick work of the first letter, then picked up the next. Again, I felt desperate. I recognized that letter, too. It bore a tea stain from the time Mama's hand shook so much, she overturned her cup while reading it. I wanted to scream. It was maddening that for once in his life, Mr. Forrester wasn't giving commentary.

My father waited in silence, using his thumb to twist a ring on his fourth finger.

Mr. Forrester turned over the last page in the file, then hooked his elbows behind his chair. "I don't understand."

"Neither do I, which is why I'm keeping her here." My father sanded the document he'd been working on, folded it, and slid it into the shoulder bag he'd worn home that evening.

Mr. Forrester shifted in his chair, allowing me to see his face. "This is Macy we're talking about here. How do you know he didn't plan this, too?"

My father withdrew a new sheet of paper. "Because no one would expect this bold of a move. Consider it from my point of view, Robert. I never wanted her here either. But now that Macy's forced my hand, I'm calling his bluff and raising the stakes."

Mr. Forrester snorted again. "And what if he's not bluffing?"

"He's stalemated, and he knows it." My father's voice

softened as he picked up his glass. "Think on it. He lacks proof of the marriage. He lacks proof she's the girl he married, and even if he could prove it, the legality of the union is debatable at best."

Mr. Forrester lifted the portfolio and waved it in the air. "No proof?"

My father glowered. He looked askance, taking a swallow of his drink. A look of sadness crossed his face before he stood and held out his hand. When Forrester handed him the portfolio, he hesitated for a second as if regretting the action, but then, seemingly emotionless, tossed the entire correspondence into the flames.

A NOTE FROM
THE AUTHOR

SOME STORIES insist upon being written. This is one of them. When I first started writing this book, I was nineteen. My intent was to tell a story about a Victorian girl who unexpectedly falls in love while visiting a Gothic estate. It didn't take me long to realize the true story was happening behind the scenes—and it was far more sinister. I liked what I had written, but I didn't see how *that* story fit into a Christian worldview. So I set it aside.

Yet the story haunted me. Over the next decade, each time I sat down to write, no matter what I intended to put on paper, I always ended up sketching a quick vignette about that girl, or the estate, or about the other characters. In my late twenties, I realized if I was ever going to write anything else, I needed to get this story out of my system, so I began in earnest. This time, I incorporated God into the picture and began to see spiritual themes developing too. As I wrote, I shared my work with my sister-in-law and my best friend. They grew so interested that they encouraged me to get it published. Little did we know it would take still another decade to learn the craft, the industry, and the necessary marketing skills.

During these years, the story has gone through several transitions. At times, the faith element has been too strong, while at other times it's been buried except through symbolism. It's always been Gothic. After many years of working on this story and these characters, I'm thrilled that this book is now finally in your hands.

Please feel free to contact me via my website, www.jessicadotta.com.

Blessings,
Jessica

ACKNOWLEDGMENTS

I AM INCREDIBLY BLESSED by and grateful for the people who have poured their wisdom and time into this novel.

Kelli and Lynn—can you believe Julia's story is now an actual book? How can I thank you enough for taking such interest in the growing story? Without your encouragement, I never would have undertaken the publishing journey.

My heartfelt thank-you to Kingdom Writers for setting up a forum where newbies can receive critique and feedback. I am especially thankful for those of you who followed an early version of this story and took the time to make me a better writer by providing feedback. A particular thank-you is owed to Jean Olsen. You were such an encouragement. A very special thanks to Janet Jones, Angela Joseph, Rich Maffeo, Chris Egbert, Brian Reaves, Sally Murtagh, Barbara, Darlene, and Andrea.

I am so grateful for my personal critique group, Penwrights. I couldn't ask for a more dedicated and talented group of writers to work alongside. Yvonne, you are a brilliant writer and editor. I am so thrilled to have your books on my shelf. Reni, your enthusiasm for this series has helped me persevere more than you'll ever know. Michelle, I hail thee as president and head of the Macy fan club. Lisa Ludwig, thank you for your awesome insights and wisdom. Mike Duran, thank you so much for

your encouragement and for rejoicing with me. Noel De Vries,
I used to so look forward to your comments; they were so valu-
able. I can't wait until one of your books is on my shelf. Terri
Thompson and Eunice, thank you for your faithfulness. A spe-
cial thanks also needs to go to Jamie Driggers, Cindy Sproles,
Steve Wallace, Patty Kyrlach, Louise M. Gouge, Donna Gilbert,
Kelly Klepfer, Heather Smith, and Felicia Mires.

To Ane Mulligan: I think I owe you a medal. You've read nearly
every version of this story without fatigue, and you know as much
about this story and its characters as I do. There aren't words to
express how much your friendship and support means to me.

To Gina Holmes, I couldn't ask for a better coach or best
friend. You never gave up on this story. Thank you from the bottom of my heart.

Chip MacGregor, you are one amazing agent! I can't tell you
how much I appreciate your time, thoughts, and willingness to
take on this series.

A very special thanks to Karen Watson, Stephanie Broene,
and Kathy Olson; Babette Rea and the publicity team. I can't tell
you how thrilled I am to be working with you!

I am so grateful for the amazing community here, too. To my
brother, Joshua, your faith in me has always been an inspira-
tion. To my sister, Joy, thank you for your feedback and willingness to chat when I need a break. To Anna and Howard
Vosburgh, thank you for the endless cups of coffee and help
with the edits. I would tell you how much I appreciate it, but that
would be floccinaucinihilipilification—you already know. And to
Star Marcrom, thank you so much for all those nights you vol-
unteered to have my daughter over to play with yours, so I could
meet deadlines. You rock!

Lastly, to my beautiful daughter: your amazing love and support is such a wonderful gift. I thank God every day for you.

DISCUSSION QUESTIONS

1. Much of the story line depends on people thinking they know what is best for other people. For example, Henry and Elizabeth think it best to keep the news of Edward's ordination from Julia, and Lord Pierson conceals his identity from her—both as her guardian and as her real father—until Macy forces his hand. In what ways have you seen people withhold information or make decisions for others? What are some of the reasons people do this? Do you find yourself doing it—or tempted to? Is it ever justified, and if so, when?

2. Edward struggles with competing values of spiritual integrity—being true to his faith and what he believes God requires of him—and seeking his own personal happiness. His challenge is further complicated by his sense of responsibility for Julia. Do you approve of the way Edward prioritizes his values in the book? Why or why not? What competing values do you face in your own life or relationships? When faced with grey areas or complex choices, how do you determine which value or guideline takes priority?

3. Julia's circumstances make it difficult for her to attain what she considers happiness: independence, an appealing marriage, a comfortable income. Have you ever felt like you were dealt an unfair hand in life, or do you know someone who feels that way? How did you respond to the feeling, or what would you say to someone in that situation?

4. Do you agree with Julia that Edward's joining the church is a personal betrayal of her and their relationship? How much consideration do life partners owe each other when making major decisions? Does that dynamic change when it comes to matters of faith? Give some examples and explain your thinking.

5. Discuss the relationship between Mr. Macy and Lady Foxmore. Are they more friends or enemies? What makes you think so? In what ways is their relationship based on their own self-interests? Do you have—or have you ever had—a relationship like this? What are the benefits? What are the drawbacks?

6. Much of the writing describing Lady Foxmore uses bird terminology. What symbolism do you think the author is hoping to convey?

7. What do you make of Mrs. Windham's character? Ultimately, do you believe she has Julia's best interests at heart? Why or why not?

8. Consider the different ways Lady Foxmore and Mrs. Windham view themselves. Lady Foxmore appears to be self-aware, while Mrs. Windham considers herself to be nobler than she actually is. To what degree do you struggle with self-awareness? Are you more likely to view yourself as better or worse than you actually are? How can we know when our self-image is distorted in either direction?

9. At one point, Mr. Greenham admits to murdering Julia's mother. Yet Julia doesn't seem to struggle with a lot of fear or anger toward him. Why is that? How should we treat people who are guilty of wrongdoing yet seem repentant? How has this played out in your life or the life of someone you know?

10. What is your final opinion of Mr. Macy? Do you share Edward's conviction that he is an evil man, or is there still reasonable doubt? If we judge a tree by its fruit, how much circumstantial evidence do we need before discerning someone's character?

11. Some elements of this story can be seen as an allegory of the Christian life. Which character, if any, reminds you of God the Father? Of Christ? Of Satan? Of fallen man? Do you enjoy reading stories that have an underlying message? Why or why not?

12. Does the ending of the story live up to your expectations? Why or why not? What do you think lies in store for Julia, Edward, and Mr. Macy?

ABOUT THE AUTHOR

JESSICA DOTTA has always been fascinated by the intricacies of society that existed in England during the Regency and Victorian eras. Her passion for British literature fueled her desire to write in a style that blends the humor of Jane Austen and the dark drama of a Brontë sister. She lives in the Nashville area with her family and works as a freelance media consultant and publicist.

Jessica is always happy to accept tea invitations from book clubs, especially when they serve Earl Grey and scones.

Visit Jessica's website at www.jessicadotta.com.